C000028918

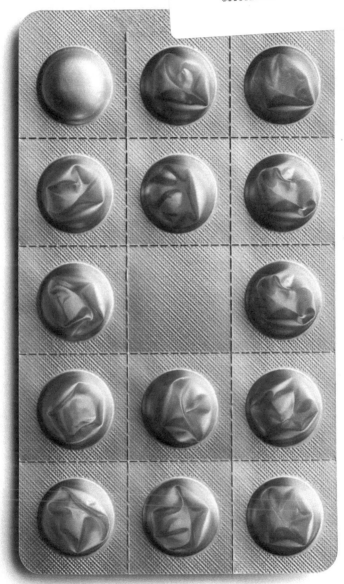

Feeding

the

Gods

Elizabeth Harrison

The Book Guild Ltd

First published in Great Britain in 2021 by
The Book Guild Ltd
9 Priory Business Park
Wistow Road, Kibworth
Leicestershire, LE8 0RX
Freephone: 0800 999 2982
www.bookguild.co.uk
Email: info@bookguild.co.uk
Twitter: @bookguild

Typeset in Adobe Garamond Pro

Printed and bound by CPI Group (UK) Ltd, Croydon, CR0 4YY

ISBN 978 1913551 636

British Library Cataloguing in Publication Data.
A catalogue record for this book is available from the British Library.

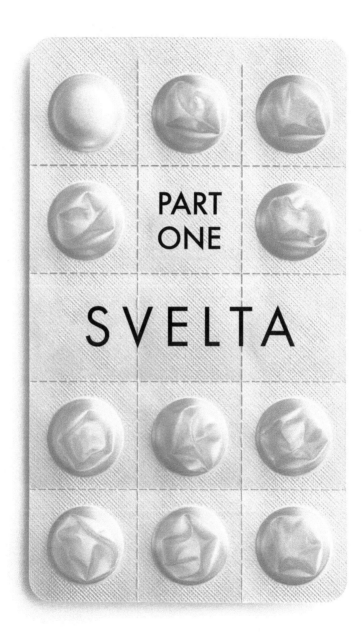

PART
ONE

SVELTA

ONE

October 2005

Linda knew she was dying. As she lay on the cold tiles, she felt an unbearable pain radiate from her back through to her chest.

A heart attack?

She was a nurse, and the irony of diagnosing her own death made her want to laugh, but all that escaped from her mouth was a gurgle, and she vomited.

The kitchen was in semi-darkness. A row of inadequate spotlights on the ceiling provided isolated pools of yellow light on the kitchen worktops, leaving large areas of gloom. The effect was dated, but Linda liked the cosy atmosphere and the residents of the Women's Refuge seemed to agree, often gathering here for coffee and a smoke at night. Now, though, it was deserted, and she saw only the shadows.

She'd been walking through the doorway when she felt an excruciating blow to her back, so powerful that she lost her balance and stumbled. She felt the strength drain from her limbs, as if it was urgently needed somewhere else in her body, and, unable to help herself, she fell violently against the corner of a worktop. Something warm ran down her face and her vision blurred. Still helpless, she slumped, hitting the floor heavily. A crushing weight descended on her chest and knocked the rest of her breath out of her.

Was it only a few minutes ago?

She was slowly regaining her senses.

She didn't know how long she'd been lying there. Her breathing was coming in ragged gasps. She tried to move her body, with no success.

Am I paralysed?

She tried to call out, but she had no breath, and instead she mewed like a kitten.

Is that someone moving past the doorway? I can't see.

Her shaking hand brushed her face and came away red with blood.

What's that?

She felt alone, vulnerable, ready to panic and run, but only her mind responded; she still couldn't move.

As the minutes went by, the slow realisation that there was nothing she could physically do seemed to calm her. She was strangely comforted by the old building where she and her friends had helped so many women and children, the security of the Women's Refuge, with its strong walls and secure locks.

I'm only forty-eight… what happened to all those years?

Her pain, her fear and the smell of blood were bringing back reluctant memories of a long night thirty years ago. Memories of her younger self, the hedonistic lifestyle she had led during her training and the consequences she had tried to forget. She was back in that tiny, sordid hotel room. She was lying on bloodied sheets, focussing on the swirling orange and brown patterns on the peeling wallpaper and trying not to scream as each wave of pain racked her body. She felt ashamed that Simon, her friend (the father?), had taken such a risk in getting drugs for her. He'd had to leave her, his involvement a well-kept secret just between the two of them. She had felt alone then.

And I've felt alone since Eddie left me. Is this my final punishment, a life for a life?

Simon. Hadn't she seen him again recently? She was struggling to remember. She seemed to be floating above the pain now and people were appearing. She was no stranger to ghosts from the past; they appeared constantly in her dreams – usually the creations of whatever anti-depressant she was taking. Her friends – Sandra, Rosie and Roberta – were standing in the distance, silently watching.

Why don't they help me?

She tried to call to them, but they faded away.

Sister Teresa's menacing face, with her steely blue eyes and whiskery chin, abruptly pushed itself into hers, her mouth whispering grim warnings of sin and sex.

'Go away! It's too late now, I am lost, and you are the devil.'

The unholy words sprang off Linda's lips, and Sister Teresa's face crumpled and disappeared, to be replaced by Eddie, her ex-husband.

Still handsome, she thought, *with his blond hair and blue eyes*. He was back in their house and he grinned as she reached out to him.

'Why did you leave me, Eddie?'

'Obsessive,' he muttered, his smile disappearing as he backed off.

She ran her hands across her stomach, surprised to find that it was slim and firm and that she was young again.

'Wait, Eddie.'

Will he love me again now; will he come back?

Then she remembered all the years that had crept by, having children, the damage to her body and her growing feelings of insecurity. They weighed down on her now and her body sagged, no longer young. She was losing the battle to keep slim. It would have been total defeat if it hadn't been for Svelta.

I wonder...

She felt the pain returning in waves so intense it was stopping her from thinking. Her chest felt sore; her breathing was becoming more difficult. She took a gasp of air and tried to call for help from her friends.

Haven't I just seen them?

Adam, one of her post-Eddie boyfriends, was hovering nearby, the last person she wanted to see. He was looking concerned, but all Linda saw was another of his false faces and she tried to shout at him. Eventually she managed a hoarse whisper.

'What are you doing here? You're a fraud, a pretender. Everybody knew you were a total tosser – it just took *me* longer to find out.'

Adam was now looking politely puzzled. Then a sly expression came over his face and he smiled. 'Yeah, and everybody knew you were the village bicycle.'

She tried to push him away, but her arms wouldn't move and he hovered around, just like he had in real life.

She was becoming distressed and disorientated.

Where am I?

The images were so real now that she lost touch with her surroundings. She turned her head slowly towards the door, but a film over her eyes put everything into soft focus. She heard voices and thought she saw the shadows of several figures.

The voices faded. An overwhelming sensation of cold coursed through her body. Her vision finally failed her and the visitors in her mind were gone too. Then finally there was nothing; the fight was over.

I wish I could tell someone what a relief death is.

TWO

2005

A scream pierced the silence of the Women's Refuge. Other screams followed, high-pitched and belonging to small children. Rosie ran out of her office, down the stairs and found the Green family in a huddle in the kitchen doorway. Their screams had been replaced by sobs and they were all shaking. Wendy Green was crouching down by her children, her arms round them, shielding them from something.

Rosie's first thought was that an angry husband had found his way in. She sighed in exasperation; despite whatever the men had done to drive them here, the women regularly gave them the door code. Then she looked beyond the wailing group and saw a trail of blood down the door of the nearest kitchen unit, ending up in a pool on the floor. Linda was lying in it. Her forehead was covered in blood, spiky blonde hair saturated with it, her normally sparkling blue eyes dull, milky and expressionless.

Rosie instinctively knew she was dead. She had never seen a dead body before, but Linda's unnatural stillness was palpable. She was lying at an awkward angle and had turned her head to one side as if looking for something. Rosie felt like screaming too.

'Come on, come on…'

Years of dealing with frantic situations kicked in, and she herded Wendy and the children away from the doorway.

'Linda has fallen, and we need to call an ambulance.'

Her voice sounded deliberately calm and had the effect of quietening the little group. Inside, though, it didn't seem to belong to her. She was fighting to keep hold of her emotions.

Hasn't this family come to the Refuge to get away from this sort of thing?

Returning to the kitchen, she sat on the floor beside the friend she had known for thirty years and stifled her sobs that now threatened to get out of her control.

What on earth's happened here?

Linda looked so horribly exposed, and she thought of getting a blanket to cover her up. There was blood everywhere. She wondered if she should close her friend's eyes.

Isn't that what I'm supposed to do?

Linda was wearing a tunic dress with long sleeves that had become a uniform for the staff at the Refuge. Rosie was an advocate of dressing simply, to signify neutrality, anonymity, being part of a united group, there to listen and not make judgements.

Rosie noticed for the first time how thin her wrists were. She saw the prominent bones in her neck and the sagging skin on her face. She stroked Linda's hand and talked to her as tears ran down her cheeks.

'Linda, I'm so sorry I didn't find you in time. I love you and I feel so guilty. I know you thought I had the ideal life, but it's not been like that at all. I should have been more honest.'

She kissed the paper-thin skin on her hand, stroked her hair, then gathered her into her arms. Linda felt heavy, and Rosie's tears fell unchecked.

The paramedics and police arrived. The police then explained that they would need access to the kitchen for at least the morning as it was a potential crime scene.

A crime scene?

The words shook her to the core, and she felt heavy and drained. She dragged herself up the stairs back to her office. There were phone calls to be made. A quick self-assessment found her hands were bloodied, her face streaked and her dress marked. She opened a cupboard and pulled out a spare dress. She walked to the nearest cloakroom and stripped off, washing as best she could, then donned the clean outfit. She checked her reflection in the mirror, but there was no evidence of her shock. She only saw clear green eyes in a heart-shaped face. She returned to her office, sat on the chair at her desk and pulled her body up straight.

Rosie Jennings, cool, capable and in control.

What she needed now was the support of her friends, Roberta and Sandra.

*

An hour later, the paramedics and police had been and gone, and Rosie had arranged a meeting with her friends for later that afternoon. She felt drained; she just wanted to go home, clean up and rest. She felt too upset to drive, so she ordered a taxi. David's chauffeur sometimes collected her from the Refuge; it all depended on his schedule. Right now, he would be well on his way taking David to a meeting in Reading, so she was surprised to see the Range Rover was still in the drive when the taxi pulled up at her house.

She zapped the front gate with a remote fob, musing that one of the advantages of being married to David was that money smoothed out the wrinkles of everyday life. Once inside the front door, and not for the first time, she paused to admire the entrance hall that took up two storeys, with its curved walnut staircase, feature window and Theo's baby grand in the corner. David spent long weeks away working as a senior VP of Sipher Pharmaceutical, but she could not fault the lifestyle that his money and position gave her and their children. Rosie fully intended to take advantage of the facilities and de-stress in the jacuzzi, followed by a short nap.

She was stopped in her tracks at the sight of David in the family room. He was wearing a smart Armani suit, Gucci shoes and was hunched over the breakfast bar on one of the stools. Something didn't look quite right, and she realised that he never normally sat there during the working week, only at weekends, when he was casually dressed. He turned his face and for a moment she thought she saw turmoil and uncertainty there. When he saw her it vanished, like wiping a slate. In its place appeared the inscrutable mask that she sadly felt was more familiar.

'Eddie phoned me with the news about Linda,' he said.

Rosie thought the words sounded rehearsed.

He's trying to be careful.

'I was on my way to the Reading meeting, but I thought I'd better come home. I knew you'd be upset, and I thought you might need a bit of support.'

And since when have you put my feelings before your job?

'That was very thoughtful of you, David. I'm sure there will be a few phone calls, but I'm shattered. It would be a great help if you could field them.'

He's hiding something.

Rosie made her way wearily up the stairs. She ran a bath and slipped gratefully into its warmth. She wondered, not for the first time, if she and David had ever had a meaningful and heartfelt conversation. She had been brought up to be polite, loyal, to play the game; and that's what she did. Over the years, however, she had learnt that for him these attributes were only on the surface, and below that was a different person that she only glimpsed. She instinctively knew it would be unhealthy for her marriage to examine things any further.

She sighed and turned on the bubbles. They had started their marriage with an unspoken agreement that she supported his career and he supported her. Now, they led separate lives.

THREE

2005

Sandra parked her car on the tree-lined Didsbury street and stepped out onto the pavement, slamming the door on the seatbelt buckle in her haste, chipping the paintwork.

Jesus Christ.

She stepped backwards onto the grass verge and her high-heeled shoes immediately sank into the soft ground.

Bloody hell.

She swore again under her breath as she extricated her shoes, locked her car and wrapped her scarf round her unruly hair.

An elderly man grinned as he walked past. 'Watch that temper, redhead,' he said.

'Get stuffed, Grandad.' She grinned at him to soften the blow. Her unfortunate swearing habit was second nature, learnt from her dear departed dad. She sometimes regretted it – when she noticed it, that was. But the old man was right; she was angry.

She walked the short distance to the Refuge. It was a cold day in Manchester, with scudding grey clouds, and the wind had blown dried leaves into the entrance porch, making a mournful scene in keeping with her thoughts of Linda's death. Uppermost were

11

denial, grief and anger. On top of these was the constant irritation she felt that she, Sandra Marsden, notoriously self-centred, had been coerced into devoting an increasing amount of her time to a women's charity.

Somehow Rosie had contrived to lead her, Roberta and Linda into volunteering. It took a special kind of management style to achieve that and she had to admire it. She and Rosie were quite different personalities, though, and outside the dynamics of the group of friends, she wondered what they had in common.

Now there's a subject not to be pursued.

She was met at the door by a police officer who was a new face, not one of the regulars who visited from time to time to check on the whereabouts of women reported missing. She thought he looked terribly young, as most of them did now – well, to her, anyway. Detective Inspector Graham Porter was polite and well spoken.

Graduate Intake Programme. He's never going to pound the beat.

'May I see some identification, madam?'

Madam? It's hardly a brothel, sunshine.

Sandra fished in her handbag for her driving licence, handed it to him and deliberately held his gaze, watching with satisfaction as he coloured up.

He checked it and handed it back. 'Thank you, madam. We've finished for the moment, I believe.' He avoided looking at her again, seeking refuge in the familiar jargon of policework. 'Are you aware that there has been an unexplained death?'

'That's why I'm here,' said Sandra, her good humour vanishing.

As he exited the door, he collided with a breathless Roberta who stumbled up the steps straight into him, her long hair flying into his face, her eyes wide with alarm. Sandra was then diverted by the sight of them shuffling around one another, the officer attempting to keep his body at a modest distance before making his escape. She decided not to torment him further and embraced Roberta instead, stifling her with a bear hug.

'Man, am I pleased to see you.'

Her eyes suddenly filled with tears that she angrily wiped away. Roberta hugged her hard.

'Come on, we need to see what's going on in there. Everybody is bound to be shaken up.'

For so many women there, the sight of the police reopened memories that they had forced to the back of their minds. Roberta and Sandra agreed that a tea party for the children would be a useful diversion, and soon everyone was distracted by drinks and biscuits, and the mums were visibly relaxing.

'Sugar works every time,' said Sandra.

When Rosie arrived back at the Refuge in the afternoon, things appeared to be running smoothly again. A new shift of staff came on duty and Rosie sought out her friends, suggesting they all go to the top floor staff room to talk, away from the residents.

The Refuge was a large Edwardian building with the attic a long walk up two flights of stairs. Sandra and Roberta were noticeably subdued as they climbed in single file, and the stairs creaked and groaned as if in sympathy. Rosie had commandeered one of the rooms long ago for their private meetings. It used to be the kitchen of a flat, and she had kept the cooker, sink and kettle, adding a cosy sofa with squashy cushions, and a table and chairs to snack at or talk.

Once they were behind the closed door, Roberta started to cry. 'I can't believe Linda isn't here anymore.'

Sandra tried to comfort her friend, but Roberta's body was racked with sobs, and for some time she was beyond speech. Finally, she was all cried out, her face red and puffy, her big eyes swollen. Sandra looked at her with exasperation. Roberta had always been the same. She couldn't contain her emotions at all; in fact, you could read her like a book.

'Any wine around?' Roberta croaked at last.

Rosie went to the fridge and returned with three glasses and a bottle of rosé that she put on the table. 'Oh, bad luck. It's always the rosé that's left, isn't it?' She winced. 'Sorry, that was my social voice, entirely inappropriate at this moment. It *is* always the rosé that gets left till last, though, isn't it?'

Sandra and Roberta cracked a smile and came to sit at the table. Rosie poured them each a generous glass and they raised them together in silence.

Emboldened by the effects of wine on an empty stomach, Sandra began to speak. 'I'm so angry, with Linda and myself.' She took a large gulp of wine. 'Her life's been on a downer for yonks. She had some bizarre experiences trying to pull a man and there were times when I feared for her safety. Now I wish I had done something to help her sooner.'

Rosie and Roberta looked at each other, both horrified and fascinated at the mention of Linda's escapades.

'Why did you think she wasn't safe?' asked Rosie.

'Trying to hook a husband on the internet, mainly,' said Sandra, then abruptly changed the subject. 'I was more concerned about her health. She was looking very skinny. Of course, she's been taking that slimming drug Svelta on and off for years. Now why does she think men find that attractive? I like my curves, and men still go silly when I show my cleavage.'

Sandra stared into her glass of wine for a moment, and then moved her gaze to Rosie. 'I've heard there's been rumours about the safety of Svelta.'

Rosie looked stunned, then quickly composed her face. 'Svelta has been widely used for over ten years. The regulators wouldn't have given their approval unless it had passed stringent clinical trials?'

Sandra face showed anger and pity now. 'Maybe you should ask your husband David. Wasn't he the lead scientist behind the discovery?'

*

Rosie was feeling increasingly uncomfortable. Linda's dating was a stark contrast to her marriage to David; she couldn't remember the last time they had been intimate. Then there was that direct attack about Svelta, the success of which furnished her lifestyle.

Why is Sandra attacking me?

'I've always worried that Linda was envious of what she saw as my privileged life,' she countered.

'Let's face it, that's true,' said Sandra, adding to her angst. 'She often mentioned Rosie's gilded cage. Don't you feel a little bit responsible for leading her on? Maybe she couldn't cope with the pressure?'

A wary look appeared on Rosie's face and she clammed up. She had her pride and she couldn't tell her friends that her marriage was not as it appeared. That she was actually treated with casual indifference by a husband whom she suspected of infidelity.

'David is always away, and I know very little about his work.'

'You don't know what he gets up to then?' Sandra leant back in her chair and folded her arms, her face showing a grim satisfaction.

Rosie was used to angry women; she met them daily and she rarely lost her cool. Nevertheless, she was stung by Sandra's accusations.

She chose her words carefully in reply and launched her own verbal salvo. 'It's normal for people to feel guilty and angry about a death. If I have fuelled Linda's angst, then it was unintentional. But you both took drugs as nurses. Do you think taking drugs is okay?'

She paused to sip her wine and softened the attack. 'You know, it was the violence, the abuse and sexism that you, my friends, have all have experienced over the years, that led me to begin work with the Women's Movement.'

I never think to look for abuse on my own doorstep, though.

Halfway down her second glass of wine, Roberta found her voice again. 'To me, Linda seemed to have a great life. She had independence, self-confidence and a good career, which many women would die for – oops!' She broke off at the irony of her words and subsided, draining her glass. 'We have known each other for so many years. Do you remember that Christmas party when we met in 1975? Weren't we so young and full of dreams?'

'Yes, it took me all my courage to turn up on my own then,' said Rosie. 'I was so glad to see you all.' She caught herself as a sob threatened. 'Including Linda.'

FOUR

November 1975

It was almost thirty years previously, that Rosie, the student, stepped off the bus in Fallowfield outside the entrance to the Owens Park student campus for an evening that would define the direction of her life. She paused for a moment, then, summoning up her courage, headed in the direction of the tower block. As she neared the building, she first heard the beat of music, then a riot of sounds, voices and laughter, and her pulse quickened. It sounded promising. She joined a flood of students, homing in on the main entrance, forming a queue to check in. They seemed to be in pairs and groups, and she felt isolated and conspicuous on her own. Was she dressed correctly? She shot a furtive glance around her, then lowered her head, fumbling in her bag for her students' union card, making it look as if she was too busy to care.

Rosie was in her first year studying sociology at Manchester University and had a room in the Victoria Park campus not far away. It was quiet there, too quiet, and with no common room to meet the other students easily. Plenty of time to study, though. She wondered if her mum had chosen it deliberately. She had been at the university long enough to have heard about Owens Park and its

17

reputation for socialising and parties. Now she was here for a closer look, and, if she was honest, hoping that David Jennings would be there. She had met him several times. First at freshers' week, then after that, she had recognised him walking in the corridors between lectures, where he had made a point of giving her long looks. After that, he somehow managed to turn up when she was in the canteen and sit at her table. They had chatted, but no more than that, deliberately on her part. She had been swiftly told about his reputation as a womaniser and had kept him at arm's length. Still, she found him interesting. His upbringing in a coal-mining village in Yorkshire was so different to hers and she could hear in his stories the determination that had gained him a place at university. Her interest was piqued, and he posed a challenge, but could she handle a naughty boy?

Rosie noticed three women hovering near the queue. They looked a bit lost. She hadn't seen them around and she immediately felt empathy for them. Someone else for whom it was clearly their first time here. She walked over to introduce herself.

'Hello, I'm Rosie. I'm a first-year student here, doing sociology. I've not been here before. Have you?'

The pretty woman with long brown hair looked relieved and gave Rosie a beaming smile. 'No. We weren't sure whether we had to pay or not and whether our student cards would be accepted here. I'm Roberta, by the way. I'm studying fine art at the art college down the road. I'm in my first year too.'

Rosie looked at the other two women. One had bright blue eyes and an unruly mop of red hair that she'd attempted to subdue into a tight bun. Bits of hair were escaping everywhere and, although not immediately attractive, she looked sexy and was aware of it too.

'I'm Sandra,' was all she said, not looking at Rosie directly but blatantly scanning the crowds of students.

The words 'talent scouting' came into her mind, and Rosie raised her eyebrows at Sandra's rudeness.

Roberta hastened to fill the gap. 'Sandra's my school friend.

She's training to be a nurse at Manchester Royal. We meet up quite often. And this is Linda.' She indicated towards the third woman. 'She's training to be a nurse too.'

Rosie warmed to Linda, who gave her a little wave and smiled. She was striking too, with a pert little nose, bleached blonde hair and blue eyes. She listened as Roberta explained at great length how they came to be there.

'There was a poster on our notice board inviting art students to an Owens Park party. I thought it would be okay if I brought Sandra and Linda too. You see, I haven't really gelled with the art students yet. In fact, I find them a bit way-out. I've never been to the university before and this is intimidating in a different way, but at least the students look relatively normal here. The fine art students dress so weirdly, and their speech is all nonsense because they're permanently high from smoking pot. I should probably have done 3D or sculpture; you have to be more practical there.'

Rosie choked back a laugh and managed to smile at her politely instead. She was entertained by this stream of consciousness and decided she liked Roberta's honesty.

They joined the queue together, chatting at first, then, as they got nearer the entrance, there was too much noise to hear each other, and they were hard pressed to keep their places. They were pushed past two bouncers, who gave their student cards a cursory glance, and then into a bar area with tables and games. Aside from people queuing for drinks, this seemed to be deserted, and the main crowd were heading to a vast hall. The students who lived in the tower seemed to be bringing in their own stuff: cushions, posters and decorations. *Like an extension of their room*, Rosie thought, liking the personal touch. Music was belting out from a DJ's desk. A martini-based fruit punch, together with kegs of Watney's Red Barrel, was on a trestle table which served as a bar. Once they had helped themselves to punch in plastic cups, Rosie watched in amazement as Sandra opened her handbag and took out a half-bottle of vodka.

'Drink a bit,' she ordered, and then topped up their cups with the vodka. 'They're all the same, these student parties: no decent booze, just pot, and I don't do that.'

A couple of students next to her were already holding out their cups. Sandra put the bottle firmly back into her handbag. 'Get your own,' she snapped.

They moved away from the bar and for the next hour they talked about their courses, what they were hoping to achieve, where they came from and what they had left behind. Rosie felt they must look an odd group with their very different styles of dress and personality, yet they seemed to establish a rapport between them. Roberta was disarmingly open, with a self-deprecating sense of humour. Rosie found Sandra frighteningly direct at first, the opposite to the way she was brought up, but gradually her horror turned to fascination. Once she got used to her, Rosie realised she was quite funny, and she had some hilarious nursing stories. She also kept casually topping up their punch with vodka. Linda seemed in her thrall but had an equal fund of stories about the convent where she was educated. They both made Rosie feel that she was the most reserved of the four. Once the women knew she lived near London, they wanted to know all about the club scene there. She had to explain that she had never been allowed into the city at night by her over-protective parents, much to the astonishment of the other three, all of whom said they would have just gone and dealt with the consequences later. She wished she had some interesting stories.

She watched in fascination as Sandra continually looked round the room. She saw her stare intently at a man who was singing along to 'Bohemian Rhapsody' and who obviously saw himself as Freddie Mercury, gyrating with a snooker cue in place of a microphone, but he was too far gone in his Freddie persona to notice her, so she gave up and continued looking elsewhere. Her gaze fell on to the tall, good-looking man who kept glancing their way. David Jennings. He'd been watching Rosie since they came in.

Sandra cut to the chase. 'That man over there can't keep his eyes off you. Do you know who he is? Not for you, I don't think. Classic good looks, but more than a touch of bad.' She tossed her head, making her red curls bounce and shimmer in the spotlights, catching his attention. She held her palms out. 'You see? Takes one to know one.'

'He's got a dreadful reputation. Well-deserved as he's slept with at least seven girls in my year this term alone,' Rosie said with a conflicting mixture of disgust and regret.

Sandra smiled knowingly at the accuracy of her earlier assessment.

Linda had taken to the dance floor after a few more cups of the vodka-enhanced punch. She clearly loved dancing to the earthiness of the Rolling Stones music and now, along with many of the men, was performing a Mick Jagger-inspired dance to 'Honky Tonk Women'. Rosie and Roberta exchanged surprised glances, taken aback by the overtly sexual performance which was attracting a lot of onlookers.

'That woman knows how to move her body,' chipped in Sandra, her face full of unabashed admiration.

As Linda danced, the three others continued chatting. Their conversation brought it home to Rosie how straightforward her life had been so far. It soon became apparent that Roberta was unhappy with her course and was considering switching if she could.

'It's difficult to feel enthusiastic about art college right now. I've been going out with Will for two years now and I do love him, but he says studying art has got nothing to do with real life. I was always good at art at school, but I'm not sure how I can make a living afterwards. I'm lucky my parents are supporting me, but, you know, I don't think they're bothered about what I do.'

'Well, my parents refused to support me after I was sixteen,' said Sandra. 'I was working in insurance and got fed up of handing my wages over to them. I'm not thick, I have nine O levels and I realised I could leave home at eighteen, live in the nurses' home, get a wage and train at the same time. You should have seen their faces when they realised they would be minus a few bob each week.'

Rosie looked shocked. She couldn't imagine parents seeing their children as a source of income, but it would seem her life so far had been very different from the others in so many ways. She felt increasing respect for Sandra, who was clearly someone who knew what she wanted.

As the evening wore on, Roberta's face was looking pale.

Too much punch, maybe the heat or the smoke?

Rosie had noticed how quiet Roberta had become, with beads of sweat on her forehead. 'Do you want to get some fresh air?' she asked.

'Yes, please. Can you show me the way to the door?'

They weaved their way through the sea of sweaty bodies that crowded the room until their faces were hit by a blast of cold evening air. Rosie looked on, aghast, as Roberta vomited the contents of her stomach all over some grass.

'I think I'd better go home. Can you point me in the direction of the bus stop, please?'

Rosie walked with Roberta to the stop just outside the hall. Both shivered in the cold, damp December air, staring in the direction the bus would come from, hoping as each one rounded the corner that it would be the 51. Roberta thanked Rosie for keeping her company, explaining that she'd felt unusually tired these last few days and thought she was sickening for something. By the time the bus lurched around the corner, their feet felt like blocks of ice. Roberta climbed on board among the throngs of early Christmas revellers and an overwhelming smell of beer and stale cigarettes filled the night air as the doors closed.

Rosie had briefly wondered whether to join Roberta on the bus, but she was reluctant to give up on the party just yet. It felt like her first real student experience. It had a demob spirit that she put down to the fact that most people would be going back home after this. There they would face the real world with temporary work on the Christmas post or one of the large department stores where extra staff would be taken on for the pre-Christmas rush and the post-Christmas sales. As she entered the hall again, the good mood was palpable, the atmosphere heightened by the lethal fruit punch, regularly topped up with a bottle of Martini Rosso. A smoky fug created by a combination of tobacco and pot gave everything a dream-like soft focus.

Sandra and Linda are working the room, Rosie thought, leaving her standing alone. At first, she was puzzled; it wasn't something she would have done, leave someone on their own. It was... well... bad mannered. Then she felt she should be more independent, like them. She noticed that they seemed to have no problems socialising. Perhaps nursing exposed them to all manner of humanity, unlike her stifling upbringing. They were both demonstrating a huge capacity for alcohol that meant that they were left standing when many others had crashed out, comatose, on the cushions scattered around the room. When she let them know that Roberta had gone home feeling ill, they seemed unconcerned and carried on enjoying the music and dancing.

David was still watching Rosie from across the room. She had felt his eyes on her all evening but had ignored him, focussing on making the three new women feel welcome. Now she was on her own, she kept looking back at him. As the evening wore on, she chatted to other people who kept topping her glass up; someone passed a joint around and she had more than one drag. Her senses felt heightened; her inhibitions were dissolving. Now their looks were creating a sexual tension that she had never experienced.

David appeared at her side and they immediately danced closely, kissing deeply. Rosie could feel his erection pressing into her stomach. She was no stranger to this phenomenon, which she had previously dismissed as an unfortunate side effect of being a teenage male. In fact, she usually burst out laughing at this point. She had never gone further than heavy petting before.

Good girls don't go 'all the way'.

Now, she was experiencing a stab of pleasure that centred itself in her groin. She felt her knickers becoming wet, and she thought of Sandra, Linda and Roberta, who were all sexually experienced. She was suddenly fed up with herself. Feeling nervous and excited, she silently let David lead her by the hand to his room.

She was enjoying the touch of his fingers between her legs, feeling her body respond with increasing pleasure, when suddenly the fingers were replaced with something warmer, smoother and much larger. She knew what was happening and didn't resist, but her pleasure diminished as David thrust into her until he shuddered and collapsed on top of her.

They lay there for a short while before he rolled off her and broke the silence.

'Well, best get back to the party before you're missed by your friends.'

Rosie retrieved her knickers and tights from the floor, pulled her bra back over her breasts, and smoothed down her skirt. It all felt a little sordid.

They returned to the party, David with his arm around her shoulder in a way that made her feel like he had chosen her. They found a group of David's course mates discussing the day's football matches. Rosie felt an uncomfortable wetness gathering in her knickers but didn't want to break the moment by going to the toilet to clean up. Eventually the discomfort won, and she turned to David.

'Just nipping to the loo. I'll be back in a couple of minutes.'

David briefly flashed a bland smile at her, then carried on talking to his friends about Leeds United's victory over Everton.

When Rosie returned to the room, she made her way to where she had last been standing with David and his friends, but there was no sign of him. As she approached the group, one of the men nodded towards the other side of the room. Rosie followed his gaze and saw David with his back to her, his arm resting on the wall above a girl whose face she couldn't see.

The bastard.

A lesson learnt. I'll trust my instincts in future.

She made her way across the smoke-filled room to grab her coat and head for the door. As she was picking her way through the pile of coats which had been thrown one on top of the other inside the hallway, she saw Linda coming to collect her coat as well.

'Are you leaving? I thought you and Sandra would be here for a few more hours. You seem to be having a great time.'

'Sandra's pulled,' Linda said in a matter-of-fact voice, 'and we have an agreement that when one or the other pulls, the other leaves them to it.'

Rosie was shocked. 'Aren't you worried about her getting home safely?'

Linda looked slightly puzzled. 'Sandra can look after herself, Rosie.'

*

Rosie's bus seemed to take forever to arrive. The night air was bitterly cold and it sobered her up quickly as she reflected on the events of the last few hours. Damn the man and damn the drugs that had made her forget the rules of her careful upbringing.

FIVE

December 1975

Rosie was surprised when Roberta phoned her a week after the party, suggesting that she, Sandra and Linda meet for lunch at the music school canteen on Oxford Road. Roberta sounded nervous and said she had some news. She said that the canteen was right next to the art college and they served a superb hot dinner there for not very much money at all.

Rosie made her way gingerly along the pavement from the bus stop on Oxford Road. The previous night's snow had turned to slush under a bright sun, and the canteen air was humid with the smell of hot food and wet clothing. The women were all wrapped in layers of scarves, gloves and Afghan coats that they deposited onto a spare chair. Seeing each other after the party in the sober light of day, there was an initial politeness that lasted until Sandra saw the food on offer.

'Wow, groovy, man. You should see the shit we have to eat at the hospital canteen.'

They all laughed.

'I've got something I have to tell you all,' Roberta began. 'I've had a miserable first term at college and I've had a terrible week last week. The only good thing that has happened to me has been meeting you all, and from now on I probably won't see you as much. I'm leaving college.'

'Oh, I'm really sorry to hear that.' Rosie's response was automatic. 'You weren't happy with your course, were you?'

Roberta shook her head impatiently. 'It's not that. It's because I'm pregnant,' she blurted out.

There was a stunned silence all round. Whatever they had expected her to say, it wasn't that.

'Oh, Roberta,' exclaimed Sandra, sitting back and folding her arms. 'Were you just careless or is it a get-out-of-college card for you? I could have got you the pill, you know.'

'Why didn't you then?' Roberta shouted, half rising from her chair. 'It's too late now, anyway.' She sat back down abruptly and burst into tears.

Sandra had seen this side of Roberta before, but Rosie and Linda froze, exchanging worried looks.

Sandra got up, flung her arms around Roberta's neck and hugged her. 'Sorry, sorry,' she said gruffly. 'I always forget how sensitive you are. You're like sunshine and showers.'

Rosie looked totally nonplussed at the little drama, but Linda went into nursing mode, giving Roberta's hand a little pat and handing her a clean handkerchief. 'Okay now, love?' she said automatically, which made Roberta laugh.

Roberta made a rapid recovery, much to Rosie's relief, and, to her surprise, carried on as if nothing had happened.

'It was an irresponsible accident, that's all. Will and I have been getting away with it for so long, I guess we thought it would never happen. I don't know where unmarried women can get the pill, anyway. It's supposed to be only for married women to plan their families, isn't it?'

'The pill is a banned substance in my Catholic world,' Linda chipped in.

'There's a certain amount of pre-meditation involved in taking the pill that makes an unmarried woman look like she's making herself available,' said Rosie, unconsciously using her mum's voice. She stopped abruptly. She had no room to talk after last week.

'I'm never having children, and I'll make sure I don't,' said Sandra. 'My parents treated me like an unpaid servant and punished me like one too. After my upbringing, who would put a child through that?'

'What are you going to do?' said Rosie. 'Does your mum know?'

'Of course my mother knows,' said Roberta in an exasperated voice. 'She's the one who made me go to the doctor and have a pregnancy test. She noticed my period was late and asked me if Will and I had been up to anything. She thinks that women should wait till they are married to have sex because that's what she and my father did. She's been dropping hints for the last year about getting married in disgrace.'

'What does Will say?' asked Linda. 'Surely he'll want to marry you. You've been going out together for over two years, you said. Doesn't that mean you're in love?'

'We do love each other – well, we did… yes, still, I think. We've talked about me having the baby and then getting a job. I think he'll be glad I don't continue at college, but he's not talked about marriage. I don't think he wants the responsibility just yet. Mother isn't giving him time to think, though. She collared him and said it was his duty to marry me, and quickly, before the pregnancy shows. She says it's his and his family's responsibility, and there's no way she wants the disgrace of an unmarried daughter with a bastard. We had a horrendous meeting on Wednesday with his parents where his father muttered about an abortion, but we both felt that wasn't right either. So, we're getting married. I'm in disgrace and Will is reluctant. It looks like we can live in a cottage on the farm.'

Linda reached across the table and took her hand. 'I sympathise. My mum would be just the same. She's devoutly Catholic – God's will and all that, sex for the procreation of children. It's taken getting away from home for me to realise that a lot of single women my age are enjoying sex, and why shouldn't I? I couldn't take the pill, though. I just have to be careful too.'

'I was nursing a pregnant woman last week,' said Sandra. 'She was after her boyfriend for money, but he says he's not the father. Your mum's afraid that if your baby's a bastard it'll have no rights and nor will you. She can't make you get married, but she's making it clear that Will has to share the responsibility. She does care about you really, Roberta. You can't live on romance forever. Be realistic and face facts. You're lucky, you have people willing to offer you support, unlike that poor woman.'

'I don't know what my mum would say,' said Rosie. 'My parents have invested so much in what they consider to be the right upbringing and education for me, and now they're supporting me through university. They would feel horribly let down.'

There was a pause in the conversation while the women ordered their lunches.

'If I hadn't had the pregnancy test, I wouldn't know anything was different,' said Roberta. 'I'm hungrier than usual, and I was sick after the party, but I just thought I'd drunk too much.'

Sandra looked at Roberta, with her long, parted hair and her innocent flushed cheeks. 'When's the baby due?' she asked. 'I find it hard to believe you'll be a mum next year.'

'The doctor says it will be the end of July or early August. I'm not going to change, you know, I'll still be Roberta, your friend,' she said. 'Won't I?'

'Of course, you will,' replied Sandra.

'We'll all be around for you,' said Linda.

'We won't lose touch,' promised Rosie, 'but never mind what your mum wants or what Will feels. What do *you* want?'

'Oh, dear, I don't know what I want to do, I never have done. I mean, what is there for a woman to do? Teach, work in an office or make a good marriage? I said I don't feel pregnant, but already I feel a sort of nesting instinct. I kind of saw art college as filling in time till Will and I were ready to get married, so it's easy to think that this has just brought it forward, however inconvenient that is.'

'I still don't see why you should have to give up your studies, though.'

'There's no one to look after the baby. Besides, my mother says I've made my bed and I have to lie in it.'

Sandra pulled a face. 'That makes the whole thing sound like a punishment.'

They paid and took their trays of food back to the table.

'Did you get off with Dave the charmer?' Sandra asked Rosie suddenly.

Rosie blushed in embarrassment. She was trying to forget the whole episode. 'Let's just say his intentions turned out to be dishonourable,' she replied carefully.

Sandra looked at her searchingly for a second. 'You're too good for the likes of him,' she said.

SIX

December 1975

At that same moment, David had been seated in the bar at Owens Park, regaling his friend Eddie with the story of his conquests at the party last week. Over the last two years, he and Eddie had been at university together, and they always took full advantage of freshers' week, which involved new students, often away from home for the first time, experiencing university life and consuming vast quantities of alcohol. The legless freshers were easy targets, and David and Eddie couldn't resist the opportunity. Eddie now had a job with a leading water treatment company and David was in his final year.

'Despite your absence, Eddie, freshers' week followed the usual pattern.' David was on form, reminding his friend just what he was missing. 'There were the usual victims, then there's been the weekly parties.' He paused for effect. He was leaning back in his chair, speaking in a drawl that Eddie found intensely irritating. He knew David was doing it to wind him up, and he refused to react.

'Sounds a bit boring to me. Now myself, I prefer a bit of a challenge.'

Nice one, Eddie, a neat thrust.

David seemed not to have heard, but then he frowned and sat forward, placing his hand on his chin, as if in deep thought. 'There was Rosie, of course. I was surprised at the cool reception I received from her.'

'Losing your touch, Dave? Your one hundred per cent record with women must be in danger in the common room.' It was Eddie's turn to lean back in satisfaction, watching Dave's face for signs of discomfort.

'Hmm, I thought at first she was probably frigid or a rug muncher.'

'You got there in the end then?'

'I was intrigued by her indifference, so I decided to play the long game and get to know her. I saw her most weeks and she chatted with me but showed no interest whatsoever beyond that. She was elegant and well spoken – posh totty, definitely a challenge. Then I saw her at the party. To be honest, it wasn't one of my best performances. We'd both had too much to drink and I suspect it was her first time. Still, she's worth pursuing – she's from money, I can tell. The second one was better, I think the dope was wearing off, but wow, she definitely knew what she was doing.'

Eddie often wondered about David. They had both been bright students who had worked and played equally as hard as each other. They had had a shared interest in laddish banter and pranks, combined with a quest for sexual experience with no strings. Yet sometimes he was taken aback at how ruthless David could be when it came to getting what he wanted. At these times, it was as if his outer persona switched off, and a mindless force took over. He didn't really know him behind the banter, and when he sensed this about him, he didn't really want to.

He shrugged his thoughts away.

Men don't take friendships that far anyway, do they?

*

Eddie left David to his pint, and David turned his attention to congratulating himself on his path to university and quite how far he had come already.

He had been born in Fryston, a South Yorkshire mining village where his family lived in near poverty in a terrace of Coal Board houses tightly packed in back-to-back rows. His dad was a 'hewer', who came home black with coal each night and bathed in a metal tub in the living room in front of the range. David despised his dad and his lowly occupation. Some of the lads, whose parents had better jobs, tried to bully him, but they just got such a chilling stare that they backed off.

David's schoolmates accepted that they would go into mining, but his mum had other ideas. David was her only child and she groomed him from an early age to expect far more. She whispered in his ear constantly about how clever he was and what wonderful opportunities he would have if he worked hard at school and got into grammar school and university. But she warned him that it was their secret. He was not to say anything about these things to his dad or his friends, and to take care not to shine too much at school in case others began to resent him.

David's strategy became one of 'getting out whilst fitting in'. At junior school he was always top of the class, but he gained respect and kudos from the other kids by lending out his homework for a small fee. He was still in all the schoolboy scrapes, but his quick mind formulated the lies that would get him and his mates off the hook. He was nicknamed 'Teflon', and when he passed the exam for the grammar school, he received grudging admiration.

Manchester was his first experience of the world outside his pit village. He could still recall the sensations he felt when he stepped off the bus from Leeds, as if it was yesterday. A mix of bewilderment and excitement at the buzz of a big city. It promised everything he could want: bars, pubs, clubs and two top-class football teams, all of which he could take advantage of with his new-found freedom and a full grant. His choice of biochemistry paid dividends. The subject fascinated him and he hit it off straight away with his tutor, Steve

33

Finch, who recognised his ability and his determination to make the most of the opportunity.

Steve too had been a working-class boy who had passed for the grammar school and gone on to university, and he was quite open about how he saw something of himself in David. Towards the end of the previous summer term, Steve arrived at David's tutorial with a big grin on his face, and what unfolded served to broaden David's horizons much further.

'I think I might have something of interest to you. One of my former PhD students is now a researcher at UCLA.'

At that point, UCLA meant nothing to David, and he looked slightly puzzled.

'University College Los Angeles,' Steve explained. 'It has a world-renowned biochemistry department. One of my former students is leading a research project into aspects of DNA that may well play a significant role in the future of drug development. He has funding for a student to spend three months working with him over the summer. Are you interested?'

David couldn't believe what he was hearing and had no hesitation in accepting. For the remainder of the tutorial they talked about the exciting implications of DNA research and life in LA. A month later, he arrived at Los Angeles after a long journey via London and New York, flying on a new jumbo jet. Steve's former student, Mark, met him and took him to the student accommodation where he would stay for the next three months.

The research project proved fascinating, and the other researchers were especially patient with him as he grasped the new ideas that DNA manipulation involved. They were also great socialisers and made sure he got to see the city and had a good time outside of work. One long weekend they invited him on a hiking trip to 'Wet Beaver Creek'. David wasn't sure whether they were joking with him; they weren't, and it was a great trip.

They took a Greyhound bus from LA to Flagstaff. It was a long journey, but the coach was far more comfortable than anything in

England and he slept most of the way. The hike was great fun and the scenery so different from anything he'd seen before. He couldn't resist sending a postcard to Eddie with the caption 'Having fun in Wet Beaver Creek'. He smiled at the memory.

Two aspects of America took him by surprise. First was the size of the servings of food, and the fact that people consumed the lot. Secondly, and probably not totally unrelated, was the size of some of the people. They weren't merely fat; they were huge, and some had to waddle rather than walk. On one occasion when he was visiting one of the many parks to take photographs, he came up behind a man and a woman who were waddling along side by side, totally blocking the path. He took their picture there and then, as he didn't think anyone would believe quite how big they were.

The summer passed all too quickly. Mark was impressed at how much David had progressed and told him so. His time at UCLA gave him an insight into what could lie ahead for him and cemented his interest in drug development. He was now determined to get a first at Manchester.

After flying back to London, he caught a coach up to Yorkshire to visit his parents. Thinking about it now, he could still feel the shock of the stark contrast to the life he had been living in Manchester and LA.

The image of the uniform lines of dark terraced houses now seemed alien. The whole landscape looked drab and depressing. The blue skies of LA had been replaced by solid grey clouds that hovered low over the houses that clung to the hillside. The slag heap had increased in size since his previous visit and dominated the village even more, providing a grim reminder of the dangerous and dirty work undertaken by generations of Fryston men. There were no sparkling glass skyscrapers, no sun, no escape. The visit reinforced his decision to leave that world behind him. He felt acute embarrassment these days when he remembered how his parents lived. He despised his former schoolmates who had no ambition. He had escaped and was going to pursue every opportunity presented to him, and that included Rosie Jennings.

Well, the long game paid dividends there, he thought as he drained the remains of his pint.

SEVEN

October 2005

Lizzie was the younger of Linda's two daughters, but it was she who took charge of the proceedings following her mum's death. She and Louisa came straight from London by train, the day after Rosie's phone call. Pragmatic by nature, she had recently qualified as a barrister. By contrast, Louisa was artistic and creative, working as a fashion designer. Despite their different interests, they had formed a strong bond as children of a single mum and regularly met up.

Lizzie was waiting impatiently at Euston Station.

She's always late.

True to form, with minutes to spare to get to the platform, she spotted Louisa, head and shoulders above the crowd as usual, long blonde hair swirling as she ran, scattering people in her wake, her long legs skittering in all directions. She arrived with a flurry and linked Lizzie's arm to drag her along too.

As if it's my fault.

Lizzie couldn't help laughing out loud, despite the situation. This was so typical of Louisa; she was also laughing at the difference in their appearance, something that always amused her. Louisa was wearing a denim jacket, tube top, hipster jeans and a wide belt, while

Lizzie, when not in court, favoured an unselfconscious 1990's student grunge, from her brown-framed glasses to her Doc Martens boots.

They focussed on boarding the train, finding their carriage, adjoining seats, and then they hugged and started to cry into each other's shoulders.

'It's great to see you,' they both gasped simultaneously.

*

They were discussing their mum on the journey, and Lizzie suggested that they first go to the mortuary to pay their respects and formally identify her.

'Rosie has offered to meet us off the train and take us straight there. She's insisting we stay at her house for a while.'

Louisa talked a lot with her hands. Her response was to wave them around in a dramatic manner, causing Lizzie to duck.

'I'm hoping there's been a mistake and it's not Mum after all.'

'I think that's highly unlikely,' said Lizzie in a level voice, hoping to restore calm. 'I'm keen to seek out the truth behind Mum's death, though. There's a lot of questions to ask. Let's face it, we've not been a part of her life much since we both moved to London.'

'I feel guilty about that.'

Lizzie gave Louisa another hug. 'Don't be sad. Mum has a strong circle of friends. They must surely be able to shed some light on what's been happening.' She paused and frowned. 'You know, they are all so different, Rosie, Roberta and Sandra. I don't know much about them, apart from the fact that they all met up when they were students, and I intend to find out a lot more.'

'There you go again, yer honour,' said Louisa. It was one of their in-jokes.

'Why do you speak as if Mum is still here?'

'To me, she still is.'

*

A few days later, the post-mortem results arrived at Rosie's house. Lizzie was grateful that she was on her own, Louisa having gone out to visit a friend. She read the documents through, then arranged a meeting at the Refuge to share the news with the women whom they both saw as aunties and mentors.

Safety in numbers too.

They gathered in the staff room upstairs and sat round the table.

'It says Mum died of a heart attack,' Lizzie began, and was immediately interrupted by a shout from Sandra, who jumped up and started pacing about the room in her agitation.

'No way! She was only forty-eight.'

'I can't believe it either,' said Roberta, pulling Sandra gently back to her seat.

'Nor me,' echoed a shocked Rosie.

There was a wail from Louisa.

Lizzie waited patiently till they all finished, then carried on, in a noticeably shaky voice. 'That's not quite all. She had some injuries, but they were all consistent with the shock of the heart attack and the fall. No evidence of foul play or an accident, but there was a question mark as to why she died so quickly. Some tests were run and a toxicity report has found traces of several different drugs in her system. The coroner has ordered further tests and an inquest to establish if there are other factors that contributed to her death. In the meantime, he has released the body for a funeral.'

She sat back, looking strained by the news and waiting for another outburst from Louisa or Sandra.

'Is there any wine in the fridge?' asked Roberta.

'It's just too awful,' wailed Louisa, flapping her hands. 'They have inquests on TV dramas, don't they? I just can't help thinking of Mum's body. What pieces have they taken out?'

'You can stop that right now,' said Sandra firmly. 'I know for a fact that Linda has donated just about every organ she can for transplant, so she will be definitely missing a few bits at her funeral, but for a good cause.'

Surprisingly, this plain speaking seemed to shut Louisa up, for now.

'Did you know that Linda was taking the slimming drug Svelta?' Sandra said abruptly.

Lizzie's reply was equally direct. 'Yes, of course. It's been her job recently promoting it for Sipher, hasn't it? I've expressed my concern about her taking it several times. I even think I may have suggested she should watch it at her age. That didn't go down well. By the way, did any of you see that programme on Channel 4 recently about the safety of Svelta?'

Rosie looked shocked. 'No, I didn't. Don't Channel 4's documentaries aim to sensationalise rather than inform?'

Lizzie appeared to be choosing her next words carefully. 'I have already been in touch with the producers, and they've given me the names of a journalist and a researcher. I've arranged to meet with them next week.'

'How clever of you,' said Roberta.

'I'm glad you're dealing with this,' said Sandra, looking at Rosie. 'I think we're all too close to have a detached view.'

'I wonder what other drugs they are talking about,' Rosie said.

Lizzie's reply was again quite straightforward. 'You mean drugs in general? Mum gave us a pep talk, years ago when we first went down to London, about the perils of taking them, and she talked quite openly about her nurse training years then. But that was a long time ago, surely?'

'Yes, it was,' said Sandra. 'But when you are a drug-taker, it gets hard-wired into your system and it's always there, waiting for a weak moment.'

'Is that how you would class Mum?'

'No, I don't think so. Linda was determined that she would enjoy life and have fun,' replied Sandra. 'But drugs are unfortunately more of a temptation for doctors and nurses, and like I said, when you get older, you can return to those habits for whatever reason. I don't think she ever got over your dad's rejection, you know.'

Lizzie felt that Sandra would be biased to defend her mum and so turned to Roberta, seeking another opinion. She liked Roberta, whom she felt was inherently honest. 'What do you think, Roberta?'

'Linda was definitely pursuing her lost youth, hence taking Svelta to stay slim. She may have taken other drugs to recapture the mood as well. The media is obsessed with appearance over experience.'

Sandra laughed, easing the tension. 'That's a good line, Roberta.'

'Aunt Rosie, do you know anything about Svelta? I understand that Mum's job was promoting it to GPs. What did Uncle David have to do with it?'

Rosie answered carefully, 'It may sound surprising to you, but when I married David, my life was controlled by him and my parents. I found my corner, looking after my sons and then working in the Refuge here. In fact, I know very little of David's business life.'

'That's truly weird,' said Lizzie.

'How did you end up marrying him then, Aunt Rosie?' asked Lizzie.

EIGHT

December 1975 Rosie's story

Rosie had arrived back home from Manchester and immediately started her Christmas job at Marks and Spencer in High Wycombe. The pretty village of Amersham where her parents lived was a picture-perfect Christmas scene when coated with a blanket of snow, and she hoped it would happen again this year.

She still felt a strange excitement after having slept with David, despite his behaviour afterwards, and her stomach flipped each time she thought about it. She felt different now, more grown up, a woman not a girl, although she had expected full sex to be a more intimate and pleasurable experience. Having to hastily rearrange her clothing, and then leave early after being snubbed by him, had taken the edge off it.

Each day until Christmas, she sat on the bus to High Wycombe and wondered what David was doing. She knew he had a job lined up in Pontefract delivering the Christmas post. They had exchanged addresses, along with most other people in the students' union, with promises of cards that were unlikely to be sent. Rosie had given David her home phone number, but David had explained that there was a problem with his and he would let her know when it was repaired.

Another brush-off, probably.

She loved the sound of Christmas songs which were played continuously in most of the shops in Wycombe. Her mum, on the other hand, spent most evenings, arms folded under her ample bosom, complaining. 'I dislike how Americanised and commercialised Christmas is nowadays.'

Rosie's dad kept his head down under cover of the *Daily Telegraph*, and Rosie wondered at what point her mum had lost the ability to enjoy anything. She would be different. She would see the good in everything, and her children would know love, affection and an unbridled joy in living. Christmas would be magical.

Christmas Day at the Clarks' home passed in the same way as every Christmas Rosie could remember. Her Aunt Sheila, who had never married, would arrive mid-morning, bringing with her a sherry trifle. Its presentation was greeted by Rosie's dad with the words, 'Nobody makes a trifle as good as you can, Sheila.'

At this point, Rosie invariably left the room in fits of giggles while her mother glared at him, and Sheila blushed and smiled coyly.

Christmas lunch was followed by the Queen's speech at three o'clock, and teatime saw further praise heaped upon Aunt Sheila's trifle. *The Morecambe and Wise Show* even succeeded in putting a smile on her mum's face.

Most of Boxing Day was spent in front of the television eating turkey and stuffing sandwiches and watching reruns of old films. The following day Rosie planned to escape and maybe see some of her old school friends or spend a few hours at the local library doing research.

Waking up on Saturday, Rosie felt dog-tired and just wanted to go back to sleep, but her mum seemed to be deliberately banging around outside her bedroom door.

Eventually, Rosie could stand no more and was forced to drag herself out of bed. In the kitchen, warmed by the Aga, she poured herself her favourite childhood cereal and went to the fridge for a fresh pint of milk. Pressing her thumb into the silver metal top, she looked at the layer of cream on the top and her stomach suddenly heaved, forcing her to rush to the sink and gag. Normally she would have drunk it straight from the bottle.

What's wrong with me today?

Grabbing her duffle coat and Manchester University scarf, she shouted down the hall. 'I'm off to the library. Don't know what time I'll be back.'

She quickly let herself out of the house before her mum could delay her with questions.

As she walked to the library, the pavements were crunchy underfoot from a thin coating of snow. Once inside the building, she immediately felt at home with the smell of books and the quiet atmosphere of calm. She immersed herself in Margaret Mead's writing, which had been what had inspired her to apply for the highly sought-after sociology course at Manchester. Her enthusiasm for the subject meant that the hours passed quickly, and she was surprised when the librarian came over to explain they were about to close. She had been totally engrossed and, strangely, she hadn't felt hungry.

Rosie set off home, feeling suddenly empty and weary, trudging her way up the long gravel drive that led to her parents' house. She let herself in quietly, slipping off her shoes and tiptoeing across the parquet floor, a practice she had perfected over the years. She could hear her mum speaking in her best 'telephone voice'.

Rosie cringed.

'To whom am I speaking?'

She started to beat a retreat towards the stairs.

'Oh, I think she has just arrived back from the library. Just one moment, I'll go and get her.'

Marjorie swept into the hall. 'Darling, there is a young man with a broad northern accent on the phone for you. I am having trouble understanding him. I think he said his name was David.'

Rosie came to the phone, wishing she had been able to gather her thoughts before having to speak to him.

Marjorie Clark stayed put, looking at her daughter. 'Well, speak to the boy. I think he said he was in a phone box and his money was running out.'

Rosie tried an overly cheerful, 'Hi,' which was at odds with the way she felt. David's accent did indeed sound more pronounced than when she had last spoken to him.

They chatted about Christmas and he explained that he had been delivering post 'eight while eight', but was now in London staying with a friend. 'Can I come over to see you on Monday?'

Do I really want to see him after the way he behaved?

Just as she was about to come up with an excuse, the telephone beeped repeatedly and David was cut off.

Rosie felt totally mixed up. He had obviously been thinking about her and had kept her address.

But how many other addresses does he have?

She sat on the bottom of the stairs, hugging her knees to her chest, alone with her thoughts.

Marcus Clark walked out of the living room, a glass of Glenfiddich in his hand. 'Penny for them?' he said as he sat down next to Rosie and put his arm around her shoulder. She rested her head against his chest and felt like a little girl again. They sat together quietly for a few minutes before Rosie felt the need to restore normality.

'Oh, I'm just not sure I want to be sociable. One of my new friends from Manchester is coming over on Monday and I was hoping for a day to relax and get more research done at the library. Still, I can't get in touch with them, so there's nothing I can do about it.'

'Well, I will look forward to meeting her,' Marcus said as he got up to top up his glass.

'It's a him, Dad, not a her.'

Marcus tried unsuccessfully to conceal his surprise. 'Well, I will look forward to meeting *him* then,' he quipped, smiling as he headed to the kitchen to find more ice cubes for his next Scotch.

*

David's friend worked in construction and had to be on site by seven-thirty, which meant that David arrived at Marylebone Station on Monday amid the early-morning rush. He was amazed at the throngs of people. He was pushed and jostled as he fought his way against the prevailing direction of commuters. He found it all very exhilarating.

You have to know where you're going.

Once inside the station, he studied the departure board and bought a ticket for a train that would get him to Amersham for ten. He then entered the comparative calm of the station buffet and bought himself a cup of tea to pass the time. Watching the other passengers, he admired how they walked with a purpose and dressed so smartly. He felt a buzz of excitement at what the world outside his home in Yorkshire could offer him.

Just before nine he settled in his seat on the train and placed his copy of *Private Eye* out on the table. The cartoon on the front cover was so irreverent, he couldn't help laughing out loud, startling the woman opposite. She sniffed and turned her head away from him.

When he arrived at Amersham Station, he realised he had no idea exactly where Rosie lived; all he had was her address. The problem was solved by the friendly stationmaster, who scribbled some directions on the back of an old timetable. Amersham was nothing like the pit village he came from. There were no similarities whatsoever. This main street was like the pictures in the magazines he'd only seen in his doctor's waiting room. There were no terraces of grey houses here. As he followed the stationmaster's directions, he noticed most of the houses were large and had at least one car parked on their long driveway. David looked around him and saw the world that one day he intended to inhabit.

He turned into the drive leading to Rosie's house and realised that you couldn't see the house from the road because of the many mature trees. His feet crunched the stones underfoot and as the driveway bent to the left a Jaguar car came into view, parked to the side of a double-fronted detached house.

There's brass here.

His mind raced to recall his taped lessons on 'Speech and Etiquette'. On his arrival at university he had become painfully aware that his strong accent and use of certain phrases often made it difficult for his fellow students to understand him. Although not intending to hurt his feelings, they mimicked him, and he had realised there and then that to be successful and accepted as an equal, he would need to lose the excesses of his Yorkshire dialect.

Oh, bugger.

He feared the three weeks on the Christmas post had eroded any progress he had made. He gazed down at his shoes and gave each a quick polish on the back of his trouser legs, then stepped forward to ring the bell before moving back to the bottom step.

Marjorie Clark opened the door and looked down her aquiline nose at David. 'Good day,' she said in a voice that sounded to him like she was reading the BBC news. 'What can I do for you?'

'Er, I've come to see Rosie. I phoned her on Saturday to let her know.'

'Ah…' said Marjorie. 'I recognise that accent. You are the young man to whom I spoke on the telephone.'

To David's relief, a smiling Rosie appeared behind her mother. She winked at him. 'Come on in, Dave, and have a brew.' Rosie caught sight of her mum's expression and rolled her eyes. 'Okay, Mum, I mean a cup of tea.'

The Clarks' kitchen was warm and homely with oak units around three sides, an Aga, a huge refrigerator and, in the centre of the room, a large farmhouse-style table and chairs. David thought of his mother's kitchen with its hotchpotch of units covered with peeling Fablon, her old gas cooker and the small folding table pushed into one corner.

David felt a warmth towards Rosie that took him by surprise. In the months he had known her, she had never given the impression of coming from a wealthy family. There were students who bragged about their parents' cars, colour TVs and foreign holidays, but Rosie was not like them, and he liked her all the more for it.

They chatted about their respective Christmases while drinking tea from identical mugs. Her dad walked into the kitchen, and David stood up and shook Marcus's hand firmly. The men chatted easily. Marcus was an Arsenal fan with a season ticket, which surprised David.

Never judge a book by its cover.

'So, tell me about your course, David, but remember, I'm not a scientist,' Marcus quipped. 'What class of degree are you hoping for and what are your plans when you graduate?'

'I'm doing biochemistry and I'm hoping for a first. Biochemistry allows me to follow a number of options, but my main interest is drug discovery. I've had an interview with a pharmaceutical company, Sipher.'

Marcus, who had retired five years ago from the civil service, was impressed with David's single-mindedness. 'Well, you seem to know what path you want to follow, David. I wish you every success.'

Their conversation was interrupted by the arrival of Marjorie. David stood up, as he now knew to do when a lady entered a room, and Marjorie smiled. He had established his credentials.

NINE

Rosie

As New Year approached, Rosie started to worry about her period. It was due the week before Christmas and was unusually late. She felt tired but put it down to the frenzied crowds looking for bargains in the post-Christmas sale. She was beginning to panic. She had gone to the library to read up on the symptoms of early pregnancy, and what she had read did nothing to allay her fears.

This isn't happening to me, I only did it once.

In January, Rosie was sitting in the doctor's waiting room. She remembered it from countless childhood visits when her mother had brought her to see Dr Edmonds with stomach aches, sore throats and high fevers, and a variety of minor childhood illnesses and accidents. The sick feeling she now had in the pit of her stomach heralded an accident of an altogether life-changing type. Her palms were clammy and she kept trying to wipe them on her skirt. Beads of perspiration gathered at her temples, turning her neatly blow-dried hair frizzy at her hairline.

Earlier that week, she had handed a urine sample to the officious receptionist, who seemed to look down her nose at her with a knowing sniff. The days between then and now had seemed an eternity. Each morning she woke up knowing something was different and her mind immediately brought her predicament centre stage. A heavy feeling of dread would hit her again, making her feel heavy and lethargic. Throughout the week she kept examining her knickers in the hope of the slightest sign that her fears were unfounded, but they remained stubbornly bloodless.

The surgery operated a system in the waiting room where patients took a number on arrival and enquired of each other who went before and who went after them. Keeping the correct order was important, especially to those who had turned up before surgery opened to get seen first. The numbered discs were held on a rack by the door and those already waiting stared silently at each new arrival as they took a disc and found a seat. Rosie looked around the waiting room with its magnolia walls and smell of disinfectant, wondering what the other people waiting had wrong with them. Many of the older ladies sat with arms folded under their ample bosoms. It had always puzzled Rosie why women's breasts grew larger and seemed to compete for space with their tummies once they had got past forty, and why they all wore their hair in the style of a rigid, permed helmet. Her mum, who was now in her early sixties, had been an example of both shape and hairstyle for as long as Rosie could remember. Men, on the other hand, all seemed smaller, as if shrivelled by the passage of time. Rosie imagined those seaside postcards with fat ladies and little men, and absentmindedly went around the room pairing people up.

She was brought back to reality by the shrill voice of a statuesque lady sitting on the front row. 'You're number 13, aren't you? Number 12 has just gone out, so you're next, dear.'

Dr Edmonds was a kindly man who had known Rosie from birth. He had a passion for horses and frequently left afternoon surgery for short periods to sit in his car listening to the racing results. He had a younger, good-looking partner, Dr White, who had joined the practice ten years ago, and for many of the older patients was still regarded as 'learning the ropes', so Dr Edmonds' surgeries were always full.

The kindly doctor looked at Rosie over his glasses and then looked back at the piece of paper in front of him which held Rosie's future in black and white. 'You are pregnant, Rosie.' His words confirmed what she already knew. 'I'll book you into our next antenatal clinic here at the surgery and write to the hospital.'

He took a piece of cardboard from his desk drawer, which, on closer inspection, Rosie saw was actually two wheels, a smaller one fixed on top of a larger one.

'What was the first day of your last period?'

Rosie's mind went blank, so she made a guess at the second week in November.

Dr Edmonds rotated the top wheel and peered at the date on the outer wheel. 'That gives a confinement date of mid-August.'

Rosie's eyes filled with tears and she bit her lip in a futile attempt to stem their flow. She felt like a child again and wanted it all to go away like a bad dream on waking up.

'Does the baby's father have any idea of your situation?'

She shook her head.

'You will need the support of your family, so that is a conversation you will need to have sooner rather than later.'

Suddenly the reality of telling them hit home. She shivered and felt a cold sweat envelop her. She felt scared. The doctor gave her a sympathetic smile, concluding the five life-changing minutes. As she got up to leave, she felt lightheaded and unsteady on her feet, and she grabbed the back of the chair. She walked out through the waiting room and felt all eyes upon her. She lowered her head to avoid the other patients seeing her red eyes and putting two and two together.

As she walked back home in the cold, damp winter evening, Rosie pulled her coat around her and buried her nose in her scarf and felt angry.

How can I have been so naive?

She walked the roads of the town, along the High Street and back before reluctantly making her way back to her parents' house. She wondered what her options were. Abortion was now available under certain circumstances, but Dr Edmonds hadn't mentioned it. He had merely assumed that she would drop out of university and return home. She gave in to tears of frustration at the unfairness of it all.

She wondered whether to tell David now or to handle matters herself.

What will his response be?

She knew he was the father, but with all his other conquests, David might believe that she had slept with other men. She decided to find out more about an abortion once she was back in Manchester the coming week. Maybe once she knew more about her options, she might talk to David. Then again, she might not.

*

On arriving home in Yorkshire, David felt like a fish out of water. The couple of days in London, with the constant buzz of people enjoying themselves, had broadened his horizons. It energised him, made him feel that anything that he put his mind to was possible. He had enjoyed seeing Rosie and he had been bowled over by the lifestyle her family enjoyed but clearly took for granted. Here in the shadow of the pit and the slag heap, all he wanted to do was escape. Though his ageing parents had spent their lives working to give him the best they possibly could, he'd had sight of the world he wanted to live in, and the contrast was stark. It was another week before lectures began and he couldn't stay in the grime a day longer. It drained his energy. His thoughts drifted back to the comparative opulence of Rosie's family kitchen. The Scotch on the rocks he had enjoyed with Marcus.

Can I chance another visit?

He still had enough funds from the Christmas post to cover the cost of a trip to Amersham.

He walked to the village telephone box, a bright beacon of red in a sea of grey and a lifeline to the world outside the pit. There were two people in front of him. Few houses in the village had telephones, so there was often a queue. David had given some thought to how he would address Mr or Mrs Clark should they answer but was taken aback when he heard an unfamiliar voice.

'The Clark residence. Who is speaking, please?'

David pushed his money into the coin box. 'May I speak to Rosie, please?'

'One moment.'

David could hear footsteps tap-tapping on the parquet floor, and he could almost smell the wood and sense the welcoming warmth of the Aga.

'Hello, Rosemary Clark speaking.'

'Hi, Rosie, it's me, David. Thought I'd phone for a chat and see when you're planning to come back to Manchester.'

David heard a muffled, 'Thank you, Sylvia.' There was a pause while the footsteps tapped away again.

'Hello, David. Sorry, that was the cleaning lady.' She sighed. 'I'm not actually sure what I'm doing.'

David had hoped for a more enthusiastic response. The pips went on the telephone, so he put more money in the coin box and cut to the chase. 'I'm down in London again tomorrow, so I was wondering if I could come over to see you again.'

He waited for a reply, but there wasn't one, and he was worried his money would run out. 'Is that okay? I'll get an early train so we could make a day of it.'

'Okay. See you then.'

He was puzzled by her apparent lack of interest. This was something that had never happened to him where women were concerned.

Two days later, David took the first train of the day down to King's Cross, took the tube to Marylebone and was once again amazed at the swarms of people criss-crossing one another's paths yet appearing totally self-contained. He loved the dynamism of the place. The people were all dressed so smartly, and the women's hair was clean and glossy. Many of the young men wore shirts in a wide range of colours and had collar-length hair with curls created by wash-and-wear perms. They would have been described as 'Nancy boys' back where he came from. The city seemed to ooze fun, wealth and success, and it seduced David completely.

Arriving in Amersham, he realised again this was the type of place he wanted to live in: an affluent small town within striking distance of a vibrant metropolis. The job offer he had just received from Sipher Pharmaceuticals was his first step on the ladder of success. At Rosie's door, he glanced down at the small bunch of flowers, bought at the High Street florists for Marjorie. He rang the bell, Rosie answered and he thought she looked pleased to see him. Marjorie was on Rosie's heels and her eyes quickly fixed on the small bunch of pink roses David held.

'These are for you, Mrs Clark, to thank you for your kind hospitality.' David hoped he had structured the sentence correctly. Marjorie beamed with delight and David knew he had won her over.

Rosie had arranged to borrow her mum's Vauxhall Viva for the day, so they drove over to Marlow, where they sat by the lock watching the boats come and go. By lunchtime David, who hadn't eaten anything but a chocolate bar at King's Cross, was starving and he suggested they find a pub for a bite to eat. They strolled along hand in hand, eventually finding The Two Brewers and taking a table next to a roaring log fire. David ordered at the bar and, before returning to Rosie, took a quick look around the pub. He was amazed at the opulence of the place. No peeling linoleum and cigarette butts, just oil lamps and antiques, none of which were nailed down.

Their meals arrived. David tucked in and was halfway through his chicken pie when he looked at Rosie. He thought she looked tired. She was definitely not her usual chatty self. She had hardly eaten any of her 'scampi in the basket' and she just sipped the Coke she had ordered.

'Is something wrong with your dinner, er, I mean lunch, Rosie?'

'I'm just not that hungry.'

The next half hour continued in a similar vein, with Rosie taking sips of Coke while David attempted banal conversation.

'Would you rather I go?' David eventually asked in frustration.

'You probably will anyway,' she countered.

'What are you talking about? I don't understand the sudden change, Rosie. Is it something I've said or done?'

'I'm pregnant.'

David's mind raced.

Could it be mine?

Rosie was not one of the girls who slept around. That was what had made her an interesting challenge.

'What are you going to do about it?'

David knew friends who had girlfriends who got pregnant and had paid for abortions.

'I'm going to find out about an abortion when I get back to Manchester. The baby is yours, David, in case you were in any doubt.'

They drove back in silence. David's mind raced as he struggled to come to terms with what he had just heard. Back at the Clarks' home, Marcus and Marjorie welcomed them warmly and asked about their day. Oblivious to any tension, Marjorie asked David if he would like to stay for dinner. He tried politely to decline, explaining that he would miss the last train from King's Cross, but Marjorie was having none of it.

'You can sleep in the guest room, David. We would love you to stay.'

Rosie looked at David. David looked back at her and then turned to Marjorie. 'That's very kind of you, Mrs Clark. I would love to stay too.'

Marjorie glowed.

Dinner was coq au vin, dauphinoise potatoes and a selection of vegetables, accompanied by a smooth red Burgundy, and dessert was Marjorie's pièce de resistance: Black Forest gateau. Conversation flowed and David talked about the job offer from Sipher which he had accepted in writing. The Clarks approved of their daughter's new friend. Marcus had found a bottle of Gevrey-Chambertin for the occasion. David savoured the wine, which was totally different from the Spanish reds that were the staple of many student parties. After port and cheese, Marcus and Marjorie retired to the living room to watch *This Week* on television, while Rosie and David cleared the dinner things into the kitchen. He watched as Rosie opened a door in one of the kitchen units, revealing the dishwasher. He had never seen one, other than in an advert, so he watched in amazement as the contents of the dinner table were removed from sight in under five minutes.

Marjorie, meanwhile, had swung into action, closing the curtains in the guest room, putting on the Tiffany bedside lamps and turning on the electric blanket.

'Rosie, can you show David the guest room and bathroom, please? David, I've just turned the blanket on low to take the chill off the bed, so you might want to turn it up. Do you need anything else?'

Marjorie was in full hostess mode and Rosie wanted to shrink with embarrassment.

'No, ta, Mrs Clark, you've spoilt us rotten.' He was about to compliment her for dinner with 'and a reet good scran' but managed to stop before the words were out of his mouth.

Marjorie looked perplexed. Rosie smiled. David stood uncomfortably with his hands in his pockets.

'Well, goodnight then, and sleep well.'

David and Rosie were left alone. Taking hold of her hands, David smiled and pulled Rosie gently towards him. He kissed her deeply, as he had done that night at Owens Park. Despite his obvious arousal, he knew that tonight would stop at a kiss.

Rosie smiled back at him as she left for her own room, just as a voice from the galleried landing followed her. 'Bedtime, Rosie.'

David lay in his warm bed, absorbing the luxury of the Clarks' lifestyle. The huge house was centrally heated and even the guest room had its own bathroom. At home his parents had only had an inside toilet installed relatively recently. He thought more about the situation and reviewed his options. He felt sure he would be able to find out how to sort an abortion. However, as he looked around, he wondered what the downside would be of making a go of it with Rosie. Tomorrow he would ask her to marry him.

*

The next morning, the four of them enjoyed breakfast together around the large kitchen table. David took hold of Rosie's hand and gave it a gentle squeeze.

'What are your plans for today, David?' Marjorie enquired.

'I was hoping that Rosie could show me around again. The area is really beautiful.'

'Well, I'm afraid I need the car today. It's the AGM of our local WI over in High Wycombe and I won't be back until this afternoon.'

'It's a lovely day for a walk, so we can do that if you like,' Rosie suggested.

'Just what I was thinking,' David said, and squeezed her hand again.

Marcus lowered the *Daily Telegraph*, winked at David and raised the paper again.

Perhaps this is going to be less of a problem than I thought.

Out in the winter sunshine, David and Rosie walked through the woods hand in hand, stopping every now and then to share a kiss. David looked at Rosie and reaffirmed that she would indeed be an asset, with her classic looks, slim figure and her knowledge of how to behave in every social setting. He chose his moment with care. As the sun lit up the rivulets in a picture-perfect stream, he turned towards her, tilted her chin towards him and looked longingly into her eyes.

'Marry me, Rosie. I've loved you from the moment I saw you. I tried sleeping with other women to get you out of my mind, but I'm in love with you. I have never felt like this about anyone, and now we're having a child together, I know this was meant to be.'

Her legs began to tremble, but David caught her and pulled her close. As he held her in his arms, he felt her body relax into his, the top of her head nestling under his chin. They stayed like that for several minutes.

'Say something, Rosie.' David gently lifted her chin so he could look into her eyes. It was a technique that had never failed him. 'Say you will be my wife and I promise to care for you and our child.'

'Yes, David. I will marry you.'

'I want to do this properly and ask your father.'

Marcus had just finished the *Telegraph* crossword and was in a good mood when they arrived back at the house. Marjorie was still at the WI meeting.

'Are you going to mention the baby?' Rosie asked in trepidation.

'No, not today. We can raise it in a month or so – no point upsetting the apple cart just yet.'

David asked Marcus if he could have a word with him and the men disappeared into the living room. Rosie sat on the bottom stair with her arms clasped around her knees, rocking gently. After what seemed an age, both men appeared, smiling.

'Well, this is a surprise, no question about it, but a nice surprise.'

Marcus gave his daughter a fatherly hug, which was interrupted all too soon by the sound of tyres on gravel as Marjorie's car made its way up the drive.

She bustled in with WI papers under one arm and a basket full of homemade jam in the other.

Marcus looked at her in a way that stopped her in her tracks. 'Marjorie, darling, David has asked me for Rosie's hand in marriage and I have said we would be delighted.'

David caught sight of Marjorie's expression and sensed her annoyance at being presented with a 'fait accompli', but he knew that once Marjorie had time to review the situation, she would find organising a wedding right up her street.

It was agreed that David would stay another night, and after a dinner of beef stroganoff and rice followed by lemon meringue pie, they all sat in the living room discussing the wedding. David and Rosie had already agreed to suggest an Easter wedding. He would be starting work shortly afterwards and most people would be able to come over during the Easter holiday. Marjorie initially thought Easter too soon – what would people think? She was eventually won around by David's argument and charm.

He was satisfied at how things had gone so far; he would deal with the pregnancy fallout when it came.

TEN

1976 Rosie

Rosie's life had then revolved around arrangements for her wedding, which Marjorie managed like a military campaign. Church and reception were booked; the latter working out perfectly, as The Compleat Angler had just had a last-minute cancellation.

'How fortuitous.' Marjorie couldn't contain her delight.

Rosie felt a strange sadness and wondered what unfortunate circumstances could have meant a cancellation for some unlucky couple. She shuddered at the thought of David getting cold feet or, worse still, leaving her standing at the altar. She subconsciously placed her hand on her stomach and replayed his words in her mind.

This was meant to be.

The invitations were printed, the cake was ordered and Marjorie's dressmaker, Daisy, was asked to make the dresses for Rosie and her bridesmaids. Marjorie was also keen to speak to David's parents about the wedding.

'I'm sure they would want to be involved in the arrangements, darling. Can you remember to ask David again for their number?'

Rosie kept stalling, and for good reason. She knew they didn't have a telephone, so the request was both futile and embarrassing.

She also knew her mother's motivation was to find out more about the family she was marrying into and their 'suitability'. She herself had yet to meet her future in-laws.

By early March Rosie was over three months pregnant, and David said that they ought to tell her parents but suggested that they explain that she was only a few weeks along.

'Doing it this way means the baby was conceived while we were engaged. They'll be shocked, but I think this will just be a bit more acceptable.'

The invitations had gone out. He knew Marjorie could not call things off without losing face.

'You've thought this through, haven't you?' Rosie said with an anxious smile.

In the lounge at Amersham, David was seated, holding Rosie's hand tightly as they waited for her parents' reaction to the news. Her father accepted it with benign resignation. He liked David and he quite liked the idea of a grandchild. Her mother, on the other hand, stared straight ahead, stony-faced and speechless. Rosie looked at her face and could imagine what she was thinking. Something along the lines of…

My daughter, who has all the advantages of a middle-class upbringing, is descending to the level of a trollop from the local council estate.

David rose to the occasion by declaring his undying love for Rosie. 'I have loved Rosie from the first moment I first met her. I'm sorry about what's happened, but I will take great care of Rosie and your grandchild.'

Rosie looked from her dad to her mum and realised that from their perspective there really wasn't an alternative path to pursue.

Rosie, Roberta, Sandra and Linda continued to meet up regularly in Manchester. Rosie was spending most weekends with her parents until the wedding but had kept her room on in Manchester after leaving university and found a job working for the gas board during the week. One weekend, her parents came to see her. Rosie knew her mum's views on girls living with a man outside marriage and had made sure that David had removed all evidence of his presence in her room. Her dad found one of David's socks by the bed and discreetly hid it from his wife behind his back, winking at Rosie as he did so.

How can my parents be so completely different and be married? Do David and I have such different outlooks on life?

She quickly dismissed the thought. He loved her and she loved him.

David's job with Sipher Pharmaceuticals was not conditional on his class of degree, so future income would not be a problem. They now had to find a house, which meant getting together a deposit and arranging a mortgage. As well as paying for the wedding, Marcus had generously offered them money as a wedding present, plus three hundred pounds to tide them over till David started work. Rosie was his only child and he could afford to be generous.

The wedding was to be a grand affair on Easter Saturday, and she had asked Linda and Sandra to be her bridesmaids. There had been two visits to Amersham where they were all seized by Rosie's mother and taken to see Daisy to choose fabrics, patterns, accessories and colours.

Rosie thought her mum looked like a galleon in full sail as she barged down the street, her coat and scarf billowing out behind her. The women struggling to keep up, were like flotsam in her wake, clutching her shopping bags and lists. Roberta had come too. She was very good at picking style and colours, not only for the dresses but for table decorations, flowers and the multitude of other items to be chosen.

Rosie had had a quiet word with her friends beforehand. 'Just let my mum have her way. I'm her only child and I feel badly enough about the circumstances of this wedding so I'm trying to make it up to her.'

The third and final dress fitting took place two weeks before the wedding. This was to check how much Rosie's figure had altered and to see if anything had to be let out. Daisy had cleverly styled the dress with a high waist and a front pleat.

Rosie was lucky and hardly showing so, after much discussion, it was decided the dress would do. The bridesmaids' dresses were tried on again, just to be sure. They were in deep magenta chiffon, strapless and falling softly to the floor. Sandra's and Linda's were tighter round the waist than at the last fit. Daisy looked at Marjorie in consternation.

Ever-intuitive, Roberta blundered in. 'Don't worry,' she said, 'nobody else is pregnant.'

Marjorie rolled her eyes at Daisy.

'Oh, don't worry,' Sandra echoed, 'my stomach balloons at the slightest thing. We had a big dinner last night, didn't we, and I haven't been to the loo yet.'

Marjorie turned her head away and sniffed at this further undiplomatic revelation.

'I'm due on at any moment,' Linda said. 'I'm sure I'll be fine in two weeks' time.'

Marjorie looked slightly faint and went to sit down. It was left to Rosie and Daisy to discuss the final details, while Linda and Sandra struggled to suppress their giggles.

*

David couldn't put it off any longer and had finally taken Rosie to meet his parents. On the train from Manchester to Leeds, he embarked on what sounded like a well-rehearsed speech.

'You will see a different way of life than the one you've been used to,' he began. 'The mining villages are not pretty, like Amersham. They are rows of blackened houses, grim and dirty. Work in the mines is hard and manual, and there is only so much that can be done to earn a wage. It doesn't take long to bring a fit man down, and most of the families live in poverty and some form of sickness.'

Rosie looked appalled.

'My mum took in washing and mending to help with the rent. She encouraged me to look for a life outside the pit and I have her to thank for where I am now.'

'She sounds a strong woman.'

They left the train and caught a bus to Pontefract, and then Fryston. Leeds was a compact city, and they soon left the built-up areas and tower blocks behind and travelled through miles of countryside interspersed with small villages, all with drab uniform housing, some with pit wheels and winding mechanisms standing out in sharp contrast to the green countryside.

'I've never seen a landscape like this before,' said Rosie.

David explained how the villages sprang up around the coal mines. He was feeling increasingly uncomfortable at the contrast between his upbringing and hers. The bus stopped at Fryston, where they were the only people to get off. David looked around quickly then pulled his jacket collar up, grabbed Rosie's hand and set off at a march towards the lines of back-to-back terraces that clung to the hillside. He didn't look up until they arrived in front of a mid-terrace with the same green front door as every other house they had passed. A small woman with gunmetal grey hair and a deeply lined face opened the door. Her face lit up when David greeted her.

'Hello, Mam. This is my fiancée, Rosie.'

Rosie extended her hand to Mrs Jennings, which the woman took, covering Rosie's hand with both of hers.

'George, it's our David with his young lady. Come in, love, come in.'

Mona Jennings kept hold of Rosie's hand and led her into the small kitchen at the back of the house, where George Jennings was reading the *Daily Mirror*. He looked up and smiled. 'By 'eck, lad, thought you'd forgotten where we lived, but it's grand to see you.' Turning to Rosie, George shook Rosie's hand enthusiastically, and she was surprised at how rough it felt.

'This is Rosie, Dad. We're going to get married.'

Mona's eyes immediately dropped towards Rosie's stomach, which was still almost flat. Weddings in the pit village were often necessitated by girls getting caught.

'We wanted to come and invite you to the wedding ourselves. I've got a job and we don't see any reason to wait.'

Mona relaxed. 'Nice to meet you, Rosie. Come over here and rest your legs.'

George stubbed out his Capstan Full Strength among the pile of that morning's cigarettes that filled a heavy glass ashtray. His voice was gravelly from a lifetime of coal dust and smoking, and he wheezed as he got up to offer his chair to his future daughter-in-law.

Mona excused herself and disappeared upstairs. When she came back down, she had a bulky envelope in her hand, which she handed to David. 'Well, go on, open it.' Mona looked fondly at her son.

The envelope contained two hundred pounds in ten-pound notes. David was unusually speechless and couldn't work out where so much money had come from, as his dad had always had one of the lowest-paid jobs in the pit. It turned out that it was money left to him by his grandfather, who had been the head clerk. David had always suspected his grandfather thought his daughter had married beneath her. He too wanted his grandson to escape to a world beyond the pit, and he had made sure he was aware of a wider world. The money had been left in his will to be given to David on his marriage.

David watched Rosie take in the kitchen with its peeling work surface and mismatched furniture, the tin bath standing up in the corner. He had told her George took a bath in front of the fire.

'That is so very kind of you both. Thank you very much.' Rosie gave both George and Mona a kiss. David, shamed by Rosie's affectionate gesture, kissed his mum and shook his dad's hand.

'Let's have us teas, Mona,' George instructed his wife, 'and some of that seed cake will go down a treat too. Mona's seed cake always wins first prize at the miners' welfare.'

Mona poured the tea out of the dark brown teapot; there was little difference in colour between the teapot and the tea. Sterilised milk was then added, together with two teaspoons of sugar.

'There you go, love, that'll put hairs on your chest,' quipped George.

David tensed with embarrassment, but Rosie took a sip and pronounced it, 'Just what I needed, Mr Jennings.'

'Oh, please call us Mona and George; after all, we'll soon be family.' David's tension grew and he pulled out his bus timetable to check on the next bus back to Leeds.

Mona was looking at David with a smile of contentment, which he hoped meant she was happy with his choice of wife.

A mother's love.

David told his parents about his job with Sipher and saw the look of satisfaction on Mona's face. All the sacrifices she had made had been worth it. George clearly didn't understand the world of pharmaceuticals, but he was impressed that, on starting his first job, David would be earning twice the wage that he had been.

Before their visit, David had explained to Rosie that his dad had expected him to go into mining, and how when he took his A levels instead of starting a mining apprenticeship, he had told George it would help him to start in mining at a higher level. Then, when he enrolled at university, he said it would help him to go into management.

'Little by little, I've eased myself out of there.'

Rosie realised what drive and determination David must have needed to break away from the traditions of Fryston. She admired her future husband's ambition.

Early that evening, as they travelled back towards Leeds, David relaxed as the distance grew between him and Fryston and he got closer to the world he now belonged in. The visit had gone well. He had won the secret battle he and his mum had been fighting to get him out of there, and his dad didn't even know about it. His parents were impressed with his job and they had got on well with Rosie.

Back in Manchester, they found a lovely detached house to the south of the city. While David arranged the house purchase, Rosie set about registering with the local doctors, met the midwife who would look after her for the length of her pregnancy, and booked herself into St Mary's, the nearest hospital, for her baby's delivery.

'Big changes ahead,' Rosie said to David a week before the wedding as they stared into Mothercare's window. She turned towards him. 'I don't know if I'm frightened or excited or both. Do you like this colour?'

David looked at the yellow-themed nursery display. 'Daytona yellow,' he said dreamily, thinking of the colour of his new company car.

ELEVEN

April 1976 The Wedding

David and his best man Eddie had been sitting on a hard pew for nearly half an hour at the front of St Mary's Church in Amersham. As the organ began to play Handel's 'Arrival of the Queen of Sheba', he turned back to see Marcus and Rosie walking up the aisle towards them.

David realised again how effortlessly elegant Rosie was and what an asset she would be to his career. She looked stunning. Her full-length ivory dress had a veil, part of which covered her face and the remainder, edged with crystals and pearls, fell in line with the train of her dress. As they arrived alongside David and Eddie, David watched Rosie turn and smile at her dad, who wiped a tear from the corner of his eye. Then she turned back towards the man she was about to marry.

As David lifted the veil back from Rosie's face, revealing flawless skin and perfectly applied make-up, she smiled radiantly at her soon-to-be husband and David heard an involuntary low whistle from his best man. Sandra and Linda stood behind Rosie, wearing extremely tight-fitting dresses which were under great strain as they bent down to arrange the veil and train.

David's gaze followed Marcus as he returned to Marjorie, who was dressed head to toe in powder blue.

I wonder when her body became like a sack of potatoes.

Behind them were relatives he supposed they hadn't seen for years together with Marjorie's friends from the WI and old work colleagues of Marcus.

David felt pleased with himself. The pregnancy news had been delivered at just the right time.

He took a quick look over his right shoulder at his parents. Mona was beaming with delight and George was pulling at his shirt collar. He didn't have a suit and the one he had hired was ill-fitting. David was embarrassed by him.

David's friends from Fryston had hired a coach and come down late last night. He knew the tradition on such journeys was to lay on crates of Tetley's and barley wine for the journey. He looked across a sea of pale faces, some struggling to keep their eyes open, all obviously suffering the after-effects of the previous evening. His spirits lifted when he saw friends from university sitting behind them.

The service was short and simple, and when the couple made their vows, Rosie promised to 'love, honour and obey', to Sandra's dismay. When it came to 'all my worldly goods I thee endow', David felt a sense of satisfaction. This was another step towards acquiring all the good things life could offer him.

After signing the register, they made their way back down the aisle to Mendelssohn's 'Wedding March'. David glanced across towards the Fryston contingent as he passed their pews and became full of trepidation for the hours ahead.

Once the photographer had finished taking pictures, by which time many were complaining of jaw-ache, having to smile so often and for so long, Rosie and David were driven in a cream vintage Rolls Royce to the reception at The Compleat Angler in Marlow. As none of David's family possessed a car or could drive, his friends from university had given them lifts to the reception. The contrast between Rosie's family and his own made David extremely uncomfortable. As they headed the family line-up to greet guests, his discomfort increased. Marcus and Mona seemed to chat comfortably to one another, but David watched in despair as his dad stared at his shoes, clearly unsure of what to say or what to do, while Marjorie glared at Marcus, who was obviously enjoying himself. Once the guests had all been welcomed and had taken a glass of Veuve Clicquot, they took their places according to the seating plan which had placed like-minded people together. Sitting at the top table, David scanned the room. His eyes came to rest on the boys from Fryston, who were well-oiled and becoming more boisterous by the minute.

Christ Almighty. I think inviting that lot is turning out to be a bad idea.

David had no appetite at all and ate little of his prawn cocktail, chicken Cordon Bleu and lemon posset. After coffee, the master of ceremonies banged his spoon twice on the table to announce that it was time for the speeches.

David watched Rosie fight back tears as Marcus spoke lovingly about the daughter that had brought them so much happiness and spoke kindly about David, who he said he knew would look after his daughter. Finally, he thanked George and Mona for nurturing such an accomplished young man.

If he only knew, thought David and his mum.

They exchanged knowing looks whilst his dad sat there, as ever, a pawn in the game. Marcus finished with a toast.

'To the bride and groom,' was echoed by the guests as they raised their glasses of champagne, which had been refilled.

David stood up and thanked Marcus and Marjorie for their kindness and the warm welcome he had received from them when he asked for their daughter's hand in marriage. 'I know I am so lucky to have found the love of my life in Rosie, and I meant every word of my vows when I promised to love and cherish her.' David knew such a public declaration of love would win Marjorie over.

Sandra and Linda both took gulps of champagne.

'I want to thank you all for coming today to share this special day in our lives, especially those who have had to travel from further afield.'

The Fryston contingent gave a self-congratulatory whoop, and David turned towards Linda and Sandra to raise his glass in a toast.

'To the beautiful bridesmaids, who have looked after my wife with such diligence.'

As people raised their glasses, David caught sight of his dad, who was looking perplexed, and realised that his face spoke volumes about the collision of two disparate worlds.

You don't get it, do you?

The beautiful bridesmaids were toasted, and it was then Eddie's job to respond on their behalf. At the mention of the best man's speech, the Fryston boys banged their cutlery on the table as Eddie stood up. Marjorie looked aghast at their vulgarity and Eddie, sensing the mood, put his hand up to quieten the mob.

David felt the sweat run down his back as his best man launched into his speech.

'Ladies and gentlemen, thank you on behalf of these two lovely ladies, and what a pair of beauties they are. For those of you who don't know me – which, looking around the room, is most of you – my name is Eddie and I'm about to give my friend Dave the worst ten minutes of his life.' He paused. 'Only joking, Dave, it will probably be nearer five.'

David felt his mouth become dry and Marjorie visibly paled while the whooping started afresh from the tables from Fryston.

'I've known Dave for three years now and we met while watching a football match back at university in Manchester. I'd seen Dave the player in action – I mean football, of course, for some time as we both played five-a-side. It was a match I'd like to forget, as Dave's team, Leeds, beat my team, Arsenal, 6-1.'

This brought about cheers of 'Mighty Whites, Mighty Whites', from the back, which Eddie managed to silence with another raising of his hand. David was unsure where this was going, and

71

beads of sweat appeared on his brow while Marcus, enjoyed the banter.

'That night cemented our friendship and I can honestly say we've been partners in crime ever since. I realised that night that Dave likes to win, and today I can see he has clearly hit the jackpot.'

Marjorie's face went puce. 'Like a prize at some ghastly fun fair,' she muttered to Marcus.

'In putting together this speech, I thought I should ask some of Dave's ex-girlfriends for some advice to offer Rosie, but due to the foot-and-mouth outbreak, many are no longer with us. Seriously, though, when Dave met Rosie I knew none of the previous incumbents could come close. So now that she's making a decent man of you, Dave, I'll need to be a little discreet about the years at Manchester. But for those of you who might like to know more, I can be persuaded to talk in more detail after a few sherbets. We have a few telegrams here for Rosie and Dave. The first is from Aunt Sheila, who is on holiday in Beaver Creek in Arizona. Dave, wasn't that the area you frequented in your gap year?'

David smiled weakly, realising Eddie was on a roll. The younger guests collapsed in fits of giggles while Marjorie looked puzzled. Marcus bit his lip in an attempt to suffocate a smile and the older guests wondered what the joke was all about.

'*Wishing you both the very best for the future. I'm sorry to miss your big day but send you both my best wishes for your future together. Aunt Sheila.*'

And one final telegram from Christine.

'*Congratulations to you both on your special day, Christine. PS Dave please return the keys to the flat.*'

Eddie looked out at his stunned audience with a cheeky grin, and after what seemed an uncomfortably long time, laughter erupted when they finally realised the last telegram was a joke. Marjorie was not laughing and sat rigidly with what seemed to be a nasty smell under her nose.

'Ladies and gentlemen, please raise your glasses to the bride and groom.'

72

After the final toast, the master of ceremonies explained that the room would be cleared to make way for the evening's dancing and that a free bar was in operation in the next room. The Fryston contingent got up with such gusto that they knocked over a couple of chairs in their haste not to waste a moment's drinking time. Having only just survived Eddie's speech, David now turned his fears to whatever mayhem a night's drinking would inflict on the sensitivities of middle England.

David led Rosie onto the floor for their first dance. He had chosen 'The First Time Ever I Saw Your Face', as he knew it was Rosie's favourite and it would cement his image as the loving husband. After a discreet space they were joined by other couples, including Linda and Eddie, who seemed to be getting on extremely well. Marjorie and Marcus too joined the dancers. Marjorie appeared almost relaxed, having been assured by Marcus that Eddie's speech was amusing, if a little risqué, and was what happened 'these days'. As the night wore on, music from The Rolling Stones, Queen and ABBA, together with copious amounts of alcohol, dispelled any lingering inhibitions, and the dance floor was packed until the early hours.

At midnight, the newlyweds slipped away to the honeymoon suite. As Rosie lay sleeping after they had made love, David lay with his arms behind his head, thinking how well things had turned out on so many levels. The day had just about survived a clash of cultures. Then there was the fulfilment of his mum's plans for him, his university choice, which had led to the job he was about to start, and Rosie. She was indeed an asset.

2005

'You know, I don't think I've ever talked about how I came to marry David till now,' said Rosie, bringing them all back to the present. 'I'm quite appalled, actually, at how I came to marry someone I hardly knew. It was almost like an arranged marriage.'

'That was my first thought, but I didn't dare mention it,' said Lizzie.

'Then he was the first and only love I ever had. I think I was so protected as a child I thought that was what happened, like a fairy tale. I was lucky that my parents and David made it so easy.'

'Don't you wish you'd finished your education and had a career before you had children?' asked Lizzie.

'That's how your generation think, an attitude made possible by the pill. We were just at the beginning of that. Women didn't aspire to careers unless they were single, because the chance of a baby was always there, and who would look after it? The armed forces made women leave if they got married, you know.'

'That's grossly unfair,' said Louisa.

'Your mum got on her feet after her divorce, thanks to changes in careers for women.'

Lizzie looked puzzled. 'Yes, she was doing so well in her career – it was strange she still wanted a marriage.'

Rosie gave an ironic laugh. 'We were brainwashed and programmed at an early age.'

TWELVE

November 2005

Lizzie, with her dad Eddie's help, was starting to make the first arrangements for Linda's funeral. Together with Louisa, they were having a day at Linda's house, sorting out the necessary paperwork. The heating had been left on a timer since her death, but the house still felt cold. They had all lived there at some point in their lives, but now it felt empty. Eddie turned on the coal-effect gas fire and Louisa made a pot of coffee.

She looked for milk in the fridge. 'Oh, it's still fresh,' she said, biting her lip to try and stop her thoughts making the inevitable connection.

Only a few days ago…

Without speaking, they all settled on the familiar sofas in the living room.

'When I look back now at what we had, there was nothing bad about it,' Eddie began. 'I was just young, arrogant and ambitious. I felt stifled by domesticity and I thought I could have something better, and I now know that wasn't the case.'

He rolled his eyes at the thought of Megan, his second wife, and Lizzie chuckled despite herself. 'Don't be too hard on yourself,

Dad,' she said. 'Rosie was telling us yesterday about how she came to marry David. It sounded like an arranged marriage at best, at least you had a choice.'

'Well, yes and no. Your mum made a beeline for me after Rosie and David's wedding. Yes, come to think of it, her behaviour is very much like a bee. You know how she is when she has a "bee in her bonnet"?'

Lizzie noticed the use of the present tense and continued in the same vein. 'Yes, when Mum decides she's going to do something, she just goes for it, doesn't she, to the point of obsession.'

'That was just it, it was all about her. But there was something else driving her too. I could never put my finger on it. Sadly, we never got to know each other very well.'

'What about the drugs in her system, do you know anything about them, Dad? How did they cause a heart attack?'

'You could say I broke her heart long ago,' said Eddie.

THIRTEEN

1976–7 Linda and Eddie's story

After Rosie's wedding, Linda had focussed on her burgeoning romance with Eddie. He had all the traits she was looking for. He was fun and good-looking in an unconventional sort of way, not tall, slightly stocky with thick spiky blond hair. He was sports mad and had played football well enough to have had a trial for Arsenal in his teens. He had a good job with great prospects, lavished her with presents and left romantic notes for her to find. Rosie told her that David had described Eddie as a bit of a womaniser.

Linda was taken aback at the cheek of someone with David's track record making such a comment.

Takes one to know one.

That Christmas, Eddie took Linda to Paris for the weekend. This was the most romantic city in the world, and she'd hoped that his choice might mean a proposal could be on the cards, but the subject was never raised. She longed for more than just 'going out'; she wanted certainty about their future together. It was early days in their relationship, but that didn't stop Linda looking in jewellers' windows and buying the odd copy of *Brides* magazine which she hid under her bed, retrieving them at bedtime so she could look at wedding dresses. They had only been going steady since summer, but Linda couldn't help herself and kept dropping hints about 'their future'.

Linda and Sandra had to work some days over the Christmas period, but in between shifts they found time to visit both Rosie and Roberta at their homes. They had clubbed together to buy teddy bears as Christmas presents for their babies: a blue one for Rosie's boy, and a pink one for Roberta's little girl. It had been shortly after the wedding when they had last been to Rosie's house and at that time there was very little furniture, just a bed and a kitchen table and chairs. The house was set at the end of a cul-de-sac of new houses with integral garages and which displayed manicured lawns and neat shrubbery.

Rosie opened the door, baby Theo on her hip, before they had a chance to ring the bell. Her face lit up at the sight of her old friends. 'Come in, come in, it's so lovely to see you both.'

The house was pristine and centrally heated with fitted carpets throughout.

'Do you want a look around?' Rosie asked.

'We'd love a nosey,' said Linda.

They took in their surroundings open-mouthed. Upstairs, two of the bedrooms now had fitted wardrobes and there were new-style duvets on the beds. In little Theo's nursery, the furniture was painted white with cheery yellow bedding and matching curtains. Downstairs in the through lounge and dining room, brand new furniture was colour-coordinated with cushions and curtains, and at the rear of the room, patio sliding doors led onto a recently flagged patio area with a garden beyond. After the tour, the women sat in the kitchen drinking freshly percolated coffee, surrounded by beech units with streamlined work surfaces on which sat a range of quality kitchen gadgets.

Linda gazed around. 'It looks just like a picture from the Habitat catalogue,' she said, and raised her own expectations accordingly.

Despite being a nurse, she felt uneasy holding a baby, and Theo regularly posseted sour-smelling milk.

'It'll be different when it's your own, you almost get indifferent to the smell,' Rosie explained. But for Linda, it was too much to bear. Suddenly she felt lightheaded and hastily handed the squirming Theo back to Rosie and dashed to the bathroom, where she flushed the toilet and emptied the contents of her stomach.

Later the same week they visited Roberta. Hannah was a sweet baby who was equally happy rolling around on a blanket with her toys or being picked up and handed to visitors. Roberta, on the other hand, looked distracted and a little unkempt. Her hair looked as if she had cut it herself and the sole was flapping loosely on one of her shoes. The house was cold apart from the main room where Roberta seemed to live and work. Jars and tubes of paint covered the table, and there were canvasses stacked in every available space in amongst baby paraphernalia, piles of clothes and nappies. Everything in the house had seen better days and it was obvious that she had made great efforts to clean and repair them, but there was only so much improvement that could be made.

They huddled around the Aga, enjoying the tea and cake which Roberta had baked especially. Hannah began to fuss, and Roberta scooped her up with ease, lifting a paint-stained jumper and attaching the baby to one of her breasts.

'It saves money,' she said, a resigned expression on her face, 'but it's wearing being the only one who can feed her, and I feel like a cow.' She gave a laugh and went on. 'I'm selling quite a few paintings in a local gallery, though. The problem is affording the art materials, although that is getting better with each sale.'

'Won't Will lend you the money?' asked Sandra.

Roberta's face dropped and took on a look of such anguish that Sandra wished she had never asked.

'You don't have to answer.'

'I feel disloyal if I say anything behind Will's back. His family have been so good, giving us this cottage.'

'Are you okay?' said Linda, going into nursing mode.

'I pretend I am. I stitch on a beatific smile for my family, for my neighbours and for myself, but my life is far from idyllic at the moment.'

Sandra and Linda waited, until Roberta decided to open up. 'Will is hardly here. He goes to the pub after work and doesn't come back till bedtime. My life is Hannah and painting. Sometimes he gets angry, as if he doesn't like me having anything of my own. Then he smashes up a painting or two when he comes home.'

There was silence after her revelations.

'There you are, you see. I'm better keeping it to myself. People don't know what to say.'

'What a complete contrast,' Linda said to Sandra when they had left.

Both women agreed they were worried about Roberta.

'She seems to have lost her sparkle, and when I hugged her, she just felt like a bag of bones.' Linda herself had always been conscientious about remaining slim, but she sensed that Roberta's weight loss was nothing to do with vanity.

'Rosie's landed on her feet with David. Did you see? Posh Denby crockery on the Welsh dresser? Must have cost a fortune. That's the range *I* want. Anyway, let's hope Dave's a reformed character and keeping it in his trousers now.'

Linda looked at her friend, expecting her to add her agreement, but Sandra seemed to be staring into space blankly.

Am I being too bitchy?

'Come on, Sandra, you must have an opinion on Dave the Rave. To me, he's the most unlikely husband and father material ever. I bet he's still putting it about every chance he gets.'

Sandra was frowning and looking evasive.

Linda giggled. 'Stop pulling faces, I'm sure it was you at the party with him after Rosie left. If you're going anywhere near him now, though, you're playing with fire.'

Sandra compressed her lips and tossed her head defiantly. 'You can think what you like. Like Roberta said, I'm better keeping it to myself.'

*

The summer of 1977 had another record-breaking heat wave, and Eddie knew he was approaching a make-or-break situation with Linda. Every time he went through the pros and cons of marriage to her, he could never come to a decision. It was like walking in treacle. On the one hand, Linda was a good-looking girl, slim, good fun and uninhibited in bed. On the other hand, she kept bringing up the subject of their future together and he just wished she would let it drop; he was beginning to feel pressurised. She was also obsessed with possessions and seemed to be fixated on living the same lifestyle as David and Rosie.

Is she more interested in lifestyle or me?

She clearly has no idea of what Dave's really like, he thought, but kept his ideas to himself.

By early October, Eddie's internal debate ended when one of his friends from London visited and commented that, with Linda's good looks, Eddie was 'punching above his weight'. This tipped the debate in favour of marriage. He proposed to Linda over dinner in the opulent surroundings of the French room at the Midland Hotel in Manchester, presenting her with a diamond solitaire engagement ring set in platinum. He was sure it was exactly what she wanted, as the design had been shown to him on numerous occasions.

They set a wedding date for the following year and began to make plans. Linda's family insisted on a full Catholic Church wedding, which meant attending 'marriage preparation classes'. For both of them the content seemed irrelevant, with the discussion of 'natural family planning' in particular being at odds with their life and the lives of everyone they knew, but they had to sit through it if they wanted to get married in church. Eddie would have been happy to marry in the local registry office, but a battle with his future in-laws was something he didn't have the stomach for.

The wedding took place in early summer, at the Holy Family Catholic Church in the north of Manchester. It was where the Maguire family attended mass each week, twice on Sundays and holy days, and where their three products of natural family planning had been baptised and confirmed. Linda's sisters and Sandra were her bridesmaids and David was Eddie's best man. Linda, dressed in a fitted white satin dress with a fish tail, savoured every moment of her big day and couldn't stop smiling all the way through the lengthy service, where only the Maguire family and other Catholics were able to follow what was going on. As she and Eddie walked down the aisle, she looked as if she were walking on air.

The reception was held at the Last Drop hotel, a recently built old-world-themed complex with cobbled courtyards and beamed buildings and stunning views over the West Pennine moors. Eddie had suggested that David should take the opportunity to meet the Maguires some weeks before the big day.

'Dave, these people make your mother-in-law seem jolly. They are perpetually miserable, and they make a virtue out of suffering. I'd go for a speech that's short and bland.'

Eddie knew he could rely on his friend to assess the occasion and the players with his customary accuracy.

As the evening wore on, even the most strait-laced guests were enjoying being whirled around to the music of a Ceilidh band in air infused by an aroma of the pie and peas which had been laid on for supper.

Later that night Eddie looked at Linda as she walked ahead of him into the bridal suite. He loved the way she swayed her hips as she walked, and as she slipped off her dress to reveal a silk basque, stockings and suspenders, Eddie wondered why he had deliberated for so long before making her his wife.

FOURTEEN

1978–83 Linda

Linda was drinking a cup of coffee at the breakfast bar in her and Eddie's new home and giving herself a mental pat on the back. Her gaze strayed across the open-plan living area to the pine bench and table set, the Dralon three-piece suite, all brand new, bought on hire purchase. The house itself was on a new estate with lawned areas to the front that gave a sense of space. In Linda's view, though, it was not quite as up-market as Rosie and David's. It was semi-detached and to the east of Manchester where house prices were cheaper. Linda reasoned that this was their first foot on the property ladder and she already knew precisely where she saw their next move.

She congratulated herself on slipping easily into the role of wife and homemaker. She put this down to some simple strategies that she had devised for herself. She would be a good cook in the kitchen and a siren in the bedroom, things she knew she could do well. Then she would make their home a perfect refuge from what she imagined to be the cut and thrust of Eddie's work. She was buoyed up with happiness and confidence. Eddie looked slightly bemused at her activity. She didn't actually consult him about anything, but he seemed happy to be on the receiving end of her attention, for now.

The first conflict came when she chose a beige shag-pile carpet for the whole house. It looked good, but it picked up the dirt easily, and she insisted that everyone took their shoes off at the door. Eddie said he felt uncomfortable asking people to do this.

'It's not a bleeding show house, Linda, it's our home,' he said to her, in an exasperated voice. Linda just ignored him and diverted his attention in the ways she knew worked. She made sure she dressed to please him and wore full make-up when he came home from work. She would then ask him about his day. Her perfect life was complete when she became pregnant and Eddie was obviously delighted at the news.

*

Eddie's life was primarily focussed on his assault on the company ladder. He and David were members of the same squash club and played several times a week, which provided an escape from what for him was beginning to feel like a cloying honey trap. He was dutifully at Linda's side when she gave birth to their first child, Louisa. He was initially disappointed, having secretly hoped for a son whom he saw himself teaching to play football, but he became besotted with his new daughter.

'A boy next time will just round up our family nicely,' he said to Linda.

Meanwhile David had a second son.

'If Dave fell off the pier, the tide would be in,' Eddie muttered out of Linda's earshot.

Eighteen months after the birth of Louisa, Linda gave birth to a second daughter, Lizzie. Eddie was again at the birth and as the screaming baby was handed to Linda, she turned to him. 'Say hello to your daddy.' She handed him the bundle. He looked in shock, but it had been a fast and painful labour, so he quickly covered up, exhaling his breath.

84

'I was worried because it all happened so fast. I'm just happy you're both okay. She's perfect.'

'I'm glad it's another girl.'

*

Linda loved being at home, adored her handsome husband and got so much pleasure from watching their daughters acquire each new skill. A vegetable plot in the garden provided ingredients for healthy meals, her dinner parties were legendary and Eddie basked in reflected glory when work colleagues complimented him on his 'wonderful wife'. Linda was back into her pre-pregnancy clothes within a couple of months of giving birth and she spent some time most days exercising to her Jane Fonda workout video.

'I'm not one of those women who lets themselves go after having children,' she told herself.

*

Eddie could see that in Linda's view, this was what marriage came down to. For his part, he was supposed to provide all the material needs of the family while she provided what he knew she believed was a welcoming home. But it wasn't welcoming to him. He found the situation stifling and the more he created space for himself, the needier she appeared to be. He was a young man and he felt he was being dragged towards middle age.

*

Eddie started making frequent trips away from home, often staying overnight for meetings.

'Why can't you come home if the meeting's only an hour or so away? I miss you and you'll miss important events in the girls' lives. You missed Louisa's first steps.'

Eddie put a paternalistic arm around her. 'These meetings involve entertaining important customers, and after a few drinks, it would be frowned upon if I drove home.'

Always a keen sportsman, Eddie began running each evening.

'I want to keep fit to help cope with the stress of work,' he told Linda.

It started with a few miles several nights a week, but he gradually increased his distances so that by summer he had entered the local half marathon.

'Shall we surprise Daddy, girls, and go to watch him run?'

Linda got them ready and, with Lizzie on her back in a papoose, they took up a position near the finishing line, Linda holding an excited Louisa's hand. They cheered him across the line, Louisa shouting, 'Daddy, Daddy.' Linda recognised some of Eddie's work colleagues on the other side of the line who had obviously also turned up to cheer him along. She watched as Eddie crossed the line, waved to his colleagues and jogged round to join them. Linda looked on crestfallen as the men slapped him on the back and the women kissed him.

Louisa was still shouting, 'Daddy, Daddy,' but her little voice was drowned out by the crowd. Eddie finally caught sight of them after collecting his medal. He hung it around the neck of a delighted Louisa, and he swept her up in his arms.

'We thought we'd surprise you,' Linda explained, her voice wobbly and tearful.

'Don't get upset. I wasn't expecting you, so I didn't look for you.' Eddie's voice sounded matter of fact.

His career went from strength to strength and he was promoted to management. His new role meant he was more office-based.

'Will the girls and I see more of you now?' asked Linda.

Eddie felt the pressure. He wanted more space, not more intense domesticity. 'I can't promise to be home at six o'clock every night. I have to be seen to be leading from the front.'

The new job meant extra salary, which was a bonus. Eddie became very particular about his appearance and no longer bought suits from Marks and Spencer, preferring to go to the designer shops in Manchester, citing the need to 'look the part' and leaving a waft of Aramis in his wake. He was on the fast-track at work and he enjoyed the status that gave him and the attention it brought.

*

Linda was getting increasingly worried about the time Eddie was spending away from home. The running continued and the distances increased, meaning he would be out for hours at a time. On occasion, Linda thought she smelt perfume on his shirts as she pulled them from the linen basket. She upped her fitness programme, replacing Jane Fonda with a higher-intensity workout and made an extra special effort to look good when he arrived home from work. Invariably he just pecked her cheek as he dashed in to either pick up his squash kit or change into his running kit before shouting, 'See you later,' as he dived back into his company BMW. She worried that she was losing him, and she didn't know what to do about it. She didn't feel she could talk to Rosie, whose world seemed so perfect and who had warned her of Eddie's 'womanising'. Sandra thought marriage was for fools and Roberta seemed to accept a husband who ignored and ridiculed her.

Throughout the following year, if they went out it was with other couples, never just the two of them. If they were both at home, Eddie would retreat into his home office to catch up on paperwork. Their sex life dwindled to the few times when alcohol created a spark, but the event was brief and mechanistic, with Eddie turning his back on Linda to go to sleep immediately afterwards.

*

Christmas was drawing near, and Linda's mood improved as she got caught up in the preparations. She loved everything about it, especially the build-up, with Christmas songs in the shops and films on TV. By early December she had put up the tree, hung decorations and bought all the presents. She looked around and felt more positive about their marriage.

All marriages go through rocky patches, especially with young kids. We just need to reconnect and spend time together again.

She caught Eddie just before he dashed out of the door and suggested he could help her wrap the presents that evening. A cosy evening together preparing for a family Christmas would bring them closer again. The tree looked beautiful with red and gold baubles hanging from nearly every branch with soft white lights fading off and on. She bathed the children and got them in bed before Eddie arrived home from work. She opened a good bottle of wine before changing into a figure-hugging black dress, stockings and high heels. She looked at herself in the long mirror. 'Not bad,' she concluded, and felt a frisson of anticipation about the evening ahead. Maybe they could have sex by the Christmas tree on the shag-pile carpet, which Eddie had said was its best use. She smiled at the thought of it.

When Eddie arrived home and picked up his squash kit to go out, her anger and hurt rose in equal parts. 'Can't you spare just one evening to do something with me as any normal husband would do? For Christ's sake, Eddie. I have done all the shopping and sorted the decorations. Can't you just give squash a miss for once?'

She looked at his stony face and knew that this was the moment she had been dreading for some time. Eddie put down his kit bag and, hands on hips, stared at his wife, who by now had tears slowly rolling down her cheeks. He had a look of cold detachment she had never seen before. 'I want my freedom, Linda. This... this life... this marriage, it's suffocating me. I don't want to spend my life like this.'

Linda felt as if she had been punched in the chest and all the air had been sucked out of her. She looked at Eddie, his square jaw set as he stared at her with not a flicker of compassion.

'What about marriage counselling? All marriages go through difficult times and we have two lovely daughters.' Linda's sobs stifled her pleas.

He continued his rant, seemingly unconcerned about the cruelty of his words. 'You don't get it, do you? We want different things. I've been unhappy for a long time. This is not what I want,' he said, looking around the room. 'Our marriage was a mistake. I love the girls, but I'm sorry, Linda, I don't love you.'

Linda felt a fool standing there in the dress and stockings meant to reignite Eddie's interest. Hadn't she kept her half of the bargain and been a good wife? She began to realise just how much she had deluded herself. As her husband's cruel words hung in the air, all the concerns she had previously dismissed filled her mind and she was gripped by a sense of righteous anger.

'You pressurised me into marrying you in the first place. You kept on and on about our future. I felt obligated,' said Eddie.

'There's someone else, isn't there, Eddie? You might as well be honest because I'll find out eventually.'

'What if there is?' Eddie inflicted a final blow. 'I've been unhappy for some time. I've taken a lease on a flat near the office. I'll continue to support you and the girls.'

*

Eddie left the house and his marriage with any transient sadness replaced by the image of his secretary, Megan. She was a woman who disliked domesticity and couldn't cook but who oozed sensuality. She was a free spirit who was happy doing things on a whim and never wanted to be tied down with children. She could have any man she wanted, but she was in love with him and was waiting for him at the flat he had rented for the last six months.

Linda sat by the Christmas tree and finished the bottle of wine. The future she planned had gone forever; her dreams of living like Rosie were shattered.

2005

'Oh, Dad,' said Louisa. 'It feels so sad, hearing the story of your marriage with Mum. I don't think Mum ever "got it", you know. She was still looking for her idea of a perfect relationship. She never realised that it takes two people to make one.'

FIFTEEN

2005

Linda's funeral and cremation were organised for just over a week after she died. Both Lizzie and Louisa had taken compassionate leave from their jobs and then extended it with paid leave, but Lizzie was conscious of time and wanted to clear Linda's house as soon as possible. They had decided to rent it out for the time being.

'Neither of us can face the final break with our childhood home just yet,' she explained to Eddie. 'It's been enough coming to terms with Mum's death.'

The two sisters were at Linda's house again, going through her personal stuff. There were a lot of clothes and drawers full of beautiful lingerie. There were many tears, and a few laughs when they found Linda's store of vibrators. Even Louisa calmed down and managed to giggle as she saw her mother in a different light.

The final clear-out was in the loft, accessed by a pull-down ladder. Fortunately, Linda was not a hoarder and they found mainly nostalgic stuff: photographs of their childhood, baby books, christening and birthday cards, first paintings, certificates for good work and swimming.

'Look, I won first prize dressing the spoon at the local show,' said Louisa. 'What on earth was that about?'

Most of the stuff they ditched and, although it was hard to do so, Lizzie rationalised it saying that it was Linda's memories, not theirs, and now it was up to them to make their own. They were down to a few small shoe boxes. One was striking in that it was old, very old. The Sellotape had long disintegrated on it and left just a brown outline. It looked as if it had been opened recently. Lizzie felt uneasy as soon as she saw it. She tentatively lifted the lid.

Nothing could have prepared her for the sight of the mummified foetus. He was tiny but perfectly formed. He was about six inches long but would have been more if he hadn't been curled up. Some of his skin was black. Lizzie found out later that this was due to being injected with sodium chloride. Lizzie knew instinctively that he must be their aborted brother, but when? Louisa joined her and at first Lizzie feared another bout of hysteria, but Louisa was now more stoical, and it was she, Lizzie, who started the crying.

'Let's phone Roberta.'

Roberta hurried over to the house, shocked, then crying with them. 'I'm only speculating here, but I knew Linda was promiscuous as a student, so sorry. I guess there was a possibility that she didn't know who the father was. You know, it was the 1970s and your mum had a very Catholic upbringing that conflicted with the mood of the times. I suspect she couldn't take the precautions that women can take now.'

She paused to collect her thoughts, trying to be mindful of the girls' feelings. 'I'm sure whatever happened must have been unorthodox, otherwise she would never have been able to keep him like this. The fact she did signals that she must have regretted it and she's lived with this all these years. I never knew about it and I'm not sure Sandra or Rosie did either. Your mum did what she thought was best at the time. Let's face it, that's all anyone can do.'

They sat for a long while, looking at him, almost in homage, and then Roberta spoke again. 'We should tell the police about this.

It may be relevant to their investigations; it may not. Then I think we should tell Rosie and Sandra too.'

*

Roberta called another meeting in the staff room at the Refuge. It was late afternoon when they could all get together. They were all off duty and it was again time for a glass of wine.

Lizzie explained what she and Louisa had found in Linda's loft.

'I can't believe Linda didn't tell me,' said Sandra. 'I think I can remember now when it happened. I was living with a doctor called Richard and when I came back to the nursing home, she was ill in bed with a tummy bug, or so she said. Oh, Linda, she must have dealt with this all alone when I was away.'

'It could have been any one of us,' said Roberta.

'Hey, come on, not me,' said Sandra stoutly.

'You are an exception, Sandra,' replied Roberta. She looked at Louisa and Lizzie. 'Women have so many rights now compared with then. Please don't judge your mum. That's how it was then. It wasn't socially acceptable to be a single mother and there was no support. Rosie and I took one path; your mum took another. Both have had their repercussions.'

Lizzie looked at Roberta. 'I'd forgotten that you got married the same time as Rosie. What happened to you?'

93

SIXTEEN

1976 Roberta's Story

Roberta had been dozing at Rosie's house with her swollen feet up on a footstool, while Rosie made lunch. Pregnancy was not being kind to her teenage body, whereas Rosie, who only had a modest bump of a tummy compared to hers, was much more mobile.

She opened her eyes and looked around again at the open-plan living room and the new furniture. Roberta was not the type to be envious, and it would be impossible anyway with Rosie. She was always so disarmingly thoughtful and sweet, but it was impossible not to feel resentful at the way her life was turning out to be so very different than Rosie's.

When she and Will married, they took over one of the farm cottages in an idyllic setting, surrounded by fields, but it was old and prone to damp. There was no fitted kitchen, just a dresser and sink, and the only heating was an ancient coal-fired Aga that Roberta struggled to keep feeding. She could feel the dust settling on her skin; it got under her nails. The house never felt clean, despite her constant scrubbing. She overheard Will's mother muttering to him. 'Well, we were grateful for anything we were given when we got married.'

Roberta didn't want to be grateful; she wanted to feel valued. She was quickly realising how crucial money was, or the lack of it. She'd never really had to think about it in her life before. Now, she was facing poverty.

She frowned, puzzling, not for the first time, over how Rosie and David had managed to marry for the same reasons as she and Will, yet somehow David had stage-managed the whole event so that it was completely acceptable. Rosie's parents had now extended their ambitions for Rosie to include David. There was no one doing that in the Kenyon camp. Eva, her mother, had called it a 'shotgun wedding', and Will's parents made it clear that they had hoped for a better start in life for their son. Will was feeling very sorry for himself and was hardly speaking to her. She tried once to talk about money, and he thumped her with his fist. After that, she was wary of him.

How does David do it?

Roberta usually tuned in to people, but she couldn't get past David's easy smile that never quite reached his eyes. He seemed to be playing to everybody's expectations whilst running his own hidden agenda. To her, he felt cold and calculating. Like the Tin Woodman, in *The Wizard of Oz*, he had no heart.

And Linda and Sandra were still behaving like the teenagers they were. It was turning out to be a hot summer and they sunbathed on the roof of the nurses' home, using cooking oil to speed their tans. Roberta was beginning to envy them their freedom.

*

June was turning into July and the sun shone every day. Roberta was outside a lot, crouching on an old footstool, leaning over her bump as she tended a vegetable patch in the garden that Will had dug to save a bit of money. Her skin became bronzed and she looked healthy, even though she didn't feel it. She tended to prolong her time outside, sketching and painting subjects from the garden, or the view that endlessly changed with the seasons and the light. She painted in the evenings when Will went to the pub, often developing work she had started during the day. One of the best wedding presents they had received was a modern 'music centre', bought by all the women who had clubbed together for it. She played her old LPs and music tapes copied from friends: Bob Dylan, Joni Mitchell, The Eagles, Santana. She loved these evenings to herself. Her mind wandered as she drew and painted, and she mused over the events of the last eight months.

She thought about her wedding night and the awkwardness of it all. Her mother had given her an antiquated sex manual. The gesture was absurd and way too late, yet sadly it had some relevance. She and Will had never actually slept together before, never mind seen each other without clothes, and Roberta was aware of a chill that had nothing to do with the weather. Will had got changed into pyjamas in the bathroom where Roberta couldn't see him. Roberta pulled a pink brushed nylon nightie over her head and got into bed.

Which side?

Then it occurred to her that because of the wedding, sex between them was now perfectly acceptable.

Will it be as good, now it's no longer forbidden?

She desperately wanted to laugh at the absurdity of it all, but she knew Will would not be amused. Eventually, she reached out and he silently took her in his arms.

*

It was the beginning of August, and Roberta's due date came and went. It was two weeks later when she went for a check-up that the hospital finally agreed to take her in and see what could be done. She had to find a phone box to ask Will to bring her suitcase of clothes, already packed and waiting, to the evening visiting hour.

Roberta was in a small ward with five other women who had all had their babies. They had formed an agreement to draw their curtains during visiting hour to give each other some privacy with their husbands. One woman didn't bother. She'd just had her sixth child, and she and her husband sat in silence, glaring at the latest addition to their family. Roberta had been given castor oil and orange juice to drink, she'd had her pubic hair shaved off, and she'd had an internal examination and an enema, all very embarrassing. There was a student nurse present during these procedures, who pointed to Roberta's stomach in horror.

'What are all those purple lines?' she asked a senior nurse.

'Oh, they're stretch marks,' she replied. 'They'll go when she has the baby.'

'It doesn't look like it to me,' said the student. 'They look like scars.'

They hadn't included Roberta in the conversation, and she wept. She felt like a piece of meat. She couldn't convey any of this to Will. He had only seen her stomach once, early on in the pregnancy, and he'd told her to cover it up.

Now it was six in the morning and she woke with cramps in her stomach. They came at intervals and reminded her of a ferocious lion crouching in a corner, rearing forward and roaring, and then retreating. She would have liked to paint the scene with vivid orange, red and black. She imagined she was in a room with artists' materials, and this kept her distracted for a while, but the pains were strong, and she pressed a button on her headboard for a nurse to come. The curtains were pulled round the bed again and there was another of those dreadful internal examinations that hurt like mad.

'Only three fingers dilated, she'll be ages yet,' said the nurse to another.

Her bed was wheeled down the corridor into a narrow room, tiled in white, with a linoleum floor.

Like an abattoir. All it needs is blood on the walls.

It seemed like hours went by, and the pain increased till she couldn't bear it. She was crying out and a nurse came rushing in.

'Stop that noise,' chided the nurse. 'You'll frighten the other mothers.'

Another painful examination and, 'You're not ready for the delivery room yet,' as if Roberta had failed in some way.

She cried out again, she couldn't help it, and the nurse looked at Roberta in consternation and went out. Someone came and gave her an injection, and everything faded.

When she woke up she was groggy and lying on her back with her knees bent. The pain had changed and there seemed to be an awful lot of people staring between her legs. Some of them were shouting at her to push, and she did as they told her. She felt a stinging sensation as the head was born, and then more urging to push and the rest followed.

'You have a baby girl,' said someone.

Will came to visit her again that night. He didn't know she'd had the baby already. 'Nobody told me,' he said. He inspected his daughter. 'She's got a wrinkled forehead. Oh, David called by the cottage just as I was leaving. Rosie had her baby two weeks early this morning. It's a boy, I think.'

Roberta went home after five days. Will came to pick her up, deposited her and baby Hannah in the living room, and went back to work. He was clearly awkward around them both and happier in the more familiar environment of the farm. The Aga wasn't lit, and Roberta found herself rolling newspaper and fetching kindling wood. By the time the fire was going, Hannah was awake and demanding to be fed. This is how it was. Only just time to do a job or two, no time for herself. Hannah was a peaceful baby, though, sleeping right until the next feed.

The hot summer continued, and Roberta often put Hannah's pram in the garden under the oak tree so she could work. Rosie came to visit, Theo in a carrycot on the back seat of the car. She had been surprised by the early birth, and although it had proved to be straightforward with David by her side, Theo was a fretful baby, and no amount of feeding him, rocking him or pushing him out in the pram could stop him grizzling. Both David and Will suddenly seemed to be unavailable to help. David was often working late and at weekends, 'carving out his career path', as he told Rosie. Will was working flat out with the harvest, then it was something else going on at the farm, or at the pub. He didn't seem to find Roberta very interesting right now. She felt bulky with unshed baby weight and her body had a new softness that made her ashamed of it. However, she was too busy and exhausted with the responsibilities of looking after a household, something she always thought happened by itself, and looking after Hannah, to do anything about it. Just sometimes, in the early hours when life was at a low ebb, waking up exhausted after only two hours' sleep, she wondered at this rapid change from independent college woman to unpaid drudge.

SEVENTEEN

2005

'**I find it incredible that** women had so little power over their own lives only thirty years ago,' exclaimed Louisa.

'And that the lack of contraception was a key factor,' said Lizzie.

'We just didn't have the rights that we have now; we didn't have a voice,' said Roberta.

'This is why I became involved in the Women's Movement,' said Rosie.

'I would love to hear about that,' said Louisa. 'I've been thinking…' Lizzie was bringing them all back to the present day. 'I need to tell Dad, but I feel our brother deserves some recognition. What do you think to a double funeral? I'll go to see him and broach the idea gently.'

She paused, as if collecting her thoughts. 'I also need to tell you all that Mum left specific instructions regarding the arrangements for her funeral. To be honest, I was surprised. It seems an odd thing for someone her age to do. I did wonder about her state of mind.'

'You must tell the police about this too,' said the ever-practical Rosie. 'The funeral will probably have to be delayed while they investigate, and maybe there are tests to be done, probably DNA.'

'I wonder who the father was,' mused Sandra. 'It must surely have been before your marriage to David, and before she met Eddie.'

It was said so casually, but Rosie felt another barb. Something was fuelling Sandra's anger over Linda's death, something from the past. She was damned if she was going to rise to the bait.

Lizzie turned to Sandra. 'What's the truth about you and Mum's experiences with nursing and drugs? Now is the time to tell us.'

EIGHTEEN

1976 Sandra and Linda

Sandra rapped her knuckles on the door of Linda's room at the nurses' hostel. To call it a room was an exaggeration for the cramped cubicle containing a single bed, a wardrobe, a chest of drawers and a desk for studying. The numbered doors were made of shabby plywood and stretched along a corridor leading to a communal bathroom at the end that seemed to be permanently engaged.

'Come in,' said Linda.

She was sitting at the desk, putting on her make-up. It was evening and dark, and she had to make do with an old mirror propped against the wall and the light from a table lamp, angled on its side with the shade taken off. The burn marks on the top of the desk bore testimony to the fact that this was a regular occurrence.

They had both eaten a supper of chilli con carne in the canteen and now they were going to yet another party at a doctor's house. A lot of the junior doctors came from affluent families, and it wasn't unusual for somebody's parents to have invested in a house near the hospital that they then rented out to other medical students. Tonight's get-together was based on turning up in uniform, a recurrent fancy-dress theme because it was easy, and because it lent itself to all sorts of high jinks as the effects of alcohol took over. After Christmas, it was an event to look forward to in the bleak days of January. It was icy cold, and the only heat in the rooms was supplied by two horizontal heating pipes that ran along the skirting board under the window and along the whole corridor. If they weren't going out, the nurses often went to bed early to keep warm, which could be really boring with only books or the radio to keep them company.

'I still can't get over both Roberta and then Rosie getting pregnant and planning weddings in the space of two months,' said Linda as she drew black eyeliner across her top lids. 'Roberta, I can sort of more understand. She's been going out with Will for a long time now, but Rosie and David? They'd hardly met, and David hasn't exactly had a good track record for fidelity, has he?'

She wasn't going to say any more, partly out of loyalty to Rosie, but also because she didn't know how much Sandra knew about David and she wasn't about to gossip.

'They've given up on having an independent life too soon,' replied Sandra. 'Roberta complains about not getting enough attention from her parents, and Rosie feels stifled and overprotected by hers, but compared to me they've both been pampered. They've both had an upbringing where they've never had to be aware of money, or where it comes from. They both see college and university as filling in time till they get married and somebody else looks after them, and it's happened sooner rather than later, that's all. As for David, he's in his final year, with a job lined up and a bright future. All he needs is the right kind of wife to support him and Rosie fits the bill.'

'That's a very cynical point of view,' said Linda. 'Doesn't love come into it at all?'

'I don't know what that is,' said Sandra. 'Do you?'

'Well, now you mention it... no. My parents were always arguing, but I'd like to think I'll fall in love one day.'

Sandra was a good friend, but sometimes Linda felt that her matter-of-fact approach to life was trampling on her dreams.

'Huh,' retorted Sandra, as she had expected. 'My dad just saw me as an unpaid helper as soon as I could do the washing-up.'

'Well, that's part of family life, isn't it?'

'Not when it progresses to doing the housework and cleaning and having a meal on the table when they came home from work. I don't fancy being in love, anyway. It seems complicated, possibly painful, and I can't see why I need it. Hurry up, will you!'

Fortunately, the doctor's house was only a short distance from the nurses' hostel. The pavements were icy and there was a fog so dense they could only walk a few feet at a time. They linked arms together in case one of them slipped and, rounding the last corner, heard the noise of the party already. Despite the cold, the front door was wide open. One of the junior doctors was greeting people at the door, wearing a white coat and bow tie, with a gynaecologist's torch strapped to his forehead.

'Hi, I'm Randolph, Randy for short,' he chortled, and ushered them in.

The heat inside the house was stifling after the cold outdoors and they could see the reason for the open front door. The main living room was packed to capacity with students dancing to ABBA's 'Mamma Mia' and a log fire was burning in the hearth. The living room and dining room had been made into one, with opened sliding glass doors between them. There was a bar in one corner with mirrors behind it that reflected the room and the people in it, making the illusion of even more space. A revolving nightclub glitter ball hung from the ceiling, catching the light from the fire as it spun slowly round.

Linda and Sandra loved coming to these parties. Not all the junior doctors lived in such opulent houses, but Randolph's parties were legendary and a definite must. Neither of them had been brought up with anything but the bare minimum, things that were needed, not wanted. The idea that you could buy stuff for sheer pleasure was alien, and therefore doubly alluring. Sandra's parents were working class and had had little money to spare. Linda's were devoutly Catholic and believed in nurturing the spirit rather than the false god of worldly goods. To be invited to keep company with people who had known wealth since birth was heady stuff. Even more heady was the sex and drugs that came with the partying.

Drinks were handed to them and they surveyed the crowd, many of whom they already knew.

'Look, there's Irene Porter trying to bag a doctor,' said Sandra nastily. 'She doesn't realise that they're just looking for sex. She doesn't stand a chance, and she's too plain and needy. She needs to learn how to play the game.'

Sandra put her spare hand on her hip and boldly stared at the doctor in question until he noticed her. She thrust her chest out and had no problem diverting his attention away from Irene. She smiled at his body language as he clearly started to make his excuses.

Linda was always amused by Sandra's tactics, but she knew they weren't for her. She was small and very slim, and she relied more on appealing to a man's urge to protect.

'I can't believe Irene doesn't know what to expect at these parties. What's she done to rattle you, anyway? Personally, I think a good party is a necessary antidote to being a trainee and dogsbody on the wards. Let's face it, we're all learning on the job. We're in the front line of a seemingly endless battle and I find that there's only so much blood and death I can stand before I need some mind-blowing fun.'

As the evening progressed, the tempo increased and pockets of action started up. There was raucous laughter as one of the junior doctors attempted to intimately examine a trainee nurse on the couch, and another nurse tried to strip a doctor. All very predictable, but somehow they were attempting to make sense of the embarrassment and indignity of the things that they had to face daily.

By midnight the music had changed to Art Garfunkel singing 'I Only Have Eyes for You'. The lights had been dimmed and couples, sometimes more people, were entwined on the floor by the dying embers of the fire. Randolph was still looking after the booze and the records, the consummate host, another reason for the success of his parties. Nobody had ever seen him pair up at a party and it was rumoured that he just liked to watch. Linda had met a junior doctor called Benedict. His name was an uncomfortable reminder of her church, but not for long, as they were soon together on the floor. Sandra had met Richard, with brown eyes and hair, who seemed more down-to-earth than most. He spoke with a northern accent, and that formed an immediate bond between them. Then the alcohol and the drugs took over, and they too joined the seething mass of bodies, but not before Linda spotted a naked David in the far corner of the room.

A leopard never changes its spots.

The next day was a day off for both Linda and Sandra, who both spent most of it cuddling hot water bottles in bed under blankets and eiderdown, topped with the inevitable candlewick bedspread. By evening they shuffled down to the canteen.

'Wow, what a party. I did like Richard,' said Sandra. 'I'd quite like to see him again, not that I'm rushing to chase him. He knows where to find me.'

'I'm surprised you remember him,' muttered Linda, who had a banging headache.

She had her head in one hand and a fork in the other, trying to force herself to eat a roast beef dinner; anything to reduce her hangover.

'Yes, that would be nice,' Sandra went on. 'Cheer up, it's men's surgical tomorrow. I wonder if Duncan will get me in the sluice room again... Ooh, now he knows how to please a lady in five minutes.'

Not for the first time, Linda wondered about just what made Sandra tick.

2005

'It's no wonder Mum always said live for the moment. A Catholic upbringing combined with life and death on a daily basis.'

Lizzie seemed in a reflective mood, but Sandra wasn't fooled. This woman had a razor-sharp brain, and she would be seeking out the next nugget of information.

'What did Mum mean, Aunty Sandra, when she said, "What makes you tick?"'

NINETEEN

1975–84 Sandra's Story

When Sandra was a child, she developed a mantra that she repeated in her head every time her father lost his temper and hit her.

I don't care, you can't hurt me… I don't care, you can't hurt me…

She never dared to say it out loud; she clenched her teeth instead. She wouldn't give in; she wouldn't cry. Her dad Eric glared at the mutinous look on her face and she got an extra slap. Her mum, Fiona, looked worried but didn't interfere. 'Your father is right. It's for your own good.'

Sandra learnt to hide all her hurt feelings. Then she made herself her number-one priority, as no one else was going to. In her opinion, this wasn't selfish. You were better equipped to deal with the problems that life threw at you if you looked after yourself; you had more to give to other people. As a nurse, she saw too many carers exhausting themselves looking after sick relatives. 'Look after yourself first,' she would tell them.

Her self-help method worked most of the time, but just sometimes the hurt came tumbling out unbidden. She was never quite sure what the trigger was, otherwise she'd find a way to control it. Her mood would plummet and she would seek a corresponding high with sex, alcohol or drugs. The human race had been doing this for centuries, she reasoned, but for Sandra, sometimes the highs got out of hand.

Sandra knew the doctors who took drugs in their time off. They always seemed to have a supply of opiates and barbiturates which they would take to help them wind down from the acute state in which they had to perform their work. She sought them out when she needed them, and they would spend an evening together. Sometimes there would be a few of them; it was all perfectly safe. They knew just how much to take to feel relief and euphoria and mix it with a drink or two, rounding the evening off at somebody's house where sex would be on the agenda.

Of course, Sandra knew she wasn't addicted and felt she had the situation under control. Then she was brutally pulled up short by an accident. She was at the home of Phillip, a doctor friend. She had intended to stay the night, but things had turned nasty and they had argued violently. 'Keep your voice down, Sandra,' he hissed. 'This is a discreet neighbourhood.'

Sandra stormed out of the house, got into her new Triumph Spitfire and gunned her way back to Manchester and her flat. It had been a wet evening, but the rain had stopped. She was speeding down the glistening empty duel carriageway, when her vision suddenly swam, and she was seized with doubt. There were suddenly too many lights and lines.

Where was the centre of the road?

She braked sharply in reaction, and the car skidded on the wet road and mounted the central reservation. There was a horrendous clash of metal and it flipped over the barrier and onto its roof, spinning slowly till it reached the opposite side of the road where a tree stopped its progress with an enormous bang. The carriageway was lined with houses and soon a group of traumatised residents had gathered at the scene, some still in their nightwear and dressing gowns. Sandra was conscious but confused and puzzled why the occupants of her ward should have assembled out in the road. Someone sniffed her breath. 'I don't think she's been drinking.'

She was hanging upside down from her seatbelt and nobody dared move her till the fire service and ambulance came. She was fortunate that the car had hit the tree on its passenger side, away from her. She was taken to Manchester Royal, where X-rays showed a ruptured spleen and a cracked pelvis.

'We'll have to remove your spleen; your pelvis will heal in time, but it might be difficult for you if you have children in the future,' said the specialist.

'Then will you sterilise me, please,' said Sandra.

This episode made Sandra slow down; she was lucky to survive. She was quizzed by the police, but she lied and said that she had swerved to avoid a dog and lost control. She was breathalysed and was found to be within the limit, then emergency surgery took priority over any further tests. Despite her injuries and the necessary recuperation, she felt she had got away lightly. She had taken a stupid risk. She could have killed or injured someone else and the thought horrified her.

Sandra found her doctor friends evasive from then on. They weren't exactly avoiding her, but she was now labelled as irresponsible as far as drug-taking was concerned. There was an unwritten rule that drug use should only be recreational, taken in time off, and was certainly not for putting other people's lives at risk.

'You can get drugs from work yourself,' said one of the doctors. 'You must know that when things are busy, there's not enough staff or time to follow procedures and the keys are always available somewhere. Just don't get greedy. They will put a warning notice on the cabinet door before they take any further action.'

Sandra decided to try and take some from a geriatric ward cabinet first. She didn't have a problem with theft. She had been stealing from shops and taking money from her mother's purse throughout her childhood. If she was asked, she would say, 'Serve them right,' and that other people were too careless with their belongings. In reality, she regarded it as her swag, her reward. She waited till she was on a night shift and there were less people around. Despite her bravado, she was a little unnerved by the thought that she was putting her job on the line this time. She got away with it, though, so she tried again, and stole some more.

Irene Porter, who was working similar shifts, had noticed that Sandra was going to the drugs cabinet on her own. Irene was sick and tired of Sandra making fun of her and stealing her boyfriends at parties. She watched her closely. She would love to get her revenge.

Sandra wasn't to know that Irene would see this as an opportunity to get her into trouble. She had no idea of the resentment that festered in her mind.

Irene waited till Sandra was on her break, then found Sister King in the tiny cubicle off the ward that served as her office. Sister's head was bent over some paperwork and she looked up and frowned. 'What is it now, Porter?'

'I'm very sorry to disturb you, Sister, but I've got to report what I've seen. I can't believe my eyes, but it's true.'

'Get on with it, Porter.' Sister King took off her hat and pushed her unruly hair back underneath it. 'Why does menopause and dealing with people like you make my hair into a bird's nest?' she muttered.

'Sorry?'

'Nothing, nothing.'

Later in the week, Sister King was discussing Irene Porter's revelations at a meeting with two of her colleagues. 'In my opinion,' she began, 'Porter seems keen to blacken Marsden's name for some reason.'

'A report of drug-taking is very serious, though,' said one of them.

'If it was anything else, I would have a personal word with Marsden. She's a good nurse,' replied Sister King.

'Yes, but it might come back on you, especially if Nurse Porter is as sly as you describe.'

'You can't be seen to let this go.'

'Why don't you put her under surveillance first?'

The next time Sandra went to the drugs cabinet, she found a note on the door to the effect that drugs had been found missing. At first, she didn't register that the note was directed at her. Then she went cold. She was in denial, a sure sign that she was getting addicted. She had tried to do without drugs recently, but she was already taking them habitually, on her night off, on her own. She looked around, but no one was in sight. Just one more time then, she'd better stock up.

When she was approached by a police officer as she left the ward at the end of her shift, she knew she had been stupid once too often. They found a selection of Diazepam tablets in her pocket, far more than a prescribed dose.

'Please sit down,' said Sister King.

They were in her office for what she called a formal interview and Sandra was hoping she would get away with a telling-off.

'I'm saddened to be in this position. You're a good nurse, but you can't be allowed to get away with stealing drugs. We have been watching you for a while and we suspect that there have been more times when you took drugs from the cabinet without having a witness or recording them. I hoped you might heed my written warning, but apparently you thought it didn't apply to you. I'm sorry, but I have no option but to refer your case to the Nursing and Midwifery Council. You will be suspended from work until a disciplinary hearing.'

What followed was a dark time in Sandra's life. She was suspended on full pay and there was nothing for her to do but wait. The police were also taking her to court. She was prescribed anti-depressants and painkillers for the pain from her accident and she drank heavily. Linda, Rosie and Roberta took turns visiting her in her flat and tried to be supportive, but it was difficult. Sandra had turned inward to a place where nobody could reach her. The flat was a mess with unwashed plates and mugs everywhere. She looked as if she slept in her clothes and she seemed exist on rum and Coke and frozen meals, only venturing out to the corner off-licence or the bank to get cash.

Roberta tried a tough approach, hoping for a response. 'The trouble with you, Sandra, is you can dish it out, but you can't take it back.'

Sandra just stared at her. It was hard to see if she had taken it in.

One day, Roberta turned up with a collie puppy from the farm. 'This little guy needs a bit of looking after, I thought you might be good for each other.'

Sandra looked at her in disbelief, then she picked up the puppy, buried her head in his fluffy coat, and cried and cried. Roberta was just on the point of thinking she had made a big mistake when Sandra looked up and gave her a smile. 'Jesus, Roberta, I think he's just what I need right now.'

The appearance of Skye, as she called him, marked a turning point for Sandra. When she tried to escape into oblivion, he nuzzled her face with his soft nose and prodded her with his paws until she responded to his demands. Soon she was spending time with him and drinking less; it was impossible to see to his needs otherwise. It took weeks to sort out her life, but Skye had patience and seemed to understand. Eventually, she found some temporary work at a suburban care home that didn't ask too many questions or examine her nursing record.

Sandra had looked after a puppy long ago when the family dog was her responsibility. She had the experience from that to gain the puppy's trust and she was strict, but it paid off, and he became obedient and loyal. She also found herself responding to Skye's utter devotion in a way she had never experienced with her parents or any of her boyfriends. 'Nobody has given me unconditional love like this before,' she told Roberta. 'Skye is my number-one priority now.'

Sandra sold her flat in Manchester and bought a small, semi-rural cottage just outside the suburbs. It was cheap because it was in an area close to the airport, but Sandra wanted a large garden and to be able to take Skye for long walks.

Her case came up for a hearing at the Nursing and Midwifery Council. She travelled to London and spoke in her own defence, saying that she had intended the drugs for her use only and that she had still been suffering from pain after her car crash, both of which statements were true. Sister King made the journey too and kindly testified as to her nursing abilities. The tribunal ruled that she would be struck off the nursing register for two years, after which she could apply for restoration. Her case then came up in the local magistrate's court. It was straightforward apart from the police seeking a link between stealing the drugs and her earlier car crash, but she again claimed her motive was pain relief. She was found guilty of theft and ordered to do forty hours of community service. Sandra was struck by the irony. Her nursing job had been a type of community service and now she no longer had it.

Sandra was sent to a drug rehabilitation centre and ordered to volunteer for a day a week for five weeks in a nursing and mentoring capacity. The choice of venue was intentional and brought it home to her how close she had come to spiralling out of control. Also, being Sandra, she picked up a man. Greg had lost his company, his wife and his family through his drug addiction. By the time she had finished the five weeks, she and Greg were dating.

2005

'The story, it doesn't end there,' said Sandra.

'Do tell us,' said Louisa.

'I'm shocked at how violent those men were,' said Lizzie.

'There's a saying that a woman always looks for her dad in the man she chooses,' said Sandra. 'I didn't stand a chance, did I?'

TWENTY

1984–1990 Sandra

'Oh no,' Roberta had groaned to Rosie. 'Whatever next? Just when Sandra seemed to be turning her life around and getting it straight. I've met him, though, and he is very handsome. He could be a model if he got his life under control again.'

Sandra and Greg were besotted with each other. He had classic good looks, if she saw beyond the bloating and the soft belly that were a result of his addiction. They had locked eyes and Sandra's senses had gone into overdrive. He had a soft voice that seemed to caress her whole body. When they shook hands, she felt his touch burn her skin.

I can smell him; I want to taste him… what am I thinking of?

At the end of the day when they were free to go, they walked outside together and when they were discreetly out of sight, he took her hand in his. 'Your place or mine?'

Sandra had never met anyone before who could excite her so much or match her sexually as Greg could. What was it that could link two people who had just met so solidly in this way? Her appetite for him felt primeval, animalistic, voracious. There was no sense of fulfilment; when they had finished, they wanted each other all over

115

again. It could have been all-consuming, but the silent watcher in Sandra would never let her lose all of herself to any one person. They spent all their first weekend in bed at Sandra's, only getting up to make tea and toast and to let Skye out into the garden.

Greg told Sandra that he had been running his own mail order catalogue. 'There was a fair amount of entertaining involved and trips away from home. I wasn't exactly faithful to my wife,' said Greg ruefully. 'The opportunities were there all the time. I had this chat up line: "I'm sure that's one of our bras you're wearing." You'd be surprised at the number of women who lifted up their tops for me.'

Greg began to find it hard to cope with the hours, the travelling and the drinking. 'I started to take drugs to keep me awake, then drugs to help me sleep,' he said. 'Then the industry changed as cheaper imported goods started flooding the market and the British manufacturers couldn't compete. I hadn't got enough money behind me, or the determination to start developing an international business at that time. I had an office and a couple of staff, a hefty mortgage, a wife and two children, and I was addicted to uppers and downers. I couldn't cope. I guess I had a breakdown, and one day I just walked away from it all.'

Unable to face his family and work colleagues, Greg had gone to stay with a friend who was alarmed at his behaviour and felt he couldn't deal with him. He called Greg's doctor, and the next day, Greg was admitted to the psychiatric unit of the local hospital.

Greg never talked to Sandra about his time there, or any other details. When he met Sandra, he was off the drugs, but his business had folded and his wife had divorced him. He had little contact with his children: 'Too painful.' He had bought a house with his share of the divorce money. He wasn't working.

'I'm no shirker, but I'm wondering what I do next,' he said.

'With your good looks you could be a model,' suggested Sandra. 'You must have contacts in the catalogue industry, and it would be easier if you're going back onto familiar territory.'

'You're not the first person to have said that,' replied Greg. 'I'd have to lose some weight and get fit first, though.'

So, Sandra and Greg embarked on a shared commitment to a healthy lifestyle. Greg rented his house out and moved in with Sandra. He took Skye running twice a day and lifted weights at the gym. Sandra worked five days a week at the care home. They went for long walks in the countryside around Sandra's cottage and they made love every night. Sandra was happier than she had ever been and never missed her old wilder lifestyle.

Greg was looking leaner and fitter and planning to meet several of the catalogue companies to discuss work prospects. Apart from Sandra's work, the two were inseparable. They weren't particularly sociable, and when Linda and Roberta called round to find out how they were, they were obviously struggling to stay apart on the sofa. Linda joked that you could see the pheromones flying across the air between them.

Greg was looking good. His face had slimmed down and revealed a chiselled jawline and cleft chin, so beloved of artists, writers and photographers. His stomach was now flat, and his arms were toned. He hadn't a clue how to go about negotiating a contract, but he remembered a modelling agent he knew and enrolled on his books. With his contacts from the old days, he was soon working with several prominent catalogue companies. He and Sandra celebrated their first anniversary together.

'This is a record for me,' said Sandra.

Greg's agent felt he was on to a winner. It was the early 1980s and the era of private companies and power dressing. Greg was exactly the right age to look the part of the thirty-something experienced businessman. He had several trips to London and a major store took him on to model their executive range of clothing. Other contracts followed and soon he was spending a large part of the week away from Sandra. Sandra found it lonely and depressing in the evenings. She met up with Roberta and Linda, but it wasn't enough; she wasn't used to being on her own. She started working behind the bar at her local pub. It was sociable and she met a lot of people. After all, Greg must be socialising without her in London.

At first they had thrilling weekends, but then Sandra noticed that Greg was questioning her rather closely about her activities while he was away. It was hard to pinpoint when it started, but he seemed ill at ease when he came home; he seemed more focussed on looking around the room, checking on things, than giving her a passionate kiss. Sometimes she caught him just staring at her. She caught his eye once as he tried to look away.

'Why are you staring like that?' she asked.

'Oh, nothing,' he said, 'I just look like that sometimes.'

Their lovemaking changed. Once had never been their limit, but now, afterwards, she sensed him staring at her in the dark, waiting. It was as if he wanted to speak or he wanted her to say something; she wasn't quite sure. It came to a head one night when they were walking Skye and they met Harry, one of the pub regulars. He was a bit worse for drink and merrily insisted on buying fish and chips for them all. Skye was snaffling the chips that came his way, making them all laugh. On the way back, Greg was silent.

They got inside the house, and Sandra was kneeling down and taking Skye's lead off his collar when Greg punched her head so hard that she hit it against the wall. The next thing she knew, she was sitting up in bed.

How did I get here?

She looked at Greg in bewilderment.

'You were downstairs babbling rubbish, then you came to bed and you wouldn't stop, so I gave you a rabbit punch.' He was avoiding eye contact with her and acting as though nothing had happened.

She was confused; she had lost minutes, hours? She went downstairs and sat for a long while against the same wall as… was she remembering it right?

The next day, Greg was up and off to London before she woke. Sandra called in sick to work and then got in the car and drove to see Greg's ex-wife. She had only seen Vivien once from afar, when Greg had dropped some presents off for his children. Vivien lived in a rather rundown semi on a housing estate. Sandra noticed a broken window with a piece of cardboard behind it, and the paint on the window frames was peeling. She would have tackled reglazing a window or painting the outside of the house, but not every woman was like that. The garden was overgrown and toys lay in the long grass.

Sandra took a deep breath and, as there was no doorbell or knocker, she rapped on it with her knuckles. The woman who came to the door was pretty, with a snub nose and big blue eyes. Sandra introduced herself.

'Please come in,' said Vivien.

Vivien seemed completely unfazed by Sandra's visit. She made them both a cup of tea, apologising for the mess and chattering about her children who were at school. Then they sat down on a sofa with strawberry jam on the arm.

Sandra was direct with her. 'I came to ask you if Greg had ever hit you,' she said.

'It was why I left him,' was the unexpected reply.

Everything that Greg had told Sandra was true. He had just omitted the violence.

'A part of me knew that Greg was having affairs, but I didn't want to believe that he was lying to me,' said Vivien. 'I also suspected he was taking medication, but he was lying about that too, so I never knew what or how much. We would be okay together, and then his behaviour would suddenly change. The first time he hit me he'd had a drink, of course. The next day he behaved as if it hadn't happened. Sometimes he would just come home and smash things up. Again, no explanation, it always came out of the blue. Then, just as suddenly, everything would be alright again. His business started to fail, and we couldn't cope financially. So, then he was angry about that too. I guess once you've hit a woman, you've broken a taboo and it's easier to do it again. The violence was increasing, and I was scared to say or do anything, but if I kept quiet that was wrong too. The reason I left him was that he was violent in front of the children. They were getting older and I couldn't go on hiding it from them.'

'There are similarities to what's happening with us,' said Sandra, dismayed by what she was hearing.

'Greg has his demons. I've heard it rumoured that his parents had an odd marriage and sometimes there was talk in front of him that he wasn't his father's child. We had relationship counselling and they said it was a combination of childhood trauma with alcohol, drugs and financial worries as a trigger.' She looked at Sandra closely. 'What will you do? You know he's vulnerable.'

'Yes, and so am I,' replied Sandra. 'You acted to protect your children; I need to protect myself.'

Sandra didn't mess about. She went straight to a locksmith and ordered new locks and keys for her front and back doors. When Greg came back from London a few days later, he couldn't get into her house. There were no lights on, and Greg's belongings had been put in two suitcases in the porch. Greg went to the local pub, but she wasn't there either. He returned to her house, but it was still in darkness.

Sandra had taken Skye and gone to see Roberta for the evening. She told her the gist of what had happened.

'Oh, dear, you can never fully know anybody,' sighed Roberta. 'Are you sure it's safe to go home? You can stay here tonight if you want.'

Sandra gratefully accepted, then went to work the next day. When she returned home there was no sign of Greg's car. She wasn't scared of him, but equally she felt that he would not take her rejection easily. She spent the evening with Roberta again, but at two in the morning, she convinced herself that she should go home; she was due in the pub again that night.

She parked her car. It was pitch black and no one seemed to be around. She went into the house, let Skye out into the garden briefly and then locked the back door again. She exhaled slowly; she hadn't realised she'd been holding her breath. She double-checked the locks and climbed the stairs to bed.

Sandra woke from a deep sleep to the sound of banging, then splintering wood. Greg had smashed the front door lock until the wood gave way. He was beyond reason as he leapt up the stairs, hauled her out of bed and threw her against the wardrobe. Several punches to her head and body followed.

His face was contorted with rage. 'You're a whore.'

'No, Greg, why?'

'Yes, why indeed did Harry buy us fish and chips? You're fucking him, you bitch. Couldn't do without it, could you?'

As he wrestled her to the floor, she managed to kick him in the groin, slip away under his right arm and run for the stairs. He tried to follow her, but she stuck out her leg and tripped him over on the landing. Then she was down the stairs, out of the front door, and running barefoot and naked to her neighbour's house.

It seemed to take ages for Maggie to answer the door.

'Hurry, hurry. Oh, Christ, hurry, please.'

There seemed no sign of pursuit.

Maggie opened the door on its safety chain and was aghast at the sight of Sandra with no clothes on, a huge egg-shaped lump on her forehead, and bruises forming on her chest and face. She quickly opened the door.

I must hide those breasts from Charles!

She pulled a coat off the rack by the door, just in time before her husband Charles's face appeared at the top of the stairs, like a querulous ostrich.

'What on earth is going on, Margaret?'

Charles was a retired solicitor, used to defending 'people like Sandra', as he referred to her in conversation with his wife afterwards. He took charge and phoned the police while Maggie took Sandra into the lounge and offered her tea or Scotch. She had Scotch.

'I'll join you,' said Maggie, pouring two generous fingers each and handing one to Sandra as she took a large gulp of hers.

Charles came in and helped himself as well while surreptitiously trying to look at Sandra's body under the short coat.

'I'll be in my study if you need me,' he said, leaving the two women alone.

Maggie asked no questions and an uncomfortable silence developed. Sandra only knew her neighbours to say hello to and they were all embarrassed. She felt as if she'd landed in the middle of a play for which she had no script.

The police went straight to Sandra's house, and after half an hour, one of them came back to Maggie's door and asked for Sandra. He then stared quite blatantly at all the parts of Sandra that the thigh-length coat did not cover.

'Miss Marsden. We've persuaded your gentleman friend to leave your house for now. It is your house, isn't it?' he asked.

'Is that all you're going to do?' replied Sandra. 'He broke into my house and hit me. You can see what he did to me, can't you?'

The policeman cast his eyes over her again. 'I understand the gentleman was living at your house for over a year when you changed the locks without telling him. He had nowhere to go and he was a bit angry about that and it obviously got the better of him. I'm afraid the police don't get involved in domestic disputes like this. I suggest you go home, contact someone to board up your front door until you can get it repaired or replaced, and then work out your differences with your boyfriend.'

'I changed the locks because he hit me two days ago,' protested Sandra.

The policeman was edging away from her. Clearly his duty was ended as far as he was concerned. He paused and looked her up and down again. 'Miss Marsden, didn't you stop to think that your actions would infuriate him? I know if my missus did that I'd be annoyed. I'm sorry, the police can't get involved in the whys and wherefores of this incident, and I'm not a relationship counsellor. I hope you manage to sort things out between you. Goodnight.'

Charles and Maggie were peering round their respective doors. For the first time Sandra was aware she was barefoot and naked in a borrowed coat, and she summoned up the remnants of her dignity.

'Sorry for waking you up. Thanks, you two. I'll bring the coat back later.'

Roberta, Rosie and Linda went around to Sandra's house that evening with several bottles of wine.

'I feared the worst when I didn't hear from you,' said Roberta.

'I'm fine, really,' protested Sandra after she had filled them in on the morning's events. 'It was a treat to see old Charlie's eyes popping out, though; I left the top button of the coat undone, just to give him a thrill. I'm happy to see you three, better than drinking alone.'

'You must be shocked, you sound a bit hysterical,' said Rosie, visibly taken aback at what had happened. 'There's a woman called Erin Pizzey who has opened a refuge for women victims of what is now called domestic violence. I never thought it would happen to a friend of mine, though.'

'Rosie, I've seen plenty of battered women at A&E, and what happened to me was nowhere near as bad as that. I feel more anger at myself for trusting him. Greg and I never talked about the past. I'm a bit thrown now that he got past my radar at all.'

'Yes, I can see that you must have lost some faith in your judgement,' said Roberta. 'We've all got an emotional child inside us. Sometimes it escapes adult control and what happens next all depends on how we feel about our childhood.'

'That sounds about right,' said Sandra.

'I feel he's really let you down,' said Linda. 'I was convinced that you two were so in love and would get married. In fact, to me you were the perfect match.'

'You can't still believe in romance after what Eddie did to you?' said Sandra unkindly. 'I've always made sure I don't let anyone else take over my life and that's how I've survived. I've found from bitter experience that the only things you can trust in life are our four-legged friends.'

'Owww, owww, owww to that,' agreed Roberta impishly, and they all howled with laughter.

'Seriously, you are a survivor, Sandra,' said Rosie, 'but that doesn't mean that Greg should get away with this sort of bullying behaviour. There are women who are not independent like you and have no choice but to put up with it.'

TWENTY-ONE

2005

'Thank goodness the law has now changed, and domestic abuse is now regarded as a crime,' exclaimed Lizzie. 'Is that how you came to be involved in the Women's Refuge, Aunt Rosie? Were you thinking of your friends?'

'I wish I was that charitable,' Rosie replied. 'No, I think I was thinking about myself first. I remember the moment when Theo and Hugo became self-sufficient teenagers. Suddenly, they could take themselves to after-school activities and then they were breaking away from us. Their dad often came into the house and headed straight to his office, forgetting to greet me, and they started to do the same thing. I was feeling increasingly redundant. I had grown up in a house where my mum didn't work, but now women were starting to have children *and* careers.'

'From your stories, you have clearly all seen a lot of changes for women. Thirty years ago, you were victims of your upbringing and your parents' expectations. Today you would have rights as individuals. I can't begin to imagine what I would have done in your shoes.'

'It's not as if things ended there,' replied Rosie. 'We still supported each other, and we all went on to take advantage of the advances in women's rights and became more independent. If there's anything you want to know about Linda's recent life that we can help you with, then ask away. Otherwise, I will just ramble on. I know, I'll tell you about the Women's Club.'

'Oh, please do,' said Louisa, hungry for any snippets about the mum she had just lost.

'Like you, we have not been as close to your mum as we were in the early days, but I tend to organise get-togethers. I was an only child and I like company,' Said Rosie.

TWENTY-TWO

1990

Rosie felt she needed to take some positive action with her life, and who better to discuss her ideas with than her women friends? She organised the first of what would become a regular monthly dinner date. She had booked a local restaurant and volunteered to drive everybody. Drink driving had become a major issue recently – no longer a matter of fudging blowing into a bag and being given the benefit of the doubt, the new breathalyser was accurate. It was hard for their generation to accept, having grown up without it, but there was far more traffic on the roads these days.

And correspondingly more idiot drivers then?

Sandra and Roberta were already seated, heads together in what looked like a serious conversation.

'Hello, both,' Rosie greeted them brightly.

Roberta looked up, and Rosie saw a glint of tears in her eyes.

'Tell you later,' she mouthed.

'I really want to talk about Linda before she turns up,' said Sandra without preamble. 'I'm worried about her. She's drinking too much for a start. She turns up at my pub regularly, propping up the bar and embarrassing us both by lamenting her fate to anyone who will listen.'

'Why do you think I suggested a dinner date? A chance to soak up the wine, of course,' said Rosie. 'Oh, I see you got me some water, great!'

They all laughed.

'I blame her Catholic upbringing,' said Roberta out of the blue, and Rosie and Sandra fell about laughing. Roberta would get to the point of what she wanted to say – eventually.

'What I mean is, it's like she forsook the Catholic religion overnight and Eddie became her new religion, or being Eddie's wife did. She worked so hard at being a super wife, mum, hostess and cook. She had a great figure and, dare I say it, she liked nothing more than making the squash club wives jealous.'

'I love the way your mind works,' said Rosie, 'but isn't that a little harsh?'

'Don't get me wrong, she's not consciously vindictive – it's all about her identity. She needs something else now. I took her some vegetable seedlings, but she wasn't interested, she was still in bed. She needs something new to get up for.'

'I tried to interest her in a puppy,' said Sandra. 'You know Cleo, that collie bitch from the rescue centre that I took on? Blow me, but she went and had puppies. Linda's daughters love coming to see them.'

'Oh, dear,' said Rosie. 'I can see what's happening here. We're all guilty of trying to give her our interests. I took her to my gym and treated her to a massage and facial.'

'Here's Linda now,' said Roberta, spotting her at the door, looking for them.

They chatted between themselves, ordered food and wine, then raised their glasses together and paused, waiting for Rosie to speak.

'Yes, I guess this is down to me – the inaugural Women's Club dinner, that is. Here's to us and to the next chapter of our lives.'

They clinked glasses.

'Shakespeare talked about the seven ages of man,' said Roberta, 'so there must be a corresponding seven ages for women by now, surely? So where are we all? Let me see, childhood, adolescence, motherhood, now what?'

'Very timely,' said Rosie. 'That's along the lines that I was thinking.'

'You can substitute failed relationships instead of motherhood for me,' Sandra interrupted.

Rosie grinned in acknowledgement. 'I'm thinking career next,' she went on. 'I've decided to volunteer for the Women's Aid Movement.'

'Wow, congratulations, that's a brilliant idea,' said Roberta. 'What did David say? I can't imagine him being happy with you working for money, and you don't need to.'

She tailed off, embarrassed; she was digging a hole for herself here.

Rosie sought to put her at ease. 'Of course, it will put David in a good light if I'm involved in charity work. He was slightly unnerved, though, by my choice.'

'He probably puts it down to your friends' experiences,' offered Sandra.

'Do you know, that's exactly what he said? He also said he hoped people wouldn't think I was an abused wife.'

'All about him, eh? What did you say to that?'

'I said, 'Not in body or mind but maybe in spirit.''

'So, what's involved in volunteering for Women's Aid?' asked Linda.

'I've had an interview and they've agreed to take me on because I was studying sociology at university and I have kept up my interest and knowledge of current women's issues. I have to complete a training course, then I can start as a volunteer at a refuge.'

'Aren't you scared? I mean, you've had a cushioned life so far – how do you know if you can deal with the situations you are going to come up against? Nursing in A&E was full on,' said Linda.

'I just want to make things better for women. I don't know how I'll react to a crisis. I think it's more important to believe I can help make a difference.'

Linda was silent. She seemed to be mulling something over, then she spoke. 'I used to believe that everything that happened to people was God's will and I had a role to help make people feel better. Then something happened and I couldn't believe in God's will anymore. But, Rosie, you have just reminded me that I can still help people as a nurse. There's a job coming up at the local doctor's surgery; it would fit in with school hours. What do you all think?'

Roberta gave her a big hug, and Sandra said, 'That's my girl; we've been worried about you.'

Rosie looked around at them all. This was such a good idea this dinner, but what about Roberta – wasn't she upset about something? Will, her husband, was always upsetting her, but despite this, their marriage endured. Rosie had helped Roberta over the years with commissions for paintings, but you couldn't get involved in people's relationships. She hoped it was more tangible help she needed. She decided to broach the subject and whispered to her, 'What were you going to tell me later?'

Roberta was on her second glass of wine and whatever was troubling her had receded for the moment, so she had to think. 'You know Will's father died over a year ago? Well, the farmhouse has been empty all this time, but Will won't talk about us moving in there. I've tried to approach the subject many times, but he ducks and weaves, and lately he started just saying, "No, Roberta." I don't know what's wrong; wouldn't you think it would be ideal for us? I would love to have a go at restoring it; maybe he thinks I'm being mercenary because it's his. Mind you, I don't know how much money he has – he never tells me. I sometimes wonder if he's deliberately tormenting me. Then there's something else that's odd. The regulars at the pub hardly speak to me if I go in. Do you think Will has told them something?'

'So, what's upsetting you most?' asked Rosie. It was hard to dissect this information and there was no point in getting into the subject of Will's behaviour. She needed to focus on her friend.

'Will's been staying at the farm on his own – that's what's upsetting me. He comes home at night for his tea, gets changed, then goes out. The next time I see him is in the morning when he comes home for his breakfast.'

Rosie, Sandra and Linda had all her attention now, their faces agog.

'How long has this been going on?'

'How do you know he's staying at the farm?'

'Have you said anything to him?'

Roberta was looking tearful and Sandra filled her glass. 'One at a time now, guys, eh?'

Roberta took a large mouthful and sighed. 'Oh, dear, now I try and put it into words it does sound incredible, but it's been going on for months. I know you're all thinking, *Why does she put up with it?* The thing is, it's always been like this. I have no power and he doesn't respect anything I say. If I try and do anything to stand up for myself, I get paid back, doubly, because it's then all my fault.' She took another slug of wine. 'I'm assuming he's staying at the farm; it looks like the bed has been slept in there.'

Rosie, Linda and Sandra were looking at each other. In the end, it was Sandra who was brave enough to speak. 'There's no easy way to say this,' said Sandra. 'I'm sorry, but he must have another woman.'

'I bet he takes her in the pub when you're not there,' said Linda thoughtlessly.

'But I've asked him, and he says there isn't anyone else,' said Roberta. 'If I can't trust the word of my own husband, who can I trust?'

'Trust no one,' said Sandra predictably. 'Believe me, it's the only way.'

'I've had enough of it now. I guess if I knew what was going on, I could make some decisions and get on with my life,' said Roberta. 'I've been doing most things on my own ever since we married, but I've never had to support myself financially. I have to give Will that.'

'Oh yes, and look how generous he's been with your clothing allowance,' retorted Sandra, gesticulating at Roberta's clothes, which were usually from charity shops.

The women were a little giddy with wine now apart from Rosie, and they hatched a plan to go to Will's local, wait in the car park and then follow him. Rosie was in a car that she and David had bought for Theo to practise driving in. Will would never recognise it.

Once they'd arrived at the pub and settled down in the car, their adrenaline petered out and there wasn't a lot to do. Then Linda started giggling uncontrollably at anything anyone said, which produced waves of hysteria.

'It's a good job I wasn't driving one of Will's Land Rovers. Can you imagine hiding that?' said Roberta.

Linda yipped like a hyena, unable to tell them what was so funny. Rosie knew that Will had developed a side-line restoring four-wheel drives and ex-military vehicles, and then an image of Roberta at a gun turret sent her off into peals of laughter too.

'Really, unless we all keep quiet...' she ventured. She was just at the point of calling it off, then Will came out of the pub with a woman, just like that.

'I've never seen her before,' whispered Roberta.

They both got into a Mini.

'Oh my God, that car has been at our house. Will said he was doing some repairs on it for a friend.'

'If you'd known, you could have smashed the windscreen,' whispered Linda gleefully.

'Shhh.'

They followed the car back to a local housing estate, where Will and the woman disappeared into a house.

'I think the show's over for now, folks,' said Sandra.

They all turned to comfort Roberta, who was now crying silently.

TWENTY-THREE

1990 Roberta

That night Roberta stayed up drinking and crying all night. She felt as if she needed to punish herself.

I'm stupid to have put up with all this.

And all the time she waited for Will to come home, just to prove her wrong.

The dawn broke. It was still dark when the birds started their chorus – the blackbird first, she recognised him. He seemed to be mocking her. It was official – Will had stayed out all night. Then others joined in and the sky lightened, and it seemed like a miracle that the birds knew that another day would happen. She pulled herself together. Her eyes were red and puffy, and she felt terrible.

She spent half an hour bathing her face with cold water so that the children wouldn't notice she had been crying, then, when they woke and dressed, she mechanically organised their breakfasts and sent them off to school. At about nine Will came in. The atmosphere was charged between them and he immediately knew that she knew. Silently she cooked his breakfast, then she went upstairs and had a shower. She looked at the bed and gratefully sank into it and into oblivion.

Will ate his breakfast, had a shower and joined her.

'How could you want to have sex with another woman after what we have together?'

'It's not for that,' replied Will. 'She knows how to smile and 'ave a laugh. You don't – you're always trying to fuckin' nag me for something. Yer pushy, just like your mother. An' you're a snob, Roberta. You and yer fucking posh friends. I'm not quite good enough for you and I can tell you've kind of accepted it as fact, but it ain't right.'

'Where did you meet her?' asked Roberta.

'At the pub,' replied Will. 'She's a cleaner.'

'How could you prefer a scrubber to me?' Roberta raged.

'Her name's Frances,' said Will.

Will wanted to behave as if nothing was wrong, just as he had done when Roberta had first found out she was pregnant. Roberta pondered on the fact that in other cultures polygamy was perfectly acceptable. However, she had no intentions of sharing Will with another woman. She felt humiliated that he had been meeting Frances openly at the local pub. She was angry that he had lied to her. She would never trust him again. As with most things that concerned Will, it was a waste of time trying to discuss anything with him. He just carried on as he always did and did exactly as he pleased.

Events took over when Will's new woman became pregnant. One of the pub regulars broke silence and called in at the cottage to tell Roberta. 'I don't care how he justifies it; it isn't right, what he's doing.'

Rosie, Roberta, Sandra and Linda had been meeting up for dinner every month for the last six months. They all looked forward to sharing their triumphs and disasters and giving each other moral support. Tonight was a Chinese meal, and Roberta was driving a Land Rover, which prompted a fresh round of jokes.

'I can't believe Will has got that woman pregnant already. It would seem that it wasn't you that was careless all those years ago,' said Linda to Roberta.

'It's probably just as well it happened,' said Rosie. 'It worries me that you're still living in what was your shared house and you still rely on Will to give you housekeeping rather than having a proper maintenance agreement. You still have no freedom or respect, and he comes and goes as he pleases.'

'He's keeping an eye on you,' said Sandra.

'I've seen all sorts of domestic arrangements since I started at the Refuge, and the more complicated they are, the less the husbands or partners seem to be able to cope with it. You know, domestic abuse is not just about physical violence. There are many methods that a husband uses to control his wife and make her scared of him. Compared to the women who have to seek shelter at the Refuge – yes, right now you're in a safe place to live, but that can change at any time for anyone. It's not just about money.'

Rosie looked at Roberta meaningfully.

'It's very hard when I still love him,' said Roberta. 'It's more powerful than logic.'

'Roberta, you're as bad as Linda,' cried Sandra in exasperation. 'You believe in this all-consuming love that's just an excuse for avoiding responsibility for your own life and your own actions. All these years you've allowed Will to treat you like this. All these years you've been hoping he will change and yet I can tell you think it's all your fault. I've seen it in your face so many times.'

Sandra's mouth was dry with the effort and she paused for a sip of wine. 'You might as well put a label on your forehead saying, "I am a doormat, use me." Well, the thing you *are* doing wrong is letting him run your life instead of doing it yourself. What kind of example are you giving to Hannah and James? How do you really feel, deep down?'

Roberta started to sob, feeling attacked by her friend, but she also knew Sandra was right. She *had* just let Will take responsibility for everything. 'I feel very angry with both myself and Will,' she replied evasively.

'Then use that anger,' said Sandra. 'Take power from it, decide what you want to do and stand up for yourself – we'll all support you. It's a job waiting to happen.'

That week, Roberta saw a solicitor that Rosie had recommended and filed for divorce, and then she gathered Hannah and James together and told them what was happening.

'I don't want anything to change,' wailed fourteen-year-old Hannah. Ten-year-old James didn't really know what to say.

'I will do my utmost to make sure your life changes as little as possible,' promised Roberta. She made up a bed for herself in the spare room.

The first thing that Will noticed was that Roberta had moved herself into the spare bedroom. Then he received a letter in the post from her solicitor. He'd been telling Frances that Roberta was refusing to divorce him, so he did what he usually did and ignored them both. Unfortunately for Will, the law had changed in recent years in favour of women. His relationship model was outdated, based as it was on his father and mother, who stayed together because they couldn't do anything else.

It was only when the courts were about to intervene and award Roberta half of everything, including the farm, that Will was forced to visit a solicitor for advice. She settled for the cottage and a lump sum, and maintenance for Hannah and James till they were eighteen.

She had kept her promise to Hannah. She would still live in the same house and she could still walk across the fields to the old farmhouse and see her father.

'I'm so busy now with painting commissions, it's great,' said Roberta at their next dinner. 'And I've been offered an "Artist in Residence" post on the Stockport Foundation Course. I still need more work, but already I feel more confident.'

'The two go hand in hand,' said Linda. 'Who decided married women shouldn't work?'

'I've decided to run my own kennels business,' said Sandra. 'I want to afford more holidays.'

'We're trailblazers,' said Rosie.

2005

'So how did you end up running your own women's refuge?' asked Lizzie.

'It was just by chance, or happenstance, as some people say,' replied Rosie.

TWENTY-FOUR

1995 Sara

Rosie had been volunteering for Women's Aid for five years when, one April, she received a phone call to the helpline.

'Hello, Rosie, it's Sara. Do you remember me? I came to the Refuge four years ago.'

Rosie did indeed remember Sara. She was unusual in that she was in her late sixties when she came there, and she had told Rosie her story.

Sara and her husband Daniel had escaped from Nazi Germany just before the war. They had settled in Manchester where Daniel had relatives, and he had worked as a solicitor amongst the Jewish community. They had managed to rent the basement flat in a large house and over the years had gradually bought that and the other flats in the house until they owned the building.

The rent from the other flats should have been a nice pension for them in their retirement, but Daniel had never got over the trauma of the flight from Germany. He knew that Britain had restricted the entry of Germans during the war, but when the extent of the Holocaust became known he became very angry. Quite unreasonably, he wanted to blame the whole of Western Europe for not doing something to stop it and Sara took the brunt of his anger. He had treated Sara in a cruel and controlling manner for years, so much so that when he started locking her in the outhouse as a punishment, she believed she had done something to deserve it. It took a determined neighbour to raise the alarm and then the Refuge became involved.

Sara had spent some time at the Refuge until she had recovered and gained enough confidence to decide what to do next. She chose to go and live with her sister in Austria.

Rosie had got on well with Sara at the time and they had built up a close friendship. Although not a war baby herself, Rosie had felt the war years like a shadow when she was growing up in the 1950s. She had elderly relatives who had survived two world wars, and she heard the tales about those who did not. Almost everyone she knew had been touched by the two wars in some way and she had a great respect for that generation. The friendship was mutual. Sara, indoctrinated by her husband about an uncaring British society, had felt healed by this young woman who showed such kindness to people such as herself.

'I am coming to England,' said Sara. 'I heard that Daniel died today, and I want to go to the funeral. I will be flying with my sister later on and we will be staying with friends. It will be okay. Most of our friends knew Daniel was unkind to me, but they do not know the details; they just think we split up. I have to deal with his will too. I would like to meet up with you, Rosie. When are you free?'

Rosie arranged to meet after the funeral which, in keeping with Jewish tradition, was to be the following day, and she looked forward to seeing Sara again. They were going to meet the following day at the Pagoda restaurant in Manchester.

Sara was a tall, elegant woman, and she was looking immaculate in her black mourning clothes. She wore a long cashmere coat with a neat velvet collar. Her long silver hair was caught up in an elegant chignon under a pillbox hat. Her sister was shorter and stouter, but Rosie could see the family resemblance. She hugged Sara and looked at her closely but only saw serenity in her clear brown eyes.

Sara introduced her sister Hanna and the next hour was taken up with ordering food and catching up with the details of the funeral and then the last four years. Over coffee, Sara began to talk about the reasons she had wanted to meet up with Rosie.

'I want you to know, Rosie, that I have been happy these last four years in a way I have never known since my childhood. I have Hanna to thank for this.' She reached out and took her sister's hand over the table. 'We are back together at a time when we need each other. Hanna is a widow and lives on her own, and her children and grandchildren keep us both busy. I have no other family and they have become my family now. I have no desire to return to England. I have left everything behind three times in my life now, so it's easy for me.'

Rosie looked puzzled, so she explained. 'The first time when I married Daniel I left my very dear childhood home to go to Berlin. The second time was when we escaped from Nazi Germany to England and we had to leave all our possessions behind, and then again when I left Daniel I took nothing with me. Daniel used to call us displaced persons, but I think I was lucky.'

Rosie wondered where all this was leading, and it must have showed in her face because Sara smiled reassuringly as she went on. 'Daniel set up a small legacy for me after I left him so that I had some income of my own. Now he has willed his other investments to me and I don't need to worry about money for the rest of my life. He also left me the house in Manchester. I want it to become a women's refuge, Rosie. I have discussed this with Hanna, and she agrees with me, but there is a condition, of course.'

Rosie wondered why Sara had met her to tell her all this.

'I want you to run it, Rosie. I can see you have the organisational skills, you have the training and you really care about people. I know from our conversations that you are at a time in your life where you have the space to take on such a project and I can see in you the ambition to be involved in the changes that are happening for women in society.'

Rosie was speechless at first, then she protested. 'I would have thought I was the least qualified person. I haven't had a challenging life so far. All I know is to be the person that other people want me to be.'

'You underestimate yourself, Rosie,' replied Sara. 'You chose to be involved in Women's Aid. I think you have hidden your capabilities for too long. You can do it, and to be honest, I think you need it right now.'

Rosie was nearly in tears at the kindness of this woman.

'I would be honoured to take it on,' she said simply.

David's initial reaction was, of course, congratulatory and supportive when Rosie told him the news, but that fooled neither of them. Rosie knew that the cogs would be whirring, and David would be weighing up the advantages and disadvantages to him personally. If he disapproved, then the questioning would begin – little questions at first – questions to which she had no ready answer, questions that his clever mind had created to slow her in her tracks, undermine her certainty and eventually halt her. If this didn't happen, then she knew she had his approval. For the first time, Rosie didn't care what he said. Sara had faith in her, and that gave her confidence; she didn't want to let her down. Roberta, Linda and Sandra were all impressed, and Roberta and Linda promised immediately to be involved.

It took a few months to draw up a legal agreement for ownership of the property, and Rosie also needed to address the problem of funding for renovation and ongoing running costs, which she did with the support of Women's Aid. The house was already divided into four flats which lent themselves, with a bit of adaptation, to the accommodation that they needed. For the first time in her life, Rosie had to organise people and a project that hadn't had the path smoothed by David and his money. It was a different world, especially when people were volunteering.

Money really does talk.

She had to learn to juggle the budget while making the most of people's time and skills. She could hear Marjorie in her head as she delegated tasks to volunteers and tradesmen.

Oh, dear, I do have my mother's voice.

Unlike Marjorie, however, she never forgot to make sure that people felt valued; she knew how it felt to be taken for granted.

*

Rosie brought the women up to date when they met up for dinner.

'I'm so excited for you,' said Roberta. 'Can I contribute something? I could use my artistic skills. I don't mean for the walls, although that might be an end result. I mean, I could run art classes for anyone who wants to come, adults and children – we would soon have the place looking colourful with paintings.'

'I could bring puppies in,' Sandra chipped in, going totally against her beliefs about volunteering. 'There's nothing more comforting than cuddling a furry animal... Well, maybe one thing, eh, ha? I could talk to the children about the responsibilities of having a pet. I could also run self-defence classes.'

'Maybe self-defence is a topic a bit close to home.' Linda giggled. 'I would be willing to do nursing shifts.'

'I'm always going away, so I couldn't commit myself to a regular slot, but I could do some nursing cover,' said Sandra more cautiously.

'Aren't you ever going to tell us who the mystery boyfriend is?' Roberta asked, jealous of so many holidays.

'He's Mr Big,' said Sandra, teasing her.

'I could grow vegetables with the families,' said Linda. 'It would remind me of the time when I was married to Eddie and really happy. These days I'm finding it harder to play the role of glamorous corporate rep. There's something empty in the travelling and the one-night stands in hotel rooms.'

Rosie looked a bit shocked at the mention of one-night stands. She reflected on how the four friends' lives were now, compared with when they first met. They had all developed their independent skills and interests. All apart from Linda, who seemed stuck in a pattern that hadn't changed for years.

TWENTY-FIVE

2005

'I **can see how you** have all supported each other,' said Lizzie. 'The Women's Refuge is like a kind of hub, isn't it, keeping you all connected. Yet you have all developed such different careers.'

'I can remember going to a careers evening at school where nursing and teaching largely figured,' said Roberta. 'There really wasn't much choice then. We have all created our own path rather than jump into a career or profession. We are self-made, based on our talents and personalities.'

'We must talk about the funeral now – sorry, sis.'

Louisa's eyes were filling up at the reminder. 'Dad found these notes attached to Mum's will.' She picked up a folder from the table and began to read from it. 'She has specified a glass hearse to be pulled by black-plumed horses.'

There was a general ripple of hysteria at this, that quickly descended into sobs.

'Silly bitch was always into appearances,' Sandra eventually choked out.

'She wants to be cremated, and there is to be no involvement from the Catholic Church,' Lizzie went on, reading from the notes.

'She has left the name and contact details of a friend, Matt Cooper, who is a humanist with whom she had already spoken about her plans. She wants him to officiate at the service and apparently she has provided him with a eulogy.'

'She seemed to have thought of everything,' Rosie began.

'What state of mind was she in?' Sandra interrupted.

'You haven't told us yet about Mum, about her life recently, about how she came to work for Sipher,' said Lizzie.

There was an uncomfortable silence.

'We were worried about her,' Sandra began. 'Some of her behaviour was a bit risqué, not that it was out of character, it's just…'

'It didn't seem dignified for a woman her age?' Rosie offered.

Lizzie laughed. 'Sorry, laughter may not seem appropriate, but we do know Mum of old. Don't forget, we used to live with her.

'Louisa, I don't think her having boyfriends affected us much. That shows that we felt secure and loved.'

TWENTY-SIX

1996–2004 Linda

Linda's new job at the local GP's surgery had ticked a lot of boxes for her at first. It suited school hours and holidays, her days were full, and she met a lot of lovely people who lifted her spirits, but she increasingly felt that she was in a backwater.

'We're dealing with the "worried well" here, you know,' said one of the doctors cynically. 'It can get a bit tedious.'

Linda had been used to the pace of hospital nursing, but she didn't want to go back to it. Rosie had helped her get the courage to go out and work again; did she have any ideas what she should do next?

'I was wondering if you had any contacts that could help Linda get another job?' Rosie asked David.

'Now that's a coincidence. Eddie was telling me the other day that Linda was asking for more maintenance, I would like to help him out. Mmm.' David paused in thought. 'You know, Linda is a good-looking woman who takes care of her appearance. Sipher is about to expand its sales team and will be specifically looking for attractive nurses to sell the benefits of Svelta to GPs.'

'That sounds more up her street, and she could do it now the girls are older.'

'Will you ask her to get in touch? I think Sipher might have a job that would suit her. It pays a good salary with a company car, and it would take the pressure off Eddie.'

Linda didn't need asking twice, and once she'd started the job, she loved it. The world of pharmaceuticals suited her down to the ground. Appearance was important and she took great pleasure in planning her wardrobe so that it highlighted her slim but shapely figure. She got on well with the GPs she visited, who were invariably pleased to enjoy a wind-down chat at the end of a full surgery.

Svelta was the ideal slimming drug for people who had a weight problem but were unable to change their diet or increase their level of exercise. However, it was becoming apparent that another group was emerging: that of women in their forties for whom approaching middle age was making weight and shape more difficult to control. These women wanted to remain in the same dress size and Svelta helped them meet that need.

Linda too, despite being very slim, was seeing the effects of middle age on her body. This was brought home to her when while driving her new company Audi and, glancing to her right, she caught her reflection in the side window. She stared in disbelief at the roll of fat that lay like a sausage between her breasts and her stomach, reminding her of the Michelin man. This was something she could not accept, and she decided she had to start taking Svelta. Ironically, she read all the literature about it from beginning to end for the first time. Once she'd persuaded herself, she took it every day and it worked. Putting herself in the patient's place just made her more successful at her job.

Linda was not having as much success in finding a new soulmate, though. She had tried a few dating agencies, met men through work, had dates with GPs, but nothing ever lasted. She consulted a medium who read her cards and assured her that within the next few years she would be living in luxury with a man of considerable wealth.

*

'Do us a favour, Linda, will you? I've double-booked my dates and I don't want to let either of them down.'

Anne had collared Linda as they were leaving the step class. Linda had recently been invited by Anne to Thursdays, a singles night at a local hotel, and been introduced to a sub-culture of divorcees mixed with travelling businesspeople, all blatantly looking for casual sex. The women danced and the men stood round the room weighing them up.

Just like a cattle market, thought Linda in disgust.

Linda eventually had a dance with a man called Dennis, who bought her a drink and bored her for an hour with the story of the breakup of his marriage. Everybody her age carried baggage. Dating was definitely more difficult the second time around.

'Is your spare date anyone I know,' she ventured, 'or someone from Thursdays?'

Anne laughed. 'Don't worry, it's no one from Thursdays. I saw your look of horror when we went there – not everyone's cup of tea, but a bit of fun if you play the game. No, it's Adam. You've met him; he's a friend of Carol's at the squash club. He's asked me to dinner. It's not really a date; I think he's at a bit of a loose end. The trouble is the relationship between Mike and me is hotting up. It might be the real thing, totally the wrong timing to go to dinner with someone else. Can I ask him to phone you? He'll understand. He'll buy you a splendid dinner; he's old-fashioned and knows how to treat a lady.'

'I remember him, and I didn't exactly warm to him,' said Linda. 'He was another one slagging off his ex-wife. They all seem to do it. And I don't play squash either.'

Anne laughed. 'Neither does he. Will you help me out then?'

Linda found herself being picked up from home by Adam. It was Saturday, and Eddie and Megan had the children. She set out determined to enjoy her free night and her date, and she was pleasantly surprised. Adam was very good company: charming, thoughtful and amusing. They seemed to have a lot in common, and their conversation opened up as the wine flowed, with no mention of the ex. The restaurant was expensive, the waiter attentive and Adam seem to know his wines. Linda knew she looked good. She was slim, tanned, and wearing black Jaeger trousers and a silk top.

When Adam drove her home, they were relaxed and laughing, and of course she invited him into her house. They sat together in the lounge, drinking and playing some music. At some point he put an arm round her shoulders, and then moved it down her back, where he started to worm his way between her trousers and top. She went a bit cold at the naivety of the gesture; it reminded her of being at the cinema when she was a teenager, and she squirmed accordingly. She was just about to move away on some pretext or other, when he kissed her. Wow. Totally unexpected, the kiss seemed to hit her straight in the groin.

Minutes later, they were on the floor with their trousers down; she had climaxed already, but he was nowhere near.

'Shall we move somewhere more comfortable?' he suggested.

An hour later and she had orgasmed again and again as he screwed her slowly. He was lying on his side with a look of amusement on his face, and he still hadn't climaxed.

'Haven't you come yet?' she asked blearily. 'How do you do it?'

'I read up about it,' he replied.

'Well, I can't stand much more. I won't be able to walk tomorrow.'

Adam chuckled and entered her again, this time to a climax that they both shared. He left in the early hours. The next day he turned up at Linda's again and she could hardly look him in the face, but he seemed amused. The children were delivered by Eddie and the two men chatted, weighing each other up. Adam was very good with Louisa and Lizzie.

'I always wanted children,' he said.

A bouquet of flowers was delivered the next day, then a dozen bottles of wine. The following weekend, Adam took her and the children out to Sunday lunch. Afterwards they stopped at a confectioners and Adam bought them all a box of assorted chocolates to eat when they got home.

The following weekend, when Eddie and Megan had the children again, he took her to London and to the Langham Hotel. They went shopping in Harrods and Adam sat with a coffee, reading the paper while she chose two complete outfits which he paid for with his Platinum American Express card.

Then Adam was phoning her every day wanting to see her, but of course it was impossible. She had work, she had the children's commitments, she had her own life and her friends.

'Too good to be true,' said Sandra.

'Money doesn't buy everything,' said Roberta jealously, not having known anything remotely like it.

Anne was concerned. 'You need to experience someone like this once in your life, but is it sustainable?'

'Be careful,' said Rosie. 'He will want to own you.'

Linda couldn't help it; she was starting to float. She was appreciated by a generous and sexy man, and not just for herself. He seemed to enjoy the whole package, including her children.

When it began to unravel, it was the little things that frayed first. Adam was a man who made speedy decisions and soon he wanted more of Linda. He asked her to marry him and move into his house with her children. She couldn't say yes; Eddie paid the overheads on her house and owned half of it. She told him that she liked the idea, but maybe in five years' time she could think of getting married when the children were older, and she had sorted her finances out.

Having extracted a promise, he was starting to talk to her in a proprietary manner. He spent most of his time at her house now and he showed her how she could do things in a better way. He snooped on the children and told tales on them, he made little jokes about how seriously she took her work, and when he discovered she took Svelta he hooted with laughter and took to saying, 'How "svelte" you look, Linda.' As time went on, the flowers and the chocolates stopped, and then the tantrums started.

The first one was after a school dance when Eddie and Megan were there. Adam was convinced for some reason that Linda had wanted to avoid being seen with him, that she was ashamed of him. The next one was when Linda met an old boyfriend through work.

'You can't be just friends with an ex-lover,' he screamed at her. 'There's always something still there, isn't there?'

Adam then found out that years before, Linda had dated a neighbour.

'There's nothing like shitting on your own doorstep, is there? I didn't know I was dating the village bicycle,' he shouted nastily, and retaliated by visiting Sandra. 'As just a friend,' he stressed.

Each time he had a tantrum he went off to sulk, only to reappear the next day full of apologies. The children were beginning to get nervous. He was so changeable, and Linda was confused. Where was the lovely man she had dated, and what had she done to make him change?

The last straw was when he criticised Linda for dressing younger than she was. 'Mutton dressed as lamb springs to mind,' he said.

Linda was mortified. Adam had found her Achilles' heel. She was convinced that if she had looked after her appearance more, Eddie would never have left her. She needed someone who would reassure her that this wasn't so, and Adam was finished from then on as far as she was concerned. She was beginning to be afraid of him. His twinkling green eyes now looked like menacing shards of glass.

She tried to let him down gently and call it a day.

'You're just like all the others,' he said. 'You were just after my money.'

He drove off, car tyres squealing, with a bottle of whisky on the passenger seat. Linda couldn't face another tantrum. In the end she agreed they would stay good friends and that seemed to pacify him. She suspected this was how all his relationships ended. It wasn't until he called round one day and Stephen, one of her work colleagues, was there, that he seemed to get the message.

Stephen was, in fact, gay.

'I think you just inadvertently got rid of my ex. You have done me a huge favour.'

Stephen was a good listener and Linda opened up to him about what had happened with Adam. 'I was letting him take over my life. My mother's generation were brought up expecting to be looked after by a husband and when I first married, that's what I wanted too. But I never thought I'd get divorced. I won't let a man pay for me again on a night out. It's a signal from the start that they're entitled to own you.'

'Tell you what,' said Stephen. 'Come with me to a gay men's club in Manchester; that will be a new experience for you.'

Hero's club was in a cellar somewhere on a back street. The man at the entrance desk stared at her for a good while.

'Don't worry, you'll find a few other women come here,' Stephen had said. 'Women are accepted; we call them FOD, short for Friends of Dorothy.'

They paid their entry fees and went in.

'Wow!' said Linda. 'Another sub-culture.'

There was a large main room and a stage, on which some of the men were dancing. The décor was black, maroon red and dark blue, and the music had a beat and a pulse. Some of the men were dressed in uniforms with peaked caps and studded belts, some had chains across their chests, and others had keys on their belts. Linda even saw a teddy bear.

'Indicates their proclivities,' said Stephen mysteriously.

Just then a puff of mist shot out at floor level on the stage, onto the dancers.

'There are rumours that they put amyl nitrate into that,' Stephen informed her.

Linda stood for a while taking in the scene and Stephen left her at intervals, darting off to chat up a likely pick-up and coming back with a disgruntled look on his face.

'I can do better in a queue at Sainsbury's checkout,' he muttered.

Linda thought a lot of the men looked handsome and menacing in equal measures. One of these icons came up and started talking to her. He said his name was Karl. He wore a pilot's uniform and looked rather stunning.

'Surprisingly, I am a pilot,' he confessed. 'I just like coming here for fun. I have the pick of beautiful men and women every day at work, and sometimes I need something more exciting. Now look at you, you're interesting: very gamine, so slim, almost androgynous.'

Linda felt a frisson of danger and she was back at the medical student parties. She was suddenly fed up with socialising with divorcees approaching middle age. She wanted to feel young again. Karl asked for her phone number. They were both playing it cool; she was with Stephen for the evening, anyway, and she didn't really expect to hear from him again. She was surprised when he phoned, and they made a date on her next free Saturday.

'I'll pick you up at eight. Dress casually, and bring a change of clothes and a toothbrush,' he said mysteriously.

'Okay,' she said, a little wary but intrigued.

'You passed the first test, by the way,' he replied, 'trusting me and no questions asked.'

On the Saturday, Karl was punctual, parking outside her house in an Audi TT sportscar. He was wearing designer jeans and a white shirt, and with dark, nearly black hair, blue eyes and what looked like a permanent tan, he was just as stunning as he had looked in his uniform. He was also younger than her, Linda realised, and she was glad she had had a non-surgical facelift that day. He opened the passenger door for her, and she climbed in as elegantly as she could.

So began a pattern that was repeated many times over the next few months and was so bizarre Linda couldn't bring herself to tell any of her friends, not even Sandra. She was whisked away for miles in Karl's car, invariably playing Whitney Houston on the CD player. Their destination was different each time and was always a stunning and remote home of the very rich. Some of the parties involved a helicopter flight or a light plane trip. The venue was always a fancy-dress party where gender stereotypes were turned on their heads. Each couture outfit, which was supplied, was an extravagant and erotic juxtaposition of male and female styles.

All the guests were masked and hooded, or wigged, and fell into two categories: those who performed and those who watched. The room would be a stage set themed with costume and music, changing at every party. What stayed the same was the people, and after a few parties Linda realised they must be members of a club. There were champagne, fine wines and drugs available. She and Karl made a striking pair, beautiful people who danced and wove their bodies as they 'performed' together. Sometimes they swapped partners, male or female; sometimes it was hard to tell. It was better to stay on the dance floor, otherwise you could get pulled into one of the seats by the not-so-beautiful spectators and it was not done to refuse. The parties always ended at two in the morning promptly and guests were escorted to rooms to carry on, or sleep and recover, and depart the next day. They never met their host and there were guests who remained masked at all times.

Karl was a totally unreachable creature. He made polite conversation during the journeys there and back, but he never volunteered any personal information. As a lover he was competent and exotic. As the months went by, Linda found it harder to make sense of this part of her life and to fit it in context with the reality of children, work and friends. She was beginning to wonder *which* part of her life was real. She also needed more feedback than Karl was giving her.

I'm being silly, she thought. *Karl is fun, extremely giving and generous.*

Her lack of self-worth meant that everyone in her life had to hold up a mirror in which she could see herself reflected, and Karl wasn't doing this. Every relationship for her had to be 'going somewhere'. Inevitably she couldn't resist probing, a question here and there about his life, about the setup, about the people. She would invite him to an event in her life to see what he said. Then she would complain when he predictably turned her down, trying to get a reaction, trying to see if he cared at all. Karl just said nothing but eyed her sadly.

153

The next time he took her home, he took her hands in his. 'This is the last time, Linda.'

She was devastated. What had she done?

'This is part of my life. It's the way I'm made. I've long ago learnt to compartmentalise all the other areas; it's the only way I can survive. I'm sorry, but I've been expecting this. It always happens, sooner or later.'

Linda failed to see what he was talking about and became angry and defensive. 'I feel like I've been used,' she said angrily. 'What are you, anyway? You're neither a man nor a woman – you're a freak. You're young and it's exciting, but what happens when you get old? I hated the old perverts.'

He got out of the car and held open the passenger door, and eventually she had to get out.

'Goodbye, Linda. You took part and enjoyed it, didn't you? Even though you're getting a bit old for it, aren't you?'

His words stayed with her. In the cold light of day, she looked back on what she had been party to, and she felt grubby.

*

Linda was in New York at a promotional event for Svelta when she met Adrian. They had chatted easily and although he was slightly younger than Linda and married, it was apparent that he found her attractive. Linda found herself in the familiar situation of not having had sex for so long that just talking to him created a throbbing and a dampness between her legs. She had her vibrator back at the apartment which could bring a level of relief, but she wanted human warmth of a specific type over and inside her.

After what was an enjoyable and exhausting few hours of sex with Adrian, who seemed to be able to produce another erection at will, they lay together and talked about their lives. She told him about Eddie, and he held her in his arms, stroking her hair. 'Not all men are bastards, you know.'

Linda didn't like to point out the irony of his remark and decided to pursue a less contentious subject. 'What did you do before working for Sipher?'

'I worked for Clinmedica on the clinical trials for Svelta. I was fresh out of university and didn't understand much about how the process worked. But I was amazed that it got FDA approval so easily considering there were at least five heart-related deaths that I was aware of. Still, it's Sipher's big money spinner and it pays our salaries.'

Linda decided to probe this a bit more. 'So why did you leave Clinmedica?'

'My boss, Peter Bolton, who I liked working for, had a nervous breakdown and was replaced by a loud-mouthed American. It was about the time Svelta got FDA approval and Sipher were recruiting, so I jumped ship and it's been a great move for me.'

Linda fell into a fitful sleep and woke up with a feeling of unease.

TWENTY-SEVEN

2005

It fell to Lizzie and Louisa to make a visit to their grandparents' home to discuss Linda's choice of funeral, something they knew was going to be difficult. As Lizzie explained the arrangements, the format of the service and the double funeral, the Maguires stared at her speechless.

'Mary and Jesus, she had an abortion, God help her soul,' Mrs Maguire wailed, crossing herself before dropping to her knees in front of a set of religious figurines on a corner table that they had played with as grandchildren.

Louisa and Lizzie realised in that moment exactly why Linda had hated the influence this religion had played in her formative years. Driving back home, Lizzie fumed.

'Those tears are not for our mum. They are for Grandma and her unhealthy relationship with that bloody church. It should have a health warning over the door.'

The funeral was delayed by over three weeks while more tests were conducted by the medical examiner, and Lizzie and Louisa went back to their jobs in London. Lizzie was the first point of contact with the police, but she faithfully reported any findings to Linda's friends, not that there was anything much.

'The DNA tests on the foetus were inconclusive, whatever that means,' she told Rosie. 'The drugs in Linda's system were identified as Svelta, anti-depressants and, surprisingly, cannabis. Nothing else of any significance has been flagged up.'

TWENTY-EIGHT

November 2005
Linda's Funeral

The funeral was held on a dismal, grey November day with low cloud hanging over South Manchester, making the air feel damp and cold. The two white coffins were placed in the glass hearse and covered with white and red floral tributes, which contrasted with the shiny black paintwork of the hearse and the plumes on the horses' heads. It was all quite theatrical.

The small chapel at the crematorium was packed to overflowing with friends, work colleagues and people from nursing days. David and Rosie sat alongside Roberta and Sandra, behind Louisa, Lizzie, Eddie and the Maguires. The ever-pushy Megan had attempted to sit next to Eddie but had been redirected by Rosie to sit elsewhere. Louisa and Lizzie looked on in relief that she had been successfully side-lined.

As the coffins were carried up the chapel nave, the mourners took in the sight of the tiny white coffin which was carried by Matthew Cooper, and those that knew nothing about it gasped. The coffins of mother and child were placed side by side at the front of the chapel, and this poignant sight reduced many of them to tears. Men wiped their eyes while for most of the women it was such a heartrending sight that they could not contain their emotions. They sobbed uncontrollably, their eye make-up running and making black tracks down their faces.

Matthew stood up and spoke of his friendship with Linda. Her notes made no mention of her aborted baby boy, so it was left to him to explain in his opening remarks that Linda had given birth many years ago in difficult circumstances and it seemed appropriate for her baby to be with her now.

Lizzie and Louisa both had questions about the exact nature of this 'friendship'.

How long has he known her? Could he be the father?

Lizzie and Louisa were aware that many of the male mourners present had also dated their mum, in the main after her divorce from Eddie, but from her nursing days too. They watched out for any tell-tale reactions with a strange, detached curiosity, muted by their grief.

Which man is wondering if the child is his?

Simon, now a well-regarded cardiologist, looked on horrified, grabbing the pew to steady himself.

Is he the father?

*

Simon calmed down as he realised that he was the only person in the chapel who knew about the events that happened thirty years ago. He tuned out Matthew's voice as he remembered how Linda had come to him for help.

TWENTY-NINE

1976 Linda and Simon

Linda had been feeling anxious and was finding it difficult to maintain her usual cheerful act on the hospital wards. She heaved a sigh of relief as her shift ended and she went to the canteen for a comforting cup of coffee.

What is wrong with me?

She had everything to be excited about, having met Eddie at Rosie's wedding. Here was the man of her dreams; they'd danced romantically. She was sure the attraction was mutual – hadn't he asked for her address and the phone number of the call box in the nurses' hostel?

But there was no doubt that she was feeling jittery. She thought about Catherine, a woman who had come into hospital with suspected ovarian cysts and been diagnosed with cancer of the ovaries and uterus, too far advanced to operate. The woman was only in her twenties, and Linda was finding it hard to deal with. She was getting sympathetic pains and butterflies in her own stomach. Linda was well aware of the dangers of getting too closely involved with a patient.

And just when she needed her, Sandra, who had always helped her maintain her work-life balance, had appeared at her door yesterday and announced that she was moving in with Richard, a doctor that she'd met at one of Randolph's parties.

'Blimey, that was quick,' said Linda, more than a little hurt.

She felt she was being abandoned. Richard and Sandra had dated a few times, but she had no idea that the relationship had progressed so far.

'Won't it be noticed if you're not in the hostel?'

'It won't if you sign in for me. Be a pal, eh? Aww, don't look like you've lost sixpence and found a penny. It's just that at the moment we can't get enough of each other. The sex is fantastic, and I can't lie awake damp and throbbing in my bed alone any longer.'

Linda had to laugh. 'Well, I'm pleased you're so happy. Don't forget me, though, will you?'

'Of course not. I'll need a break when I get sore, ha!'

With a casual wave she was gone, duffle bag over her shoulder.

*

Two days later, Linda was about to enter the gynaecology ward when Simon came through the doors. Simon was a good-natured, attractive man with fair hair, blue eyes and a smile that was always playing at the edges of his mouth. Linda and he had had several fun dates. Today, though, he was looking serious.

'Hello, Linda.' He greeted her formally in front of the other staff and was about to pass by, but she stalled him.

'Have you got a minute in private?'

'Yes, of course. Shall we go into this side room? It's vacant.'

Once inside he took her in his arms and gave her a luscious, lingering kiss that sent her senses reeling and made her melt inside.

'Wow,' he said. 'It's been a long time since we did that. You taste of peaches and cream. When are you next free?'

Linda laughed and, regaining her balance, replied, 'How about tomorrow evening? But that's not what I stopped you for, although can I say that it was just what the doctor ordered.'

They both laughed at the tired old joke.

'Actually, I wanted to talk to you about Catherine Grayson.'

'Ah.' He immediately became serious. 'Yes, I've just come from seeing her, very sad indeed.'

'Her case is affecting me more than it should,' confessed Linda. 'I've started to have physical symptoms like hers. I can't help it. I'm feeling strange cramps in my tummy and it feels heavy. I don't want to report myself to Sister officially, so when I saw you I wondered if you… you know… could just check there's nothing wrong and put my mind at rest.'

'I'd be delighted, ma'am,' joked Simon, his smile reappearing. 'Meet you at my place tomorrow evening. Is eight okay?'

Linda felt slightly awkward as she knocked on the door of Simon's house. He was sharing it with four other doctors and although he was expecting her and came straight to the door, the others were in the lounge and there was low laughter as they went straight upstairs to Simon's room on the first floor. Simon was his usual humorous self, though, and soon she was laughing with him as she lay down on the bed. She rolled down her jeans, but he just lay on top of her, kissing her slowly and thoroughly till her insides turned to liquid and they both forgot about the examination as they undressed and made love.

They lay a while in a sticky torpor, then Simon began to stroke her stomach softly. 'What seems to be the problem, Miss Maguire?' he joked, then he abruptly changed mode and became serious as he intently probed her stomach with his fingers. After a minute or so his expression changed again.

'Oh, dear,' said Linda, 'what is it?'

'I just wonder,' he replied tentatively, 'is there any way you could possibly be pregnant?'

'Oh no, I haven't had any signs of it. I haven't missed a period or anything like that. Anyway, the Catholic Church wouldn't allow it.'

Simon gave a brief smile at her joke. 'Okay,' he replied slowly. 'Listen carefully to me now. Before a doctor goes ahead with tests on your ovaries and womb, he would have to rule out pregnancy. Firstly, it's possible for a woman to be pregnant and still have periods. It's unusual, but it can happen. Secondly, I felt a distinct bulge above your pelvis that is probably an enlarged uterus. This happens in pregnancy at different times for different women but usually denotes a pregnancy over twelve weeks. Lastly, I felt a flutter of movement. This can happen from thirteen weeks onwards.'

He wasn't meeting her eyes now. He could possibly be the father. He waited patiently as his words sank in.

Linda was trying hard not to panic. She thought about her parents and about God. She was in a bind, and she thought she'd been so careful. She deliberated about her feelings for several minutes while Simon tactfully dressed and went downstairs to make a cup of tea for them both. On his return, he handed a cup to her and sat beside her.

His body language seemed to say, *I'm not in love, I'm not taking responsibility, but I care and I'll help you whatever you decide to do.*

She rested her head on his shoulder as if to test him and he did not turn away.

She eventually broke the silence. 'I'm a Catholic and I can't be seen to have a child out of wedlock. I can't have an abortion in this hospital, or any other hospital, for that matter. Can you imagine what that would do to me if it was on my medical record, if my family found out?'

'Let's take it a step at a time,' said Simon. 'I'll get your urine tested for pregnancy. It takes about a week, and then we can take it from there. Can you let me have a sample now, perhaps?' He grinned at the absurdity of it.

Linda was knocking on the door again at Simon's house a week later. She had had an awful time; Catherine Grayson had gone to a hospice for terminal care. She had seen Sandra briefly at work and she was evasive, sporting a black eye concealed with make-up. She had no one else to talk to about her fears, which she thought was just as well, as they might prove groundless. To confuse things,

Eddie had phoned the nurses' hostel twice and left messages and his phone number. She couldn't think about him right now.

Simon opened the door to her again with a friendly greeting, giving nothing away. They climbed the stairs again to the seclusion of his room and he got straight to the point. 'The good news is, it's unlikely you have any problems like Catherine Grayson. Unfortunately, however, you have tested positive for pregnancy.'

Linda's eyes filled with tears. 'I expected it somehow,' she replied, willing the tears to stop embarrassing her. 'I have to have a termination as soon as possible, but I don't know how to go about it. Can you help me?'

'I thought you might ask that,' replied Simon. 'It's not easy for me as I've been trained to preserve life, but at the same time I feel it's unfair that a woman should have to face this kind of situation, whereas a man can choose to walk away. I guess we both know it could be mine. It isn't something I want right now either, so yes, if you won't go to your doctor, I'll help you. But understand, I can't be seen to be having anything to do with this. It would be devastating for my career if it were found out. It's also illegal.'

He had taken a step back from her as he talked and he was staring out of the window, as if already distancing himself. 'I've been thinking over this last week. You need to be somewhere other than the hospital, the nurses' hostel or my house. You also need to take a couple of days' leave or call in sick. I've been researching the best way to go about this.'

His voice droned on as he outlined the practicalities.

A week later and Linda was alone in a cheap hotel room with a single bed. It was a tiny space, carved out of what had once been a larger room. One of the walls was painted chocolate brown; another was covered in lurid wallpaper with psychedelic orange swirls. There was no bathroom, only a cracked sink in the corner. She would have to make do with that; she couldn't afford anything else. She hadn't seen Sandra at all, not even at work, and she was feeling very much alone and very sorry for herself. She began weeping. 'Stop it, you're just full of self-pity,' she scolded herself in her mum's voice.

She had smuggled out some equipment from a ward. Simon had come and given her two injections into her stomach. One was a drug to help start labour and one she didn't like to think about, but it was to make sure it was not a live birth. He had spent some time manipulating her cervix and inserting seaweed sticks to further encourage things to progress. Neither of them knew how far pregnant she was. He stayed as long as he could, then he had to go on duty, and he had left her alone. He would be back in twelve hours. She was a nurse; in theory she could cope from now on.

The pain, when it came, was excruciating. She did not dare take the Valium that Simon had left. She couldn't make a sound. She willed herself to think outside her body and what was happening to it.

Can this really be God's will? Am I being punished for daring to think I can disobey the Pope?

The pain was grinding her down, wearing away at what she saw now were just the opinions and prejudices of one group of people that inhabited the world. The pain was bigger than them, bigger than the universe. As it tore into her, she threw away the last of her Catholic beliefs.

She promised herself a reward for this suffering; it would be Eddie. With him, she could have a secure life, with a safe home, with children that would be wanted, theirs, the two of them, not like this one. It was working; she was distancing herself from what was happening. Just when she thought she couldn't bear the pain any longer, it changed, and as she pushed uncontrollably, an object slid out and she reached for the metal dish to catch it. She was lucky – the foetus had expelled with the placenta intact; she was free of it, the thing that was not meant to be. She looked down in horror. He was perfect. Her tears fell.

Two days later Linda was recovering in bed in her room from what she told everybody was a stomach bug, when Sandra rolled in sheepishly, her face covered in bruises.

'Oh, dear,' they both exclaimed simultaneously as they took in each other's appearances. Linda was thin and pale; Sandra had bruises up her arms too as well as a black eye and a split lip. Linda's state was not newsworthy – well, at least, not the official version. Sandra sat on the bed and told her tale.

'At first it was great with Richard. We spent all our time together – shopping, eating and fucking – then he started to walk me to work and was waiting for me when I finished. I thought it was a nice touch – gentlemanly, even – until I said I wanted to have a night out with you, and he went mad. He was in an uncontrollable rage, mouthing off all sorts of stuff, how you and I were a notorious pair, how he couldn't trust me. The first time it happened I just gave up and he simmered down and apologised, but I've been brought up with a father who has a similar temperament, and the next time I said it and he started up, I just couldn't keep quiet. We'd both had a drink and bam, one black eye. Of course, then it was my fault for winding him up. I tried to come back to the nurses' home while he was working, but he came and found me. By this time, he was distraught, saying his life wasn't worth living without me, so I felt I had to go back with him and talk to him. Today I told him I was going to see you and he wasn't going to stop me. I tried fighting back, Linda, but Jesus, I'd never realised how much stronger a man is physically than a woman till now. I waited till he got called into work and as soon as he had gone, I made my escape. I'm going to alert the caretaker not to let him anywhere near this place.'

'Aren't you worried about his state of mind?'

'You must be joking. All that'll be wrong with that big baby right now is a bad dose of self-pity. He'll just tell everyone how rotten I am, and eventually he'll believe it himself. I tell you, I'm going to enrol at self-defence classes as soon as I can. Oh, Linda,' she hugged her friend, 'it's good to see you again.'

Linda and Sandra were off work for a few days and met up with Roberta and Rosie. Sandra's face was multi-coloured – purple and yellow with streaks of black and blue – while Linda was still deathly pale.

'Wow, what amazing colours, you two look like you're going to a Halloween party,' Roberta exclaimed tactlessly.

Rosie was concerned. 'What on earth has happened to you both?' she asked.

Sandra tried to make light of her injuries. She was not that close to Rosie. They were too dissimilar, and Rosie was a bit naive. As for Roberta – well, she lived on Cloud Roberta. So, she was surprised when Rosie told her that she had been researching for a project on domestic violence at university.

'Things are being done to help women right now. They've started a women's refuge in London, you know.'

'Yes, that's all very well, but this is Manchester, so I'll just have to look after myself. It's okay for you two; you've opted out of real life.'

THIRTY

2002 Linda

Linda had been working for Sipher for some years when her path crossed Simon's again. Sipher was running a new sales campaign which targeted consultants whose patients' symptoms were exacerbated by being overweight. Simon was now a successful cardiologist with a private practice in one of the new state-of-the-art private hospitals that had sprung up around Manchester and Linda had arrived to give him the Svelta pitch.

Simon looked genuinely pleased to see her. 'Long time no see, Linda. You look well. Come in and tell me what you've been up to. It must be twenty years. You had just qualified and it seems time has been very kind to you. You've come to tell me about the Svelta slimming drug. Hasn't it had a bit of bad publicity recently?'

'I do actually take Svelta myself.' This was Linda's new opening line and it always made people look directly at her.

'It looks as if it works then.' Simon smiled back at Linda in a way that she took to mean he found her attractive.

Linda looked at the man who had helped her get rid of her unwanted pregnancy. In common with all cardiologists, Simon was extremely slim and toned, and he still had his slightly wavy blond hair. She forgot all about her pitch and provided Simon with a potted version of the last twenty years, trying not to denigrate Eddie, explaining that their divorce had given her the impetus to forge her own career.

'And what about you, Simon, are you married, kids and all that?'

'Neither, sadly. The long hours in this profession and a happy marriage do not good bedfellows make. I've been through a painful divorce recently – another casualty of medicine, I'm afraid.'

Linda was amused at his turn of phrase and she felt a comforting warmth talking to a man who had played such an intimate role in her life. They chatted for a long time until his secretary popped her head round the door to let him know she was leaving for the night.

'Gosh. Look at the time.'

Linda put her Svelta brochures back in her briefcase. She was far more interested in the subject of Simon, who ticked all the boxes as a potential partner.

'I don't suppose you are free this evening, Linda? I don't like eating alone and it would be nice to continue reminiscing.'

'Actually I am.' The girls were with Eddie and Megan that evening and Linda felt the hand of fate.

'Great. What sort of food do you like?'

'Not keen on Indian or Chinese,' Linda replied, knowing that a cardiologist would avoid ghee and MSG-laden food.

'There's a new fish restaurant opened near where I live, and I've wanted to try it for a while. I don't have to operate until tomorrow afternoon, so we can have a good night.'

Linda, for her part, took that to mean that he planned to take her home afterwards.

They agreed to meet at the restaurant at eight. Linda went home and changed into a low-cut navy silk dress which showed her figure to her advantage. Stockings and black patent stilettos completed the look, which was unashamedly 'come and get me'. She packed a small overnight bag and drove over to Didsbury where Simon lived.

They both arrived at the restaurant at the same time. Simon, who was wearing jeans and a polo shirt, was visibly taken aback by the overtly sexy dress that Linda was wearing.

'I'm sorry if I've underdressed,' he said with an apologetic grin. 'I've got into the habit of taking my shirt and tie off when I get home.'

The waiter's eyes were out on stalks, however, and Linda was loving it.

They chatted easily and after the second bottle of wine, Simon, who was not a big drinker, was full of bonhomie and suggested they go back to his apartment for coffee.

The apartment was a testimony to technology, with surround sound speakers and a host of kitchen gadgets that looked untouched. Linda was captivated. This was more opulent than Rosie and David's house. She looked around and imagined herself and the girls living in this level of luxury.

'Do you remember *Grease*?' Simon asked with a cheeky smile that took years off him. 'It reminds me of our era. There's nothing wrong with nostalgia.'

He put on the video and they sat leaning against one another. When Olivia Newton John danced towards John Travolta to 'You're the One That I Want', Linda took it as a cue and started to mimic her. She knew she was a good dancer and she closed her eyes, pouted her mouth and stood up, gyrating her hips. To a man who was interested in taking her to bed, this would have been a mind-blowing turn-on, but Simon was clearly embarrassed.

When Linda opened her eyes and saw his discomfort her fantasy abruptly disappeared, and she realised how badly she had misjudged things. She felt total humiliation. Simon hadn't uttered a word; he didn't need to. Their respective perceptions of the evening were now laid bare.

'I'm sorry, Linda. It's not you. You're a very attractive woman, but I'm just not ready for a relationship,' Simon said gently, trying to rescue the situation and get things back on an even keel.

Linda was both embarrassed and hurt at the obvious rejection of her femininity, but she had had too much to drink to think reasonably.

She turned towards Simon and, with measured malice, borne solely out of rejection, fired a verbal salvo designed to hit where it hurt. 'Never forget we committed a crime together all those years ago, and that knowledge could hurt you more than it could hurt me.'

With that, she grabbed her handbag, marched to the door and wrenched it open, walking out into the night, carrying her stilettos. She flagged down a passing taxi and went back to her empty house, burning with self-righteous anger.

THIRTY-ONE

2005 Linda's Funeral

The song Linda had chosen to be played as her coffin arrived was 'If You Could Read My Mind' by Gordon Lightfoot, which now seemed to have added poignancy. Matthew started by reading a piece that Linda had written some months earlier, which was essentially an account of her life and the people in it. She mentioned nothing of her childhood, focussing on her love of nursing and the friends she had made during the 1970s, and how three of them in particular – Rosie, Roberta and Sandra – had been 'the most wonderful friends anyone could have wished for throughout the highs and lows of the intervening years'. Her description of her two daughters, 'who are the two best things in my life and who have made me so proud', caused Louisa and Lizzie to sob loudly, and Eddie, who sat between them with his arms around each one, couldn't stop tears from streaming down his cheeks too.

Overall, her words were uplifting, thanking people for their friendship and for their support and encouragement, and Louisa and Lizzie felt their mum's kindness and humanity reach out through her words. However, she had saved some words for 'those people who fail to grasp all the good things life has to offer, seeing the world from their narrow religious perspective which snuffs out any joy of living'. The Maguires knew that although they were not named specifically, they had been singled out for a mention, and Bernadette closed her eyes and crossed herself.

Matthew paused for effect and the chapel was silent. 'It is unforgivable to deprive those around you of love. It is what makes us all human. Living involves making mistakes, I know that more than anyone, but it is far better to enjoy your life as I have tried to do. You will not get another chance. This is it.'

The mourners broke out into spontaneous applause brought on by Linda's call to action to 'live for the moment', which suited some of them down to the ground.

The curtains closed around the coffins and the mourners made their way out, many clearly lost in their own thoughts. Rosie had arranged a 'celebration of Linda's life' at the wine bar she had frequented in Didsbury village and nearly all those at the service went along, many in the hope of questioning Lizzie and Louisa further about what they had seen and heard.

After the service, Simon explained to Louisa and Lizzie that he was in theatre that afternoon so he could not come along, and he dashed off.

*

Proceedings started off quietly, but after a few drinks conversation began to flow, and old friends and acquaintances exchanged stories and reminiscences.

David took Eddie to one side.

'Did she tell you about this baby?'

'I had no idea, Dave. I think it must have been before I met her. I had a DNA test to check and it's not mine.'

David looked uneasy momentarily, but his mood changed when he turned around to see the Maguires sitting in sanctimonious misery, grasping their orange juices in silence.

What a miserable existence. Sad bastards.

'Linda was right about one thing: life is too short, and you only get one shot at it,' David said in a manner that Eddie thought somewhat profound for Dave the player.

David made a mental note to get his own DNA tested at some point.

He had always felt that his friend had made a serious mistake in leaving Linda for Megan. He watched as Eddie turned to look at his daughters. The mood was broken by the arrival of Megan, who was obviously feeling left out of things and who placed herself between Eddie and his view of them. *Linda would never have behaved like that*, David thought to himself. But Eddie had made his choice all those years ago and now he had to live with it.

Poor sod.

Rosie had taken charge of the catering and was kept busy topping up the plates of food as the alcohol spiked everyone's hunger. David watched his wife and asset do what she did so well: well-presented, well-spoken and adept at keeping up appearances.

His mobile rang and he went outside where there was a better signal and where he could take the call in private. He was beginning to seriously worry about the level of scrutiny that the Svelta trials were receiving after all the adverse reporting in the media. The call did nothing to put his mind at rest. As he walked back into the room, he met Rosie coming towards him.

'I have to go to head office – there's a problem that needs my attention. I'll phone you when I get a moment.'

He turned on his heel, mobile phone to his ear, and left without kissing Rosie goodbye. He drove off, the wheels of his Range Rover squealing on the tarmac, talking intensely on the phone.

*

Eddie retreated to a corner of the bar on his own. He seemed to be determinedly drinking now. Fending off Megan's attempts to intrude, he clearly wanted to be left alone. He was experiencing the guilt and regret of those left behind, combined with conflicting memories of his time with Linda. True, she had striven selflessly to give them all a perfect family experience, but it had been all from her perspective. He had found it obsessive; he had found her overwhelmingly needy at times, and eventually, he had to escape.

'Was her death my fault?' he murmured to himself.

THIRTY-TWO

2005 Amelia

The afternoon light was waning fast, as if in sympathy with the mood of the day. A morning funeral, too much drinking and eating at lunchtime, and most people were gratefully heading for home. Megan, her mouth set in a grim line, had called a taxi for herself and Eddie. Rosie was supervising arrangements to the last. There was an air of unfinished business, though.

'Let's get a pot of tea and talk some more about Mum,' suggested Lizzie. 'I find it difficult to leave things just yet.'

They were joined by Rosie and Roberta. Sandra had taken a phone call and abruptly announced that she had to go. They were into the preliminaries of ordering the tea when a red-haired woman approached their little group.

It was uncanny. Apart from her brown eyes, she bore a striking resemblance to Sandra. Everybody stared at her in fascination. They unconsciously leant towards each other, as if closing ranks for protection.

'I'm looking for Lizzie Hammond?'

'You must be Amelia,' said Lizzie. 'Please, join us. Let me introduce everybody.'

'I'm sorry for your loss,' Amelia said to Lizzie and Louisa when the formalities had been concluded and she had found a seat. 'I came in at the end of Linda's funeral. I didn't want to intrude.' She turned to address the wider group. 'I personally didn't know Linda, but two weeks ago, Lizzie found me through the Channel 4 researchers. I worked with David years ago, and it was me who instigated the recent investigation into Svelta that led to the documentary. I was motivated by rumours about safety, but mainly I'll admit I wanted revenge.' She paused. 'You see, he stole my idea.'

There was a collective gasp.

'I didn't want to intrude into your grief on a day like this, but since the programme, someone, who wants to remain anonymous, has come forward to expose a loophole that David exploited. The police have now become involved, and you will find out sooner rather than later. I'd rather you heard it from me.'

Everyone turned to Rosie.

'Yes, I want to hear about it,' she said. 'I need to know the truth.'

She looked composed, but her face was deathly pale.

THIRTY-THREE

1976–94 David

David had started on the graduate induction programme at Sipher, straight after leaving university. This involved working a month at a time in different areas of the business. In the animal laboratories he took and analysed samples, in the marketing department he wrote packaging instructions for taking tablets, and in the commercial department he learnt how GPs would be targeted to give Sipher drugs preference. He found this all a bit beneath him but knew he had to look eager and interested. He met several women, including an attractive redhead called Amelia, but played a straight role of new husband and dedicated scientist, even taking to wearing horn-rimmed glasses.

He quickly focussed on the area where new drugs were discovered, developed and tested, the lifeblood of any pharmaceutical company.

This is more like it.

From then on, David's ambition was to work there. He made sure that his manager could not fail to notice him and his dedication. Soon he was asked to join the team.

David was surprised at exactly how long it took a pharmaceutical company like Sipher to get from a concept to getting the drug prescribed and making profits. Some drugs took twenty years to develop. Then there was the cost; it took billions of dollars to get a drug to market, but successful drugs would return that investment many times over.

He next learnt that a lot of work was put in at the beginning of the process to make sure the idea was viable, and that the most profitable drugs were those that had the greatest number of potential users: drugs that would keep symptoms at bay but not provide a total cure, which would mean the end of that stream of revenue. The words of his boss stayed with him: 'We don't want to cure people. We want them to feel better when they take our drugs and so keep taking them.'

Profit before people.

In common with other pharmaceutical companies, Sipher kept track of population changes that could indicate new opportunities. Antibiotics had contributed to a significant increase in life expectancy in the Western world and that had driven the requirement for drugs to manage the diseases of old age such as arthritis, high blood pressure and kidney disease.

Twice every year, Sipher held a company conference in a prestigious hotel, during which each area of the company gave a presentation. These events could, on occasion, be interesting but were often an excuse for a company-sponsored booze-up where, after a few drinks, inhibitions were cast aside and room numbers swapped. David was present when his attention was caught by a research department presentation on what they described as an impending obesity epidemic. He made a note to attend.

The evidence from US researchers showed that there was a significant increase in the number of people who were obese. They had linked this trend to a change in eating habits to high-calorie fast food, combined with an increase in car use. The waddling couple in the LA park came into his mind, together with the huge plates of food he remembered. The final slide in the presentation demonstrated that the trend was beginning to be observed in the UK and parts of Western Europe.

After the Q&A session that followed the presentation, David sought out Amelia, who gave the presentation, and asked her for a copy of the slides. They exchanged business cards and a handshake that he made sure lasted a little longer than what would be usual. He knew women found him attractive and he had no qualms about using this if it furthered his career.

Business and pleasure.

The following day he engineered sitting next to her at lunch and, having been through her slides thoroughly, questioned her in more detail. His memory was exceptional, and he found it easy to retain facts and figures for future recall without being seen to make notes.

David knew that obesity as a major cause of ill health fitted the profile perfectly for a blockbuster drug to cure or contain symptoms. Potentially millions of people would need to be medicated to keep feeling well. He spent hours in his home office reading up on it. There wasn't a lot to learn. In the first half of the twentieth century, which had seen two world wars, people were slimmer because they ate less, and travel by car was restricted to the well-to-do. He also found out that for certain careers you had to be slim; he discovered that fashion models and jockeys took amphetamines to control any weight gain, drugs which were highly addictive and had dangerous side effects.

He spent the next year or so working long hours and making sure he was seen to be doing so. On the nights he left before seven, he always left a spare jacket over the back of his chair so anyone walking past would think he was just away from his desk. He kept up to date with population statistics and increasing evidence of obesity. He had frequent evening meetings with Amelia.

He chose his moment to approach his boss, Roger Littlewood, who headed up drug discovery and development. Sipher had just received FDA approval for a blood pressure drug that David knew would be a big money spinner for the next ten years while it was protected by patent, but Sipher needed drugs in the pipeline to take over when the patent expired. A number of new drugs needed to be in development at any one time, as not all of them would make it to market. Currently there were not enough.

David explained his ideas and left Roger with a paper he had prepared that backed them up with detailed data and outlined the market opportunity for an anti-obesity drug. The following week, Roger told David that he had copied the paper to other Sipher managers, and the feedback was that they would like David to make a formal presentation.

David's timing appeared to have been impeccable in another way. Sipher had just acquired Silica, a small drug development company that had been working on fat binders as a treatment for cholesterol but had run out of money. This was the first presentation David had ever given and he felt the nervous twitch above his right eye that always appeared when he was anxious. He had prepared well and knew his subject inside out, but when he plugged in his computer to the audio-visual equipment and waited for the large screen to display his first slide, nothing happened. He felt a light sweat creep down his back and he tried fiddling with the power lead. Still nothing happened.

He looked up at the managers. 'Could you bear with me a minute, please?'

He said it with a confidence that belied how he felt, then – bingo! The combination of keys he needed to transfer the display came to him and the screen flickered into life. He felt a rush of adrenaline and launched into his slides, delivering the facts with confidence.

It went well. Sipher's scientists could see that obesity was indeed going to become a problem that needed a pharmaceutical solution. He was followed by a boffin from Silica, who gave a technical presentation on their work to date and what he believed to be the next phase of development, and helpfully added in passing its relevance for obesity control. David wanted to punch the air but contented himself with a broad grin. He had raised his profile within Sipher and his rise within the company was underway.

Nothing happened for a couple of months and David felt frustrated enough to begin looking at the job pages. He was about to fire off his CV when Roger called him in to his office. 'Sorry things have seemed quiet for a while, David. After your presentation the management were so convinced of the opportunity they wanted to consult various other areas of Sipher worldwide about an anti-obesity drug and, to cut a long story short, everyone is on board. We have the go-ahead to start the feasibility phase.'

David's jaw dropped before he regained his composure. 'That's brilliant, Roger, brilliant.'

Roger explained that although he would have overall responsibility, he was freeing David up from other work and wanted him to work full time on the project. David listened with satisfaction as Roger outlined the project and his role in it.

'The pre-clinical phase is going to be somewhat different to other projects we have undertaken. Obesity itself is not a disease in the clinical sense, more a result of lifestyle and diet. There's no molecular mechanism for the disease for us to model. We'll need to look at and assess the biochemical effects of diet on the body and see what compounds we can discover that can significantly mitigate weight gain.'

David went back to his office and phoned Rosie to tell her the good news, and she sounded genuinely pleased for him.

'Sort a sitter out, darling, and we'll celebrate how clever your husband is,' he said, just as he caught Amelia walking away. She had heard the whole conversation.

I suppose it was too good to last, he thought.

Onward and upward.

It had been a long time since he found himself looking forward to going out to dinner with his wife.

Besides acquiring the fat-binding compound from Silica, other compounds which increased metabolism and suppressed appetite had been developed by the company, and their use meant the pre-clinical phase advanced quickly. David loved using his knowledge and lived and breathed the project.

After approval to move to the development phase, David, alone in his home office with a glass of Burgundy in his hand, stared at his reflection in the mirror and toasted his success. 'I own this. My idea. A game changer. Recognition.' He drained the glass and savoured the taste of impending success.

By the mid-1980s, Sipher had started the clinical trials that would take around four years and had successfully applied for a patent for the drug, now known as Svelta. Phase one trials were carried out on healthy subjects. They went well and the process then moved on to the two phases which used subjects who were obese and were key to proving the drug worked.

All this was outsourced to a company, Clinmedica. Their project director, Peter Bolton, and David got on particularly well. They were of a similar age with young families and both were determined to make it to the top of their companies. For this phase the results for each patient were recorded on report forms, with details of weight loss and any side effects. Clinmedica would collate and analyse the findings before sending them to Sipher.

After one of their regular dinners, washed down by a couple of bottles of good wine, Peter confided in David. 'We're running trials for several pharmaceutical companies and I'm afraid my team are somewhat stretched. This might add some months to the timeline.'

Silence followed, and David seemed to be mulling something over.

I spy an opportunity, but is it ethical?

'I could arrange for Sipher resources to help analyse and collate the results,' he offered.

There was more silence. Both men knew this was highly irregular, as the analysis needed to be independent of the drug developer.

Peter looked directly at David. 'I will accept your offer, David,' he replied. 'It's irregular… but I trust you, and it means we can be confident about meeting our timescales. If I do meet them, I'll get a bonus, which will help with my youngest boy's medical fees.'

The men shook hands on their arrangement. Peter felt a weight lift from his shoulders and David felt he had wrested control of the outcome of the trials.

Power.

The phase two trials took place using several hundred patients. The Svelta group lost significant amounts of weight, but in ten per cent, there were side effects of heart palpitations. This was sufficiently high enough to raise questions of safety and to potentially delay progress. David had no intention of letting such minor side effects scupper his plans. He established a process within Sipher where all the report forms were taken directly from the fax machine to his desk. By the time phase two had been completed, the reported percentage of patients experiencing heart palpitations was under four per cent and an acceptable level. Svelta had demonstrated effective weight loss with minor side effects, which could be managed by modifying the dose. He had not forgotten his manager's words when he was a trainee: *We don't want to cure people. We want them to feel better when they take our drugs and so keep taking them.*

Phase three trials followed, involving over a thousand patients, and David was only too aware that controlling the outcome of such a large-scale trial would be far more of a challenge. By this stage the potential offered by Svelta was causing great excitement at Sipher and David's star was rising. Sipher's accountants were modelling the future potential revenues from Svelta and the figures dwarfed all previous drug revenues. The demographic data supported the idea that the population was getting fatter and there was a significant increase in the number of people who were clinically obese. A large framed version of the picture of the two fat Californians now hung on the wall of David's office. It was a constant reminder of his opportunity.

David agreed with Peter Bolton of Clinmedica to continue their method of working for the phase three trials. The arrangement suited them both, but for different reasons. However, there was a major problem David needed to address. The scale of the study and the fact it was being run across different continents and time zones meant that, for David, keeping charge over all the results would be impossible. It was a chance call from a small software company that provided David with a solution. Technology had moved on apace and report forms could now be sent electronically into Sipher's IT network and routed according to content to specific users for data entry. Working closely with the company, David explained that he needed a solution which had different user types and different routes for forms within the system. Those forms reporting adverse reactions or deaths would be routed to a designated 'Super User' with the highest level of access. The system was delivered, tested and ready for use some weeks before phase three began.

Super User. Superman.

David congratulated himself on his brilliance as the final user tests were completed satisfactorily.

Over the period of the phase three trials, significant numbers of patients were experiencing heart palpitations and in a number of cases patients had experienced heart attacks, some of which were fatal.

Obese people are more likely to have heart attacks.

David had come this far and had become the face of Svelta within Sipher. He was not going to allow anything to get in the way of a successful outcome for Svelta or for his career. The idea of failure was unthinkable.

Fabricating data or replacing the records for these patients with bogus ones became his routine. Within ten years of the original concept, Svelta was given approval by the FDA and European regulators to be prescribed with few restrictions. By this time the problem of obesity was starting to become a serious concern. Women in particular wanted to be slimmer and doctors were aware that without weight loss their obese patients would suffer a number of illnesses for which they would require medication for life. Svelta was widely prescribed and David was rewarded by a promotion to the role of vice president.

By now Rosie was heavily involved in a women's refuge and their marriage, although neither admitted it, was a polite sham. Intimacy between them was a thing of the past, but for David, opportunities for sex were abundant.

'It's true what they say about a man in his forties,' he said to Eddie on one of their rare nights out together. 'You have to fight them off with a shitty stick.'

Eddie seemed to listen with a mixture of amusement and nostalgia as David gave him a rundown of his sexual conquests. David had a suspicion that all in Eddie's life was not well. He could see that Eddie had stupidly exchanged one suffocating relationship with Linda for another with Megan who had, over the last decade, transformed from siren to harridan.

David was at the peak of his career. From time to time there were grumblings in the press about the possibility of Svelta-related deaths, but Sipher always solidly backed their money spinner and David looked forward to his next challenge with a trouble-free conscience.

THIRTY-FOUR

2005

'Are you all okay? I knew nothing of this at the time, obviously. I would have done something sooner.'

Amelia broke the silence that had descended after her stark revelations of David's behaviour.

Rosie spoke first. 'I'm numb, shocked. I feel now that I didn't know David at all, that my whole marriage has been a lie.' She put her head in her hands.

'Hmmm. A miner's son. How did he learn the arrogance to play God?' cried Roberta.

'From his mum, I'm afraid,' said Rosie. 'I see it now. Amelia, I'm glad you were motivated to question Svelta. Whether it was from anger or from conscience. Tell me, which was it?'

'Well, neither, unfortunately. It took the death of my aunt to make me act.'

Roberta was looking around the room. 'Where has Sandra gone? She should be listening to this.'

THIRTY-FIVE

2005 Amelia and Melanie

Melanie, junior reporter at the *Manchester Evening News*, had woken with a start.

The phone had rung shortly after she drifted into sleep and she recognised the voice immediately.

'Amelia, what's wrong?'

'I have some dreadful news. My Aunt Antonia, she's dead.' Her voice broke.

'Whatever happened?' Melanie was struggling to wake up.

'We don't know. There is nothing obvious but there will have to be a…' Her voice cracked again. 'A post-mortem,' she said through tears.

'Darling, keep me posted.'

Melanie sat in bed, her knees pulled up under her chin after she had replaced the receiver, tears running down her face. She had been a student with Amelia, and Aunt Antonia had been a fun experience in their lives. She had taken them under her wing, showing them the best nightspots in London.

It was a couple of weeks before Amelia's parents were able to make the funeral arrangements. The post-mortem concluded that Antonia had died of a heart attack, which was a surprise to everyone who knew her because she was so slim, obsessive about eating organic food and being fit. The coroner's report also noted that she took the slimming drug Svelta but did not link that specifically to her death.

Antonia had worked as a fashion buyer for Harrods and was always surrounded by beautiful clothes and super slim models. It was a glamorous world where appearances were everything. Melanie knew all this but was still shocked that Antonia had been taking slimming pills. She had never heard of Svelta and wanted to find out more.

The newspaper's offices were open twenty-four hours and had an enviable library in their basement with desks for study and a drinks machine. Melanie loved her job and spent a lot of her spare time there. Once she had submitted her copy for the day, she signed the register at reception to indicate where she would be and made her way down the stairs.

She collected a coffee from the machine, sat at a desk with a monitor, and got out her new iPod and earphones. She had no idea how far back she needed to research, and she was expecting to be in for a long evening.

Recent items were held digitally on the company's IT system, older information was held on microfilm and there was always Google, which allowed her to look through the millions of items that were not recorded within the newspaper's systems. She was soon absorbed in her task whilst listening to The Beautiful South.

The first item she tracked down was the FDA approval of Svelta in 1994, which licensed it with only a minimum of restrictions as the clinical trials had shown so few side effects. Over the following years all the coverage she could find described it as a wonder drug that had made a huge difference to those people who had been unable to reduce their weight through diet or exercise. There were other articles, predominantly in women's magazines, reviewing its use by middle-aged women whose shape was starting to change and for whom Svelta had halted their middle-age spread.

The realisation that Antonia had taken slimming pills to keep her model-slim figure shocked her.

Why did she need them?

She continued her trawl, alone in the library. She took a break to get some food as the cathedral clock chimed twelve midnight.

Jed, the security lad, was at reception. 'Hi, Melanie, you're here late tonight.' He quite fancied Melanie. She was attractive and had an energy about her that was appealing.

'Hi, Jed, just going out for a pizza, can't stop, I'm really into something at the moment.' She disappeared out of the front door and down the street.

She's always too busy for a chat. Too busy and bright for the likes of me, anyway.

She rushed back to her desk and ate her pizza, careful not to get any of it on the IT equipment. She collected another coffee from the machine – black this time.

One article in the *British Medical Journal* from late 1998 caught her eye. It was a review of a number of unexplained deaths in middle-aged women, all of whom had been users of Svelta and who had no pre-existing history of heart conditions. The article suggested further investigation might be advisable, particularly in the light of its widespread use.

Christ. That's over five years ago.

Melanie continued working into the early hours, drinking black coffee to keep her awake.

The next article of interest, published in 1999, was from Sipher, the manufacturer of Svelta. It went to great lengths to reinforce the drug's safety record. Central to their case was its approval for use by the FDA in the US and the EMEA in Europe. Impressive case studies were included of patients whose lives had been transformed by their weight loss. Their blood pressure had returned to normal, they were no longer diabetic and they could enjoy exercise again without getting tired.

But no mention of even the slightest side effect; even aspirin has side effects.

Melanie's journalistic intuition felt there was more to this than met the eye, but before she could take the idea to her editor, she needed more information. She was on a roll, hunched over the computer screen, burning the midnight oil. She looked through coroners' reports to find cases where the deceased had been using Svelta, as well as combing through back issues of the *British Medical Journal* for more articles about the drug. What she found was alarming. In the UK alone there had been over five hundred unexpected deaths of middle-aged women who had taken the drug for several years. Articles in the medical press had been calling for the clinical trial data to be made available in order to find out what adverse reactions had been reported during the trials and if there should be any specific contra-indications.

This information was enough of a smoking gun for Melanie to pluck up her courage and request an interview with Ed Russell, the next day. 'Ed the editor' – everyone laughed about his name in the office, but she had never spoken to him personally. He was always super busy. Would he take the time to see her?

*

Melanie underestimated herself. Ed had already noticed her and her enthusiasm for her job, which was refreshing in a profession where people could soon get jaded. He was looking forward to hearing what she had to say.

*

Melanie was nervous and bursting with information, but she had prepared well. She decided to present the facts in a series of headlines.

Ed's a busy man and he'll appreciate that.

'I became involved in researching the history of the slimming drug Svelta because my friend's aunt was taking it when she died.' Her voice wobbled a bit, but she carried on. 'Here's what I found out, and it's alarming.' She held up a presentation sheet that she had prepared on her computer.

- *1994 – Svelta is launched as the new wonder slimming drug when diet and exercise fail.*
- *1994–98 – Svelta claims to halt middle-age spread in women.*
- *1998 – BMJ cites increase in deaths of middle-aged women taking Svelta.*
- *1999 – Sipher re-enforces drugs safety record with case studies.*
- *Records show over five hundred unexpected deaths amongst Svelta users in the UK.*
- *Records show ten cases in the Manchester Evening News's circulation area this year alone.*

'Now I'm alarmed too,' said Ed, who was clearly impressed. 'Are you sure of your facts? This has huge public-interest potential.' He paused and looked at her. 'Think you can handle investigating this further?'

*

Melanie realised the next stage was going to be harrowing, as the bereaved she would need to interview would still be grieving and many were left to cope with young children. So many of the phone calls she made were heart-breaking. She had to steel herself before each call.

'She started smoking again a year after giving up.'
'I loved her just as she was.'
'I told her that with a bit more weight, there was more of her to love.'
'She wanted to be a size ten again.'

'She was the best wife and mother anyone could have.'

The men left behind all said the same things, and when it came to the mention of their motherless children, that was when they always broke down. Melanie listened to them with tears in her eyes too. After a week of emotionally draining calls she had set up interviews with two men who were willing to get involved, as both suspected that Svelta was a contributory factor in the death of their loved ones. One man had lost his wife, leaving him to bring up three young children, and in the other case a young man in his third year of studying medicine had lost the mother who had brought him up as a single mum.

*

Paul Myers answered the door. He looked exhausted, his hair and complexion both grey. He wore tracksuit bottoms and a crumpled T-shirt with what looked like tomato ketchup down the front.

'Come in, Miss Scott. Excuse the mess; I'm not very good with housework.'

Melanie's heart went out to this man whose whole world had been upended.

'I never realised how hard it must have been for Jan, looking after the house, washing and cleaning and taking care of the kids. Would you like a cup of tea?'

'That would be great. The traffic was dreadful round here. Is it always that bad?' Melanie tried to make normal conversation to put him more at ease. The state of the kitchen, with piles of unwashed dishes and discarded biscuit wrappers, which Melanie hoped were not evidence of the children's breakfast, was testimony to the fact there was no longer anything normal in Paul's life.

The interview was far harder than anything she had done before. Paul explained that he and Jan had married in their late thirties within a few months of meeting.

'It was love at first sight. You probably think that's a myth, but we both knew we had found our soulmate.' Paul wiped his eyes with a dirty-looking handkerchief and Melanie bit her lip hard. He took a deep breath and continued. 'We tried for children straight away and after the birth of Charlie, Jan had got straight back into her old clothes. She took great pride in her appearance. But after the twins were born eighteen months later, she struggled to lose the weight she had put on. I kept telling her I loved her just as she was, but she was used to being slim. None of her clothes fitted. Diet and exercise didn't make much difference. That's when she got Svelta from our doctor. It worked, and Jan was happy and back to her old self. I assumed she would stop taking it, but she kept putting in a request for a repeat prescription and the doctors kept prescribing it. In the last year before she died she was getting palpitations, which worried me, but she put it down to the kids running her ragged. Do you think Svelta might have been the reason she died?'

Melanie didn't know what to say. She didn't want to compound his guilt by implying that he could have intervened more forcibly in Jan's use of the drug, but equally he knew that the reason for her visit was to investigate Svelta. She said nothing.

'Are there other people you are talking to?' Paul asked.

'Yes, there is another lady who also died last year, and I am going to meet her son tomorrow.'

'Does he have children, Melanie?'

'No, he's still at university, but his mother brought him up on her own, so they were very close.'

Paul seemed to take some kind of solace from knowing he was not alone, so she opened up to him.

'My friend's aunt died a few months ago and she took Svelta.'

*

Matthew Riley was tall, good-looking and extremely angry. His anger had been evident when Melanie spoke to him on the phone, but in the flesh he was quite intimidating. If the circumstances had been different, she would have found him extremely attractive. They had arranged to meet at a coffee shop in the city centre. Both had described themselves to the other in order to identify one another among the crowd of caffeine addicts who met in the warm, steamy shop to escape the Manchester drizzle.

'Thanks for meeting me. I understand that this is difficult for you and I really appreciate you giving me this interview, Mr Riley.'

Matthew Riley stared at her for a short period before launching into a tirade about his mother's death. 'It was corporate manslaughter, and she was one of many. There's a pattern emerging, of deaths in middle-aged women who have taken Svelta. Sipher needs to be exposed for what it has done. My dad left my mum when I was two – I suppose that's why we were so close. I had a wonderful childhood. She worked full time once I was at school to make sure I had every opportunity she could afford. She never remarried. She said she had seen her friends marry for a second time and witnessed how "blended families" don't work. She believed that it's the children who suffer to keep the adults' relationship on track and she had no intention of taking that risk. She was the best mum anyone could wish for.' Matthew's voice cracked and he looked down at his coffee.

Melanie looked at this man on his way to becoming a doctor and she saw a little boy lost, not the cocksure man she had initially shaken hands with, and she wanted to give him a hug.

Re-establishing her professional self, she asked him to explain the circumstances of his mother's death.

'Mum was always slim, but as she approached her mid-forties, she used to complain about her "muffin top" and her waist disappearing. As a medic – well, I'm not qualified yet – I understand the effects of hormones on fat deposits and the changes that occur in metabolism as people age. Her GP prescribed a course of Svelta, which clearly worked as Mum lost her excess weight. But she was experiencing palpitations, which she never had before, and I knew that wasn't right. I told her I was worried, and I thought she'd stopped taking Svelta. Then one day eight months ago I received a call from her best friend to say she'd been rushed to hospital with a suspected heart attack. She died before I could get across town to be with her. She had no history of heart disease or high blood pressure, so I believe Svelta is a contributing factor, if not the cause of her death.'

They finished their coffees and went their separate ways, Matthew with a renewed drive to try to find out more about the clinical trial data and Melanie to the office to write up what she had uncovered.

*

The published article covered a full page and carried the title 'Dying to Be Slim?' The newspaper's lawyers had reviewed the copy to ensure that there was nothing that could result in them being sued by Sipher, and Melanie included only factual evidence she had uncovered through her research, focussing instead on the impact on the lives of Paul and Matthew. The article also highlighted the use of unrealistic images of flawless young models to promote fashion and beauty. It posed the question that such images created pressure on older women to hold back the years, which, from everything she'd learnt, was why these women were using Svelta.

The article was in Monday night's paper with a précis available in the online edition and by the end of the week the *Evening News* had received hundreds of calls, letters and emails from the bereaved and from Svelta users who had recovered from heart attacks. Melanie also received an interesting email from a London-based television journalist, Teresa O'Donnell. Teresa had also been looking into Svelta-related deaths, having received an anonymous tip-off about the validity of the clinical trials. The women agreed to meet midway in Birmingham at New Street Station.

Melanie was expecting to meet a ballsy, chain-smoking, power-dressed woman and was surprised to find a tiny woman, with wire-framed glasses, dressed in jeans and a T-shirt, and who rolled her own. Teresa – or 'T', as she preferred to be called – was quietly spoken and Melanie had to strain against the background chatter of the clientele of McDonald's to hear what she was saying. They told each other what they knew, and it appeared that when the information was looked at in the round, it presented a very disturbing picture. They agreed that their next course of action should be to ask Sipher for a statement to clarify the safety of Svelta. The tip-off regarding the trials was to be kept a secret for the moment and Sipher were provided with a copy of Melanie's article and asked for a comment.

The response they received was, in T's words, 'total corporate psychobabble'.

> *Sipher HQ – for immediate release.*
> *Sipher puts patient safety at the heart of its business.*
> *Our products and processes consistently meet the highest industry standards for quality.*

This statement provided no reassurance regarding the safety of Svelta and T now believed she had enough evidence with which to go to her producer and propose an exposé that had the potential to rock the pharmaceutical and medical professions. She promised to keep Melanie informed of her progress if Melanie agreed not to publish any of T's new findings before the show went live. Melanie, for her part, had plenty of sources of new material from the people who had contacted her after 'Dying to Be Slim?', so she kept up the pressure by writing further articles about people whose lives had been shattered by the death of a Svelta user. After losing her good friend Antonia, she was writing from the heart.

*

In the summer of 2005, Channel 4 broadcast *What Price Svelta?* during prime-time viewing, having advertised it nightly for the previous week and paid for a large number of ads in the printed press. The programme featured three case studies of women who had died unexpectedly after taking Svelta. The cases T had chosen were particularly heartrending, as they involved women who still had young families and whose bereaved husbands and children were totally devastated.

The focus of the programme then moved on to the drug itself and whoever had given the initial tip-off had now provided further insight into exactly how the clinical trial process for Svelta could have been manipulated to optimise the results. The programme was careful to suggest only 'the possibility' that this could be done, thus minimising the 'possibility' of legal action. Sipher had been asked to appear on the programme to answer the questions raised but declined and issued the same meaningless statement as before. At the end of the programme a telephone number was provided for 'those affected by the issues raised in the programme'. It was inundated with calls.

Two days after the programme was aired, T's producer received a call from a police inspector from the Serious Crime Unit, who requested sight of the information that they had used for the programme. Inspector Jack Holly explained that for some months they had been investigating a number of unexpected deaths from Svelta and they believed the information used by the programme would be of considerable use to them.

Melanie and T met up again in Birmingham, not in McDonald's this time but at a trendy Italian restaurant not far from New Street. The rest of the media were now getting in on the act. The internet was awash with stories – some accurate, some not – and while they felt pleased that they were the first to break the story, neither felt inclined to celebrate when they considered the consequences of what they had uncovered.

THIRTY-SIX

2005

'How come we haven't been aware of all this?' said Roberta angrily.

'Please don't start beating yourself up on our mum's behalf,' came the reasonable voice of Lizzie. 'Of course, our immediate reaction is if we'd acted sooner, Mum might still be alive, but we didn't know, did we, and would we have noticed?'

'The reports are actually all fairly new,' said Amelia.

'And then we only latch on to things that concern us, don't we? We could equally ask Linda why she wasn't following the news. After all, she was selling the product,' said Rosie. 'We can't blame anybody.'

'What can we do now?' said Roberta.

'It would seem that there is now a police investigation, following on from the Channel 4 documentary,' said Amelia. 'I don't know who instigated it, but it involves your husband, Rosie. I'm sorry.'

Rosie became aware that she hadn't seen David for hours. She then remembered he had said he was urgently needed.

THIRTY-SEVEN

2005 David

David had left Didsbury and headed towards the M6 to drive south to Sipher's UK head office in Reading. The call was from Jacintha Wood, Vice President of Human Resources, asking him to attend a meeting at four that afternoon with Eugene Kennedy, Sipher's CEO. Her manner had been formal and when David asked her about the nature of the meeting, she explained that it was a matter best discussed face to face.

Once on the motorway, he set the Range Rover to cruise and mulled over what might be on the agenda. Jacintha's tone worried him. In the past she had always been up for a laugh, but on this occasion his charm had made no impact whatsoever. He began to feel uncomfortable at not being in full control and he didn't like the way it felt.

He had a clear drive down. It was motorway most of the way and the traffic was light. He swung into his parking space in front of the glass-fronted edifice of head office that had been funded in no small part by sales of Svelta. In fact, a new extension which had doubled the size of the building was known internally as 'the Svelta Wing'. David's rise in the company on the back of Svelta had been meteoric and his reputation had been legendary in more ways than one.

When he walked into the boardroom, he was met by three people seated at the far end of the board table. Eugene N Kennedy was a humourless American with severe halitosis. He sat at the head, flanked on one side by Jacintha Woods and on his other side by a man David had not seen before.

Eugene asked David to take a seat and then started the meeting. 'David, you know Jacintha Woods from HR already. This is Ian de Voet, who is head of legal services and who I don't believe you have met before.'

David sensed that things were about to get difficult and he would need his wits about him.

'You will be aware that there has been media coverage regarding Svelta and attempts to link it to a number of deaths. Over the years we have defended the product and its efficacy, citing the data coming out of our clinical trials. However, as a consequence of information provided to the police, which they have let us have sight of, we can no longer maintain this stance. There is a strong possibility that the data collected by the trials had been deliberately tampered with. Can you shed any light on this, David?'

'Clinmedica ran the trials,' David responded with confidence. 'You need to speak to Peter Bolton, who was their project director.'

'Unfortunately, Mr Bolton had a nervous breakdown in 1993, just after Svelta received FDA approval, and he left the employment of Clinmedica. He has been in and out of psychiatric hospitals ever since.'

David felt a sense of relief that Peter Bolton was out of the picture.

'Can I ask you about the computer system used to collate the trial data? I understand you specified how it worked.'

'That's right. I could see that we could speed up the whole data capture in a way that would allow us to get to approval far more quickly. I presented the proposed system to the UK board and they signed off on it.'

Ian de Voet was writing notes throughout the meeting, occasionally peering over his half-rim glasses. David thought he looked like a small rodent.

Eugene continued. 'The police asked for a copy of the software and the databases used for the trials, for analysis by their specialists. We have provided them with both. Should we be worried about what they might find?'

David couldn't lay this one at Peter Bolton's door and he tried humour. 'I hope they have signed a confidentiality agreement.'

His quip was met with silence.

'Should we be worried?' Eugene repeated, fixing him with a stare.

'Not for any reason I am aware of.'

'Can you please leave the room while I take advice from Ian?'

David pushed his chair back, leaving them to it, and went outside to get a coffee from the vending machine.

Ten minutes later, David was asked to return to the boardroom. He faced three stony faces. Jacintha took charge.

'Sipher is suspending you on full pay while this matter is fully investigated. You may wish to consult a lawyer, as it is highly likely that you will be interviewed as part of the police investigation.'

David left the room with a sense that the net was closing in. As he pushed the Range Rover hard, driving north again, he felt a sense of injustice.

Hasn't Sipher made billions out of my ideas? Hasn't their share price gone stratospheric on the back of Svelta? What hypocrites they are!

THIRTY-EIGHT

2005 Sandra

It was late afternoon and the rain was bucketing down as Sandra finished packing her suitcase. She had checked the dogs and was satisfied that all was in order with the kennels. Her staff of two school leavers and her manager Dawn would see to them while she was away. Star, Skye's puppy, was stretched out asleep on the rug.

She was, therefore, surprised by the knock at the door.

A man stood in the porch sheltering from the rain. He took an ID card out of his inside pocket. 'Miss Marsden, I'm DS Steven Mallory,' he began.

'For heaven's sake, come in before my carpet gets soaked with the rain,' Sandra snapped. She wasn't too pleased at this interruption to her plans. 'Put your wet coat on the end of the stairs and follow me.'

DS Mallory did just that and accepted her offer of a cup of tea. He was in his early forties and not bad-looking, with a full head of thick hair, and so far he was winning the battle against middle-age and lifestyle spread.

Regular sessions at the gym?

He was looking uneasy at her blatant once-over. 'Miss

Marsden,' he began, and then his throat went dry. He coughed and took a sip of tea while Sandra cocked her head on one side and smiled.

I'm wrong-footing him. I think I'll play with him for a bit.

He began again. 'I've come for an informal interview with you concerning the death of your friend Linda Hammond.'

The smile was wiped off Sandra's face and replaced with a slightly hostile expression. 'Heaven's sake, man, I've just come from the funeral.'

'I'm sorry for your loss,' Mallory replied mechanically. 'Can I see your passport?'

Sandra produced it from her bag and held it out.

'Do you always keep your passport with you?' Mallory asked, curiosity in his voice.

'That's my choice,' snapped Sandra.

'You should be careful, carrying it around with you,' was all Mallory said. 'Identity theft is on the increase.'

He took some time checking through it. Finally, he looked up, composed now, and started his questions. 'I understand that you and Mrs Hammond had been friends since you were trainee nurses together?'

'Yes,' replied Sandra.

'A number of drugs were found in her system when she died.'

'So, what's that got to do with me?'

'We want to establish whether she had a drug habit. At least three of the drugs were class A and B. I understand that in 1984 you were convicted of stealing class A drugs from the workplace?'

Mallory paused, but Sandra didn't oblige him by filling the space with an answer. He waited.

Standard interrogation tactics, eh? I'll wait too.

When she finally replied, he looked shocked. It clearly wasn't what he expected.

'Go on,' said Sandra. 'Spit it out. I can tell you've got more up your sleeve.'

Mallory coughed again. 'In 1982 you were in a traffic accident. At the time, no drug tests were possible, but police observations at the scene report that your responses were sluggish and suggested possible drug intoxication.'

'Oh, yeah, and how would you react if you were hanging upside down in your seatbelt with a ruptured spleen and fractured pelvis, all to avoid a stupid dog on the road? The answer is emphatically no. I don't take any drugs, and if Linda did, I don't know anything about it.'

Mallory seemed the one with no answers now. As if on cue, the dogs started barking in the kennels as they were fed, and Star woofed in response from the fireside. Sandra was a convincing dog lover.

'I notice from your passport that you have been to Morocco recently. Could you tell me the purpose of these visits?'

'No, I couldn't. It's personal, but I can tell you I wasn't coming back to England with a suitcase full of kif to kill my best friend off. Come on, Mallory, you've done your bit now. What's this all about?'

Mallory was fast losing his professional manner. 'Mrs Hammond's post-mortem tests revealed traces of fat binders, but also amphetamines, anti-depressants and cannabis. The quantities are sufficient to be alarming and your criminal record raised questions that need discounting. It is part of a wider investigation which I can't divulge to you right now. Suffice to say, the police have had a tip-off and we are conducting our own investigation. That's all I can tell you right now.'

'And are you satisfied with me yet, DS Mallory?' said Sandra. 'Or do you need anything else? You see, I am going out shortly.'

He is rather gorgeous-looking.

THIRTY-NINE

2005 Roberta

Roberta's car came slowly to a halt. Damn, she was nearly home after the funeral and everything that had followed, and now she'd run out of petrol. How could she have been so stupid? She looked at the instrument panel before she turned the ignition off, and the tank still showed half full. That was the problem with an old car; there was always something going wrong. She wished she could afford a better one; everyone else seemed to have a newer car than her.

Even worse was the fact that the nearest building was Will's farm. Roberta didn't like going there if she could help it. It wasn't because of the divorce; that was long ago. She just hated to see the farmhouse and imagine what she would have done with it if she'd had the chance to renovate it. She could walk home, but then what? There was no spare petrol there. Will would have some; it would be silly to struggle. Just then it started to rain and that made the decision for her. It was dark and she wanted to get back home.

She reached for her waterproof from the back seat and opened the cubbyhole to retrieve her torch. Fortunately, she had already changed into flat shoes for driving. She then started walking up the narrow lane. It had been raining a lot recently and there were plenty of potholes that had filled with water. She had to be careful not to stumble and get wet. As the farmhouse came into view she saw that Will's van was there; not that it mattered if he wasn't in, as she knew where he kept petrol in cans. There was another car there too. The boot lid was up and Will was standing at the back, talking to a man and woman whose faces were momentarily obscured from Roberta's view by the lid. Will must have bought the car from Tom at the pub and was selling it on. He'd bought cars from Tom, fixed them up and sold them on for years; it was another of his money spinners. He was good at mechanics, he had his Land Rovers and he had a rather messy barn full of car spares.

Roberta hated to interrupt Will, but it was starting to rain in earnest. At that moment Will pulled the boot lid down, spotted Roberta, and his jaw dropped as his mouth formed a big 'O'. A split second later, Roberta had recognised the other two people. Suddenly the sense she had of the relationships and the people in her life made no sense at all, like a jigsaw that had fallen apart and now none of the pieces fitted in the right place.

There was Will.

And David?

Roberta didn't think she'd ever seen them in the same room together.

And then there was Sandra.

What is she doing there?

At that moment the heavens opened.

'For heaven's sake, stop gawping, Will, and invite us into the farmhouse,' said Sandra in her usual no-nonsense manner.

The farmhouse was dark, chilly and untidy. Frances and the children were out, and Roberta thought the untidiness was definitely not just from the day, more like the product of messy living. They all stood uncomfortably in the kitchen for a moment. David looked through Roberta and started to talk to Will in a low voice. Roberta looked at the two of them again in disbelief. She was too naive to make any assumptions at this point, but something was very wrong.

Sandra took her arm. 'You might as well know,' she said simply.

Sandra led Roberta into the living room, which was equally cold and inhospitable, with a dead fire in the hearth that had also been used as an ashtray. Everything felt unreal to Roberta, and she sat down on the settee and waited with a sense of doom to hear what Sandra had to say.

'David and I have been seeing each other for years,' Sandra began, and Roberta gave a gasp. 'Think about it, Roberta. He's had numerous affairs and so have I. David and I are very alike in that way; an affair was inevitable between us. Can you see that?'

'Yes,' said Roberta reluctantly, 'I suppose I can, now you point it out.'

'What is unusual for both of us is that the attraction has never waned. To put it bluntly, we are both equally focussed on getting what we want, and it makes for an interesting combination. We have been planning this for a while and now we are going away together.'

'Oh, God, Sandra. What about Rosie?'

'Rosie has known that David has had someone else for a long time. She and David married because they each thought the other would provide the life they aspired to, not because they were well-suited or because they loved each other. They both got what they wanted and now that part of their life is over, hollow, a sham. They both need to move on.'

Roberta looked agitated. She stood up from the settee, took a few paces away and then turned to face Sandra. She felt her anger growing. How could Sandra be talking in such a matter-of-fact way?

'Don't you feel any guilt?' she almost shrieked at her friend. 'How could you still be a friend of Rosie's all these years?'

Sandra looked hard at her. 'Come on, Roberta. David's had just about every woman that Rosie knows,' she paused, 'including you.'

Roberta flinched and stepped back. 'How do you know about that?' she stammered, and then sat back down on the settee, her arms folded defensively.

'David told me,' said Sandra.

There was silence. Roberta could hear the rise and fall of David's voice in the next room. She hoped Will hadn't heard.

'It was totally unfair,' she muttered eventually. 'I was at a freshers' party just after I started at art college. He and Eddie got me and another student horribly drunk and I don't really remember much else. I've erased the memory from my mind.'

She glared at Sandra. 'These days it would be classed as date-rape. How can you be going away with such a man? It was bad enough when Rosie announced she was marrying him. I've avoided speaking to him if I can help it, all these years. It wasn't difficult. I can tell I'm of no further interest to him.'

'I've already told you. David and I are very alike. I'm the last one to judge him.'

'You don't know what else he's done, Sandra. You left the funeral before Amelia came. I need to tell you what she said, he's responsible for—'

Just then, David came into the room. 'We have to go now, Sandra,' he said.

And that was it. David and Sandra went out of the front door, and Roberta was left sitting on the sofa looking at Will.

She sat in shocked silence again for a while, assimilating what was happening, and Will retreated to the dining area and started looking through some papers. After a while, she realised that he wasn't actually doing anything; he seemed to be waiting for her.

She pulled herself together and stood up. 'Sorry, it's all been a bit of a shock. I came to borrow some petrol,' she said. 'My car's run out and it's just down the road. Can you give me a can and I'll be on my way?'

Will looked at her. 'On your way where?' he asked. 'You see, nobody knows about this.'

Roberta was poised to run, but Will didn't move. Oh no, was he going to play one of his games where because he knew she wanted something, he would deliberately withhold it? She'd forgotten how he could be.

'Please, Will.' She couldn't believe she was pleading, regressing to how she used to be when she was married to him. 'I'm not planning to go and see anyone; I want to get home.'

'That won't stop you phoning people, though, will it? You see, David has paid me well to keep all this quiet. And it would have been, if you hadn't come barging in.'

He walked towards the doorway and stood in it with his arms folded, as if barring her escape, then he dropped his arms and turned his hands outwards as if in surrender. 'There's some in back of van,' he said at last. 'Come wi' me.'

He went out of the front door and walked towards the van. Something in his manner told her she should make a run for it, but she dismissed it as absurd. She was forty-eight now and when had she last run? She followed him and he opened one van door.

'Other van door's stuck,' he said. 'Reach round and grab the can... no? Get a bit further in, then, just climb on the step.'

Before she knew it he had pushed her in the van, shut the door and locked it.

Roberta shouted and banged on the door, then realised she was wasting her efforts. Why had she resisted buying a mobile phone? She thought that computers, the internet and mobile phones were the 'spawn of the devil' and didn't like the way they distracted people into a virtual world, away from the true world around them. She knew they would change society irrevocably. Now for the first time she saw the value of the mobile phone in an emergency. Maybe half an hour went by, she didn't know, and then Will climbed into the cab of the van and started the engine. Where was he taking her?

She lost sense of time. She was sure she'd read about things like this in books where a prisoner in a car had a built-in radar and knew where they were being taken. She didn't have a clue. It seemed to be a similar time to being kept in the farmyard when Will stopped the van. It must be local. Will got out of the van and another similar interval of time went by. Roberta was now beginning to worry that Will planned to leave her in the van for however long it took David and Sandra to get away.

Eventually, Will came back to the van and opened the door. It was getting dark now, but she could just see that the van was parked at the far end of a car park, alongside a river.

'This way,' he said, holding on to both her arms. She tried to bite him and kick him, but she couldn't reach, and he just laughed.

She had no choice. She'd wrestled with Will long ago and knew he was much stronger than her. He frogmarched her in front of him along a well-worn path until they reached a narrowboat.

So, we must be by a canal?

The doors were already open, and he pushed her inside. It was rather nice, everything in miniature, but before she could look any further he wrapped a chain round each of her ankles and padlocked them. They were attached to two longer metal chains that Will had fixed to a metal post that formed part of the dividing wall between the kitchen and the bathroom. She looked down and recognised the chains as belonging to the yard dogs at the farm. She was a prisoner.

Roberta shouted and screamed, but Will was focussed on starting up the engine and just ignored her. Eventually he went to the back of the boat where she lost sight of him. The boat rocked, she heard his footsteps on the bank and then back on the boat. They motored for at least an hour in the gathering darkness. How Will knew where he was going, Roberta didn't know. Eventually she felt the boat bump against something, and the engine stopped. She couldn't see anything outside now. Will came back to the cabin and looked at her.

'What on earth do you think you're doing?' she screamed at him.

'Bought this boat fifteen years ago when we were divorced. Didn't want you getting yer hands on all my money, eh? Ha.'

'I've just been to Linda's funeral,' she shouted. 'I've learnt that David's behaviour at work has been criminal to say the least. You don't know the half of what he's been up to. Now I find that Sandra is running away with him. Does she know about him?' Roberta got up, suddenly agitated. 'I don't believe she would go away with him if she knew. I have to find her; I have to tell somebody.' She took a few steps till the chain tightened and then yanked at them, making her feet bleed.

'Stop that,' he growled, catching her by the waist, throwing her to the floor and pinning her with his foot.

Roberta howled in frustration, then burst into noisy sobs. The emotions of the day engulfed her, and she cried for Linda, Rosie and herself.

'Like a drink?' he asked eventually, with a grin, knowing there was nothing she could do.

Roberta felt that the whole day had taken on a bizarre quality. She calmed down and decided she would go with the flow.

They sat together sharing a bottle of wine. The hour of motoring had nicely chilled it in the fridge.

They talked about Hannah and James, then she began to feel hungry. Will got some biscuits out and cracked open another bottle of wine.

'What about Frances?' she asked. 'Won't she be wondering where you are?'

'You know me,' he replied enigmatically.

Roberta tried again. 'So, what's the plan, Will? Why am I here like this?'

'Thing is, I've gone to trouble getting a car for David that can't be traced. That's what he asked me for, an' that's what he's paid me for. I don't know where they're goin' and I'll make sure no one else will. I know you, though. Yer a fuckin' blabbermouth, an' you'll think yer honour-bound to do or say summat. No, I promised 'em two days clear, an' that's what they'll have.'

'So, you're keeping me chained here for two days?' she said

incredulously. She stood up and tried to yank the chains. On the one side, she could get to the bathroom; on the other side, she could go into the saloon and lie down; and in the middle, she could access the galley. Will had thought it out well.

'Yer in the middle of nowhere now,' said Will, catching her thoughts, 'so don't waste yer breath shoutin' an' all that, 'ave a rest.'

Roberta's head was beginning to spin with too much wine and too little to eat.

Will put his arm around her and lowered her onto the settee. 'This is for old time's sake?' He laughed.

Another piece of Roberta's jigsaw that no longer fitted.

*

Will left Roberta asleep in the narrowboat. He locked the door, stepped onto the bank, and then he wove his way unsteadily along the towpath and back to his car. He was fit, but he'd also drunk a lot of white wine. He reasoned that he would work off the alcohol during the walk. He remembered the days when you could drink and drive with no restrictions. He was in a country area and no one would catch him here.

When he got back to the van he had several attempts to find the lock with his key, a bad sign. He got in eventually and started the engine. No problem, he would be fine. He drove fast, with main beam headlights on until he'd nearly reached the farm. Then a vehicle came the other way. He focussed on it, dipped his headlights – and ploughed straight into Roberta's car that she'd left on the side of the road with no lights on.

FORTY

2005 Rosie

Rosie was preparing to leave the house for a day at the Refuge when the house phone rang, and she was surprised to hear a breathless voice on the other end.

'It's Frances, Will's wife. Do you know where Roberta is?' she asked. 'I've called at her house on the way home from the hospital, but she's not there. I don't know why her car was on the road in the first place. If it hadn't been, maybe Will would have made it home safely.'

She sounded stressed and nothing she said made sense. Rosie was used to dealing with conversations like this at the Refuge.

'Take your time, Frances, and start from the beginning,' she replied gently.

'Will drove into the back of Roberta's car last night.'

'Where was this?' asked Rosie, puzzled.

'It was parked just down the road from the lane leading to the farm. Apparently he hit it at speed in the dark. He was over the limit, of course, and hadn't fastened his seatbelt. He's in hospital with head injuries.' Frances sighed, and then sniffed. She had obviously been crying.

'Oh, dear, I'm sorry,' Rosie said automatically. 'Can Will talk about it yet?'

'No, he's been unconscious since it happened. I've been trying to track Roberta down. She wasn't in the car; she isn't at home. I've phoned the college, but she's not there either. I'd like to go back to the hospital now and I was hoping you could take over the search. I can't think about it anymore.'

'Don't worry. Of course, I will,' said Rosie.

Rosie decided to go to the Refuge as planned; she might as well be there and make phone calls. There was the usual debriefing from the other staff, a communal catch-up with the residents and then she escaped to her office with a cup of coffee.

She tried Roberta's home phone first and there was no reply. She then phoned the college and the secretary hadn't seen Roberta all day. No change there then.

Her next call was to Sandra. One of the kennel workers answered the phone. It was difficult to hear her; she had obviously left the back door open and the dogs were barking.

'Sandra's away at the moment and she didn't say when she'd be back.'

'When did she go?'

'I'm not quite sure. I wasn't here yesterday, but I do know that she left with her boyfriend, so maybe they've gone away for a few days.'

'Okay, thanks.'

Rosie felt a momentary chill. Where was everybody? Then she told herself not to be silly. She emailed Roberta's children, first Hannah and then James, telling them what she knew, being careful not to be alarmist. She had no idea where they might be in the world, only that they both worked abroad. By the afternoon they had both emailed back. James was in Berlin. He thanked Rosie for letting him know and asked if she would please keep in touch. Hannah was in New York and five hours behind, so she didn't get back to her till early afternoon, but she asked Rosie if she had Skype on her computer plus a microphone so that they could talk for nothing. Rosie emailed back saying no, but she would look into it, and they had to make do with communicating with a series of emails. Hannah would come home as soon as she could.

Back home later that day, Rosie sat at the table in her kitchen with a coffee in her favourite mug and looked around. Years ago, the place would have been littered with lunchboxes and dirty rugby kits, and finger marks would have adorned the now perfectly polished glass table. David would invariably have been away on business, but despite his regular absences and the boys' independence once they were teenagers, she had always tried so very hard to make their home a welcoming place for them. How different things were now. Would they have been any different if she had stood up for herself when David denigrated her views or ignored her completely? Should she have been more forceful when challenging him over the affairs she suspected? Probably not, she concluded. The main difference would be that she would not feel such a doormat as she did at that moment. The boys had their own lives and so, she suspected, had David.

The conversation with the girl at Sandra's kennels kept coming back to her and she couldn't shake off her unease at Sandra's sudden disappearance. She picked up the phone and redialled the kennels.

'Hello, Rosie Jennings here, I'm a friend of Sandra's. Are you the person I spoke to earlier?'

'Oh, hello, it's Dawn here. No, it wasn't me you spoke to, it was my colleague. She said you'd phoned trying to contact Sandra. I was here when she left, but I'm afraid I don't know where she's gone, and I don't know her friend either.'

Rosie's heart was pounding. 'She might be with a mutual friend of ours, but I just wanted to check the description of the car again before I bother him. Do you remember what colour it was or anything?'

'It was a black four-by-four with those tinted windows at the back and... yes, I remember, it had one of those personalised number plates. He's been here a number of times, so I recognised him and the car.'

'Thank you,' Rosie managed to whisper, before sinking to the floor as the realisation of what she had been told hit her hard.

David and Sandra?

She remained on the floor, phone in hand, for nearly an hour trying to process what she had heard, and as she did so she began to see events in the past in a totally different light. The phone rang again, shocking her back to the present. It was Marjorie wanting to discuss arrangements for Christmas. She lived on her own now since Marcus's death and Rosie usually drove to Amersham to pick her up. She couldn't think about anything more right now, so she feigned flu and promised to phone back when she was better.

Rosie realised there and then that the familiar and the banal in her world would never be the same again.

Has he told Sandra? Has she known all along about what he did all those years ago?

If Sandra knows that deadly side effects have been hidden, why hasn't she ever spoken to Linda about them?

Rosie felt a chill down her spine at the thought that Linda's death could have been prevented if Sandra had warned her. She remained on the floor until the room was in total darkness, then she finally hauled herself up. She remembered Roberta and tried her number again, but the phone just rang out.

She was just about to run herself a bath when the buzzer on the gate rang. She pressed the intercom on the entry system and was surprised when a man identified himself as a police officer.

'Good evening, madam. We'd like to speak to Mr David Jennings, please.'

'He's not here and I'm afraid I don't know where he is.'

'Is that Mrs Jennings? May we speak with you, please, madam?'

Rosie operated the gate remote, then went downstairs to open the front door. It began to dawn on her quite how serious David's situation might be.

At the door were two police officers, one in uniform and the other in plain clothes. 'May we come in, please?'

Just like a TV drama.

'Yes, of course, please follow me. What's this all about?'

They sat down in the family room. There were polite questions, most of which she was unable to answer. Yes, she had just heard about the Svelta scandal, but otherwise, she didn't know much about his work. No, she didn't know where he had gone. Eventually they nodded to each other and rose to their feet.

'I'm sorry I can't help you. I feel foolish for not knowing the man I've been married to for thirty years.'

'We'll be in touch, Mrs Jennings.'

David, Sandra and Roberta are all missing.

She slept fitfully and got up before dawn. She thought again about Roberta and the conversation with Frances and began to worry seriously about her safety. Sweet, honest Roberta was a breath of fresh air amid all the deceit. Unsure of what to do, she decided she would contact Inspector Graham Porter who had been so considerate in his handling of the situation over Linda's death at the Refuge. She waited until after nine o'clock and then phoned him on the direct line number he had given her. He remembered Roberta and took the details Rosie provided which, even to her, sounded rather vague. But he told her that he would take her concern seriously and promised to make enquiries and get back to her.

Her next call was to Simon. She wanted to ask if he had heard anything about the safety of Svelta. She phoned his rooms and his secretary, a very plummy-voiced girl called Lucy, answered. It appeared to Rosie that Lucy's job was to screen all calls to her boss, so despite explaining that she was a long-standing friend of Simon's, she was not put through. Lucy took her number and said she would let Simon know she had rung, but he had an extremely busy surgery that day. Rosie was, therefore, very surprised when Simon phoned back five minutes later.

'Hi, Rosie, how are you? Sorry I couldn't stay after the funeral, but I was operating.'

'I quite understand, Simon. It was something else I wanted to talk to you about. Do you have a minute?'

'Erm, yes, of course.' Simon's hesitation was palpable.

Rosie felt that all the conversations she'd had in the last two days had been weird and that they were getting increasingly bizarre.

I'm getting paranoid.

'Are you aware of any adverse reactions or concerns about Svelta, Simon?'

'Uh huh, yes, I am.' Simon sounded relieved and spoke confidently. 'There have been articles in the medical press for years about the high number of heart-related deaths among users. There have been a number of calls for the clinical trial data to be made available for review, but Sipher's always stood behind it. I suppose because it's such a money spinner for them, and for some patients it really had great results. Why don't you ask David, though? It was his baby.'

'David isn't here, and I don't know where he is.'

'Oh, gosh, I'm sorry. Are you okay?'

'At least I'm alive. Thanks for phoning back.'

Rosie put down the phone and tried David's mobile. It went straight to an 'out of service' message.

She was about to leave the house to go to the Refuge when her phone rang again. It was Simon. 'Hi, Rosie, I've just received an email from Sipher. It appears that Svelta has been withdrawn from the market with immediate effect. I thought you'd want to know.'

Rosie put down the phone as the enormity of David's problems became increasingly apparent to her.

FORTY-ONE

2005 Roberta

Roberta opened her eyes and for a moment wondered at her new surroundings. Then she slowly remembered the events of the previous night. She was lying on a cushioned bench that served as a sofa in the main cabin of the narrowboat. Will had thoughtfully covered her with a thick duvet that must have come from another cabin. She sat up, her head groggy. Her mouth felt parched. There was a stickiness between her legs.

All that wine last night and the barriers dividing time and people have blurred and disappeared. A social norm has been breached; the rules that govern civilised behaviour broken. I can't feel it's wrong; I know it's not right either.

Half an hour later she had thoroughly explored the extent of her confines. She had used the bathroom, which smelt damp, and a towel that smelt mouldy. She had explored the galley and found coffee, teabags, long-life milk, breakfast cereal and a stack of tins; if she could find a tin opener she wouldn't starve. There was a sizeable stash of bottles of wine and some beer; she would be able to drown her sorrows. She had to move around carefully or the dog chains around her ankles chafed. It wasn't cold, and Roberta could hear some kind of heater kicking in every now and then.

Her immediate needs seen to, she sat back on the sofa and wrapped the duvet around her. Helpless, she felt a mounting frustration and anger.

Damn Will.

She could just imagine him congratulating himself on leaving her thoughtfully provided for. He'd always managed to make her feel helpless and stupid. No doubt he would be laughing to himself, but how long did he intend to keep her here? He wasn't wired with a normal conscience like other people and anything could happen. She wondered if she could saw through the chains somehow and felt an irrational urge to smash a hole in the boat, but there were no tools within reach that would perform either of these actions. She wrapped the duvet around herself and slept.

By late afternoon, Roberta was wide awake again and realised she was probably in for another night on the boat. She had been avoiding thinking, seeking oblivion in sleep, but now, with nothing else she could possibly do, the thoughts came crowding in. She felt her life had been shattered yet again. It felt worse than the divorce, because now two people that she loved, Sandra and Linda, had disappeared out of her life without warning.

Has Sandra been seeing David all these years and not said anything?

Sandra could talk her way out of anything, and Roberta had always felt that deep down she was morally flawed. There were so many unanswered questions and Roberta had no words to confront someone like Sandra, who gave brutally honest and devastating answers.

Linda, her sudden death, the unborn baby.

Roberta was now convinced that Svelta had played a part in her death.

But Linda had been out with Simon once again, a bit of a disaster that Linda had spelt out for them all, blow by blow in a drunken monologue on one of their evenings out together.

Will Simon have known if Linda had heart problems?

Is he the baby's father?

Haven't I seen him dropping Linda off at the Refuge just before she died?

What Sandra had said about David came into her mind: 'He's had most of Rosie's friends.'

Is David the baby's father?

Linda must have had the abortion soon after Rosie's wedding.

Is the father Eddie?

It wouldn't be Will, surely. Linda was always looking for a 'good' husband. Roberta laughed out loud and then she wept, for Linda, Sandra and herself.

Will anybody miss me?

Will would almost certainly have hot-wired her car and moved it. She hadn't made any social plans. There was only Rosie left now to make them with, she realised, and tears pricked her eyes again. When she didn't turn up for work, her colleagues would be puzzled, maybe phone her home, but it would take a few days before they became suspicious and hopefully by then she would be home.

Her thoughts were driving her mad. She was feeling incredibly angry and frustrated again. She shuffled carefully to the kitchen and opened a bottle of wine, seeking another route to oblivion and sleep.

*

Roberta had been on the narrowboat for a week and was looking and feeling decidedly wretched. Her anger was all but spent, and she was becoming increasingly scared as each day went by and Will didn't come for her. He had said a couple of days, so something must have happened to delay him; instinctively she felt it was something bad. Will was thoughtless, but he wouldn't leave her alone here for this long.

Roberta was facing some unpleasant problems too. Her period had started, and she only had wads of toilet paper. She didn't know how much water was left and she had been frugal with it when washing herself, mainly using wet wipes that someone had conveniently left. Her underarms and private parts were smelly. Her clothes and her hair were becoming grubby and greasy. The toilet wasn't flushing very well and the bathroom smelt. Her ankles were developing sores from the chains. She had found a first aid box and had done her best to protect them with bandages and plasters.

Then the supply of food had dwindled alarmingly. She checked the cupboards and worked out that if she imposed some sort of rationing she could eat for maybe another week; she wasn't very hungry anyway. She had discovered some bottled water – a real find as the tank water tasted faintly of diesel. It had obviously been used as a party boat and there were several boxes of wine and beer. She drank most nights out of sheer boredom, waking each morning with a hangover.

There was nothing within reach to write with or draw on, a great frustration for her, and the only books she could find were manuals about boat maintenance and inland waterways. Roberta was never very good at reading non-fiction, but she decided to read about the marine toilet and found out that there was a tank that held all the waste to stop it polluting the canal. It would normally be emptied at a 'pump-out station'. She found out that in an emergency it could be pumped into the canal by the turning of a lever and she hastened to do that, feeling surprised and gratified when it worked.

Roberta was used to living on her own and used to her own company, but she wasn't used to being imprisoned. Or was she? She had started to draw parallels with her situation now and the life she had led.

Haven't I always been a prisoner?

When have I known freedom?

She was surviving, as she always had, but she could do better. She had actually worked out how to deal with that toilet, hadn't she? There were pink jobs and blue jobs, and that had definitely been a blue job. The whole thing was absurd, but it gave her hope and confidence. She made herself a promise that when she got out of here, she would get away from everything she had known and make a fresh start somewhere new. Freedom was a double-edged sword and with it she would also have to take responsibility for her life, possibly for the first time ever. It gave her something to look forward to.

*

Arnold was the bailiff of his local fishing club. It was his duty to patrol the waters belonging to it at least once a day, a duty he enjoyed rain or shine as it gave him an excuse to get out of the house and away from under his wife's feet, an essential thing to do since he'd retired.

Every week or so he made it a long day, walking a good five miles beyond the club waters to check the next stretch of the canal, which belonged to a landowner, for which he was paid in beer at the local pub that night. He was looking for illegal fishermen, illegally parked boats, foreign objects in the water and pollution.

He heard the sound of the diesel generator from a distance, long before he saw the narrowboat. Arnold's hearing was very good, a fact that he carefully hid from his wife. He slowed down, looking for signs of anyone on board. He didn't want to end up in a nasty brawl.

He stood for a while just watching, while he pondered his next move. The narrowboat seemed deserted, but life had taught him to expect the unexpected. He decided to go to the main house and fetch Percy, the landowner. There would be safety in numbers.

*

An hour later, Percy and Arnold were climbing into Percy's old Land Rover. They had gathered an assortment of tools, including the rope and bolt croppers that Percy insisted on taking. He had been in the navy and said he knew they were useful in emergencies.

Percy killed the engine as they neared the narrowboat and it allowed them to coast quietly down the grassy slope towards it.

'Best stop now, it slopes too much from here.'

They climbed out and looked at the boat again. There was still no movement.

'I'll get my gun,' said Percy, 'and, Arnold, you get something like a hammer.'

'Percy, I'm a peaceful man, can't we just negotiate?' Arnold had raised his voice louder than he intended.

They both saw the boat rock and a pale face appeared at one of the windows.

'It's a woman,' gasped Arnold.

Roberta began waving both hands frantically.

FORTY-TWO

2005

Hannah had come back from New York and was staying at Rosie's house. At first she said she wanted to stay at the family home in case Roberta came back, but as the days went by with no news, she found it too upsetting and eventually accepted Rosie's offer to stay with her. She was visiting Will in hospital every day and he was still in a coma. Hannah spent hours talking to him, hoping he might respond to a familiar voice. He should surely know where Roberta was.

Hannah and Rosie had a lot in common at the moment. Hannah had lost both her parents at once, and Rosie had lost her husband and two of her friends.

One of the friends is no loss, Rosie thought.

The two women found comfort in each other's company. They were both feeling angry with certain people too. David and Will came in for a lot of stick, as did Sandra.

'I don't know, you guys,' exclaimed Hannah more than once. 'I was working away in the US, secure in the knowledge that my elders are comfortably settling into middle age, and suddenly all hell breaks loose.'

'Yes, the trigger seems to have been Linda's untimely death,' said Rosie.

'It seems obvious to me that the disappearance of Uncle David, Aunt Sandra and Mum on the same day must be related, but why do I get the feeling that it's all related? Like why did Dad crash into Mum's car? Oh, yeah, I know. Apart from the fact that he'd been drinking, I mean.' Hannah rolled her eyes.

Rosie was uncomfortably aware that David seemed pivotal to everything that had happened. 'I've suspected that David has been seeing someone for years. I've also known what Sandra can be capable of, but how could they both be so two-faced, be my friends, be lovers together, and worse still, fail to warn Linda about Svelta – what sort of people do that?'

'In the US, they would be described as sociopaths,' said Hannah, blithely unaware that she might possibly be offending Rosie. She reached for her laptop which seemed to go everywhere with her.

'I'm sure having portable computers and internet everywhere you go is not good for people,' said Rosie a little crossly. 'It will become obsessive. David had this new Wi-Fi installed, but I'm sticking with a PC that I can shut away in a room and leave.'

'It's only replaced going to the library. Oh, here we are: "Sociopath: lack of remorse, shame or guilt, pathological liar"… oops.' She glanced at Rosie's face and put her hand over her mouth apologetically. 'I think I'll read this another time, eh?'

Rosie had to laugh despite herself. 'You're so like your mother, Hannah.'

It was mid-afternoon. She was just saying, 'I'm counting the hours till wine o'clock,' when the phone suddenly rang.

'Rosie,' a voice croaked.

'Roberta, is that you?' she asked incredulously.

It was, unbelievably, Roberta. Rosie gave thanks to whichever god was watching over them right now and listened intently to her halting speech.

227

'Hannah's here with me. We'll come straight over and get you,' she said.

Roberta was at Stepping Hill Hospital's A&E department. Hannah parked the car blatantly at the front entrance. 'Pushy American visitor doesn't know the rules,' she mouthed over her shoulder to Rosie, who was left with no choice but to follow in her wake to the reception.

'Mrs Kenyon was brought in this morning,' said a nurse. 'We've told her she can go home as long as there is someone to look after her.'

They were taken to a cubicle where Roberta was waiting. She was lying asleep on a trolley. She had an IV line attached to her arm and her ankles were bandaged above dirty feet. Her face looked haggard, and the state of her – her clothes, her skin, her smell – reminded Hannah of her own trips to music festivals years ago. Tears rolled down Hannah's face and Rosie struggled to keep a stiff upper lip.

'Mrs Kenyon hasn't had a drink of water for three days, so we took the precaution of treating her for dehydration,' said the nurse. She raised an eyebrow. 'She had also drunk a lot of alcohol. I'll let her tell you that story.'

She went on. 'Her ankles will take a while to heal, as large areas of the skin have been abraded, similar to burns. These will need dressing every day and you will need to take her to her local GP. She may be distressed. I would suggest you let her tell you what has happened when she is ready, rather than bombard her with questions. The police have already been here to interview her, so what she needs now is rest and reassurance. Can you cope with all that?'

Roberta was taken to the car in a wheelchair. Hannah sat with her in the back, holding her in her arms, and they made their way back to Rosie's house, where they helped her up to the first-floor living room and settled her on a sofa with a blanket. They drank tea with cake, then moved on to wine with snacks, and they talked and talked.

Roberta relaxed in this atmosphere of safety and friendship and was able to describe her period of captivity on the canal boat and the events that led up to it. Rosie then explained what had happened to Will to prevent him from coming back for her.

'It was lucky, then, that Arnold, the bailiff of the fishing club, was doing his rounds when he was,' said Roberta. 'I could have been there a lot longer. Bless him, he and the landowner were real gentlemen.'

'I knew that Dad had bought a narrowboat, but I never said anything to you at the time because I didn't want to upset you,' said Hannah. 'The police have searched everywhere for you and I never thought of looking there.'

'Well, don't beat yourself up about it,' said Roberta. 'Erm, I guess David and Sandra haven't been seen since then?'

'Nobody knows where David has gone. Or if indeed, Sandra, the bitch, has gone with him,' said Rosie.

Roberta winced. It wasn't like Rosie to use such language.

'Thanks to Will, they will have managed to get away,' Rosie went on. 'The Eurotunnel terminal and the airports have been checked, but there's no sign of them having left the country.'

'Well, it's obvious now why they went to Will to get a car that wouldn't be recognised, but I don't know about anything else. I was trying to think things through when I was on the boat, but I just got very confused,' said Roberta. 'I can't help but feel that Svelta is the link in all these events.'

FORTY-THREE

2005 David and Sandra

David swore as he tried for a third time to find fifth gear in the 5 Series BMW that Will had acquired for them. It struck Sandra that David must be unaccustomed to driving a car that was not top of the range and the latest model. It wasn't helping his mood.

With a final crash of the gearbox, the car finally shifted into gear. David moved out into the third lane of the M6 and set the cruise control to eighty. Sandra gazed out of the passenger window as they passed the steady stream of cars and lorries heading south. They planned to travel through the night, getting to the Eurotunnel terminal at Ashford by dawn to catch an early shuttle to France. From there they would head to south-west France, intending to stop there for the night to enjoy the local food and wine before crossing into northern Spain. Then it would take two days to drive to Tarifa, where they could catch a ferry to North Africa. The surveillance and internet coverage there were patchy, and they hoped to cover their tracks.

Over the many years of their affair they had joked about running away together, but neither thought it would ever really happen. It had only become a reality over the last month, as David became increasingly nervous about the questions being asked about the safety of Svelta. At the beginning of November, he had told Sandra there was likely to be an 'in-depth re-evaluation of Svelta', adding that as he was the 'face of Svelta' within the company, his work would be put under close scrutiny. If any problems were uncovered he was worried he would be well and truly hung out to dry.

At the time, Sandra had tried to ask him quite how serious any problem was likely to be, and he had been evasive. Then there was the phone call at the funeral. David wanted to get out of the country, quickly, like now. So here they were, running away together, but not quite in the way that she had imagined.

Her thoughts came back to the safety concerns over Svelta that had recently been ever-present in the media.

Linda used it for years, but she worked for Sipher, so she'd know if it was safe to take, surely?

'David, what does a re-evaluation of Svelta mean?'

He gave a long sigh, which Sandra found unusual. His demeanour was normally one of either arrogance or anger, and she sensed that now would be a good time to try and find out more.

He ran his hand through his hair. She noticed the slight tic in his right eyelid that always signalled tension. His lips were pressed firmly together, and it was some time before he spoke. When he did, she could tell he was trying to sound matter of fact, but he wasn't fooling her; she knew him too well.

'Sipher has been asked to go back through the clinical trial phases and look in detail at exactly how the process was worked, how the data was recorded and how it had been analysed.'

She watched a line of perspiration run down the side of his face as he spoke and began to wonder exactly what David's role had been in all this, so she pressed on. 'The regulators must have been satisfied. It's widely prescribed, and millions of people use it, don't they?'

'Exactly, yet they've suspended me.' David spat with barely concealed venom.

Sandra watched as his face contorted with anger, and she decided to push a little further. 'But I don't understand. Why suspend just you, David?' Sandra realised she had hit a nerve as his anger spilt over.

'Sipher is run by pen-pushers, administrators and accountants. They are devoid of vision. And they are jealous of my reputation. It's not them; it's me who's invited to speak at conferences, to be interviewed by the media. As the person most closely associated with Svelta, I am an obvious target for any Svelta-related crap that they might uncover.'

Linda took it and she died. Is that because of your Svelta-related crap?

Sandra could see David was getting really angry now. But she'd had a lifetime of experience with angry men; this was just more of the same.

'What's with the interrogation, Sandra? Why are you interested in what I may or may not have done twenty years ago? You've never been interested in my work before, so why now?'

Sandra listened to David's words and knew there was more to it, but now was not the time to pursue the subject further. She wiped the perspiration from his cheek and then, moving her hand slowly down his body to stroke his thigh, she suggested they pull over at the next services so she could 'do something to help take his mind off things'.

The thought lifted David's spirits, and as the BMW swung into Toddington services, he was already unzipping his jeans.

*

Two hours later, they were on a shuttle in the Eurotunnel heading towards France. After the meeting in Reading, David had known that time was not on his side and had spent the journey home putting his ideas into action. He and Sandra already had forged passports in different names, but he needed a car that was not registered to him. Who had the contacts for such things? Will,

Roberta's ex. The guy was not someone he would normally have any time for – a total tosser, in fact – but suitably dodgy, with the right contacts for this type of work. All dealings would be in cash and therefore untraceable. He had told Will that the car would be travelling some distance, and as he drove on he hoped that Will had been thorough in its preparation. He also hoped that Will could keep both his mouth and Roberta's shut.

They made good time to the south-west and found a small chateau advertising rooms just outside the mountain town of Pau. They both slept soundly, only to be awakened by a knock on the door which made David jump uncharacteristically. He pulled on his jeans and opened the door slightly to see who was there.

Nobody.

Looking down, he saw a breakfast tray. He inhaled the smell of freshly baked croissants, pains au chocolat and crusty baguettes, accompanied by the aroma of freshly percolated coffee.

They ate the lot.

'So much better than the rubbish you'd be expected to eat in the UK,' he said, his cool re-established.

He finished the last pain au chocolat, wiping the final crumbs from his mouth and patting his toned abs.

After paying the bill in cash, they crossed into northern Spain, driving down to the west of Madrid before stopping overnight in the old Roman town of Merida. They spent a couple of hours the following morning looking around the well-preserved Roman ruins. David wondered why he hadn't found time in the past to visit places like this. He thought briefly of his sons. He wondered if they would have been interested in seeing two-thousand-year-old buildings and realised he didn't know much about what they were interested in. He immediately consoled himself with the fact that their private school had organised trips to a variety of places around the world – he couldn't remember exactly where.

*

233

Back in the car, they continued the drive towards Tarifa. Sandra looked out of the window at the real Spain, not the one she had seen years ago through the lens of the package holidays she and Linda had enjoyed. Her friend occupied her thoughts for some time and the image of the two white coffins wouldn't go away.

'I wonder who the father of Linda's baby was,' Sandra thought out loud. 'She slept with quite a few different men, so maybe she didn't know.'

David told her about his conversation with Eddie at Linda's funeral, during which Eddie had explained that he had paid for a DNA test to establish if he was the baby's father. He wasn't.

'I suppose the police had to take DNA to check the baby was actually Linda's.'

She thought back to their wild partying all those years ago and looked at David.

Are you the father?

They arrived in Tarifa mid-afternoon to catch the ferry to Tangier. David had never been to Morocco, but Sandra had on many occasions. She had suggested it as a destination, as communications there were still in their infancy, and it would be a good place to hide. Even as the ferry pulled into Tangier, she could see he was unlikely to share her enthusiasm for the country. His face said it all.

*

David hated the place on first sight – or smell, to be more accurate. He found the stench from the harbour nauseating, the noise overwhelming. The call of the muezzin all over town sounded like a herd of sheep to him, and as the ferry left, it joined in on a mournful bass note. He had looked at the El Minzah hotel online; it was in the heart of the city, a short drive from the port, and it boasted five stars and a list of famous people who had stayed there. But now he was entering an opulent but decaying building that seemed not to have been updated since the seventies. His mood darkened, as he was shown several rooms with cramped cheap beds and dusty furniture.

Money will no doubt talk, here as everywhere.

He produced some dirham notes and immediately they were shown a luxurious room with a balcony and a bathroom with a jacuzzi. His lack of faith in human nature being upheld put him in a better frame of mind. It lasted until they sat down to dinner in the crowded dining room with tinny Moroccan music, intrusive belly dancers and an overwhelming smell of Moroccan spices.

'I'll have steak and chips with salad,' said David petulantly, ignoring Sandra's advice about avoiding raw food washed with local water.

It took him three days to get over the subsequent food poisoning.

As he lay in bed, David considered his situation and was inwardly seething at his lack of control over it, or his bodily functions. He had cleverly organised his escape, but now he found himself marooned in a place he knew nothing about, with a clapped-out banger of a car. It had been a long time since he had been in a position where he was not in control of the outcome. He felt trapped.

As he began to feel better, his mind started bouncing thoughts around that ricocheted back and forth. He wasn't entirely sure of Sandra's loyalty. How could he be? She was just like him.

How much does she know about Svelta and the drug trials?

She and Linda were as thick as thieves, and she had mentioned that in New York Linda had slept with Adrian, who had worked for Clinmedica.

Pillow talk?

Somebody had tipped off Channel 4 and Sipher. Linda had drugs in her system when she died. And cannabis? He thought of the kif farms in Morocco that Sandra had laughingly told him about and wondered why and how Linda had been indulging in that particular habit when she died. She and Sandra had taken drugs in the past.

Had they started again? Is this connected with her death?

235

Once back on his feet, David was spending most of his time at the hotel's cybercafé where he could get a half-decent internet signal. He hated Morocco: the dirt, the poverty, the smell, the noise, the food and the lack of alcohol. He had to get away.

A week after they arrived, he took Sandra out for dinner.

'I have to leave here,' he said to Sandra. 'I can't stand the place and I need to get away on my own. This isn't how I thought it would be, but I need to be in control now.'

He was deliberately vague about where he was going, but Sandra accepted it without further questioning. He found this a bit odd, but it made the situation a lot easier.

*

The morning after their final night together, a taxi picked David up from the hotel.

Sandra stood on the balcony, looking with mixed emotions at the disappearing car. It wouldn't have worked, given the way things were now. Over the years they had always held each other at arm's length with what they'd laughingly referred to as a 'mutual and healthy mistrust', but since they had left England, it had taken a more tangible form, posing too many unanswered questions. She thought through her options. She could go back to England. She could honestly say she didn't know where David had gone, but she would have to face Rosie and Roberta, and that would not be an easy meeting for any of them. She leant on the balcony, feeling the warmth of the sun on her back.

How had she ended up in this situation?

She had grown up fighting male control by using her womanly assets to manipulate. But now she felt shallow compared with Rosie, who had run the Refuge with assets that ran much deeper. For the first time she wondered how she would feel right now if she were Rosie.

FORTY-FOUR

2005 David

As David sat back in the taxi, which was taking him to the airport at Casablanca, he realised quite how glad he was to be leaving Morocco behind. He hated the place and the total lack of twenty-first-century amenities.

Added to his dislike of Morocco was his concern about Sandra. He liked her, the sex was never a disappointment, but he was beginning to feel there were too many questions being asked about Svelta. That belonged in the world he was leaving behind for good and he didn't need any reminders. He had woken up one morning to hear her on the phone outside on the balcony, which was unusual. He thought she mentioned Svelta, but maybe he'd dreamt it. The whole situation had been getting to him and making him jumpy.

In planning his exit, he had the good fortune to get talking with a fellow Brit, Ali Mahmood. Ali was evading the UK authorities, who wanted to question him about a VAT scam involving mobile phones. Ali spoke with a strong Brummie accent. He had made millions by importing phones, VAT-free, from the EU and then selling them on in the UK, charging VAT which he then pocketed. He had now established himself and his family in Dubai, where there was a lot more money to be made, tax-free, and he was in Morocco offloading the last of his phone stocks onto an unsuspecting Africa that was largely devoid of a landline structure and hungry for mobiles.

David was taken aback at quite how forthcoming Ali was about his circumstances. He was the fount of all knowledge as to where in the world was best to go to avoid the long arm of the law.

Ali had used his wealth to buy into projects in the property market which were going to provide significant returns. David had listened intently.

Dubai worked for him on a number of levels. He had visited the city several times for Sipher-sponsored conferences, and the standard of the hotels and restaurants was excellent. The UAE did not have an extradition agreement with the UK so if, as he expected, he was going to be the subject of a European arrest warrant, Dubai would be a safe haven. It appeared that there was a demand for presentable people with good sales skills to sell property. There were few, if any, background checks by employers and the tax-free position was an added bonus.

Not exactly using my first in biochemistry, but needs must.

As the old taxi bounced along the pot-holed roads towards Mohammed V Airport, he thought about Sandra. She had taken his departure in her usual matter-of-fact way without any histrionics. Maybe their paths would cross again, or maybe not. He was ambivalent. He needed to move on.

At the airport he went to the Air Arabia check-in desk. The airline was a new low-cost operator and he paid cash at the desk. His flight from Casablanca landed in Sharjah, an hour north of Dubai, and a regular coach service took him from there to the centre of Dubai. As he looked out of the coach window, he was reminded that the skyline of Dubai at night never failed to impress; the illuminated buildings and the newly built network of fast roads were so futuristic. The city was inspirational, oozing opportunity, and he felt a surge of excitement at the possibilities it held.

He had made a reservation at the Meridian Hotel for five nights, which should give him time to find work. Ali had given him the contact details of someone he knew, who he thought could use someone like David. He checked in and unpacked his small suitcase before going into the bathroom to rid himself of the film of North African dust that stuck to his skin.

The toiletries he found in the bathroom welcomed him back to civilisation, and as he relaxed in a deep bath with a cold beer from the minibar, he inhaled the luxurious scent of Bulgari. As he lay there, his former life came back to him and he considered how dramatically things had changed since Linda's death.

Thank God she ended that pregnancy; that could have been a seriously difficult problem for me.

FORTY-FIVE

2005 Rosie

On the Monday following David's disappearance, Rosie was sitting in her office at the Refuge, reliving recent events. She felt uncomfortable about the way she had abruptly ended her phone conversation with Simon. Her upbringing had never left her, and good manners were a part of who she was, so she picked up her mobile and tried Simon's rooms. Her call was answered again by Lucy's plummy voice. This time she was put through immediately.

'Rosie, how are you? It's lovely to hear from you. I have been worried about you.'

'Oh, I'm okay, Simon. I just wanted to apologise for the abrupt way our last call finished. It was unforgivable of me, especially when you were phoning with information you thought I might need.'

'No problem. I didn't think anything of it. You obviously have a lot on your mind. How are things regarding David? I've read in the press that he's wanted for questioning by the police and that he's disappeared. I've wanted to phone you, but to be honest, I didn't want to intrude. You don't have to talk about it to me if you don't want to.'

'I haven't seen or heard from him for a week and I don't think I'm going to any time soon. I think wherever he's gone, he's with

Sandra. I feel a bit of a fool for not knowing about them, but Sandra and I are like chalk and cheese, and I would never have guessed that David would find her attractive. Now I can see that they are actually quite similar; they are both unscrupulous.'

'Is there anything I can do to help?'

'No, I'm fine really. Just a bruised ego and smouldering anger at two people I thought were my friends. Not to mention that they both allowed Linda's death to happen. It's funny, you think you know someone, but then something like this happens. I've been forced to accept that I knew little of what my husband did, and even less about one of my best friends.'

Rosie stopped herself at that point; the deep influence of her mother's example pulled her up short. She realised that she was unburdening herself and she was beginning to sound undignified.

'Would you like to go out for a drink one evening?' Simon asked. 'No strings, I promise, and I totally understand if you don't want to.'

Why not?

Everyone else in her life seemed to have disappeared, and she had known Simon for thirty years, so what would be the harm?

'That would be lovely. I'm in danger of becoming a recluse.'

'How about tomorrow evening? Is there anywhere you'd like to go?'

'I haven't been to the city centre for years. That would be a lovely change.'

'Good. I'll pick you up at seven-thirty and I'll ask Lucy about a good place to go. I'm afraid I'm a bit of a recluse too, so I'll have to get a recommendation from her.'

'See you tomorrow, and thank you for being a good friend.'

The following evening was cold and crisp, with a clear sky and a twinkle of frost on the pavements of Manchester. They walked along, linking arms. Simon twice had to catch Rosie as her feet went from under her. They went to a couple of bars just off Deansgate and chatted for hours. It transpired that Simon had been brought up in Beaconsfield, just down the road from her family home in Amersham, and so they reminisced about their respective childhood haunts. The night was good fun and they agreed to do the same the following Friday.

Arrangements were changed when Roberta was found two days later, safe and sound, if a little fragile. Rosie insisted Roberta stay with her until she rebuilt her strength and so she phoned Simon, explained the situation without going into too much detail, and asked him if he would like to come round on Friday and she would cook dinner for them all.

Dinner at Rosie's turned out to be a fun evening too. Simon entertained them with stories of his time as a junior doctor in A&E. His tales of the sexual proclivities of some of Manchester's citizens had them in fits of giggles. Men with vacuum cleaner attachments stuck into or onto places they were not designed for and women whose jaws had become dislocated as a result of over-enthusiastic foreplay. These were a not-uncommon occurrence and were seen alongside the regular parade of drunks and drug addicts, together with more serious accidents and emergencies.

'I sometimes miss the excitement of not knowing what will come through the door. Now my work is quite predictable. Most of my patients have either inherited their problems or acquired them by lifestyle choices. But I have to be honest, the hours and the pay are definitely preferable.'

Simon smiled in a self-deprecating way that Rosie thought charming and such a contrast to David's arrogance.

Rosie had cooked a green Thai curry, coconut rice and pad Thai noodles, which Roberta and Simon devoured with gusto. She was so glad to see Roberta relaxed and enjoying herself, and it struck her that she had never really seen her like that. Will's presence in her life had meant she was always on edge. Although he was still in a coma, and she would never wish ill of him, she hoped that he would be consigned to history as far as Roberta was concerned.

It's so important to have the right people for you in your life.

'What are you doing for Christmas, Rosie?' Simon asked her, bringing her back into the conversation.

'I've not thought about it with everything else that's happened. Mother has been coming here since Dad died, but it's not really a family event anymore. The boys are at the age where they prefer to be with their friends.'

'And what about you, Roberta?' Simon asked.

'Staying away from canals and kidnappers.'

'Well, it doesn't sound like either of you have major plans, so I have a proposition to make to you both. Not an indecent one, I promise!' Simon guffawed at his own joke. 'My parents have a holiday home overlooking a beautiful bay in Grenada. They've had it for years and it's a great getaway at this time of year. The weather's warm, the sea's warm and the views over Woburn Bay are to die for. I've spent Christmas there for the last couple of years and I've booked my flight for this year as well. I would love it if you ladies would come and share Christmas with me out there. I just think it would do you both the world of good to get away. Promise me you'll think about it.'

Rosie and Roberta sat in stunned silence before Rosie's innate good manners took over. 'Gosh, Simon, that is so kind of you. However, my first thought is, what will my mum do at Christmas? When do you need an answer?'

'As soon as you can. The only problem could be getting flights. It might just mean you can't get a non-stop flight and have to fly via the US. Think about it over the weekend and let me know on Monday.'

'I don't have to think about it,' said Roberta. 'I can't think of anything better right now, I'd love to come. Come on, Rosie, let's think about ourselves for once. Your mother could just as easily go to that friend of hers. You know, the one who invites her every year. Who does far more for her than you ever can because she lives nearby? Call her bluff for once.'

Rosie's mind was racing. 'I'd need to make sure the Refuge would be okay. Sharon is my right-hand woman and knows how things work; I'm sure she could manage without me for a week or two.'

Simon looked at the two women with a paternalistic smile. 'Everyone needs a refuge from time to time in their lives and I think that now, ladies, it is your turn.'

Rosie smiled at his turn of phrase. 'I'd love to come but on one condition – that you stop calling us ladies.'

'What's wrong with that, Rosie? I've never met anyone as ladylike in my life as you. And Roberta, of course. Okay, condition met, girls.'

'Noooooo!'

'Women!'

Rosie and Roberta collapsed in fits of laughter and, after a pause, Simon joined them.

They were interrupted by the sound of the gate buzzer. Still laughing, Rosie went to the intercom. 'I wasn't expecting anyone,' she said.

'Hello?' She couldn't hear the voice clearly. 'Hush a minute, you two. Sorry, who is it?'

'It's Sandra!'

Rosie sprang away from the intercom as if it was red hot. 'I don't want to let her in.'

'She's come to you. Don't you at least want to hear what she has to say?' Roberta suggested.

Rosie looked at Simon, who looked clearly out of his depth. She shrugged her shoulders and opened the gate with the remote control. A car drove in and parked outside the house.

'I'll get the door,' said Simon gallantly.

The dining room was on a mezzanine floor above the front door, and Rosie and Roberta could see clearly, as Simon went down the stairs, when the porch light came on and he opened the door.

Sandra was in the doorway, looking up at them. 'I know I'm the last person you want to see right now, Rosie, but there are things I want to say. May I come in?'

Rosie was silent. It was left to Simon to let Sandra in and he looked unsure as to what to do next. For a long moment they all stood in frozen tableau, Simon and Sandra on the ground floor, Rosie and Roberta on the first floor, looking over the balcony rail.

Sandra looks diminished. I like that. She can stay down there as far as I'm concerned.

'Has David forgotten something?' Rosie asked her icily.

'I don't know where he is,' was Sandra's unexpected reply.

They glared at one another.

I'm damned if I ask her any more questions.

Another pause, then Sandra turned to face Roberta. 'I came home this afternoon and heard what had happened to you, Roberta. I wanted to see if you were alright. Jesus, I feel so bad. I wouldn't have left you with Will if I'd known he'd put you through all that.'

'You've shocked me many times over the years,' said Roberta wearily, 'but what you did this time went too far. It's hurt too many people.'

'I came to tell you how sorry I am, Roberta,' Sandra began, then stopped as she saw the disbelief in Rosie and Roberta's faces. 'Okay, I understand if you don't believe me. I know I've been selfish, and I've looked after number one all my life, but I swear I didn't know the real reason why David was running away. Linda was my best friend. Do you really think I'd have gone with him if I had?'

Rosie forgot herself and retorted angrily, 'Just to be clear, you've been shagging David for thirty years and now you've come back because you've been dumped?'

'I could say the same about you, Rosie. There's only a piece of paper that makes your relationship with David any different than mine. He's used us both, and now he's discarded us, hasn't he?'

Rosie stepped backwards, visibly shaken. There was an unpleasant silence. Simon had disappeared into the kitchen and they turned at the welcome distraction of clinking crockery.

'Leave that, Simon.'

'I'll come and help you.'

When they turned back, Sandra had left, closing the door behind her.

FORTY-SIX

Christmas 2005
The Caribbean

On Christmas Day, Simon rose early with the Caribbean sun and walked out onto the balcony of the house that his parents had built ten years ago in Grenada. He could hear the tree frogs making their 'gloop' noise as he gazed across the bay beneath him at the yachts at anchor and at the exotic display of tropical trees. He loved this time of day here, when everything felt fresh. By nine the heat would have started to sting, the humidity would have settled like a stifling blanket and the mosquitoes would be about unless it was windy. He had heard that the female mosquito bit during the day and carried dengue fever, so he was always extra vigilant with insect repellent. The forgiving thing that made the Caribbean islands bearable during the day was the breeze. But for now, it felt like a warm summer's day in England. He padded noiselessly down the steps and into the lush tropical gardens, down to the wooden veranda by the water that housed an outdoor bar, dining area and sunbathing platform, and onto the wooden jetty where a motorboat was tied up. He dived into the water and swam.

Simon's parents had been lucky to get away with minimal damage to the property when Hurricane Ivan hit Grenada the previous year. The landing stage and all its buildings had been washed away, but the house itself had escaped. Woburn Bay was a hurricane hole, a place of shelter in such events. Now Grenada was struggling to recover and the spice plantations, for which the island was famous, had largely been destroyed. The island needed to reinvent itself, and tourism, yachting and rum looked like the way forward. And drugs.

As a student, Simon hadn't really smoked pot, as it was called then, but when his marriage collapsed, he spent quite a few holidays alone on Grenada. If you knew where to go, there were rum shops away from the tourist areas where you could live like the locals, share a chicken oil down, a beer, a tot of rum and a spliff of ganja. He found smoking cannabis helped him relax, and he regularly took some back to the UK. Nobody questioned a cardiologist at customs.

Simon had persuaded Rosie and Roberta to stay for three weeks. Rosie had come up with a brilliant idea. Her boys, Theo and Hugo, and respective girlfriends would invite Hannah and James over on Christmas Day. They all knew each other from childhood, and they would enjoy a young people's Christmas for a change. Marjorie was horrified and had taken up her friend's long-standing invitation to Christmas dinner.

When they arrived, Rosie and Roberta had both looked pale and listless with the trauma of recent events. Now, after just over a week, they were already rested and tanned. Simon had taken them by boat to the 'Jump Up' on Hog Island the previous Sunday, where there was local cooking, a bar and a band playing all day and night. Then there was barbeque night at Clark's Court marina and a yacht race at Le Phare Bleu; there was always something going on. These events were frequented by the community of live-aboard yachties who anchored their boats in the bay. Roberta was entranced by the stories of their nomadic lifestyle and particularly by Jan, a tall, blond, tanned Danish sailor. He and Roberta had quickly become an item and Jan stayed over on Christmas Eve.

Today, Simon decided, would be about hanging around doing not very much. In the evening when it was cooler, he planned to cook a roast turkey and all the trimmings. He mentally went through the ingredients and the timing as he swam.

Later that evening on the veranda, Simon, Rosie, Roberta and Jan were chatting over more wine and listening to Simon's iPod shuffle through all the greats from the 1980s.

'I stopped following the latest bands long ago,' said Simon apologetically. 'I guess it's a product of age, but who could follow on from Band Aid and Live Aid?'

Mellow and relaxed, he ventured to broach the subject of Linda. They hadn't talked about her at all since they'd come away together and Simon was keen to make it clear to Rosie that there hadn't been anything going on between them. He and Rosie weren't an item… yet. But they enjoyed each other's company and Simon thought it would only be a matter of time. But right now, she could do without a man that had enjoyed another of her best friends.

His fling with Linda was long ago, after all.

Jan had been filled in by Roberta about recent events and listened amiably.

'I would like to say this to you two women, as Linda's closest friends,' said Simon. 'I have regretted my behaviour when Linda and I met up again. I insulted her by turning her advances down. I think the problem was that I just saw her as an old friend, whereas I think she saw me as… well, at one end of the scale she maybe just wanted sex, but I felt like it was more, like she was looking for a potential husband. It's normal to feel guilty when someone dies, but I was too busy dealing with the situation to spot any warning signs that she might be ill.'

Both Rosie and Roberta warmed to his frankness and honesty in declaring something that they had both separately wondered about.

'Linda didn't confide everything to us,' said Rosie. 'We didn't know she'd had an abortion; we didn't know she was taking anti-depressants and the cannabis is news to us. We did know she was taking Svelta. I also suspect she wasn't eating healthily, and she seemed to be drinking steadily. All those things could have played a part in her death.'

'You were quite right, she *was* looking for someone to marry,' said Roberta. 'She never got over Eddie leaving her, and she was always looking for what she had with him, rather than appreciating new people. It was rather unhealthy, really, and men sensed it. If you were concerned about her, she might have interpreted that as renewed interest. Mind you, didn't I see you drop her off at the Refuge not long before she died?'

Simon thought quickly. So, they didn't know that he was involved in the abortion. Linda's threats had resonated with him and stayed with him, despite his trying to rationalise that she would be very unlikely to go to the lengths she had described.

Hell hath no fury like a woman scorned.

He had gone round to Linda's house two nights before she died. Linda had been drinking and was incoherent. He had sat with her for a while and listened to her rambling. At one point she had become quite agitated and he had given her a joint to calm her down. She had relaxed and fallen into a deep sleep, hardly breathing. Simon was concerned and had stayed the night with her.

Simon decided on the disarmingly honest approach again. 'Yes, Roberta, I decided to visit her and see if she was okay. When I turned up she had been drinking heavily and I could smell cannabis. She passed out in the lounge and she looked so terrible I stayed with her. When she woke late the next morning, she of course thought I had stayed for different reasons. She told me she had a shift at the Refuge, and I offered to give her a lift there when she was ready. She seemed okay but deathly pale, and I noticed how thin she was. I suggested she went to her doctor, but she would have none of it. What more could I have done?'

He put his head in his hands, as if reliving the enormity of it had been too much for him. He felt Rosie's hand on his shoulder and raised his head.

'We all feel guilty,' said Roberta. 'I admired her so much. The way she coped with being a single mother; the way she created a new career for herself with Svelta. I am guilty of not noticing how she was struggling of late.'

'I knew she aspired to the lifestyle that she saw David and I were heading for when we got married,' said Rosie. 'I really think that she went for Eddie because he had similar prospects, and when my marriage started to show its cracks I papered over them and pretended that everything was alright. I wasn't honest with her. I think I felt superior to her. Now I realise that the reasons why David and I married were no better. We each used the other to further our ambitions, to create this sham marriage, and all the time he was having an affair with one of my best friends, the bitch!'

Rosie stood up abruptly, and not realising how much she had drunk, fell to the floor. Simon crouched down to help her up and they both ended up falling over. The resultant hilarity broke the mood and they eventually staggered together to a hammock in the corner of the veranda and collapsed, laughing.

When they had quietened down, there was a silence that Simon didn't try to interrupt. The hammock was swinging gently. A breeze took away the heat of the evening and the stars winked in a tropical sky. They could hear the purr of an outboard motor as a dinghy returned to one of the yachts.

Roberta snuggled up to Jan on the sofa and broke the silence. 'I have decided that I'm not flying back to England with you both. Jan has invited me to sail up the islands with him. If I like it, I'll sail back across the Atlantic with him in April.'

'Blimey, Roberta,' said Simon. 'That's a bit of a bombshell!'

Simon was immediately worried she was making a hasty decision. How could she really know Jan yet? Simon didn't. But

Roberta had changed so much in this last week; she positively glowed. Was that enough?

'When will I ever get another opportunity like this?' said Roberta. 'What do I have to rush back for? All there is waiting for me are the reminders of the last two months, an empty house and a job that someone else can do if I don't turn up. I'm excited by the different colours here in the tropical sun and I'm dying to paint them. I've always wanted to run away, and I'm being offered the opportunity to do it.' She looked at Rosie and waited.

'I'm in shock,' said Rosie. 'I think it's a wonderful opportunity and I'm really pleased for you if it's what you want to do. But I also know how impulsive you can be. I need time to take it in. We should talk about it when we're sober.'

'I'm not changing my mind,' said Roberta, and Jan grinned with delight.

FORTY-SEVEN

Christmas Day 2005 UK

Frances was spending Christmas Day at her sister's house, together with her two sons. She was grateful for the invitation; she was exhausted from visiting Will in hospital every day for weeks and working at the pub, as well as overseeing the farm. Fortunately, her children joined in willingly. They were dutiful and loving boys; Frances couldn't believe her luck sometimes. They didn't take after Will.

They had all visited Will that morning in hospital. He was unresponsive and just looked asleep, as he had been since the accident. They chatted to him, wished him 'Happy Christmas' and then kissed him goodbye.

'His injuries have healed, and his head scans are clear. It's just a matter of time till he comes out of the coma, Mrs Kenyon,' the doctor said.

Christmas dinner was wonderful, and everybody made sure that Frances relaxed and did nothing. Her sister had promised to drive them all home, and before Frances knew it, she had had a glass of sherry before dinner, a glass of white wine with the turkey, a glass of red with the pudding and a glass of port afterwards. She was tiddly and laughing, till her mobile rang. What she heard wiped the smile off her face.

'Okay, I'll come as soon as I can,' she said.

There was silence in the room.

'Will has recovered consciousness,' she blurted out, and burst into tears. 'Oh, thank the Lord, even if his timing is a bit inconsiderate. That is typical of Will.'

The whole family burst out with a series of exclamations, not the least of which was the question of sobering Frances up before she went. In the end, they fed her a couple of cups of coffee and then all set out together for the hospital in two cars.

Will was propped up with pillows, amazingly awake and talking – or grumbling, to be precise. The staff had just fed him some soup which had gone down well, but apparently that wasn't enough.

'I bet you lot 'ave just had a Christmas dinner,' were his first words. 'You brought me some then?'

'Oh, Will,' said Frances, bursting into tears again. 'We've been so worried for you.'

'I know, I know, I've 'eard you. I know everyone who's bin to see me, I just couldn't move or speak. It was weird.' He sniffed. 'Have you been drinking, Frances? Bloody 'ell, I could murder a pint.'

They all laughed. It would seem that Will was his old self.

'I'll tell you who ain't bin to see me, that ex of mine, Roberta.'

There was silence.

'Don't you remember what happened to her?' Frances eventually asked.

Will thought solemnly for a minute and then a slow smile appeared onto his face. It broadened into a grin and then he started laughing.

*

Eddie and Megan had booked Christmas dinner at their favourite restaurant in Prestbury. Louisa and Lizzie had been invited to join them but had declined. They were far more interested in the 'young person's Christmas' going on at Rosie's house.

As they sat together at their table, a silent oasis of two among the tables crowded with raucous families, Eddie remembered the Christmas dinners that Linda used to cook, with a plump turkey and all the trimmings, vegetables that she had grown. Their meals were in packets from Marks and Spencer or Sainsbury's, so the idea of Megan cooking a Christmas dinner was never on the cards.

Meals out and takeaways washed down with wine and followed by uninhibited sex had seemed exciting in the early days of their affair, and the total contrast with his home life was what had turned his head. But it wasn't long before the attraction wore off and he missed Linda's home cooking, cuddling up with his daughters, bathed and in their PJs watching TV, and a welcoming home.

Linda had tried so hard to be what she believed he wanted, and he had stupidly been flattered by the attentions of a younger woman.

Eddie sighed and brought himself back to the present. 'Happy Christmas, darling.'

He raised a solitary glass to Megan, who was picking turkey from between her teeth.

*

Peter Bolton served up the last of the Christmas dinners at the walk-in centre for the homeless in central London. It was something he did each year. It was one of the few things that he could *still* do.

Peter's life had been plagued with mental illness for over twenty years, brought on by his feelings of failure and guilt over the way he had allowed the clinical trial data of Svelta to be compromised. It was a drug that had gone on to kill people. He had found it hard to live with the knowledge and no amount of chemical cosh had been able to give him the peace he craved. He had had several breakdowns and was taking lithium. It kept him stable, but his brain was dulled, he'd ironically put on weight and his physical health was poor. He felt lucky that his wife and family coped with him, but he would never again be the husband and father they had known.

He had done his best to make amends in his own mind by helping others, whom society had left behind, but it was not enough, and the root cause of his guilt had to be faced.

He felt he had to do more.

He also had nothing more to lose.

He had written to Teresa O'Donnell, the investigative TV journalist, to explain how the trials for Svelta had been managed inappropriately and how it was beyond doubt that the data had been manipulated within Sipher to produce a positive outcome.

*

Sandra was cooking a token chicken for Christmas dinner. As there was only herself, there would be scraps left over for Star and the other dogs.

She didn't have to invite parents; they were both long gone: her dad quite early on of a heart attack, her mum four years later from breast cancer. Sandra reflected cynically that given their respective temperaments and lifestyle, as a nurse, she could have predicted their ends for them both.

She thought that Christmas was an outdated religious event, overtaken by a children's folktale, then swamped by rampant consumerism. Her only problem in holding this view was everyone else's expectation that she would feel lonely or sad if she were on her own. Since her parents died she would have been happy to avoid it, but she usually got invited somewhere and had to endure a stuffy room, spoilt children, and too much to eat and drink, never mind having to buy token presents. This year, though, nobody had invited her.

So why, when I should be feeling grateful to be left alone, do I feel sad and neglected?

There was a knock on the door.

'If that's Father Christmas, we don't want any,' she shouted crossly.

'No, it isn't. Will I do?' The reply came through the letterbox.

Intrigued, Sandra went to the door and opened it.

DS Steve Mallory was standing in the porch. His arms were full of a bouquet of flowers, a gift-wrapped parcel and a bottle of champagne.

'At least it's not raining this time,' Sandra quipped.

Steve Mallory looked a bit taken aback, so she relented and treated him to a voluptuous and lengthy kiss.

FORTY-EIGHT

February 2006 The Inquest

The inquest into Linda's death took place on a cold and sunny morning in mid-February at the Coroners' Court in Stockport, Greater Manchester. Louisa and Lizzie had travelled up from London to attend and were seated next to their father on the front row. They were joined by Rosie and Hannah, who said she was there 'in loco parentis' on behalf of Roberta, who was still in Grenada. Also in attendance was Melanie Scott representing the *Manchester Evening News*. She was seated next to Teresa O'Donnell from Channel 4 who had also travelled up from London. Some members of the public had seated themselves on the back row and hiding among them was Ian de Voet from Sipher Chemicals.

Just as the coroner entered, the door opened for two latecomers who seated themselves next to Ian de Voet, much to his annoyance. They created a bit of a disturbance and the coroner frowned as he took his seat and waited.

Sandra, who was accompanied by DS Mallory, caught Hannah's gaze and gave her a big, beaming smile and a wave, which caused the coroner to frown again in disapproval.

Having thoroughly quelled Sandra with an icy look, the coroner began the proceedings, which he explained were to investigate in more detail how Linda Hammond had died of a heart attack. He explained that, since the post-mortem, he had ordered more tests and he had also asked for an investigation into the drugs that Linda had in her system at the time of her death.

The first witness called was the pathologist who conducted the original post-mortem. He began by repeating what they all already knew, that Linda had died of a heart attack and there was a question as to why she had died so quickly when she had no previous history of heart problems; that after some further tests had been run, a toxicity report had found traces of several drugs in her system, namely fat binders, amphetamines, anti-depressants, alcohol and cannabis. He then went on to the recent more detailed tests that had been ordered by the coroner.

'I can confirm that the anti-depressants in Linda Hammond's system were as supplied on prescription by her GP. However, the amount in her system was more than double the dose prescribed.' He paused. 'The quantity of fat binders and amphetamines was also more than double the amount recommended for her body weight. This was an overdose of Svelta.'

There was a buzz of conversation throughout the courtroom at these revelations.

The second witness was DS Mallory. He explained that the police had made enquiries concerning the various drugs in Linda's system and that they were satisfied that there was no large-scale drug abuse on Linda's part, and that the cannabis, though unexplained, was a negligible amount. He made his way back to his seat, straightening his tie as he went and revealing his shirt hanging out at the back.

The third witness was Linda's GP, Dr Paul Grey, who looked a picture of ill health with a face colour that matched his name. He was covered with a nervous sheen of sweat.

'I c-can confirm t-that I prescribed anti-depressants to Linda Hammond,' he began nervously.

258

He stressed that at the time she had not disclosed that she was taking Svelta. He went on, almost pleading, that if she had disclosed this, he would have checked the different brands and types for contra-indications.

'There is no way of recording a drug that a patient is taking privately unless they voluntarily disclose it.' He paused, hoping he was done, and then drooped gratefully back to his seat.

The fourth witness was DI Jack Holly, who looked over in disapproval at DS Mallory. Jack Holly spent some time outlining details of the police investigation so far into the deaths from heart attacks in women taking the slimming pill Svelta. He then made the following statement: 'There is now no doubt that these deaths were due to taking Svelta, and furthermore, it has been discovered that all the deaths so far appear to be of people who were also taking a certain type of anti-depressant. There are no warnings or contra-indications in the Svelta instructions that the drug should not be taken with these anti-depressants.'

He concluded that investigations were still ongoing and a full statement would be issued when they had been completed. He abruptly sat down again.

There was a volley of exclamations among those assembled. The press was scribbling frantically on their notepads, and Louisa and Lizzie looked at each other, aghast, each thinking the same thing: that their mother's death had been caused by an overdose.

The coroner called for order and there was silence once more, with everyone poised to hear his verdict. Would he blame Svelta for Linda Hammond's death?

The coroner took the floor again for the final summing-up. 'The prescription of anti-depressants was made in good faith and without a full disclosure by Linda Hammond. I cannot find any evidence of malpractice. However, the combination of a type of anti-depressant and the amphetamines in Svelta has been proved to cause heart problems, leading to death. There is evidence that these drugs were taken by the deceased in larger quantities than prescribed or advised. It must be concluded that this only made them a more lethal cocktail.'

The coroner paused for effect. 'I therefore conclude that Linda Hammond, who died on October 31st, 2005 in the county of Greater Manchester, died from a heart attack caused by taking the slimming drug Svelta, which contains amphetamines, in conjunction with anti-depressants. I have sent a recommendation to the chief coroner, that there should now be a review of similar recorded deaths.'

He collected his papers and exited the room.

A hubbub of conversation broke out as people made their way out of the room and congregated in groups in the lobby. The journalists were excitedly discussing the coroner's verdict. They would have a field day looking for more case studies. That's what they were paid for.

Lizzie was crying and Eddie had an arm round each of his daughters.

Rosie and Hannah stopped by the little group, clearly offering their condolences, then leaving discreetly, together.

Sandra was looking at the little group hesitantly from a distance; Eddie had no axe to grind with her.

DS Mallory was standing red-faced, tucking his shirt in at the back and getting a dressing-down from DI Holly.

A few people slithered out, obviously trying not to be noticed. Dr Grey looked relieved that he had got away with no more than a verbal lashing. Ian de Voet marched out, looking directly ahead of him, his jaw set. Peter Bolton emerged, unknown by anyone, a look of satisfaction on his face.

With Steven Mallory otherwise occupied, Sandra looked across at Eddie hugging his daughters. She was relieved when he signalled to her. Sandra crossed over to the little group and Louisa detached herself from the others.

'Come to lunch with us, Aunt Sandra,' she said simply.

Eddie took them all to the Arden Arms in Stockport, where there was real ale on tap and a fire in the hearth to warm them. They ordered food and drinks and the conversation flowed as they caught up with all the things that had happened over the last three months.

*

That evening, Sandra sat gazing into the flames of the fire. A glass of red wine in her hand, with Star at her feet, she still felt alone in a way she never had before in her life. Linda was dead, Roberta was living in the Caribbean, David was missing and Rosie would probably never speak to her again.

Hard-faced, Sandra Marsden sighed, pursed her lips and blew out a long breath.

What was it that Linda had said?

You will not get another chance. This is it.

FORTY-NINE

2006

The withdrawal of Svelta from the market was bound to unnerve the shareholders, whose immediate reaction would be a rush to sell. Knowing this to be the likely course of events, the Sipher board had taken the decision to ask for a temporary suspension of their shares, to allow the company to respond to serious allegations.

This was new territory for Eugene N Kennedy, Sipher's CEO, and he sensed that the Svelta story was going to be the ultimate exercise in crisis management.

Sipher had already provided the police with the database and program code that was used for the phase three clinical trials, and Kennedy knew he needed to be prepared for what they would find. The board agreed to commission a forensic IT company to undertake a parallel evaluation with the remit to provide them with a 'warts and all' report within a week.

As luck would have it, the local university had a well-regarded computer science department that had recently set up a company specialising in just this area. Forensix was awarded the contract, after assurances of total confidentiality and an obligation to report their findings ASAP, but at the latest within the week. Kennedy hoped this would allow them to prepare for the undoubted questioning that would accompany the next meeting with the police.

As well as an analysis of the software used for the phase three trials, the handling of the first two phases would no doubt come under scrutiny. Kennedy knew that most companies had an effective internal grapevine that was usually well-informed, and he felt sure that someone would have known how these phases had been managed. He called his key managers together, asking them to talk to staff who had been involved to try to get a better understanding of exactly how the process had worked.

Finally, at the inquest into the death of Linda Hammond, one of their own representatives, the coroner had recorded death due to a heart attack caused by taking Svelta with an anti-depressant. Kennedy expected the media would now be searching for heartrending stories to launch a campaign, none of which would reflect well on Sipher.

The next few days involved long meetings with Sipher's lawyers, who sensed a potential goldmine in fees. From these initial meetings, it became apparent that the board would need to put assets aside for any future compensation claims from patients, their families and Sipher shareholders. A figure of $10 billion was discussed. In the worst-case scenario, the litigation could go on for years.

The report from Forensix was presented to the board of Sipher within four days of the work being commissioned. The academics that presented it could not contain their excitement and delight at how they had been able to uncover a complete picture of what had happened. Not for the first time, Kennedy was struck by the disconnect between commerce and academia as he stared down the barrel of the smoking gun that pointed Sipher's way. His worst fears were confirmed:

'Data records deleted where death occurred.'

'Data records amended to downgrade adverse reactions.'

'Forms with adverse reactions and deaths were routed to a Super User, who was always the same person, David Jennings.'

Kennedy and his board sat there in stunned silence. The

academics gradually lost their self-congratulatory smiles. Kennedy cleared his throat before asking the question he suspected he already knew the answer to: 'So, are you saying that all the data entry and analysis of the Svelta phase three clinical trials was done entirely within the Sipher IT network?'

'Yes, that's correct. All the input of data and the routing of the forms was from computers whose addresses identify them as within the Sipher network.'

Kennedy knew that he had to confirm his worst nightmare. 'And you are telling me that David Jennings, who you call the Super User, was able to input data that could have varied from what was recorded on the original form?'

Kennedy watched as the academic puffed himself up to reveal more of his brilliant work. 'Exactly. We were also able to evidence records being amended by David Jennings more than once.'

The board were left shell-shocked. They had yet to hear feedback from the Sipher managers as to what happened in the phase one and phase two trials.

The feedback, when it came, provided no comfort. While there was no real concern about the phase one trials, in the phase two trials all the report forms with adverse reaction were put on David Jennings' desk for analysis and data input.

The arrogant upstart.

Kennedy hated the man.

He also despised the former Sipher board members who had stonewalled the safety concerns and were now retired, sunning themselves in luxury courtesy of their gold-plated Sipher pension pots. He would be the man in the firing line, the man whose picture would be on the front pages. He downed a double dose of his antacid tablets to quell his rising heartburn.

By the time the police came back to meet him, he had spent many long hours with Sipher's lawyers, and the agreed strategy was to not admit liability but to cooperate as far as possible without compromising this position. The police presented their findings to Eugene Kennedy, facts of which he was now well aware. He went through the motions, his face and manner portraying shock, incredulity and then decisive action.

'I would like a copy of your report and time to digest its contents, but I can tell you now, the first thing I plan to do is organise a robust internal inquiry to understand what happened and why. This will run alongside an urgent review of the handling of any adverse reaction reports received before Svelta was withdrawn.'

In reality, Kennedy knew that some potential claimants would be old and in poor health. The longer they could protract the process, the greater the likelihood that many of these would die. It would be a lengthy and costly process.

Those implicated by association also moved quickly to appear to act. The regulators who had licensed Svelta, and who had not been persuaded to review the data after the high number of deaths, were suddenly demanding meetings. 'Damage limitation' and 'crisis management' became the bywords.

Outside of Sipher, law firms specialising in personal injury started to gear up for what could be a bumper few years. Millions worldwide had taken Svelta, and if just a small percentage had died or experienced cardiac problems, the value of claims would run into the billions. Advertisements were placed in newspapers and on television to track down potential claimants, and the newspapers were full of stories about Svelta-related personal tragedies. Under instructions from their lawyers, Sipher issued a further carefully worded statement relating to the safety of Svelta:

'Sipher has acted responsibly every step of the way from research to drug approval and has voluntarily withdrawn Svelta from the market.'

Law firms in the US and UK, specialising in personal injury claims, took no time at all, orchestrating a class action suit on behalf of those affected by their use of Svelta:

'Our clients allege that Sipher falsely promoted the safety of Svelta and failed to disclose the full range of the drug's dangerous side effects.'

When Sipher returned to the market, its shares opened at the level of 'junk', wiping billions off the value of the company. Employees with stock options saw the cash value of their years of hard work reduced to nothing. Shareholders saw their investment wiped out.

After the company had received another accusation of 'relentless greed' by the frenzied media, Kennedy informed his board, 'That bastard Jennings appears to have gone to ground. The police can't trace his whereabouts. I hope he rots in hell.'

*

David, for his part, stood on his balcony after an excellent breakfast and surveyed Jumeirah Beach. The Burj Al Arab gleamed in the early-morning sun as he watched a helicopter land on the deck halfway up the sail-like building. His meeting with Ali's contacts had gone every bit as well as he had expected, and now he was about to embark on a lucrative second career, selling property on the Dubai Marina.

FIFTY

2006 Rosie

The phone rang early, before her alarm, waking Rosie with a start. She immediately recognised the voice at the other end. It was Mona, David's mum, and she sounded upset.

'Hello, love. Sorry to trouble you, but my George has taken bad and he's in hospital. Can David come up and see his dad? I don't think he's got long. I thought you might know where he is.'

Rosie knew that George had been suffering from pneumoconiosis for some years, a consequence of a life down the pit. It was known as 'black lung disease' in Fryston and was common amongst the older miners.

Rosie felt the woman's pain. Mona was a good woman. She had given her son the very best she could. She had married for love and as a result struggled daily with the difficulties of an impoverished life with George.

'I'm afraid I still don't know where David is, Mona.'

'If he gets in touch, can you let him know what's happened?'

Rosie felt desperately sad. Mona was such a decent person and she didn't want to burden her further with details about David's absence.

'If you can speak to him, tell him his dad is at Jimmy's.'

Rosie was confused, thinking it sounded like George was being looked after by a friend or relative before Mona added, 'St James's Hospital in Leeds, love. He's on oxygen. He'd love to see his lad.'

Rosie heard Mona's voice crack with grief.

'If I hear from him I'll tell him, Mona. Give George my love.'

Rosie put the phone down and cried bitter tears, for Mona, for George and for herself. She was glad now she had sent them a Christmas card and a food hamper from 'David, Rosie and the boys' even though she was tempted at the time to remove his name.

It was still dark outside. There was no chance of sleep now, so she got up to make herself a cup of coffee. She put on the news and fired up her computer to catch up on her emails. One from Simon caught her eye. They had been seeing one another since coming back from Grenada, and the relationship had moved up a gear, with Simon staying at Rosie's most weekends. They had been apprehensive about sleeping together. It had been a long time since either of them had had sex, and they didn't want to lose a friendship that had come to mean so much.

In the end, though, sex had been wonderful, each seeming to know what the other wanted. They revelled in every aspect of their deepening relationship. They felt young again and life for both of them had a new meaning.

Simon's email was a cheeky declaration of his love.

'You are the person I think about when I go to sleep.
You are the first person I think about when I wake up.
My body and I would like you here.
Why aren't you here?'

It made her laugh out loud. Here was a man she could rely on, and he was straightforward and honest. The contrast with David was not lost on her.

Why did I waste so many years with a man who loved himself more than anything or anybody else?

Over the previous months, she had looked back over the years of her marriage and seen everything in a new light. She realised how ruthless David had been in every aspect of his life from the moment they met.

It was six-forty. She wondered if it was too early to phone Simon. No sooner had she dismissed the thought than the phone rang. She recognised the number; it was Simon. She picked it up and burst into tears.

'What on earth is the matter?' Simon could get no sense from Rosie's sobs. 'I'm on my way. I'll be there in fifteen minutes.'

After years of David's indifference to her feelings, Rosie still couldn't get used to having someone who cared for her, someone who would put her first. She was frightened it wouldn't last, that Simon would gradually retreat from the relationship just as David had done. Thirty years of marriage to him had well and truly crushed her confidence.

Simon arrived in joggers and a sweatshirt, unshaven and unwashed. He ran up the stairs two at a time into the kitchen where Rosie sat hugging a cushion, tears streaming down her face.

'What's happened, Rosie?' Simon sat down next to her. He put an arm around her, pulling her close, stroking her hair gently.

She relaxed into him and she told him about Mona's phone call. 'I don't know where he is. What can I do?'

They sat there for some time. There wasn't an easy answer.

'Well, you don't have to do anything today.' Simon's rational thinking was one of the things she liked about him. 'Back to bed,' he ordered.

'Only if you come with me, Doctor.'

Rosie looked at him in his scruffs and his bedhead and loved him all the more. Simon held her in his arms, and she fell into a sound sleep. When she woke up some hours later, the early spring sun was streaming in through the window. Simon had gone, leaving her a note on the pillow:

Off to work.
Will come back later.
Don't worry, we'll sort something.
Doctor's orders.

Rosie felt a warm glow. He was a good man. She busied herself for the rest of the day, finishing a bid for further funding for the Refuge. Her role there was now less hands-on and more advisory, which suited her down to the ground. She was preparing Simon's favourite meal of sea bass on a bed of risotto when the phone rang. Her heart raced, sensing it might be bad news from Leeds. Mona's sobs confirmed her worst suspicions. George had died that afternoon.

The funeral took place the following week. Simon drove Rosie over to Fryston, tactfully dropping her off nearby to attend the funeral on her own. In a grey stone church, under a grey sky, George Jennings was dispatched to a 'better place' according to the officiating minister. As she gazed around at George's fellow miners and their families, she saw their complexions were also grey. She hoped the minister was right. Hacking coughs and wheezes accompanied the hymns. Not for the first time, Rosie thought, *You can't choose your womb well enough.*

She was dreading facing Mona, but to her surprise, when she found her after the service, Mona took Rosie's smooth hands between her cold and gnarled hands, squeezed them and gave her a knowing look. 'You look after yourself, love. You're a good girl.'

And with that she walked away to rejoin the other mourners.

'Simon. Can you pick me up, please? Yes, where you dropped me off. Thanks.'

She got into Simon's car and smiled at him. 'She knows, Simon. I think she knows David isn't coming back. She didn't say anything, but I'm sure she knew.'

'Let's get you home. I don't like you in black.'

Rosie laughed. She felt so lucky to have Simon by her side, especially today. She realised quite how different this relationship could be to the one she had with David. Simon was kind, considerate and a great lover.

'I've got something I want to talk to you about,' Simon said that weekend as they walked along the canal banks of the Cheshire Ring. 'I have been approached about a job in Abu Dhabi. It sounds really interesting. They've built a new state-of-the-art hospital that specialises in cardiology. Heart disease is a big problem in the Middle East. They've asked me to consider the post of director. If I'm interested, I would need to go out for an interview in the next couple of weeks, but I'd only be interested if you wanted to come with me.'

'Well, I'm always up for a holiday in the sun, Simon. You know me, I'm a hothouse plant.'

'Rosie, I meant if I get the job, I'd only take it if you came with me. I want us to spend the rest of our lives together, and if this place doesn't work for you, then it won't work for me.'

Rosie was stunned. Simon's feelings were as deep as hers. But it wasn't straightforward. Her rational mind took over. 'I'm still technically married. What about my house?'

'You could rent the house out. I know it may be a while before you can get a divorce, but we can look into how best to progress that.' Simon looked hesitant, as if he'd gone too far, then added, 'That's if you want to get divorced and—'

'Are you asking me to marry you, Simon?'

Turning to face her, he held her gaze. 'Rosie. I love you and I want to spend the rest of my life with you, if you'll have me. I've never felt so comfortable in someone's company before. I even know what you're thinking most of the time. Haven't you noticed we finish each other's sentences? And you are the most beautiful woman in the world.'

Rosie looked back at him. She was so happy she didn't know whether to laugh or cry, so she did both.

Two weeks later they sat side by side, sipping champagne in business-class seats on a flight from Manchester to Abu Dhabi.

Once the seatbelt signs had gone out, Simon fetched his briefcase from the overhead locker and pulled out a small turquoise-coloured box. Rosie recognised it immediately as coming from the jeweller Tiffany.

He handed it to her. 'Open it, darling.'

Rosie's hands shook slightly as she opened the box. Inside was a fine chain holding an emerald-cut diamond, set in platinum.

'Do you like it?' Simon asked tentatively.

'It's beautiful.' Rosie gave a huge smile as he fastened the clasp at the back of her neck. Both were unaware of the passing flight attendant who paused, smiled and then hurried away, not wanting to intrude on an intimate moment.

'The diamond can be made into a ring at some point in the future.'

'At the first possible moment, please.'

Their champagne glasses recharged, Simon looked at the woman who had changed his world. 'I love you, Rosie. I have no intention of ever letting you go.'

'And I have no intention of going anywhere.'

As the plane began its descent into Abu Dhabi, Rosie's thoughts came back to Linda.

How desperate Linda had been to find love and happiness and someone to share her life.

Desperation leading to her untimely death.

Revelations leading to changes in the lives of so many people.

She looked at the handsome doctor seated beside her and felt mixed emotions, knowing that her good fortune in finding love with Simon had come at a time of unhappiness for so many. She intended to grab what life offered her with both hands.

We have a second chance.

FIFTY-ONE

2006 Roberta

Jan pulled Roberta down into the cockpit of his yacht.

'Hold the wheel, stay down there,' he ordered, 'and I would take your clothes off if I were you!' He grinned at her startled expression. 'You will soon be soaked.'

A moment later, conflicting blasts of wind smashed the mainsail's metal boom across the deck and crashed the main and jib together. Rain began bucketing down and visibility suddenly plummeted to zero.

Jan started the engine. 'Steer into the wind,' he shouted urgently to Roberta, as the boat bucked wildly, the rigging howled and waves crashed on the hull.

'Where are the rocks now? I can't see them,' wailed Roberta.

Jan wrestled and fought with the sails. Every time he tried to lower them, they filled with wind again. Roberta was terrified, but Jan was relishing the challenge with an enormous grin on his face. It took all his strength, but gradually he was winning, the boat was calming down, the engine was taking control. Roberta took a moment to appreciate his physique: fit, bronzed, with white-blond hair and flashing blue eyes. They called him Viking out here.

'Now steer 180 the hell away,' he bellowed.

Suddenly it was all over; the rain and the wind stopped, the waves petered out, and Jan slowed the engine till the boat was drifting. He was pumped with adrenaline, and at the sight of Roberta's wet, naked body he seized her and they made love on the slippery deck.

*

When the squall struck, Jan had been sailing his yacht north of Grenada in the West Indies, between a group of small islands and the site of 'Kick 'em Jenny', an underwater volcano. He had persuaded Roberta to come close to them both and view a colony of birds, and that despite the fearsome-sounding names, there was nothing to worry about.

'I saw the squall coming over the water,' said Jan. 'It's okay when you know what to do; now you must steer for a while, please, while I clear up the deck and set sail again.'

Roberta braced her body as she steered Jan's yacht. The feeling of harnessing the wind with the sails and then using them to propel the yacht forward was exhilarating. She trusted Jan's expertise completely. These few months since she had been sailing with him, every day had held a new experience or adventure. She felt in control, she felt good, she was travelling free. The sun shone, the Caribbean Sea hissed under the bows of the yacht and sparkled on the hull.

Roberta thought of her friends, Rosie and Simon, who had flown back to England after their holiday in Grenada, whilst she chose to stay with Jan. They had all needed a break after the series of events and revelations that had followed Linda's sudden death. When Jan invited her to sail with him, she didn't have to think twice. Jan was single and a handsome forty-six-year-old; Roberta was single and forty-eight, and her life so far had been a failed marriage, bringing up her two children and working as an artist to pay the bills. To her, it was a no-brainer, but Rosie was, as always, concerned for her. She sent her a thought message.

You don't need to worry, Rosie, I'm very happy.

FIFTY-TWO

2006 Sandra

Sandra had been helping Dawn put the dogs away in their kennels. They were one person down and she had felt obliged to go out there, rather than watch through the window. It had been raining all day, and the encroaching gloom of a late afternoon in March had made conditions outside utterly miserable. She left Dawn to finish up, grateful to come into the warm house. She stripped off her wet clothes, lit the log fire and put the kettle on. As she sipped her tea, she stared out of the window, watching the lights of aircraft as they glided slowly across the darkening sky, bright stars in a line following one another towards Manchester Airport. She wished she was on one.

Bored again, Sandra?

Yes, I am bored.

Nothing to do with winter then.

More to do with having no friends left.

And the gravy train has disappeared.

The visit to Rosie's before Christmas had made it clear that the two of them would never be friends in the near future. Then there was Roberta. She had fully intended to make it up with Roberta, who was far more accepting of human behaviour, but she had never returned from the Caribbean. She thought about her oldest friend, Linda, now dead because of the hubris of David. She felt betrayed by him. She hadn't known about Svelta, she really hadn't, all those years when he hadn't told her. Now Rosie and Roberta thought she had known all along.

She thought back to the party at Owens Park, where they had all met. She had fancied the pants off David, but he clearly only had eyes for Rosie. She had waited until he was left on his own and made her move; she decided she would give him an experience he would never forget. She spotted Rosie scanning the room for him and swiftly pulled him to her and gave him a lengthy kiss. When they broke apart, Rosie had gone.

It had been an even playing field until Rosie became pregnant. Sandra was initially disgusted that he could fall for that old trick, until David had pointed out how Rosie would benefit his career in a way that Sandra never could. Then she was coldly furious. No way was she hanging around with this chancer.

Yet over the years they came together, again and again. It was inevitable that they would meet up socially and the physical attraction between them was strong. Rosie was steeped in the bible of civilised behaviour and didn't notice at first. Then there were near-misses, and Rosie had to reluctantly accept that David was unfaithful, but she didn't know who with. Her relationship with David cooled, but it was beneath her dignity to investigate further. Sandra thought they all had a good bargain.

Until Linda's death.

Sandra didn't dislike Rosie – she had many qualities that she admired, mainly the ones that were lacking in herself – but Linda's death had reminded her of the snub she had felt thirty years ago.

I've hung around David all this time. That's what my life has been about.

She thought about her nursing ambitions, and how they had lapsed.

I need something to feel zealous about, other than sex, for once.

FIFTY-THREE

2006 Louisa and Lizzie

Linda's daughters were up in the north again. They were staying with Rosie's sons, Theo and Hugo, in Chelford and meeting up with Melanie in Manchester's trendy Northern Quarter to grab a meal, see a band and maybe end up in a club, if they still had the energy.

They had enjoyed Christmas together at Rosie's house, and coming back was now a monthly event. Theo and Hugo were fast becoming like a second family, especially with Rosie away. It did the boys good to have to tidy up and Lizzie would make sure the cupboards were replenished before they left.

They had also had regular interviews with Melanie, who was writing diary pieces, following the lives of the people who had lost loved ones to Svelta. Although it was instinctive to bury unpleasant things, they both found it cathartic to describe their feelings on a regular basis, and to read the experiences of others.

'Better than counselling,' said Louisa, who had had plenty in her time. 'We've felt everything from denial, anger, bargaining and guilt and depression, to a form of acceptance.'

'Yet that acceptance is fragile, and easily invaded by triggers in the present that bring past events tumbling back as if they were yesterday,' said Melanie. 'Then you have to go through the whole thing again – what if... what if – until you realise you can't go back.'

They were drinking in a bar, waiting for Theo, Hugo and Theo's girlfriend to arrive. They were perched uncomfortably on barrels, cut down to make seats, yet they made an eye-catching group: Louisa with her long blonde hair; Lizzie with a spiky crop and horn-rimmed glasses; Melanie, whose dark hair tumbled in curls over her face.

'Hey, Melanie, you're getting a dab hand at this, ever thought of a career change?' said Lizzie, grinning.

Melanie grimaced and rolled her eyes. 'No way. Some of the people that I interview talk about very strange things, like making a pact with God or the Devil, whichever force they believe can change things. Someone else was researching time travel; another visits the grave three times a day. I tend not to print those. I refer them to bereavement counselling instead.'

'People are so individual and have their own ways of dealing with grief,' said Lizzie.

'I get upset when I think she will never see my children.' Louisa's eyes suddenly welled with tears.

Ever-practical, Lizzie stepped in. 'You and your boyfriend had better hurry up then. Don't you know that women's fertility declines after the age of thirty-five?'

Rosie's boys turned up. Theo, with his fair hair and green eyes, like his mum; Hugo, handsome like his dad, with curly dark hair and brown eyes, and a restless air, as if he would leave if something better came along. Theo's girlfriend was pretty, with long auburn curls, like a Rossetti painting.

Lizzie felt an overwhelming sense of love, of time passing, a new family, things moving on.

This feeling won't last; just hold on to it and enjoy the moment.

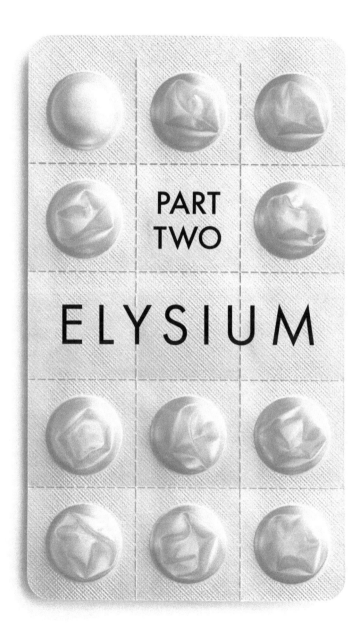

PART
TWO

ELYSIUM

ONE

November 2006

The woman was aware of a dull, insistent ache radiating from the back of her right hand and up into her arm. She tried and failed to lift it, then began willing other parts of her body to move, but she seemed to have no control over them.

I'm in a dream. That's it.

She forced her mind to apply itself to the business of breaking out and up, like a swimmer trying to reach the surface of the water. She had done this before with bad dreams.

The realisation came slowly.

She was trapped, and she was already awake.

Where am I?

A memory emerged of being wheeled on a trolley.

What's happening to me?

She sensed light through her eyelids and fought hard to open them, but they were too heavy. She tried again to lift her head up and failed. She was lying on her back, immobile and paralysed. Her tongue inside her dry mouth felt like a thick, gritty sponge.

I can't even speak…

She was alarmed now, her breathing coming shallow and fast,

her heart thumping. She tried to calm herself, to disengage her mind from the present, but every time she captured a thought it floated away. She began to struggle for breath.

A cold sensation was oozing through her body like a tide of viscous fluid, numbing her, seeming to seep into every corner of what remained of her former self.

Soon it will reach my brain, and I will be engulfed.

A man and woman were talking.

'How are the others this morning?'

'They are peaceful, only this one is fretful.'

'Are they all being treated within the guidelines?'

'Of course.'

She managed to move her head slowly from side to side and tried again to speak, but although she moved her lips she could make no recognisable sound and the effort made her gasp.

She sensed the man leaning over her, watching. 'I gave her the usual dose. Why doesn't she respond like the others?'

She felt his breath on her face. He lifted her eyelid and shone a light directly into her eye. 'Check her pulse.'

There was a pause, then she felt the light touch of the woman and heard her murmur. She was now desperate for breath, and for them to realise that she knew they were there. She failed to open her mouth again and inhaled noisily through her nose.

'She's panicking. Her heart is racing. I'll give her another dose.'

She heard a chair being dragged towards her bed. The man took her hand in his and placed his head close to her ear. 'I know you are frightened, but there is no need. We are going to make all the pain and anxiety go away and you will feel wonderfully relaxed.'

She felt something tug at her hand and the cold sensation began to course through her veins with a renewed purpose.

TWO

January 2006 Jason

Jason Brown, civil servant and recently promoted Director of Business Transformation, glanced with satisfaction at the view of the Thames from his new office. The river today was a dark sludgy-grey, and while he waited for his computer to fire up, he watched the activity on the busy waterway and ran his hands over the smooth leather and polished mahogany of his new desk. The quality and craftsmanship were lost on him; he only saw an expensive object in keeping with his status.

Barely two weeks into his promotion, he had ordered a complete breakdown of Department of Health spending, giving his staff an impossibly short deadline. Jason was an expert numbers man with a shrewd mind. His staff viewed him with a mixture of fear, respect and amusement. His dark eyes never missed a thing, and together with his demonic eyebrows, he was intimidating enough to make them jump to it and burn the midnight oil. It was his wife that unwittingly drove his ambition. She was a city banker and they had a lot of common aims, like no children or pets, and spreadsheets for everything. She earnt twice as much as he did, though, and his resentment made him power-hungry.

In front of him now were facts and figures that he could use to enhance his career.

All he needed was specialist help.

The whole issue will be a hot potato, though.

He scribbled a few figures on a pad, paused, then crumpled the paper into a tight ball with one hand and, with a well-practised aim, flicked it into his waste bin. The action always gave him great satisfaction.

He buzzed for his PA.

Andrew Gordon had recently left university and had a near-photographic memory. Normally, Jason hated graduates on principle, but he tolerated Andrew, whose gift was proving very useful.

Andrew knocked tentatively on the door and entered.

'Can you name a specialist in elderly care?' Jason asked, not taking his eyes off the computer screen.

'Professor Richard Hawley is a leading gerontologist and Government advisor on older people—' Andrew began.

'I've heard of him, but I don't know anything about him,' interrupted Jason.

'Well, he's been on TV a lot—'

'He'll provide kudos then. Find out everything you can about him for me, please, and put a report on my desk by tomorrow.'

THREE

January 2006 Richard

Richard Hawley was examining his face in the shaving mirror. It was part of his daily ritual to check for any early and unwelcome signs of ageing. Today, the early-morning sunshine in suburban Manchester filtered through the tree branches outside his bathroom window, creating distracting patterns.

No nasolabial folds, firm jawline, clear eyes.

He walked back into the bedroom he shared with his current girlfriend, a medical student and part-time model, twenty years his junior. He was drawn to women with youth and beauty, always moving on when it started to fade, and she bore a distinct likeness to his previous girlfriend.

Tall, blonde, slim, toned… young.

He looked at her sleeping peacefully, admiring the perfect symmetry of her facial features and the tantalising outline of her breasts, which rose and fell beneath the silk sheets as she breathed. He was tempted to return to bed to enjoy her perfection once again, but the importance of his gym routine came first, and he grabbed his kit bag and headed out.

As he pounded the treadmill he kept track of the display,

pushing himself harder, and was rewarded with a new personal best time. Wiping the sweat from his face he glanced around the gym at the other members. There were a few new faces, most of whom were out of shape and overweight. A large middle-aged woman in skin-tight top and leggings, which emphasised her rolls of fat, smiled at him. He returned her smile despite his distaste for what he saw and what it meant.

Why do they let themselves get so fat? She's obese. Type-two diabetes, high blood pressure, a total and unnecessary drain on health services.

There was another reason for his thoughts.

He was adopted shortly after birth. His new parents were doctors and they were both kind and affluent, introducing him and his sister to the finer things in life. He took this happy upbringing for granted and it was understood that he would follow his parents into medicine. Yet for some reason, in his early twenties, he decided to track down his birth mother. What he discovered had shocked and revolted him in equal part. He had traced her to a hostel and found she was both an alcoholic and a drug addict, who had not only given him up for adoption at birth but had also given up two further children. Although in her forties, she looked twice that age. Emaciated, her face skeletal, her skin grey and her few remaining teeth badly discoloured, she had been unable to remember the name of his father. He felt helpless in the face of such obvious self-destruction and found it hard to accept the reality of his blood family. He tried to help her, but he was way too late; she told him she didn't want to live any longer. She died shortly afterwards from a drug overdose.

He had tried to eradicate the memory, but it lay dormant in the dark recesses of his mind. By the middle of his medical training, he decided that he hated the ugliness of injury and disease. In his view, many of the cases brought into hospital were a result of unhealthy or dangerous lifestyles. His decision to specialise in elderly care might have seemed contradictory, but he realised his interests lay in researching approaches that would promote healthy ageing and then a dignified death, something he had been unable to do for his birth mother. His dedication had seen him rise to the top of his profession, a fact that gave him great self-satisfaction and made him appear more than a little pompous.

*

Richard switched off his reminiscences and focussed on the rest of his gym session in the weights room, then showered before driving into central Manchester for a meeting with one of the Government's most senior civil servants, Jason Brown.

They must be looking at something high-profile or sensitive if Brown is personally getting involved.

FOUR

Jason and Richard

Jason had arranged to meet Richard at a serviced apartment at the top of the Hilton Hotel on Deansgate. Richard took the lift to the forty-fifth floor.

Very clandestine, I'm intrigued.

Jason was waiting in the foyer to show him to the apartment. As they walked, they exchanged pleasantries about the great views from the panoramic windows and the Manchester weather, which was unusually sunny.

Richard disliked civil servants and found this social chit-chat both banal and insincere. When they were seated in comfortable sofas with glasses of Perrier water, he decided to cut to the chase. 'I know the minister would only send Jason Brown if the issue is sensitive,' he began. 'So, what's going on?'

Jason remained unruffled. 'Professor, you are an expert on all aspects of elderly care, so the minister wants you to be involved in a new project that needs to remain completely confidential. We have been looking at the implications of the rising number of elderly people and the cost to public services of caring for them. In ten years, seventy-five per cent of hospital beds will be occupied by them, preventing surgery taking place.'

He paused to sip his water and let his words sink in. 'The project is code-named Avalon, and one aspect will be looking at the way palliative care is delivered. We are aware of your academic work on the End of Life Pathway project and we think it will have great merit.'

Richard wanted to correct the man about the name. It had always been called the Palliative Care Pathway. He sensed that this was not just an oversight on Jason's behalf, but nevertheless, he spoke carefully. 'The Pathway was originally created as a programme of palliative care, divided into stages that could be monitored and the boxes ticked before moving on to the next stage. The irony is that, by its very nature, it became known as the End of Life Pathway.'

There was a pause, and he waited with curiosity for Jason's response.

'For some time now, there has been concern about the appropriateness and cost of keeping the elderly alive for an extra few weeks or months with mechanical and surgical interventions.'

Richard could see that the man was trying to gauge his reaction. 'It is common knowledge that I am an advocate of pro-choice euthanasia and a member of the group A Dignified Death.'

Jason's dark eyes bore into his. 'And less well known is the fact that you have been involved in the development of a new palliative care drug, Elysium.'

Richard was taken aback but held his cool. Of course, Jason would have done his homework and found out everything about him – everything. Elysium had recently been approved, but he shouldn't be seen to be using it exclusively, which was exactly what he had been doing.

After a moment, and with a slight nod of the head, Jason continued. 'The minister is very keen to get you involved from the outset. We need you to continue your work as you have been doing and provide us with case studies of the dosages given at each stage.'

Richard couldn't let this opportunity go to anyone else. It would herald the most important change in UK society's management of the elderly and the dying, and he wanted to be part of that. 'It sounds very interesting and I'm sure I could bring my knowledge to bear,' he ventured cautiously. 'Can I ask who I would be working with?'

'Well, actually we would be looking to you for suggestions. We need to keep things tight and under wraps, so it will be a very small team. You can imagine if the media were to get a sniff, all hell would break loose. So, can I tell the minister you are interested?'

'It would be a pleasure to become involved, Jason.'

As the men shook hands, Jason Brown smiled at a task accomplished.

'Great stuff, Richard, I'll be in touch.'

Richard, for his part, was stunned at the turn of events.

So, the Government finally realise that they have a problem to solve.

FIVE

April 2006 Dom

Dom Maxwell glanced around the prestigious suite on the top floor of The Gherkin in the heart of the City and felt a buzz as his adrenaline kicked in. Most people hated public speaking or giving presentations; not Dom – he positively thrived on them.

Prepare well, dress well and know your subject inside out.

Over the last two years, Dom had been the property developer behind Summerlands, a luxury retirement complex. Today was about securing funding to build a further two and the invited audience were hopefully going to provide it.

He had planned his presentation meticulously. He would explain the commercial opportunity presented by a large and growing number of healthy and wealthy older people. He had drawn on the comprehensive data provided by the well-known and well-regarded Professor Richard Hawley to quantify the size of the market opportunity. To add gravitas to the project, he had asked Richard to join him on the board from the start, two years ago.

Dom checked his tie and buttoned the jacket of his Armani suit which covered a toned stomach, courtesy of lengthy workouts at the gym. He was a handsome man in his late thirties, well over six foot, with a classic profile, blue eyes and a full head of curly dark hair.

'Ladies and gentlemen, thank you for your time today. Let me introduce you to Summerlands, a luxury proposition for retirees wanting to "downsize without compromise".'

He pointed to a screen and a video began to the strains of 'The Flower Duet'. Dom had deliberately chosen this British Airways television commercial classic to set the scene and denote a strong and trustworthy brand. It worked. He had the audience's full attention straight away. The video began by showing an aerial view of Summerlands in mid-Cheshire. Central to the complex was a lake with an island. Properties around the lake were built into the hillside to preserve the countryside setting. The camera panned through large rooms, tastefully decorated in creams and pale greens, to bathrooms and kitchens with top-of-the-range fittings. A lift glided from the basement garage to upper floors, where from the opulent living room you could stroll onto a balcony with a hot tub discreetly housed in one corner.

Other properties set further back from the lakeside were single-storey and were built at angles around landscaped gardens to ensure total privacy. They too enjoyed the same level of interior luxury.

The audience appeared captivated. Dom had been watching their reactions throughout the video and he knew he was winning them over. He thought of how proud his mum and dad would be to witness this.

I owe this idea to them. They wanted to downsize without compromise too.

The facilities available to residents came next, a soothing voice extolling the virtues of each one. 'As you can see, there is a state-of-the-art leisure complex with a pool and gym, and a range of classes are timetabled each week. And finally, we have The Retreat, which, as its name suggests, is a place where people can take time out and recuperate if they become ill. It is managed by our own on-site medical team who have been recruited to provide the very best of care and who have access to the latest in medical developments.'

The audience watched as an older woman, dressed in a designer tracksuit, walked confidently out of the gleaming glass doors of The Retreat, waving farewell to smiling nurses, who waved back.

'This team is led by Professor Richard Hawley, who has acted for some years as the Government's advisor on healthy ageing.'

Dom gestured towards Richard Hawley, who was sitting on the front row. Richard stood and turned to face the audience and, with a short bow of acknowledgement, offered a nugget of information they would all remember: 'In my opinion, old age doesn't begin until eighty.'

The audience became animated at this statistic, smiling and scribbling notes at the same time. It combined evidence of a compelling commercial opportunity with a positive feeling amongst those listening that they had many more good years ahead of them.

Now he had their attention, Dom moved on to the facts and figures he had put together, profiling the wealthy clients the company targeted and the cost of living the Summerlands lifestyle. This was the detail that his potential investors needed.

As he looked around the room he was surprised to see many of the audience already had calculators on top of their slide packs and were using them.

He felt a surge of adrenaline as he realised his presentation had hit the mark.

'I'd like to thank you all again for your time today, and if you need any further information, please do get in touch.'

On cue, the lights came on as the automatic blinds rose to reveal the London skyline, its glass-fronted buildings in the city glistening in the midday sun.

As the audience made their way to the lifts, Richard came up and slapped him on the back. 'Cracking presentation Dom. Celebratory lunch?'

SIX

Richard and Dom

Richard and Dom's taxi pulled into a cobbled courtyard in front of the restaurant, where people were seated outside, drinking champagne in the spring sunshine. Richard paid the driver and Dom followed him across the yard to an ivy-covered doorway. He obviously knew the place.

'Best food and wine in the City,' said Richard as they were shown to a table.

The maître d' was chatting to him like an old friend, so Dom looked around. The walls were oak-panelled and the chairs a mixture of red leather and burgundy velour. Crisp white tablecloths and shining silver cutlery lightened the ambience a little, but to Dom, the place had the touch of a bordello about it. Richard looked very at home in these surroundings and Dom had to control the urge to laugh at the implications of this thought.

'I've never had a bad meal here, Dom. It's spot-on for a celebration after this morning's success.'

There was a pause while they ordered, then Dom replied, 'Yes, today felt really good. I like presenting and I honestly think Summerlands is a brilliant concept, and that makes selling the story so much easier. It's a great business model.'

'And it's a growing market, which makes investment so attractive.'

The restaurant was now filling up, predominantly with businesspeople from the City. There was a buzz about the place that seemed to ooze success and Dom couldn't help thinking that its patrons would, in future years, be ideal prospects for Summerlands.

'So, Summerlands Cheshire is almost sold out, Dom?'

'That's right. To be honest, I'm amazed it went so quickly. We pitched the prices at the top of what we thought we could achieve, and it doesn't seem to have put people off. The only ones who have brought up the issue of costs are their families.'

Richard put down his knife and fork and placed his hands on the table. 'Dom, would you expect anyone to tell you where you can live or how to spend the money you've earnt? Of course not. So why, just because people are older and in the final decades of their life, should anyone else tell them what to do with their hard-earned cash?'

Dom smiled. He recognised Richard's television persona being played back to him. 'I totally agree, but I have been surprised at some of the uncomfortable conversations I've had with relatives who obviously had plans for what they thought they would inherit.'

Richard put down his fork. 'The present elderly generation suffered the after-effects of two world wars and learnt to save and work hard. Their reward was buying and owning their own property.' He was on his soapbox now. 'After the Second World War there was a surge in property prices and investments… and births. Those born in the years after World War Two are known as the baby boomers. They were born at just the right time to benefit from a dramatic increase in property prices and their wealth increased, with not a lot of effort on their part. But the next generation has not fared so well, with stock market crashes and a series of recessions. They look to their parents and sometimes their grandparents for money.'

'I hadn't really appreciated this,' said Dom, feeling as if he had been on the receiving end of a short history lesson. 'I guess it was before my time.'

A slight frown crossed Richard's face at this backhanded assessment of his age, and Dom thought him a little vain.

Shortly after Richard had called for the bill, he checked his phone and stood up. 'Sorry, Dom. Something's come up. Can I leave you to settle?' He shook Dom's hand and, as he left, shook hands with the maître d' before pointing towards Dom. Richard had ordered the best of everything and the bill, when it arrived, was eye-watering, even by the standards Dom was used to.

Richard Hawley, you know how to play the game.

SEVEN

2006 Roberta

Roberta Kenyon, one of Richard's baby boomers, was at this moment sailing the Caribbean seas with the new man in her life, Danish skipper Jan Larsen. No longer did she have to put the needs of others before her own. She had brought her children up single-handed, and now they were grown up and independent. Her elderly mother was thousands of miles away. She felt free for the first time in her life.

When Jan had invited her to sail with him, she didn't have to think twice. Jan was single and a handsome forty-six-year-old. Roberta was forty-eight and her life so far had been a failed marriage, bringing up her two children and working as an artist to pay the bills, with the care of her elderly mother looming on the horizon.

Roberta looked at the handsome Dane and couldn't believe her luck; she was falling in love with him fast.

This is my time.

*

Jan glanced at Roberta. He was becoming quite fond of her. Her light brown hair tumbled past her shoulders, bleached in streaks by the sun. She had a curvaceous figure and looked stunning in or out of a bikini, yet she seemed unaware of this. She showed a childlike fascination with everything to do with sailing. He had travelled with a good number of female companions on his yacht, and they usually became tired of the Spartan life and the lack of modern amenities.

Jan was taking his yacht south. They were sailing downwind and it was almost unbearably hot on the deck. He explained to Roberta that the speed of the boat cancelled out the breeze, but she didn't really understand. With the sails set, there wasn't much else to do. They sat in the cockpit under the shade of the Bimini and, in this enforced intimacy, told each other about their lives.

'I don't know much about Denmark, to be honest,' confessed Roberta. 'Bicycles and hippies spring to mind.'

Jan laughed. 'Yes, Denmark is very flat. The hippies are now one of the tourist attractions in Copenhagen; they live in a government-free town called Christiania, where cannabis is openly sold.'

'How did you come to be sailing like this?'

'All of Denmark is near the coast. My father worked in shipbuilding and we always had a sailing boat in Skudehavnen.' Jan smiled in reminiscence. 'I took maritime studies, then I went to work on big sailing yachts as crew, then I bought my own boat.'

'I envy your upbringing,' said Roberta.

'Yes, it was happy, wasn't yours?'

'Oh dear, how can I explain middle-class English parents like mine in the 1950s and '60s, especially regarding daughters. They stifled our voices with old-fashioned values, yet we were supposed to make more of ourselves than they did. Make money and marry well. I got pregnant, anyway, at eighteen and had to leave college. This is my first experience of independence.'

'Oh, Roberta, how sad,' teased Jan. 'In Denmark, our children have an independent voice from very young. Then the state looks after everyone, young and old, and there is no very rich or poor. But we Danes do pay fifty per cent tax for this.'

'Sounds like you've got it right in Denmark.'

'Yes, it's supposed to be the best country to live in, apart from the weather. But Danes, they just dress for the weather, like you and me now.'

They were both naked, and Jan reached over to Roberta and pulled her down onto the cockpit floor, stopping her from talking further with his kisses.

*

When they made landfall, Roberta was surprised that the marina was fenced, with security guards at the gates.

'Why hasn't it been like this at any of the other islands we've been to?'

'This island has oil, and that means very rich and very poor people,' said Jan. He seemed to know a lot of locals and was often out 'trading cargo', as he called it. He didn't elaborate and didn't seem to like too many questions being asked.

Roberta took his explanations at face value. Everything had to be imported to these islands and it stood to reason that Jan was fetching and carrying things to earn a bit of money. She didn't like to go out of the marina on her own, though.

Eventually, they set off for a long trip north. Roberta sat in the cockpit watching the sun sink into the sea, followed by a burst of pink and red streaks like brushstrokes that spread across the sky and reflected in the water. Darkness fell quickly in the Caribbean, and as she lingered, watching the last of the colours fade, she became aware of the lights of a small powerboat. 'My God, they're heading straight for us!' Roberta was becoming increasingly alarmed.

'Not to worry, these are my friends. I want you to go into the cabin and wait. It'll be safest for you.'

Roberta heard the boat moor up alongside them. There followed a lot of rocking and scuffling as something was loaded on board the yacht and transferred to the aft cabin. At last, the movement stopped, and she heard the outboard engine splutter, start up, then fade into the distance.

This feels too, too familiar.

Roberta's ex-husband Will had been involved in more than a few shady dealings during the time they had been married and she had learnt it was better not to know the facts. It was a long time ago, but she didn't want to go back there.

She felt angry and helpless. She was having the best time of her life, but she had been unconsciously tuning out any bad vibes – a coping strategy that she had developed over her years with Will but wasn't aware of. Now she was.

Smuggling?

Why do I always fall for plausible rogues?

Jan was busy starting the boat engine once more as Roberta stormed up the ladder to the cockpit. 'Jan, I can't live with this kind of fear.'

'I'm sorry, but how do you think I make the money to keep my boat?'

'I will get off this boat when we land.'

And, despite Jan's pleading, she refused to discuss it for the rest of the trip.

EIGHT

2006 Rosie

Rosie stirred at the gentle ring of a bell which brought her back from a sense of profound relaxation. She breathed deeply and inhaled the aroma of expensive oils that enveloped her. Back in England, she had been a regular at her local beauty salon, but this experience was something else. In fact, everything about the Emirates Palace in Abu Dhabi was something else. Simon had secured a job here as a cardiologist and his employers had provided them with a suite at this prestigious hotel while they found a suitable villa or apartment. The hotel was indeed a huge palace with more staff than residents and every luxury you could wish for. It was the most opulent-looking building she had ever seen, decorated with gold and marble throughout. Each guest had a personal butler that catered for their every need and were transported around the grounds on golf buggies. Everything about her current circumstances felt like a dream.

The soothing voice of her therapist interrupted her thoughts. 'Madam, the treatment is finished. I will leave you to put on your robe and I will be back in a few minutes. Take your time.' With that, the tiny Filipino therapist quietly left the room.

As Rosie lay on the bed and again inhaled the expensive scent of oud which provided a subtle backdrop to the subterranean spa complex, she felt strangely insecure.

This is too good to last. Something will go wrong; someone will need me.

One of my sons, who should be independent? Or my mum, who is getting old?

Rosie got up and put on the soft white robe just as the therapist returned with a tray of herbal tea and an envelope. 'A message for you, madam.'

Rosie thanked her and opened the envelope, which contained a note from Simon.

Will be back by six. Have booked us into Le Vendome for eight. Hope you are having a lovely day.

Thoroughly relaxed, she wandered back to their hotel suite, which was also decorated in traditional Arab style, the walls adorned by elaborate artwork and needlework. She lay on the bed and sank into its cool softness, thinking how her life had changed.

Last year I was in a loveless marriage to a man I clearly didn't know.

Tears unexpectedly trickled down her face onto the pillow and self-doubt dogged her.

Adding to her feelings of foolishness was the knowledge that David was now wanted by the police and seemed to have disappeared off the face of the earth. Surely someone knew where he was.

A gentle knock on the door disturbed her thoughts. She wiped away her tears. 'Come in.'

Jashmin the butler entered carrying a tray of sweets and her favourite cappuccino. 'Shall I put the tray on the balcony, madam?'

Rosie smiled and nodded at the young man. He looked immaculate in his freshly laundered white dish-dash, his neatly trimmed beard and, in common with all the staff who encountered the guests, a slight but subtle hint of an expensive scent.

She watched as he placed the tray on an ornate table, before quietly leaving the room.

She picked up the paperback she was halfway through reading

and walked out onto the balcony. She settled herself on the huge daybed, keeping her head in the shade of a billowing white canopy, and looked out over the gold balustrade at the view. The sand on the man-made beach was as smooth as a velour carpet, kept that way by a team of beach boys whose job was to remove any intrusive stone or footprint. Beyond the perfect sand, the turquoise sea was crystal-clear and merged at the horizon with a cloudless blue sky. As if on cue to make the scene perfect, a school of dolphins swam the length of the bay, breaking the surface as they leapt in and out of the water. Even her favourite cappuccino was sprinkled with twenty-four-carat gold flakes. She absentmindedly scooped them off the top as her thoughts turned to Hugo, the younger of her two sons. He had phoned a couple of weeks ago asking if she could lend him ten thousand pounds for a business venture. Unfortunately, or maybe fortunately, the money her father had left her in his will was tied up in a bond, so she was unable to help him. Hugo had suggested she ask Simon. She had declined, and the call had ended badly.

I see David in Hugo, always driven by money and possessions.

Then as she viewed her opulent surroundings, she felt just a little hypocritical at her analysis of Hugo and his love of all things material. This perpetual holiday was very enjoyable, but not enough for her if she and Simon were going to be here for some years.

She turned her thoughts to Simon; he was so attentive. A good-looking man with greying blond hair. Earnest, decent, dedicated, not the sort you noticed – not in your teens, anyway. She'd known him for years but never really considered him in a romantic way till they'd holidayed together at Christmas. Then the dynamics between them had quickly changed to friendship, and then love.

This relationship feels different, a meeting of minds and souls, yet here I am again, financially dependent on a man, why?

Her book dropped into her lap unopened as her thoughts turned to her first marriage and how it began.

*

I was the only child of older parents, their late blessing. Lots of love and attention and always a Daddy's girl. But I was cushioned and naive and so unprepared for the real world. No wonder I fell for David's seduction. Pregnant at eighteen, what a fool. He saw me as an asset, the right upbringing, and as he climbed the corporate ladder, I enjoyed the material benefits too. My parents thought I had married well, if only they had known the reality. I'm not sure Mum would have wanted to know; her daughter's affluent lifestyle went down well at her WI. Thank heavens for the Women's Refuge; it gave me a purpose. Those poor women and children lived each day in fear of their men. I only had to put up with indifference.

Her book dropped to the ground, breaking her thoughts of the past and she revisited her earlier thoughts.

I have never had to worry about money and I still don't have to now. Am I a kept woman again? But Simon is nothing like David.

*

Later that evening, as she and Simon ate lobster in Le Vendome, Simon talked excitedly about his job as Director of Cardiology at the new purpose-built hospital. He was full of enthusiasm for the role and the opportunities it presented. Rosie loved the way he shared his world with her, something her errant husband had never done.

'Did you know that in the UAE, as many people die from heart attacks as die on the roads? They eat too much and drive everywhere. It's a cardiac ticking time-bomb. Which reminds me. I have something that may be of interest to you. The sheikh whose foundation funds the hospital is setting up a charity, Al Wahah, to help people with addictions to drugs and alcohol. Many of the potential patients will be expats and I thought you might be interested in getting involved? No pressure, you can be a lady who lunches if you prefer?' Rosie saw him raise an eyebrow as he said it; he knew her so well.

'Simon, you've read my mind. It sounds exactly the sort of thing I'd love to get my teeth into.'

NINE

2006 Sandra

It was a bright spring morning. Sandra was drinking coffee in her living room and studying a glossy Summerlands information pack. She had applied for a job there because she needed something more than her dog kennels to occupy her. She felt bereft and was missing a deeper meaning to her life.

The shared experiences of old friends?

I wonder if Roberta and Rosie will ever forgive me.

From her window she could see the activity in the yard and hear the dogs barking as her staff went through their morning routine. The kennel business had grown, and these days her manager Dawn and a succession of school leavers ran it so efficiently that she wasn't really needed. It had been her long-term plan to be away more. Now she was back in the UK, her lover David had done a runner and she felt very alone.

It seemed incredible now that she had been having an affair for over thirty years with the husband of one of her best friends. True, it had started before David and Rosie married, but then it had just carried on. Rosie and David were never a convincing couple, anyway; their marriage seemed a lifestyle choice for both.

And that's my justification, I suppose.

She knew she had behaved badly. What was once exciting and liberating now seemed tawdry.

You reap what you sow.

*

Sandra had expected to be called to interview.

After all, I'm grossly overqualified for this job.

As she drove the short distance from her house, she realised that she knew very little about Summerlands, apart from the brochure. What had appealed to her was that it was a luxury retirement complex with state-of-the-art medical facilities. Now, as she approached the imposing entrance, she could feel her confidence draining away.

At the gate, there was a lodge with a sexy-looking uniformed guard who checked her credentials and allowed her to pass. She felt on unfamiliar territory and unable to banter with him as she would normally have done. She swore under her breath as she drove through a lawned area, past a lake with luxurious villas, then through a collection of smaller housing with gardens and courtyards, ending up at what looked like the main administration building.

Hell's teeth; talk about posh.

She parked her ten-year-old car discreetly out of view, and entered a glassed atrium, stocked with exotic plants. She eventually located a reception desk at the far side with an elegant woman behind it.

'Please take a seat, Ms Marsden.'

Sandra walked over to a group of settees arranged around a marble-topped coffee table. She sank gingerly into the overstuffed cushions on the nearest one. A collection of magazines was rigidly arranged on the table: *Cheshire Life, Horse and Hound, Tatler*. Everything was brand new and screamed 'money' at her.

'Can I offer you some tea or coffee?' droned the receptionist, not even looking up.

'No, thanks,' Sandra replied. A drink always posed problems, better not.

Fortunately, at that moment, a young woman opened an internal door into the reception and addressed her directly. 'Ms Marsden?'

Sandra stood up, mesmerised. She was suddenly unsure of herself; her hands felt clammy and sweat broke out at her hairline. The woman before her was exquisite. Tall and slender, she looked to be in her late thirties with a mix of East Asian and European blood that she found disturbingly exotic. Sandra felt her large, expressive brown eyes drawing her in.

Jesus Christ, I feel like I'm on a date.

She straightened her shoulders and mentally pulled herself together as the woman smiled, and the spell was broken. 'I'm Yume Yamamoto,' she said simply, in perfect English. 'Please come this way.'

Sandra followed her, along pristine corridors that she felt could do with some of Roberta's paintings.

Yume stopped ahead of her, pointing her to the manager's office. 'In here, please.'

Like everywhere else so far, the room was luxuriously furnished too. Sandra cast a practised eye over the layout, starting with the leather-topped desk, high-backed swivel chair and formal chairs at the front and side of the desk. It also helped her regain her cool.

Staff briefings and interviews here, then...

A sofa and chair were grouped around a low table with a box of tissues positioned in the centre. A drinks machine stood next to them.

...meetings with relatives and residents over here?

Sandra thought of her early nursing experience and the spartan rooms at the Manchester Royal Infirmary that were designated as family waiting rooms. She wanted to work here in this luxury, and she wanted to find out more about the enigmatic Yume. She was introduced to Paul Drury from HR and Nicky Grimes, the manager of Summerlands. Then Yume was introduced again as Dr Yamamoto.

She's a doctor?

Sandra struggled not to show her surprise.

Nicky was a large woman with a cheerful smile who plonked herself on the swivel chair and gestured for Sandra to sit across the desk from them all.

The interview progressed. Paul gave a brief outline of the scope of the Summerlands project and the job specification. He then focussed on Sandra, asking questions about her background and experience. There was a difficult moment when Paul wanted to question her in detail about the time she was struck off the nursing register in the 1980s, but Nicky seemed intent in steering him away from the subject.

'This part of the interview is concluded,' said Paul, whose face clearly showed that it wasn't as far as he was concerned. 'Can you accompany Dr Yamamoto to The Retreat, where she will explain the medical services we provide.'

They all shook hands and Sandra left the room, following Yume again. They had barely got out of the door when they heard Paul's indignant tones.

'Why did you stop me asking more about her conviction for stealing drugs? Surely that's important?'

To Sandra's surprise, Yume put her hand to her mouth, trying and failing to suppress a giggle. She motioned Sandra to get away from the room till they could not be heard, then stopped and turned to face her. 'I'm so sorry, so unprofessional of me,' she whispered. 'I've done a lot of interviews with Paul and he goes by the book, which is fine, but Nicky and I look for qualities that are not mentioned in the tick boxes and you have them in spades.'

She carried on walking, and Sandra fell in step with her.

'You have the right qualifications and expertise, but more importantly you show resilience. So, you took drugs twenty years ago? You made your way back and you were reinstated. You are a strong woman.'

To the surprise of them both, Sandra's eyes filled with tears.

'Don't worry, Nicky and I want you.'

Sandra made her way back to the reception after a tantalising half hour, checking her knowledge of the equipment whilst checking the vibes between them. She felt distracted and wasn't at all sure how the interview had gone. She had a strong feeling, though, that she would be offered a job. She had felt the silent sisterhood of understanding from Nicky, and as for Yume… She uncurled her fingers and looked at the piece of paper that she had pressed into her hand. It was a phone number.

TEN

Roberta

Roberta's time on Jan's yacht was coming to an end. Jan had said that all being well, they would make landfall sometime the following day. She took turns at the helm and produced meals and drinks from the tiny galley, all the while plagued with conflicting emotions. One minute she hadn't ever wanted to leave Jan; but he seemed to have ignored her ultimatum and her feelings. Her new-found pride would not let her back down, and a terrible silence had developed between them. Now she couldn't wait to go.

On the last night, she woke abruptly. The ship's VHF radio was making spluttering noises and she jumped as a loud, disembodied voice called Jan's boat's name. As she raised her head, she saw Jan spring into action as if he had been scalded. In one fluid motion, he turned from the helm, grabbed the cargo from the aft cabin and heaved it over the side of the boat into the sea. No sooner had he completed the task, a fast powerboat came into view and a spotlight was trained on them.

'Po-lice! Stop your boat an' we board you.'

Jan acted cool as he motioned to Roberta to stay down below. He then put out the anchor and prepared for the police launch to come alongside.

'I'm fed up of being kept down here,' Roberta shouted to him. Her indignant face appeared at the top of the steps, then she saw two policemen climb into the cockpit, armed and unsmiling, their guns glinting in the beam of the spotlight. She gasped and vanished back down.

One of them pointed his weapon at Jan. 'So, it's you, Viking. Whassup tonight?'

The other looked in the cabin and saw Roberta. 'American white leedy?'

'Actually, I'm English,' squeaked Roberta with as much voice as she could muster.

'My, oh my, we was once your slaves, preety leedy,' he sneered, smacking his lips to frighten her.

'Your passports,' shouted the first one, and when Roberta had them in her hand, he motioned with his gun for her to come up on deck and give them to him. He kept the gun pointed at them both. The other began to search the deck, throwing stuff about; he then went to the aft cabin and did the same. In the main cabin, they heard him opening cupboards and emptying containers into the sink. After about an hour, when he had not found what he was looking for, he became angry and started smashing things up down below. The noise he made was horrendous.

Jan's face remained expressionless, his eyes looking ahead. Roberta was terrified and wet her shorts.

Eventually, he returned to the cockpit and both policemen stood in menacing postures, their white teeth gleaming in the dark.

'Okay, we know somethin' goin' up t'night. We have powerboat crew grassing you up right now, man. You're comin' in with us. You too, leedy.'

Roberta and Jan had their hands cuffed behind their backs, then they were manhandled to the edge of the cockpit and roughly thrown onto the deck of the police launch. With no hands free to break his fall, Jan gave a practised roll as he landed, but Roberta hit her head and was knocked unconscious.

*

Roberta woke on the floor of a wooden shack that was empty except for a desk and two chairs. A fly-coated fan whirred lazily in the ceiling, doing little to combat the humidity. In the dim light from an equally filthy bulb, she discovered she was spattered with dried blood.

She sat up slowly and vomited. Her head swam as she painfully lay down again.

'Well, darlin'. You a mess.' A grinning face pushed itself close to hers. 'Come, clean up.'

The woman helped Roberta slowly to her feet and walked her out of the door, onto a veranda and into another room with a grimy toilet and washbasin.

At least the towel and soap are clean.

As she washed, she could hear the woman mopping the floor next door.

'Sorry.'

'S'okay, darlin'. Dem men is rough.'

When Roberta had finished, she was taken back into the first room. A different policeman was sitting at the table and he motioned her to take the other chair. A glass of water was placed in front of her which she drank greedily.

Then the interrogation began.

'How long you know Jan Larsen?'

It soon became apparent that Roberta knew nothing of Jan's activities, and the policeman changed tack to focus on her status. 'We take boat. Without boat, you ain't crew. You must buy return plane ticket now,' he ordered firmly.

'Where is Jan?' asked Roberta.

'Either you go with him to jail, or you go home now. You choose, leedy.'

*

As soon as it was light, Roberta was escorted to a travel agent by the grinning policewoman. The travel shop was grubby and hot. The woman at the desk was clearly used to the situation and, while she exchanged polite greetings with the policewoman, she ignored Roberta with her foul, slightly stinky clothes. She kept her at arm's length throughout the interview and maintained an air of hostility and mistrust, asking monosyllabic questions and completing the paperwork at a snail's pace.

Despite her situation, Roberta was fascinated by this little interplay. *She doesn't know what I've done, but clearly I have been classified as a bad 'un.*

Once out in the fresh air, though, her amusement disappeared and she felt groggy, bruised and generally badly done-to. The policewoman was kind, though, and a couple of hours later she had showered and had some clean clothes and a little to eat and drink.

'I'd better phone someone at home.'

The policewoman took her to an internet café, another stifling room without air-conditioning. Roberta missed the sea breeze, the only thing that kept the temperature bearable in these islands.

She was surprised to see an email from her sister. She knew immediately it would be about her mother. Her sister didn't email her about anything else. She also knew it would be bad news.

'Mother has had a fall and has been diagnosed with osteoporosis. She is in St Joseph's Hospital, which is a long drive for me to visit every day. I'll put her address at the bottom of this email, and you can phone the ward on this number. I don't expect she will be able to look after herself when she comes out and I can't have her here, I'm still working. She will have to go into a home. When are you coming back?'

Roberta felt a weight descend on her shoulders; her new life had ended abruptly in more ways than one.

You pay a price for everything. Jan is right: this life has a cost.

The computer had Skype and Roberta was soon connected to the ward that her mother was in.

'Mummy, it's Roberta.'

'What did you say? Who?'

'It's Bobbie,' said Roberta. She hated her pet name, but the family still used it.

'Yes, where are you? Aren't you on a boat somewhere?'

'Yes, Mummy, I'm in the Caribbean. What's happened?'

'I can't hear properly. There's a group of nurses talking and laughing near me. Be quiet! My daughter is phoning from the Caribbean and it's expensive.'

'It's okay, Mummy. It's only one point four pence a minute, I'm using Skype.'

'You're what? When are you coming back?'

*

Roberta was feeling wretched. She had loved everything about Jan and the life that he led. Jan was a free spirit. He worked admirably hard on his boat, and he had an infectious zest for the sailing life. He was easy-going, thoughtful and kind. She had only ever lived with her ex-husband Will, and she didn't have much experience of different relationships; but Jan had his shady activities, like Will.

But there the resemblance ends.

Jan would never be deliberately cruel to her like Will. And he was so handsome and sexy. She steeled herself to stick to her guns.

Later, waiting at the airport with the policewoman still dogging her steps, she allowed herself to weep for the happiness she had found and abruptly lost.

ELEVEN

Rosie

Rosie touched up her lipstick as the Lexus purred up the sweeping drive of the Al Wahah clinic. Simon's driver, Rashid, took her here each day. The clinic provided treatment for drug and alcohol addiction, a problem that was becoming an increasingly large aspect of life in the Emirates. The patients were mostly expat executives who had overdone the excesses that a tax-free salary afforded, bored expat wives and young people from wealthy Emirati families with lots of money and time to spend on booze and cocaine.

Rosie loved working there. She had found her niche and was able to use the expertise she had gained from running the Refuge.

But what a contrast this is to the lives of those women.

'We are here, madam. Shall I pick you up at the usual time this afternoon?'

As she got out of the car, the heat of early summer hit her in a sharp blast. Looking up at the ever-perfect blue sky, Rosie felt a sense of contentment as she considered her good fortune.

'Yes, thanks, Rashid. Same time as usual, please.'

Walking through the ornate Arabian arch at the entrance to

the clinic's central courtyard, she stopped to appreciate the cooling sound of water cascading from four fountains into a square pool. The calm environment was a contrast to the chaotic lives of the patients who came to Al Wahah to get clean, and most of the patients would spend part of their day sitting there and perhaps contemplating.

Rosie's reveries were disturbed by one of her colleagues, another Brit called Gail. 'Hey, Rosie! You and Simon up for brunch this Saturday? Richard has chartered a boat again and we plan to have a party on board.'

Rosie turned towards the tall, striking blonde woman, who could be mistaken for a Scandinavian with her fair hair and blue eyes. Despite having had three children, Gail still looked good in a bikini and would no doubt be sporting a little La Perla number on Saturday. Rosie liked her very much. She was good company, had a wicked sense of humour and could always be relied upon.

'Count us in. Simon and I still talk about your last brunch party, although, note to self, I must not drink too much in this heat!'

As the two women walked to their office, Rosie's mobile phone rang and, glancing at the caller ID, she saw it was her son Theo. He didn't normally phone and a sense of unease overcame her.

'Hi, Mum, just phoning to say hello and to let you know I got that job in Manchester.'

The unease melted away and was replaced by delight for her eldest son. He was the quieter and the kinder of her two sons. He just got on with life, whilst his younger brother, Hugo, seemed to lurch from one money-making scheme to another, without any obvious success. Both lived in the family home in Cheshire, which meant at least it was occupied and, she hoped, looked after as well.

'Well done, darling. I knew how much you wanted that one, so I'm really pleased for you.'

Rosie turned to Gail, who had been all smiles as she listened to Rosie's side of the conversation.

'Well, that means we will definitely be celebrating this Saturday. There go my good intentions.'

*

The Saturday brunch was looking to be every bit as good as the last one, if not better. The boat was moored at Yas Marina, and was to set sail from there at ten-thirty am. The marina had been purpose-built to stage motor racing in the Emirates. Simon was a fanatic and Rosie knew this would make his day.

'We need to get there in good time so we can have a look around the circuit first.'

Rosie laughed at his boyish excitement.

Arriving early, with the sun already blazing hot in an intense blue sky, they walked around the marina to follow the track that was used each year for the Abu Dhabi Formula One.

Simon had a beaming smile like a child in a sweet shop. 'Look! That's the pit lane, and do you see that huge hotel over there? The track actually runs underneath it, and when the race is finished, it's illuminated like a black-and-white chequered flag!'

As the boat cruised out into the Gulf, the party went into the large air-conditioned cabin below deck to enjoy a brunch of steak, lobster, and a huge variety of salads and breads. While the men discussed F1, the women gathered around Gail, who was animatedly telling the story of a charity dinner she had attended in Dubai some weeks ago, held at the Burj Al Arab Hotel on Jumeirah Beach. She was showing them photos on her phone of the hotel's interior, explaining just how lavish it was, as was the food and the guests.

'I felt positively like Orphan Annie amongst these women.' She laughed.

Rosie thought that Gail could probably wear a bin liner and still look stylish.

Gail continued her tale. 'I'm not exaggerating, they all wore

317

designer dresses, shoes and carried designer handbags. Their husbands must work just to keep them in clothes!'

The phone was passed around, eventually reaching Rosie, who politely flicked through the pictures. Just as she was about to return it to Gail, she looked again at the last picture. In the background she saw a man who bore an uncanny resemblance to David, but this man had a beard. She looked again before dismissing it and passing the phone back.

Just at that moment, Simon arrived at her side with two glasses of pink champagne. Life was just perfect. Nothing was going to stop her from making up for the unhappiness of the last thirty years.

TWELVE

Roberta

Roberta came off the flight from Heathrow to Manchester, collected her luggage and took it through security. She had contacted Sandra, who was waiting for her at arrivals, anxious to make amends. Roberta had let her house out and was going to stay with her initially and see how they got on.

'Are old friends forgiven?' asked Sandra, straight to the point as usual. 'Let's get back to mine and talk about it.'

It was March, and although it was sunny there was a chill in the air. Sandra had organised a brunch on the table in front of the French windows, and Roberta felt immediately nostalgic at the sight and sounds of the kennels that Sandra ran as a business.

How quickly the other life is eclipsed.

Over lunch, they avoided the topic that hung between them and talked about tangible practicalities. Then the wine relaxed their inhibitions.

'Roberta, I'm really sorry that I left you alone with Will…' she began.

Roberta looked blank for a moment.

'You know… your ex-husband?'

I'd like to forget that my ex-husband kidnapped and raped me.

'It seems like another life,' murmured Roberta.

'I'm trying to apologise for that day. You interrupted Will helping David and me to run away together, but I didn't know the whole picture. I didn't know David was escaping from a police investigation as well.'

Roberta breathed a sigh as Sandra continued. 'I never gave it a thought that you weren't safe with Will.'

'It was selfish the way you just left me there. You were totally focussed on yourself and David.'

'It was only when David left me in the lurch that I realised what a bastard he was, and I had been a bitch.'

That's exactly what they all call you.

'So, you only realised what you had done when it hurt you? You are *so* self-centred.'

'Give me a break. I know I've looked after number one all my life, but what happened to you really hurt me and it's made me see that I do care about what effect I have on people, especially you. I want to make amends, even though it may be too late.'

'Sandra, the worst thing for me was thinking that you knew how David had abused his position at Sipher and falsified the drug trials for Svelta.'

'Jesus, I didn't know about it, I swear. Is that what everyone thinks? No wonder they hate me.'

'You're my oldest friend and I've always known you have a caring side. After all, how else could you be such a good nurse?'

'Roberta, you seem different, you're more confident somehow.'

'I've experienced a lot in the last six months. I've grown up, I've loved and lost. I'll tell you all about it.'

'Before you get started, I have to tell you something that you might find interesting for your mum. I've had an interview for a job at a retirement complex called Summerlands. They will buy your house, then you buy your own property there, and it has all the facilities for the older generation on one site, from when they are still active through to elderly care. It's expensive, but I'm wondering if there might be something that would suit Eva if she can afford it?'

'Now that *is* interesting,' said Roberta.

Sandra refilled their wine glasses. 'I've got a brochure here you can look at, but first, tell me all about your lover.'

*

Later that day, Roberta and her sister met at the door of the house where they both grew up. An Edwardian semi with attics and cellars, it seemed to have shrunk from the viewpoint that she best remembered it as a child. Inside it was chilly, and she thought it smelt of dust and old age.

Does old age have a smell?

Roberta was caught up in the nostalgia of familiar things: the furniture, the ornaments and pictures on the walls. It was all very 1960s and Danish style, she realised.

Her sister broke her reverie. 'I can't stay long; I've got to get back to work. Mother obviously must go into a home of some sort. I've had a look at the costs and it's not cheap.'

Roberta watched her sister's eyes roll, emphasising the element of cost.

'I've looked at a range of accommodation; it all depends how long Mother lives and how much we get for this place. I've arranged for a couple of valuations; they're booked in for next week.'

Roberta was taken aback at how impersonal her sister sounded.

I suppose this is the practicality of the situation.

'I've had a key cut for you so you can accompany the estate agents. Obviously, I can't do it as I'm still working full time.'

Roberta winced at her sister's barbed comment.

'No need to look like that, Bobbie. The fact is that while you've been swanning around the Caribbean, I've been at Mother's beck and call, *and* holding down a job.'

Roberta didn't have the energy for a row, so she changed the subject. 'The house could do with a good clean and some fresh air through the place. I'll make a start, but can you come over at the weekend to help?'

'Okay, Bobbie, good idea. Then we can decide what to do with her.' Roberta watched her sister sweep up her car keys and head for the door, continuing the conversation as she went. 'Oh, and by the way, why don't you visit Mother later this afternoon? Get a taxi.'

The door slammed shut, leaving Roberta stunned by her sister's attitude. She decided she'd put in a couple of hours' cleaning before visiting her mother. She rummaged through the musty-smelling cupboard under the sink, which contained a small selection of cleaning materials, the contents of which had dripped down the outside of most of the bottles.

When she got to her old bedroom, she opened the door gently and what she saw brought a lump to her throat. Still the same furniture and wallpaper that she had chosen all those years ago.

Life was so much simpler then, she thought, wiping away a tear. She knew the tables had turned. The thought depressed her.

I hope my daughter never has to feel like this.

THIRTEEN

Rosie

Rosie was awoken by the early-morning sun creating a pool of light through the billowing white drapes of the bedroom. It energised her for the day ahead and was such a contrast to the grey clouds of the UK. She stretched out her arm to touch Simon but felt only the cool sheets. A moment of unease gripped her until she heard the shower running and realised that he was already up and getting ready for work.

She got out of bed, put on her silk dressing gown and walked barefoot down the cool, tiled stairs towards the kitchen to make herself some breakfast. She could hear her mobile ringing, but it had stopped by the time she got to it.

Drat. Who can be phoning at this time?

She glanced at the screen and saw she had missed two previous calls from the same number. They were from the UK and she recognised the code as Amersham. Her mum Marjorie still lived there. Rosie felt a sense of dread begin to overwhelm her.

It's the middle of the night back home. Oh my God, what is happening there?

She saw that the caller had left a voicemail. Her hands were shaking as she retrieved the message; it was from her mum's next-door neighbour.

'Hello, Rosie. It's Doreen Robinson here. I don't want you to worry, but your mum has had a fall. Nothing's broken, but call me and I'll tell you the details.'

Rosie let out a deep sigh. She felt hugely relieved. She had feared far worse. She phoned Doreen, who picked up almost immediately. After a short exchange of pleasantries, Doreen explained that Marjorie had climbed onto a chair to get something from the top shelf of her Welsh dresser and had lost her balance and fallen. She had managed to crawl to the phone to summon Doreen, who decided to call an ambulance.

'As you can imagine, my dear, Marjorie didn't want to go to the hospital, but I convinced her she needed to be checked over. I went with her and stayed while she was X-rayed. The good news is there are no broken bones, but she is badly bruised, and they want to keep her in for observation. I'll visit again later and then phone you with an update.'

'Thank you so much, Doreen. I know how difficult Mum can be, so I am very grateful to you. I think I'll come back to the UK and see what help she needs.'

Rosie ended the call, made herself a comforting cup of tea and began considering the implications of the morning's news. First, she needed to phone the hospital. It sounded as if she could be away for a couple of weeks and that would throw a curveball into several things in her diary. She had been asked to give a presentation on her previous work at the Women's Refuge to a group looking to set up a similar service in the Emirates. This was scheduled for the coming week and she was really looking forward to the whole thing. It was her 'cause célèbre' and she was hoping that they might ask her to become involved.

Your timing is not helpful, Mum.

Then there was the weekend brunch, now a weekly event, that had become a mainstay of their social life. Sun, sea and excellent food – what was there not to like? She felt a tinge of resentment towards her mother for undermining it and immediately felt guilty.

No doubt it's raining in the UK as well.

Checking the time, she realised that Rashid the driver had returned from dropping Simon off and was waiting outside. She dressed hurriedly, grabbed her bag and dashed out the door.

It was mid-afternoon by the time she managed to speak to someone at the hospital and she groaned at the news. She would have to be away longer than she thought.

Back at home, she decided to phone Hugo and Theo and tell them she was coming to the UK. She tried Hugo's mobile first, but it went to voicemail, so she left him a message asking him to phone back.

And I bet he won't bother.

Her thoughts were interrupted by Simon's return. She turned to him with tears in her eyes and saw the look of concern on his face.

'Don't worry, I'm okay, but Mum is in hospital, I'll tell you all about it.' She relayed the day's events to him. 'I've spoken to the doctor this afternoon and apparently she hit her head when she fell and that is why they are keeping her in hospital for observation. When she comes out she'll need someone with her until she's back on her feet and can live independently.'

'Oh, dear. That's not what you wanted to hear, is it. Chin up, darling. We're a team and we'll sort it.'

Rosie wanted to cry. Simon was such a kind man.

'I'm going to go back and sort things out, Simon. It's my duty.'

Simon didn't say anything and just wrapped his arms around her. She buried her head in his shoulder and they stood there for several minutes holding each other close, a silent bond of understanding between them.

*

Marjorie was to be discharged the following Friday, so Rosie arranged to fly into Manchester where Theo would meet her and take her back to the family home. Here she could pick up some clothes more suited to the English climate and hopefully see Hugo, who still hadn't phoned back, before driving down to Amersham to pick up Marjorie from the hospital.

As she walked through into the arrivals hall at Manchester Airport, she caught sight of Theo waving widely. Her heart swelled with pride at what a lovely young man he had grown into.

'Hi, Mum, you look great! Here, give me your case. I just need to pay for the car park and then we can get going.'

Theo drove on the short trip from the airport to Chelford, so Rosie was free to appreciate anew the luscious green of the Cheshire countryside. As he turned the car up the sweeping drive to her old home, she felt the juxtaposition between her two lives. This house also represented years of a loveless marriage and contrasted in more than one way with what she had left behind in Abu Dhabi.

Theo opened the door and Rosie walked in. She looked around. It didn't feel like home anymore.

'Where's Hugo?'

Theo sighed. 'Probably in bed, he was late in last night. I'll give him a shout.'

Rosie wandered around the house, picking up photos she had long forgotten. There was one of her and David at a company party. It must have been at least ten years ago. As she looked at his face, she remembered the photo on Gail's phone taken in Dubai. She tried to recall the man who had reminded her of her missing husband, but her train of thought was interrupted by the sight of Hugo in his dressing gown, coming towards her, arms outstretched. A smell of stale cigarettes and booze wafted towards her. It had obviously been a heavy night. Maybe it was thinking about the photo or the fact that she hadn't seen him for a while, but she suddenly caught a glimpse of David in him.

'Lovely to see you, Mum. Sorry about Gran. What are you going to do with her?'

Hugo seemed a bit jittery, avoiding eye contact with her, and she wondered if he had been taking anything.

'Are you okay, Hugo?'

Just then, his mobile phone rang upstairs and a look of horror crossed his face before he turned and ran out of the door.

When Hugo eventually came down again, showered and dressed, he looked more presentable. They all chatted over coffee and caught up on jobs, girlfriends and the neighbours. Hugo was vague about still pursuing a 'range of business opportunities', whilst Theo was enjoying his new job in Manchester. Rosie tried to pin Hugo down with more questions, but she had missed the moment and his self-assured mask was firmly back in place.

I'll have to question him another time.

After filling a small suitcase full of clothes more suited to an English spring, Rosie loaded up her old VW and turned to her boys. 'I'll probably bring Grandma back up here next week. I think it will be easier to look after her here.'

She thought she caught a look of displeasure pass across Hugo's face.

'Okay, Mum,' said Theo. 'Let us know so we can get a room sorted for her.'

As she drove slowly down the gravel drive, she looked in her rear-view mirror and saw Theo waving. Hugo was nowhere to be seen.

FOURTEEN

Richard

At the Department of Health's colossal headquarters in London, Richard Hawley negotiated the revolving glass door with a flourish that attracted admiring glances from the four women behind the main desk. He was no stranger to the building and was aware that most people struggled with the doors, giving the receptionists repeated entertainment.

In their otherwise boring day.

The women continued to watch him as he walked across the atrium towards them. He knew he looked good: handsome face, toned body, well-cut suit, open-necked shirt, dark hair with a slight hint of grey at the sides and all topped off by a perfect white smile.

'Should be on a magazine cover,' murmured one, under her breath.

'Good morning, Professor Hawley. Here for the Pathway meeting?'

He held the receptionist's gaze a little longer than would be normal before replying, 'Yes, Chantelle. Usual room?'

Chantelle blushed at the mention of her name and looked down to confirm the room booking. 'The meeting is being held in Mr Brown's office,' she replied.

Richard smiled and ran a hand through his hair. All four looked at him with poorly disguised lust as he took his visitor's lanyard and put it on, making sure the lapels of his suit were undisturbed.

'Sex on legs,' whispered Chantelle to the others, who nodded their agreement. Their eyes continued to follow the charismatic professor through the automatic barriers and towards the lifts, oblivious of the next visitors waiting in line. A gentle cough and a sigh brought them back to earth and the mediocrity of their day.

Jason Brown's PA, Andrew, met him at the lift and escorted him to the office. 'Good morning, Professor. Black coffee?'

Richard was impressed at Andrew's extraordinary memory for matters both material and banal. He wondered briefly quite how far the young man's discretion went.

Hard to believe he doesn't know about the purpose of Avalon.

Jason stood up, shook Richard's hand and introduced him to two men sitting at the conference table with him. They all had computer screens in front of them.

'These guys have been seconded to Avalon from the Home Office. They have high-security clearance, obviously, and they're used to data analysis in highly sensitive projects.'

Richard greeted them warmly and shook hands, which contrasted sharply with their almost robotic demeanour; they barely looked up.

Accountants, humourless.

Richard had been used to the formality of previous Pathway meetings, however, and Jason Brown launched straight in. 'We have decided to keep a tight team for the Avalon project, so there will just be the four of us. We have reassigned "the lifers", as I call them, from the Palliative Care Pathway project to other activities, and we now have the people on board to allow us to push ahead.'

Richard was taken aback by Jason's scathing description of the original Pathway team and the way they had been summarily removed and reallocated. He thought particularly of Catherine Day. She had worked on the Pathway for several years and although they had often disagreed on things, she had always put the hours in.

He also recalled that Jason had said he would be looking to him, Richard, for team suggestions and realised that Jason had just been pandering to his ego and had no intention of asking his advice. He felt distinctly ruffled and underwhelmed by the meeting and the team, but he still badly wanted this opportunity to experiment further with Elysium, so he stayed silent.

Jason was speaking again, and he pushed his thoughts away to concentrate.

'Richard, let me outline the respective roles. Central to this project is going to be an analysis of current costs and this will be divided into two work streams. One will be looking at the costs associated with drugs, specialist equipment and specific interventions. The other will be looking at the impact of freeing up beds currently blocked by the elderly, making way for elective surgery on younger people who can then get back into the workplace and add to the tax take.'

There was silence as Richard realised that Jason was determining the direction the project was taking and he felt his expertise was being disregarded. But the moment passed, and his inflated ego re-established itself.

I am the only person in the country who can do this, and they know it.

Without looking up from his laptop or waiting for an answer, Jason continued. 'Richard. How is your work progressing with the use of Elysium?'

Richard glanced around the table at his three fellow team members, all fixated on the screens in front of them. He affected a cough to attract their attention; he was used to people hanging on his every word.

Jason looked up. 'Do you need a glass of water, Richard?' He pressed the intercom as he spoke. 'Andrew, a glass of water in here, please.'

Richard took a sip of the unwanted water and then began to explain. 'As you are aware, we have enhanced the palliative care in

Summerlands so that it includes the use of Elysium in incremental doses along the various stages. We have used it for all our patients who have been diagnosed as entering the final stages of their lives. The results have been completely in line with what we hoped for. So far, three patients are being managed in this way and none are experiencing any distress or pain.'

Richard looked at the others, expecting a reaction, but all he saw were inanimate faces.

Why are they not excited? Elysium will be a fundamental element in what is being proposed, and it's already demonstrating that it works well at The Retreat.

Jason closed his laptop and pushed back his chair, signalling the end of the meeting. 'Good, good. Next meeting in three weeks. Andrew will send you the details. We should have some initial data by then.'

What makes these people tick? They don't even recognise the ground-breaking nature of what's in front of them. The Retreat will be the model for end-of-life care in the future.

FIFTEEN

Yume and Sandra

Yume Yamamoto was sitting alone in a wine bar in Alderley Edge, a glass of viognier in front of her. She was thinking about how she came to England from Japan three years ago when her licence to practise medicine was withdrawn. Because of this she had felt an immediate empathy with Sandra Marsden during her interview that morning. If she was honest, though, she had been drawn towards the woman from the moment she saw her and was surprised and happy that Sandra had wasted no time in calling her. She sipped her wine and quietly assessed her reactions.

Sandra's unruly red hair, with an attempt to subdue it into a bun on the top of her head, spoke to her of a passionate nature barely held in check. Never mind the grey hairs threatening at the hairline; they just denoted experience. Her body was not slim, but it still had firm curves; her stance was confident, her blue-eyed gaze faintly challenging. She was not a beauty, but she was striking, and Yume thought she would like to get to know her better, right down to the vulnerable child inside her. She flushed and broke off from her delicious but dangerous reveries as the door of the wine bar swung open and Sandra entered. It was raining, and Sandra had an umbrella which was tricky to close, showering Yume's legs with droplets. They both laughed.

*

'That was a great interview for me,' said Sandra when she was seated with a drink ordered. 'I felt that you and Nicky were rooting for me, and Paul was trying to trip me up. Mind you, that's blokes for you, eh?'

'I liked your confidence; the fact that you had made a comeback in your career – that takes a lot of nerve. I know because I have been in the same position,' replied Yume.

Sandra turned to look at her directly. Yume was beautiful with her liquid brown almond-shaped eyes, like fathomless pools, her long jet-black hair, her slim figure. Sandra was taken aback by her honesty.

Yume reached her hand over and touched Sandra's arm. The gesture radiated empathy. 'I will tell you as briefly as I can, then you can tell me?' suggested Yume.

'Okay.'

'Well, at school in Tokyo I loved sciences, particularly chemistry and biology, so I went to university to study medicine. I specialised in geriatrics. I wanted to help people with end-of-life illnesses to have as dignified a death as possible. Many life-prolonging treatments are distressing for both patients and their relatives. In Japan, like here, euthanasia is illegal. So, I did my best to make a dying patient comfortable.'

She sipped her wine, her eyes focussed on the past. 'I never discussed my views, but people came to know of them anyway. One night I was on call. The family of an elderly patient wanted his intubation removed. They wanted him to die peacefully. He'd had a catastrophic stroke and it was obvious that he would not recover. His children and grandchildren were gathered around his bed, all looking emotionally and physically drained. The noise of the ventilator was constantly in the background and the eldest son asked me if his father was being kept alive by the machine. I told him yes, it was breathing for his father and if we removed the tube, he would just breathe on his own for as long as he could. The family decided they wanted him to die a quieter and more dignified death as if he was at home.'

Tears began to form in Yume's eyes and her voice wavered. 'It went very wrong. When I removed the tube from the man's airway, he started to breathe on his own, but with difficulty, each breath becoming more of a desperate gasp. I had never seen this reaction before. The relatives were horrified; the old man began to arch his back in his effort to breathe. His eldest son asked me to do something. So, I gave him a strong sedative, and he died a short time later.'

The tears were running freely down her cheeks now. 'I listened to the relatives' pleas for me to act. I believed it was the right thing to do, clinically and morally. I was suspended from working as a doctor immediately, then I was struck off.'

Sandra reached across the table and hugged her, drying her tears with a paper napkin. 'Jesus, I wish my story was as noble,' exclaimed Sandra when Yume had recovered. 'I ended up taking drugs from the ward cabinet to bury my feelings. I didn't think about it much at the time; I dealt with life and death daily and I just partied hard with other like-minded doctors and nurses. Now I realise it was the hurt from my childhood. My father used to beat me, and I never remember any love or hugs.'

'Ah yes, the hurt child you carry inside. I have one too.'

Sandra wasn't quite sure what Yume was saying, but it sounded appropriate.

'I just wrapped a shell around myself and said, "Look after number one."'

'I was always left alone,' said Yume. 'My mother is American, and my father is Japanese. My father was always working, and my mother was busy with charity work and socialising, a familiar tale in the lives of expat families. Except I was different. I was a *hafu*, or "halfling". That means mixed-race. In Japanese families, a pure bloodline is important, and the Japanese part of my family didn't like the idea of me. It was the same when I went to school or socialised. When people found I could speak in both fluent Japanese and English they were incredulous. Then the Japanese girls in my class all wanted to look like me: a bit more Westernised, larger eyes, more defined nose and mouth. They admired me, but they left me alone.'

'So how did you come to be in England?'

'My grandfather worked as a US diplomat in Tokyo. He and my grandmother made up for everything that was missing in my life, taking me on their holidays to the Miyako Islands each year. When he retired, they moved to London. As soon as they heard what had happened, they asked me to come and stay with them. My grandfather helped me get a lawyer and although it took three long years, my case was eventually dismissed and I could practise again.'

'It was my friends who rallied round me, not my family,' said Sandra. 'I couldn't have got through it without them.'

And I betrayed two of them, but I won't tell you about that just yet.

'And Summerlands?'

'My grandfather is a friend of Professor Richard Hawley. I worked unofficially for him while I was waiting for my case to be heard. No money changed hands; it was for my sanity, really. So, when I was reinstated, he offered me a job.'

Yume paused and looked intensely at Sandra. 'You know, I've never really told anyone my story like this before.'

Sandra held her gaze. 'Well, I'm glad you were there today, and I'm looking forward to our new relationship.'

'Me too.'

They clinked glasses.

SIXTEEN

Roberta

'**It's not easy living back** at home with your mother at the age of forty-eight.'

Roberta rewarded herself with a slug of wine as she and Sandra sat in a local Italian restaurant discussing Eva's proposed visit to Summerlands. The walls were decorated with scenes of family life in Italy.

It's another culture there.

'I feel like I've got a temporary pass out tonight, just like when I had young kids.'

Sandra burst out laughing. 'Jesus, I'm not surprised. I wouldn't do it, but then I didn't have to. My dad lost his temper once too often and had a fatal heart attack at fifty-eight. Mum worried herself to death four years later.'

'Mother is frail, yet she has all her marbles. The thing I find difficult is that she's turned inward mentally. I've tried to suggest trips out, things to do, tell her about the Caribbean, but she's not interested. She was always blunt, but she has got so used to just thinking of herself now that she's downright cantankerous. She's issuing orders and I'm reverting to being five years old and thinking about being deliberately awkward to score a point.'

'That's old people for you. They get impatient and cross, but it's usually because they are exhausted or in pain. They use up their manners with acquaintances and family gets what's left. Living together is the worst thing for both of you.'

'Hopefully it won't be for long.'

*

Outside the Summerlands main building, Roberta waited patiently, holding the car door open as her mother slowly got out. She refused to have a stick.

'People will think I'm an old lady.'

Well, you are, and your pride makes it harder for everyone else.

Roberta had been shocked at how Eva had deteriorated since her fall. A mixture of pain, lack of strength and confidence had rendered her virtually immobile.

A pity it doesn't stretch to her tongue.

Roberta went towards her to take her arm and, as she spun around, a momentary dizziness made her collide into Eva.

'What are you doing, trying to kill me?' snapped Eva.

Roberta pushed unwelcome thoughts from her head. 'Don't be silly, Mother, I just seem to have trouble with balance at the moment. I think it's being on a boat for so long.'

Roberta had taken Eva straight to the front entrance with the car. 'I'll drop you off here, find you a seat, then park. Can you cope?'

Fortunately, there was a woman waiting for them at the entrance who was happy to help out. 'Hello, I'm Anna, and you must be Mrs Phipps.'

Roberta got a good feeling about the quality of service here.

Money talks.

When Roberta returned, they were seated in reception on upright chairs, not the squashy sofa, obviously out of deference to Eva. They had been joined by a man in uniform who introduced himself as Sam and her mother had a walking stick in her hand. Roberta couldn't hide her amazement.

'It's just a precaution,' muttered Eva to Roberta, not looking at her. 'Sam says it's because of health and safety.'

Yes, and he's a man, so he must be right.

They were greeted by Nicky, the manager, and joined by Sandra.

'Anna and Sam will give you a tour of Summerlands and its facilities, and then we'll meet back here for coffee. We have another group touring this morning, so if you don't mind, we'll talk to you both together. Is that a plan?' She gave a huge smile.

'I have duties this morning, but I'll join you for coffee,' said Sandra.

Eva was exchanging comments with Sam. 'Everybody is very pleasant here,' she told him in theatrical tones.

In fact, from the very moment they had driven through the entrance gates, Roberta had realised that Summerlands was in a different league to the other retirement properties her mother had viewed.

'It's like a country estate,' Eva said, and Roberta tried not to build her hopes up at this positive observation.

Anna and Sam were leading them across a huge lawn towards the villas that they had agreed were within Eva's budget, when they spotted a party coming the other way that looked identical to theirs. An elderly lady and two women following, heads together in discussion. There was something familiar about one of the women: tall, slim, an expensively bobbed haircut and a heart-shaped face.

'Rosieee!'

Roberta ran over to her and they embraced, then stepped back and observed each other at arm's length, noticing the changes since they last met over six months ago. Both were looking healthy and sporting a deep tan, but there the resemblance ended. Roberta was casually dressed, long hair curling past her shoulders, tousled and sun-streaked, and Rosie was, as always, immaculately groomed with a professionally cut and highlighted bob. They searched each other's faces, finding happiness and a common present worry, and both laughed at the irony of it.

'So, we meet again to share our lives. It must be fate,' exclaimed Roberta.

'Roberta, you're positively blooming. I'm so used to seeing a skinny waif.'

'Rosie, I can see that your new life is making you happy.'

They were forced to carry on with their respective tours, but Roberta was buoyed up with the knowledge that Rosie was here to share and discuss things with her. Then she remembered Sandra.

She looked around, but Rosie had already disappeared.

Oh, God, how can I warn her?

Roberta still didn't have a mobile phone.

The villas were stunning inside and out. Each one had a small terrace situated to make the most of the daytime sun. There was a through lounge, a dining room, a kitchen fitted with every modern appliance. A cloakroom with toilet and shower, a master bedroom with a fitted bathroom and a spare bedroom.

How many old people will use all this?

Roberta then remembered Summerlands was not marketed as a home for old people. She glanced down at the glossy brochure they had been given and smiled as she read, 'For people who want to downsize without compromise.'

'Not far then, if you need the loo,' she quipped.

Eva gave her a withering look.

It was a nervous Roberta that trailed back to the manager's office. As they entered the room, Rosie and Sandra were already there, not looking at each other, an awkward distance separating them. Sandra didn't meet Roberta's eyes and soon made an excuse to leave.

Eva and Marjorie had been introduced and were swapping pleasantries about the coincidence of meeting up together like this, whilst shrewdly appraising each other for social standing, intellect and worthiness. Roberta observed that they were not displeased.

339

After all, they are very similar.

Coffee was served to everybody. Somebody droned on about details and finances, but she tuned them out, wondering if Sandra and Rosie would ever make up.

'Any questions, anybody?' asked Nicky, jerking her back to the present.

I will have to crib off Rosie afterwards.

One thing was certain: she could tell they were all impressed with the place, and that included Eva and Marjorie.

Despite themselves, they both look as if they've found the Holy Grail.

As Roberta looked around, everyone was getting ready to leave, and she mouthed over to Rosie, 'I'll phone you tonight.'

SEVENTEEN

Roberta

Roberta hadn't expected to see a blue line on the pregnancy test kit that Sandra had advised her to buy.

'I've put on weight and I've not had a period for months,' she had confided in Sandra soon after she returned. 'At my age it's bound to be menopause, isn't it?'

Now in her mother's downstairs toilet, she stared at it in horror. Her head swam, and dancing lights crowded her vision. Half-blinded, she groped her way to the lounge and flopped onto her mother's ancient and bony sofa, leaning her head back into a cushion.

'Watch those springs,' said Eva from her armchair, peering over her reading glasses. When Roberta didn't move, she craned her neck, trying to see her more closely. 'You're looking very white. Sit up and get your head between your knees. I remember you used to do this a lot at school, trying to skip off lessons.'

'Yes, it was appendicitis,' muttered Roberta.

'It's nearly four o'clock and I usually have a cup of tea and a biscuit, when you're ready to make it,' said Eva.

*

That night, Roberta lay in her childhood bedroom, reliving the moment thirty years ago when she had found out she was pregnant. She reflected on how things had improved for women since then in terms of choices. She acknowledged to herself that she was also older, wiser and independent. Now she could choose what she did.

She could earn money anywhere as an artist and she had her own house. She didn't see Jan as part of the picture; she realised that she loved him and his free spirit, and so for that reason, she had to let him go. She had experienced enough with her first marriage of living with someone who had been forced to be with her.

And I don't want another rogue.

*

'Have you made any decisions about where you are going to live yet, Mummy?'

Roberta's sister had come for tea and they were all sitting at the round dining table that was supposed to make everyone at it equal.

So how come it feels like Mother is at the head?

'What's wrong with my house here?' replied Eva obtusely, not looking at either of them, focussing on struggling with her food.

'You know you're too frail to look after yourself and the house now. What if you fell and broke something? With osteoporosis, it's a major thing.'

'I have a panic button! I have Susie who cleans, George does the garden, you do my shopping and Roberta here helps with the rest.' Eva was mushing her food up on her plate now and it was hard to watch.

'What about Summerlands, Mummy?' said Roberta. 'You liked it there, didn't you, and it could all happen so quickly with their scheme where they'll buy your house off you.'

Her sister glared at her. 'Why are you still going on about that money-pit? They're fleecing you even before you get in there with their so-called "cash for your house" deal.'

'Rosie's mother may be going there,' retorted Roberta.

'I like Marjorie,' said Eva perking up. 'She's more my social standing.'

'Social standing my... my foot!' Roberta's sister leant across the table angrily. 'Now look here, we're not in the same league as Rosie and her posh family. Listen to me, Mummy. I'm the executor and if we sell your house, that money plus your savings will give you twenty years in a care home.'

That's ridiculous, she won't live another twenty years.

'It isn't all about money,' Roberta shouted back. 'Mummy liked Summerlands, I could tell, and it's her choice at the end of the day.'

'Are you so sure she's capable of making the right choice?'

'Be quiet, the pair of you!' Eva crashed her fork down onto her plate. It was an unusual gesture for her, being normally so controlled, and it silenced them both.

I'm five years old again.

'I'm staying in my home. I'm staying here.'

'I knew this would happen. Look, you're only here, Mummy, because Roberta agreed to come back.'

'Mummy, I have to tell you I'm pregnant.'

There was complete silence.

*

Eva was frowning. Her eyes seemed to bore into Roberta's, but it was hard to read any expression in them through her varifocal lenses. Her sister had started to cry with the stress, and Roberta felt tears prick her eyelids too.

Now I'm eighteen years old again.

With an effort, she tried to break through to them both. 'You know I have been telling you about Jan...'

She hesitated. She had never said he was a boyfriend.

Do people have boyfriends at forty-eight? Is Simon Rosie's boyfriend?

343

'I thought he was just a sailing colleague,' said Eva eventually, dragging out Roberta's misery.

'We fell in love,' said Roberta simply.

'How could you...' Eva didn't finish her sentence; she didn't have to. She was making her feelings clear enough.

There was a further silence where Eva was obviously considering the implications of this news.

When she spoke again, it was in a reasonable tone – concerned, even. 'What will you do?'

'I'll stay in the UK for the moment.'

'And this sailor, what will he do?'

'I'm not going to tell him about the pregnancy.'

'What do you mean?' Eva looked agitated.

'Mummy, I lived for fourteen years with a man who was forced to marry me, and I won't do it again.'

'You sound like a hippy, Roberta. What will you do for money?'

'I am self-sufficient, Mummy, thank you.'

'Who will look after you then?'

'I don't need looking after, Mummy.'

'The baby, if it survives, will be a bastard. Doesn't that bother you?'

'Mummy, it's the twenty-first century and a lot of people, who are not religious, choose not to get married now.'

'Well, I'm not having a bastard in this house, I can tell you.' Eva's voice faltered as she realised that this statement effectively ruled out Roberta as well, and she abruptly clamped her mouth shut.

Roberta's sister, who had her elbows on the table, head in her hands, looked up in despair. 'Yes, that's right, Roberta. You get out of everything as usual. You escaped, didn't you? Don't you think I would like to?'

'I'm sorry you feel like that.'

Eva got up from the table slowly and headed for the entrance to the room, painfully clutching at furniture along the way. At the doorway, she paused and turned.

What now?

'I have decided I am selling this house and buying a villa in Summerlands,' she announced dramatically.

Good on you, Mother. I hope it won't be like this when it's my turn.

EIGHTEEN

Rosie

Rosie walked around the kitchen, the phone between her ear and shoulder, leaving her hands free to tidy away the breakfast things.

'That's right, darling, probably another couple of weeks while they get all the paperwork in place. I know, I miss you too.'

She ended the call with a broad smile on her face, which then faded as she looked across at Marjorie, who was ostensibly doing the *Telegraph* crossword. Rosie was all too aware that she'd been listening.

Marjorie's face had a pinched look which caused her to raise her eyebrows slightly, giving the impression that she had a nasty smell under her nose. Rosie recognised the look and waited for the inevitable criticism which would come from Marjorie's pursed lips.

'I don't know why you have to talk to him every day. And I don't like you discussing my affairs. It's nothing to do with him.'

Rosie knew her mum was jealous and disliked sharing her only child.

Please, God, when I am elderly, don't let me become like my mum.

Rosie took a deep, calming breath and went to sit next to Marjorie on the settee. 'Mum, Simon is a doctor and he wants to

346

make sure you are getting better and receiving the appropriate care. He also wants to look after me. I feel so lucky to have met him and found love at last. I lived in a wretched, loveless marriage for thirty years.'

Marjorie was not about to be assuaged by any of this. 'Well, I knew David was not out of the top drawer the minute I first spoke to him, but we both know the circumstances which led to that marriage, Rosemary. David provided well for you and the boys despite the marriage being loveless, as you call it. You can't take away from him the fact that he gave you all a very comfortable life.'

Rosie didn't know whether to laugh or cry. Throughout the years of her marriage, she had kept her suspicions of David's affairs to herself, and even now, her mother had never asked anything about the police investigations into the clinical trials that David was responsible for. Marjorie just saw what everyone else saw. A luxurious lifestyle.

'Simon and I have a good life in Abu Dhabi, but what's more important to me, Mum, is that I can trust him, and he involves me in his life. I never had that with David. I thought you'd want me to be happy! Once you are settled into Summerlands, why don't you come out and visit us?'

Rosie hoped against hope that Marjorie might soften her stance and accept the new circumstances they found themselves in.

Marjorie feigned interest in another clue and returned to the crossword. Rosie got up and turned on the coffee machine. A hit of caffeine and a chocolate biscuit might lift her spirits.

'Would you like a tea or coffee, Mum?' Rosie said in a cheery voice that belied her true mood.

'Tea and one of those shortbread biscuits would be nice, thank you.'

The drinks and biscuits were consumed in a chilly atmosphere that Rosie suspected her mum intended to perpetuate. She couldn't stay in the house any longer. 'Right, I'm off to the shops. Do you need anything, Mum?'

Marjorie made a point of slowly counting the spaces on the clue she was working on. 'No, thank you,' she said without lifting her head.

Rosie grabbed her car keys and as she walked towards the front door she was greeted by a dishevelled-looking Hugo coming in.

'Coffee machine's on, Hugo. Can you spend a bit of time chatting to Grandma, please? She seems a bit down. I'll see you later.'

Rosie shut the door behind her, putting a welcome distance between her and her mum. In the car she loaded her Gloria Gaynor CD, selected 'I Will Survive' and sang along with gusto.

*

'Morning, Grandma. How are you?'

Marjorie looked up from her crossword, put down her pencil and smiled at her eldest grandson. 'I'm fine, Hugo, darling. Come over here and tell me what you are doing these days. You seem to be working very long hours.'

Hugo made a coffee and sat next to Marjorie on the comfy sofa that had filled one end of the kitchen for as long as he could remember. 'You are very perceptive, Grandma. I have several projects on the go. I don't want all my eggs in one basket, so I am operating a diversified portfolio. It means I need a lot of working capital so I'm meeting finance people all the time. I could certainly do with more hours in the day.'

Seeing that Marjorie was impressed, he continued. 'The problem is one of knowing which of the business propositions that people bring to me I should take on. It would be easy to over-stretch myself and some of the projects are such bankers it's hard to turn them down, but I have to.'

Marjorie looked at him with a puzzled expression. 'How do you invest in a banker, Hugo? Surely they are paid by the bank that employs them?'

'A banker, Grandma, is a deal which is certain to do well. It's a term used by entrepreneurs like me, and it's usually the sort of deal that you need to move on immediately, so you must have the cash in place. Cash-flow for me is always a problem.'

Marjorie looked at Hugo with a benevolent smile. 'Well, Hugo, you and your brother will inherit my estate when I die. Your mother doesn't need any financial help from me. By the way, did you know I'm buying a property at Summerlands? I'm hoping to move in within the next fortnight. It's only about ten miles away, so I hope you'll pop round and see me.'

Hugo's mind was racing.

How much is her estate worth? How long will she live for? Maybe I can ask for an advance on my inheritance?

'Of course, I will, Grandma.'

And, uncharacteristically, Hugo put his arm around Marjorie and kissed her cheek.

NINETEEN

Rosie

Rosie gazed out of the aircraft window at the blue sea and sky as the plane made its descent into Abu Dhabi. She had butterflies in her stomach at the prospect of seeing Simon again and feeling the warmth of his arms around her. He had worked out regularly for years and his broad shoulders, taut body and strong arms paid testimony to the hours he had put in. She loved the feel of him and she had missed their lovemaking too. She intended to make up for lost time.

I can't believe the desire I'm feeling.

Once the plane had reached the stand, she took her trolley bag from the overhead locker and walked out across the air bridge. She got through passport control ahead of everyone else and, with no other luggage to collect, she took a minute to brush her hair and top up her lipstick before hurrying out into arrivals, where a grinning Simon was waiting for her.

Her stomach flipped at the sight of him and she walked quickly towards him, wishing she could fling herself into his arms and kiss him with the passion she felt. Mindful of the decorum expected in the UAE, she just stood looking up at him as tears of joy ran down her face.

'Hey, what's the matter, darling? Has something happened?'

'You've happened, Simon, and I'm so happy to be back here with you.'

They stood there grinning at one another until Simon suggested they get back to the villa where he had prepared a welcome-home dinner.

'That sounds wonderful. I've got so much to tell you.'

*

They ate seafood and salad, washed down by a crisp white wine. The pleasure of warm evenings and eating al fresco was one aspect of her new life that Rosie loved. She set about updating Simon on everything that had happened over the preceding weeks.

'Mum has settled in surprisingly well at Summerlands. She gets on with Roberta's mother, Eva. They are both a tad stuck up, if I'm honest, and they discuss how the UK is going to the dogs, etc., etc. God, I hope I can be more positive when I get older. The boys are as different as they've ever been. Theo was so helpful; he was great with Mum, who can be so cantankerous at times. She even had him getting her clothes out for her. Hugo was conspicuous by his absence. He was coming and going at all hours and I never got a straight answer as to what he was doing for work. If I'm honest, I don't think I want to know.' She paused to sip her wine. 'But the biggest news is, and you're never going to believe this, Roberta is pregnant!'

Simon's jaw dropped. Rosie recognised the expression he pulled when his mind was racing. 'She's in her late forties, isn't she? Could it be the menopause?'

Rosie saw he had gone into 'doctor mode', but she continued with what she knew. 'Well, at first that's what she thought too, but she's done the test and she's pregnant, sixteen weeks now. We are all quite excited about it. Jan is the father, but Roberta doesn't want him to know, in case he feels he has to be with her just because she's pregnant with his child.'

Simon sat back in his chair, arms folded, and Rosie waited for his next response. 'Gosh, Rosie, is she aware of the risks to her and the child with a pregnancy at her age? There is a higher risk of abnormalities in the child and the risk to the mother from pre-eclampsia rises considerably. She would probably have to have a C-section. Has she considered a termination?'

Rosie was a little rattled by this negative response. 'I thought you were a cardiologist, not an obstetrician?' she joked.

Simon looked distinctly unsettled for a moment.

'What's wrong, Simon?'

'Oh, nothing. I was reminded of a difficult event in my student days.'

'I know you are thinking of Roberta's best interests, but she seems quite happy about what's happened. Let's drink to Roberta and new beginnings.'

They clinked glasses, and Rosie got up and walked around to Simon and sat on his knee. They looked fondly at one another, feeling the need to re-establish their close connection. Simon gently undid her silk blouse and, releasing a breast from her flimsy lace bra, he took her nipple into his mouth. It had been three long weeks since they'd made love and the excitement built so quickly it took her by surprise. She could feel Simon's erection under her and she pressed against him, her body aching with desire.

'If you carry on with that, I will come.'

He took up the challenge and increased the intensity. Rosie's breath quickened as she held his head and gave herself up to a mind-blowing orgasm.

Simon picked her up and carried her to their bedroom, gently laying her on the bed before undressing her and making love to her, slowly this time.

The following morning, Rosie woke with a smile on her face as she remembered their lovemaking on the balcony and then again during the night. She looked up to see Simon walking out of the bathroom, a towel wrapped low on his hips. He reciprocated the look of appreciation and she beckoned him to come back to bed.

Simon moaned like a wounded animal. 'Oh, God, Rosie, please stop it, I can't resist you. I've got to go to work. I'm operating this morning. There's nothing I'd like more. Rain check until I get home tonight?'

Rosie smiled. She found him fiercely attractive, but she admired him even more for being principled. 'Off you go and patch up some more hearts, Doctor. I love you.'

It was good to get back to work at Al Wahah. Gail welcomed her with a big hug and wanted to know how she had got on back in the UK. The clinic had seen more new patients and Rosie was kept busy all day, so the time flew by. As they packed their bags to leave for the night, Gail picked up her mobile phone, which reminded Rosie of the photo she had seen of the David 'look-alike' at the Dubai charity fundraiser.

'Gail, there was a photo of someone I thought I knew from the UK amongst those photos you took at the Dubai fundraiser. If I showed it to you, could you send it to me?'

The women looked through the photos until Gail pointed out the one in question and sent it to Rosie's phone. 'Hope it's who you think it is,' she said, oblivious to Rosie's discomfort.

Back home that evening, Rosie was staring at her phone when Simon arrived back from work. She couldn't decide whether the man in the picture was her missing husband or not.

'Simon, have a look at this photo and tell me what you see.' Rosie passed the phone to Simon, who walked around the kitchen, phone in one hand whilst loosening his tie and turning on the coffee machine with the other.

Then he stopped in his tracks. 'Christ. This looks like David. Where was it taken?'

Rosie felt a sense of relief having been able to share her fears with him and explained the photo's origin. 'Gail took it at a Dubai fundraiser a couple of months ago. I don't know what the event was.'

Simon looked thoughtful before suddenly becoming energised. 'I know most of these people. It was the annual event to raise funds for heart research in the Emirates. It's invariably held in Dubai. We got an invite, if you remember, but we didn't go because I was working late that night, and anyway, we decided it would be full of pretentious people.'

Rosie wondered quite how she would have reacted if she had come face to face with David.

What to do next?

Simon handed the phone back to her and put an arm around her shoulder. 'Let me think about what I can find out, darling. Can you send me the photo?'

TWENTY

Sandra and Yume

A sexual tension was building up between Sandra and Yume. Every time they met at work, Yume contrived to touch Sandra with a brush of her hand on hers – seemingly innocuous, except for the rippling effect it had on her senses.

This is something I have never felt from a woman before.

Sandra had had a healthy appetite for sex ever since early adolescence when her magnificent breasts had made their sudden appearance. She had noticed a corresponding new interest from men and had lapped up all the adoration and attention that she had never had as a child. She liked sex for pleasure, never thinking of seeking a mate. However, the idea of sex with a woman had never entered her mind. If anything, she tended to make women nervous.

But now I'm curious.

It wasn't long before they were in bed together. She couldn't remember whether it was the second or maybe the third time they met for a drink that Yume had invited her back to her flat. It was simply furnished, with low lighting that immediately created an intimate atmosphere. Yume led Sandra quite naturally to her bedroom.

Touching and exploring another woman intimately was a revelation. She could feel the result of her actions as if it were her own body, a double whammy. She knew how it would feel, where the trigger points were and the secret places to explore. She laughed out loud.

'What is it?' said Yume drowsily. 'Don't stop what you're doing.'

'Jesus, how come it's taken me so long to discover this?' She hooted with laughter again. 'No tedious instructions needed for the location of the G-spot.'

'Less talking.'

*

'So many things are down to chance and coincidence,' mused Sandra. 'Our meeting up, I mean. I didn't really intend to specialise in elderly nursing, but at one time it was the only option open to me. Tell me, why did you choose it?'

They were lying in bed, catching up with each other's lives.

'I am fascinated by toxicology. The exact amount of a drug needed to get the right result must be measured so precisely. Did you know some poisons are medicines in a lower dosage? For a while, I thought I would be a toxicologist, but we made a visit to a hospital and I saw how difficult it was to prescribe for end-of-life care. People develop chronic conditions and are faced with a mix of medications that can inter-react badly. It seemed more important to be working directly with patients than in a laboratory.'

'So, what would you do now if you had the same thing happen? You know, when you were struck off.'

Yume sighed. 'Ah, the right to die with dignity is such a complex subject and there are different rules in different countries. In Japan, if a person has made a declaration on paper that they have a terminal condition and do not wish to be kept alive by artificial means, then it is okay to remove the device. I thought, because the family asked for it, the man had written one. I was eventually reinstated when the family testified for me. I wasn't actively ending his life; I was passively ending it.'

'I think the world has gone legislation-mad. For centuries doctors have been making their own judgements, just as you did.'

'I still believe that what I did was morally right. Since I have been in England I have joined a society called A Dignified Death. There are organisations like this all over the world, campaigning for changes in the law and supporting individual cases. Put simply, we believe in euthanasia. We believe that all mentally competent, terminally ill people should be allowed to opt for assisted dying.'

'Wow, that is controversial,' said Sandra in amazement. 'So, who assists them? I thought doctors took the Hippocratic Oath.'

'Yes, all doctors swear an oath, but the old text is often modified, and the words euthanasia and abortion omitted. There are many doctors who are members of A Dignified Death.'

'I'm shocked. So how does this help older people, especially those with dementia?'

'People at the end of their lives should also be able to choose euthanasia. Then, by extending the Powers of Attorney, relatives can make that choice on their behalf if they are no longer capable. Did you know that euthanasia is legal in the Netherlands, Belgium, Canada and India? And assisted suicide is legal in Switzerland, Germany and in many US states. You could say all the other countries, including ours, are lagging behind.'

'I know from experience that so-called passively ending life can cause more pain and distress than actively ending it,' said Sandra. 'It's a no-brainer, really.'

Yume hesitated as if choosing her next words carefully. 'What do you think of Richard Hawley?'

'Really and truly?' Sandra laughed mischievously. 'He's a looker, a bit of a narcissist and a pompous arse!'

They both laughed.

'Hmm, that may be so, but he's well thought of in high places. I ask because he is now working with the Government on something.

It's all very secretive, but a new palliative care drug, Elysium, is involved. I wonder if this is a move in the right direction.'

'Surely you know, you work closely with him.'

'No, I don't know everything he does. He is being very secretive. Perhaps he doesn't trust me completely because of my history?'

'You did not deserve to be struck off. I, on the other hand, deserved everything that I got.'

'I think I like you bad. Come here and stop talking.'

TWENTY-ONE

Dom

Dominic Maxwell was seated at the head of a huge oval glass table that dominated the boardroom at Summerlands. It was a stiflingly hot day outside, but the room was minimalist, cool and comfortable. The neutral colours, the ultra-modern furniture and the windows shuttered by light-sensitive blinds had all been specified by a prominent local design team.

The board meeting was coming to an end. The four men seated around the table were responsible for the management and direction of the Summerlands project. Besides Dom and Richard Hawley, there was Kevin Charles, head of legal, and Andrew Crompton, financial director. They had all given their reports and were basking in the reflected glory of an excellent set of accounts. The atmosphere was relaxed and self-congratulatory.

Dom had mixed feelings. While the overall figures were good, there was an over-spend at The Retreat that needed investigating. Then there had been more conflict with relatives over contracts. He was reminded of his conversation with Richard Hawley over lunch.

None of this showed in his face as he turned, smiling, to address the other board members. 'In summary, Andrew has reported that we are running ahead of budget and we now have one hundred per cent occupancy in Summerlands Cheshire. In addition, we already have reservations for half of the properties in Summerlands Berkshire and Surrey.'

The other board members nodded their heads and there were mutterings of approval.

'Now, there are a couple of issues I would like to discuss.' He paused to get their full attention again. 'There has been a marked increase in the cost of pharmaceuticals in The Retreat.'

All turned towards Richard Hawley, who nodded and smiled sagely but did not respond.

'I would also like to raise the subject of some relatives and their reaction to the contracts.'

There was an uncomfortable silence that was broken by Kevin, who was a newcomer, keen to make his mark. 'It is probably worth explaining our contracts,' Kevin began. 'We buy our clients' old property. Then, in addition to the cost of their Summerlands property, we ask for five years' annual fees up front, plus ten thousand pounds on account for the use of our medical services. We also include a buyback clause, which means if the resident wishes to sell, we offer to buy their property at the current market value. Any balance on their account is then returned to them.'

Dom spoke. 'How do the purchasers and their relatives react to this?'

'The wealthiest who buy the duplexes are unfazed by the costs; the villas are a different matter. There are often relatives who can see a dramatic erosion of their inheritance and they are not happy, I'm afraid.'

There was silence around the table at this news.

'It's unavoidable,' Kevin continued. 'The figures are there in black and white in front of them. There have been a number of occasions where this has caused friction within families.'

Dom looked over at Richard Hawley who, he could tell, was keen to provide his input. 'Richard. Do you think there is an ethical point here?'

Richard sat with his hands on the table in front of him with fingertips touching as if in prayer.

'We mustn't forget that older people are just that... Older,' he repeated with emphasis. 'Their right to decide on how they live their lives should not be taken away from them. If these people were thirty years old there would not be a discussion about ethics.'

'Thank you, Richard. Good point well made. Perhaps you could elaborate on the spending at The Retreat?'

The professor smiled, sat back in his chair and spoke without reference to his papers. 'We have not had much demand for our regular medical services as most residents are relatively young and healthy. By that I mean they are under the age of eighty.

'However, this month we have had to admit four elderly people into The Retreat with underlying issues. It is a fact that for some people, life will end sooner than for others. At The Retreat, we are committed to making that journey compatible with their wishes. It is the management of this process that has incurred the increase in the drugs bill.'

The other board members nodded their understanding. After all, the professor was an expert in his field.

TWENTY-TWO

Hugo

Hugo paced back and forth the length of the living room, mobile phone clamped to his ear. He took a deep breath and spoke, his voice husky from the previous night on the Bells.

'You know I'm good for the money, it's just a temporary cash-flow problem. Yes, I know, the interest. By the end of the week.'

Hugo sank down on the settee.

Three thousand pounds to find.

He had heard what had happened to others who had fallen foul of these people and the sweat began to run down his back. With shaky hands, he went to light a cigarette, his mum's voice echoing in his head: '*And please, Hugo, no smoking in the house.*'

He went upstairs, and as he walked past her bedroom, an idea came to him. He needed to make sure he was alone, so he leant over the stairs and shouted down, 'Theo, mate, any chance of a brew?'

He waited for his brother to reply, then called him for a second time just to make sure. Silence.

Once in the bedroom, he walked across to the window and saw Theo's car was not on the drive.

He was alone.

Rosie's polished walnut jewellery case on her dressing table lured him like a magnet. He turned the small gold key.

Bingo!

It was full of jewellery he had never seen her wear. The top tray held a diamond and sapphire ring and matching bracelet and necklace.

Dad must have bought her all this and I've never seen her wear any of it. She probably doesn't know what she's got.

He paused as he thought of his absent father. He remembered David's cool, mocking voice when he was growing up, his indifference, the cruel comparisons made between him and his clever older brother. He had felt his mum's love, but she had never interfered or taken his side. He had learnt to bury his feelings and ape his dad's indifference. He decided both his mum and grandma were dazzled by David's money and were still enjoying it, despite his fall from grace. Money, he reasoned, would buy him power and respect. It was their fault he had taken risks and got himself into debt.

I don't owe them any loyalty.

He lifted the top tray and put it to one side. On the tray beneath was a fine gold chain with a large teardrop-shaped diamond, together with a diamond-set bracelet. He felt a sense of elation and knew what he could do.

If this is real – and if I know Dad, it will be – it's worth thousands. One of those top-end pawn shops in Manchester will lend against it. She'll not be back for months and once I'm on a winning streak again, I'll get it back. Result!

After putting the necklace into his shirt pocket, he carefully put everything back in its place. He felt pleased with himself for his inventiveness, which he saw as a mark of his entrepreneurial skills.

Always one to think outside the box… and in this case, the jewellery box.

TWENTY-THREE

Hugo

Hugo let himself into Marjorie's Summerlands villa. She insisted he kept a key in case she was out when he popped round for his weekly visit. He made himself at home with a cup of coffee and his grandmother's daily newspaper.

Why does she get the Telegraph? *It's such hard work to read. Nothing of interest.*

He turned on the TV and flicked through the channels until he found one showing reruns of reality shows.

Easy viewing, and the women are easy on the eye.

He wished he could forget his problems, but they loomed large. The career he saw for himself as a professional gambler had faltered big time and he was in debt up to the hilt. Pawning some of his mother's jewellery had bought him some time, but he knew the pressure would be on him again soon.

I hope she is going to be her usual generous self today. I'm due a run of luck and maybe tonight's the night.

Hearing his grandmother open the front door, he turned the TV back to the BBC and got up to greet her. 'Hello, Grandma. I let myself in and made myself a brew. I hope you don't mind.'

Hugo knew she wanted him to feel at home in her house; she had said as much. But he knew it would be prudent to let her know he wasn't taking it for granted. 'I brought a different type of cake this week – it's a lemon drizzle cake. I saw it in the window at the village cake shop. I know you like the Madeira cake, but I thought we'd have a change.'

Marjorie glowed with appreciation and smiled broadly, which highlighted the spinach that was stuck between several of her lower teeth. Hugo felt the urge to gag and needed to get out. 'Just popping out for a cigarette. Won't be long.'

Hugo lit up outside the door and surveyed the grounds surrounding his grandmother's new home. Fountains babbled amongst the landscaped gardens. The whole design gave a sense of space and privacy between the Summerlands properties.

There must be some serious money locked up here, including my inheritance.

He made his way to the gazebo where the smokers gathered. Kevin Charles, Summerlands' lawyer, was already there and raised a hand to greet Hugo. Both men were smokers and their paths had crossed most weeks when Hugo was visiting Marjorie.

'So, how's business then, Hugo? Still having trouble with cash-flow? It's the one thing that holds most businesses back. Summerlands is an exception; its business model generates cash. It's a veritable goldmine.'

Hugo wondered quite how honest he could be with the man. 'Well, your goldmine is my inheritance. My grandma has left everything to me and my brother, but as I see it, with your business model, my inheritance diminishes year on year. And if she becomes ill and needs expensive medical care, then we'll be wiped out.'

Hugo wondered if he had gone too far. He watched as Kevin drew heavily on his cigarette and paused before answering. 'Mate, people don't live forever. Old people die. In fact, we have four people at death's door right now. Though Summerlands is not explicit about this and I would deny it if anyone asked, The Retreat caters for people entering the final stages of their lives. Once one of our residents is so frail or so confused that they need twenty-four-hour care, they are moved into The Retreat to be looked after.'

Hugo thought about what he had just heard. 'Does anyone ever come out of The Retreat?'

'Not many, Hugo. From what I can see, it's a one-way ticket.'

Hugo began to see that all might not be lost. 'So, if I understand what you are saying, The Retreat is a way to hasten the inevitable.'

Kevin took another long drag on his cigarette before responding. 'I don't know about you, but I don't want to be kept going when I can't remember what day it is and I'm incontinent. I know the Government are involved in the work Hawley is doing, so what does that mean? To me it must be the way to go, if you'll pardon the pun.'

Stubbing out his cigarette, Kevin bid Hugo farewell, leaving him to his thoughts.

Hugo considered what he had heard.

A one-way ticket.

He popped a peppermint into his mouth and hurried back to Marjorie's villa, where he found her busy making them some tea and slicing cake.

'I'm back, Grandma. Sorry I took so long. I got into a conversation with one of the directors. It was very interesting talking to Kevin about business. I always enjoy talking shop with like-minded people. He was explaining the Summerlands business model to me, you know, all about the annual payments.'

'This really is the best cake you've brought me. Can you bring another one when you visit next week, please?'

Hugo persisted with the account of his conversation with Kevin. 'He was telling me they look into the financial position of everyone who purchases a property here to make sure they can afford to keep paying the fees for the time they are here.'

This seemed to register with Marjorie. 'Oh, I left all the facts and figures to your mum to sort out. Would you like another slice of cake, dear?'

Hugo took another slice.

I'll just have to try another tack for a short-term gain.

'Kevin had a really smart grey business suit. I'm sure it was Armani. Not much change from a thousand pounds, but appearance is so important in business. I'm going shopping for a new business suit tomorrow, but I won't be looking at Armani. Cash-flow is a bit tight right now.'

Hugo looked across at his grandmother with his practised look of a little boy lost, then sighed. He picked up the plates and glasses and took them into the kitchen. On his return, he saw Marjorie sitting at her writing desk.

'I'm off now, Grandma. See you next week.'

As he walked towards the door his grandmother handed him a cheque which she had folded in half. He knew he couldn't open it to check the amount there and then – his mum *had* instilled some good manners in him – so he kissed his grandmother and ran back to his car to find out how generous she had been this week.

Five hundred! Thank you, Grandma. Tonight, I will claw back my losses.

TWENTY-FOUR

Marjorie

Marjorie was enjoying herself. The luxurious modern villa appealed to her vanity, and a care package gave her back her independence. She no longer had to rely on the goodwill of neighbours – a fact she didn't hesitate to tell everybody, including her old neighbour, Doreen.

Marjorie was seeing a lot of Roberta's mother Eva, and she was also surprised and gratified by Hugo's frequent visits. She listened vaguely to his business aspirations and found herself giving him money, fondly imagining herself as a supporter of his new ventures, a philanthropist.

'Be careful he doesn't take it all,' observed Eva, jealous of the attention.

'I think Hugo likes talking to me about his ideas and I enjoy helping him,' replied Marjorie. 'I think of it as an investment in the future generation.'

'Make sure you keep a tally of what you are giving him; you should give the same to Theo. That's what I would do.'

*

It was Eva who first noticed Marjorie behaving oddly. Marjorie had invited her for coffee on her patio as it was a sunny morning. Eva found her in the kitchen spooning ground coffee into two cups.

'You do know that's not instant coffee,' she remarked tartly.

Marjorie gave her a strange, unfocussed stare, then shook her head slowly. 'Oh, how silly. Will you make the coffee, please? I'm a bit tired,' was all she said.

Eva took over, thinking how unusual it was for Marjorie to betray any sign of weakness. She watched her make her way outside, clutching at things to steady herself, breathing heavily. When they were both seated, Eva kept the conversation general, whilst keeping a keen eye on her. Marjorie was obviously struggling, and she was worried. She decided the decent thing was to leave as soon as she could.

She called in the next morning and Marjorie seemed brighter. She was just making conversation about how their first two months had flown by, and how pleasant they had been, when Marjorie suddenly swayed. She clutched the back of a dining chair, but it was too light, and she and the chair crashed onto the floor.

Eva flapped her arms, knowing she was useless. 'Shall I get help?'

'No.'

Marjorie took some time, but she managed to haul herself upright and into an armchair.

'How are you now? Can I fetch you anything?'

Marjorie seemed confused for a moment. Eva could see the panic in her eyes and felt the tremendous effort she was making to regain her composure.

'Just some water, dear. I felt dizzy, but you do at our age, don't you?'

She took a sip, refused to phone the doctor and suddenly fell asleep, dropping the glass on the floor. Eva left with a heavy heart but resolved to respect Marjorie's decision and check her later.

*

Later that day, the care team were summoned by Marjorie's panic alarm and found her lying awkwardly between the armchair and a table. She had no obvious injuries, but she was confused and didn't know how she'd got there. After a brief examination, they sat her back in her chair and questioned her.

'Dizzy,' she muttered. She was too scared to say any more. There were rumours circulating about The Retreat, and she didn't want to go in there.

*

'Can you call in to see me next time you're visiting your mum?' Yume was speaking on the phone to Roberta.

She sounded cool and calm to Roberta, but then she always did.

'I'll come and visit tomorrow,' Roberta said, and proceeded to fret about her mother.

Yume's office had the imprint of her taste in the simple décor, with two of Roberta's Caribbean paintings hanging on the walls, creating a bright focus.

'Your mum is fine,' was the first thing that Yume said.

Roberta heaved a sigh of relief.

'It's Marjorie Clark. She's suddenly become very unwell and it's been going on for a few days now. She's dizzy and she keeps falling over. This is making her very confused and nauseous. We've checked her, but we can't find anything sinister. It's hard to make a diagnosis in someone so elderly, it could be anything. I have phoned Mrs Jennings, but we haven't met. I wanted you to know because you are friends. She said she would phone you tonight.'

Rosie was predictably both concerned and irritated at the news when she phoned. 'Poor Mum, it was too much to expect that moving her would cure her physical symptoms. I guess I'll have to come back to the UK again or I'll never forgive myself. I wonder if Simon could come. He would know the right questions to ask.'

*

Hugo was visibly upset when he next visited Marjorie.

'How do you feel?' he asked her, reaching out for her hand.

'Better, thank you. You're so thoughtful.'

Marjorie felt more inclined to open up to Hugo. Eva was too judgemental and she dreaded being moved into The Retreat if she talked to the doctors.

'I am frightened of what my symptoms mean, where they will take me if I don't improve.'

'Don't worry, Grandma. I don't suppose you're up to having a slice of this Madeira cake I brought you?'

They both grinned conspiratorially.

'I'll take that as a yes then. Tell you what, I'll go and fetch Eva.'

Hugo brought Eva back with him and she settled into an armchair while he busied himself in the kitchen making tea and slicing the cake.

'It's so nice to be made a fuss of by Theo,' said Marjorie. 'I feel better already.'

'You mean Hugo,' muttered Eva. 'You're getting mixed up, you know.' She leant over to whisper so that Hugo couldn't hear. 'I've said before, this attention comes at a price. Make sure Theo gets some money too.'

'You're right,' said Marjorie. She would write a cheque… if she remembered.

*

Marjorie woke to find the care team at her bedside. It was dark.

What time is it?

She tried to speak but her words were coming out all jumbled up. She began to wave her arms in panic, a searing pain gripped her head, then her stomach, and she vomited.

'Never mind, luv,' said a friendly faced carer, expertly placing a tray under her chin. She had magenta-coloured hair, a nose ring, and a broad Mancunian accent. 'Doctor's comin' to examine yer.'

'Talk prop'r,' said Marjorie thickly, annoyed that she could do no better.

She had her eyes closed and the girl stuck her tongue out, displaying a stud in the centre.

Sandra and Yume came in the front door. Sandra had picked up the alarm call and decided to go with Yume when she found out who it was. 'Maybe I can earn some brownie points with Rosie,' she said hopefully, once they were in the bedroom.

Marjorie had heard. She wanted to know who these people were who knew Rosie, but she couldn't coordinate her brain and her speech. She forced her eyes open.

'Hello, Marjorie,' said Yume.

She recognised Yume and Sandra briefly, but her eyes closed again as if they had a will of their own.

Yume proceeded to examine her. 'What happened?' she asked the carer.

'We did a visit last thing, and when I shook her gently she sorta contorted all over, in spasms, like.'

'Marjorie, your heartbeat is rapid and your face is flushed. I want you to think calm thoughts and focus on your breathing.'

'No.'

'Please do as I ask, Marjorie. It will help.'

Marjorie responded by suddenly vomiting again.

When it was over, Marjorie's breathing slowed and she fell into a light sleep.

'I am puzzled,' said Yume to Sandra. 'Dizziness and confusion are not unusual at her age, but the vomiting could indicate either a migraine or something she ate that disagreed with her digestion. I think we need to get her into The Retreat and do some tests, just to be on the safe side.'

In some far region of her consciousness Marjorie heard this, and her body shuddered.

'I don't like these symptoms,' said Yume to Sandra. 'It's almost six am. I will speak to Richard when he comes in. We should give her a CT scan.'

TWENTY-FIVE

Rosie

As Rosie packed a suitcase for a week's visit to the UK, she felt resentment at having to leave Abu Dhabi again. The only consolation would be exchanging the searing heat for a cooler English autumn.

Oh, well, needs must. Curse of being an only child. It's only a week and Mum will be glad to see us.

Rosie had been unsettled by the news that there was concern over Marjorie's health, and Simon had insisted on accompanying her, for which she was very glad. He was hoping that the doctors at Summerlands would be willing to discuss her medication with him.

Rosie suspected that her snobbish mother would have been making great social capital out of Simon's job amongst the residents and staff at Summerlands. Thinking of Simon, her mother and her new relationship led her thoughts back to her husband.

He must be somewhere.

Damn the bastard.

As she threw clothes into the case, her thoughts turned to her sons. She was looking forward to seeing them, albeit with some slight trepidation as far as Hugo was concerned.

She shuddered and zipped up the suitcase, symbolically shutting down these uncomfortable thoughts, just as she heard Simon being dropped off by Rashid. He had cancelled his operations for a week to accompany her. Their plane was scheduled to depart early evening, arriving in Manchester later that night. Theo had insisted on meeting them and rebutted any ideas of their picking up a taxi.

No chance of such an offer from Hugo.

*

Theo was waiting at arrivals as promised and drove them back to the family home.

'I expect you're tired, so I'll see you tomorrow. I've taken the morning off so we can catch up.'

Rosie felt a surge of pride at quite how decent a young man he was. Then her mind automatically segued to Hugo. 'Is Hugo in?'

Theo stared ahead, his face expressionless.

'Is there something wrong? Is he ill?'

Rosie looked at her son. Minutes before, he had been in a great mood, and now he suddenly appeared to have the world on his shoulders. She moved towards him and put her arm around his shoulder, and she felt his body relax slightly.

'Oh, Mum, I don't know what's happening with Hugo. People phone and want to speak to him but never give a name. When he takes one of these calls, he is always on edge afterwards and his hands shake. From the little bits I've overheard, I think it's about money. He's also behind with his share of the household bills. I'm sorry, Mum. I didn't want to bother you with all this.'

Rosie stroked the back of his head as she had done when he was a child.

They're always your children, even when they are grown up.

'I'm glad you've told me. Did he know I was coming to visit Grandma?'

'Yes, he did. In fact, when I told him, he insisted he go round to her house to check everything was tidy.'

*

Rosie and Simon briefly spoke about Hugo before going to sleep and Simon was concerned.

'It could be drugs or maybe gambling. Both tend to incur debts that are recovered by thugs.'

Neither explanation made Rosie feel any better.

I could do without this, on top of worrying about Mum.

Next morning, a full English breakfast around the old oak farmhouse table was a welcome start to the day. The sun was shining, but it was much cooler than the Emirates and Rosie was appreciating the difference.

'No Hugo?' she asked. Turning to Theo as she asked the question, she immediately felt guilty. This was her problem, not his. 'Simon and I are going to visit Grandma this morning. She doesn't know, so I hope it will be a nice surprise. Do you want to come with us?'

Theo looked uncomfortable. 'Mum, when I visited Grandma last week I'm not sure she knew who I was. She seemed quite confused.'

What am I going to find?

She looked over at Simon, who attempted to reassure her. 'I'm hoping the medical team will let me look at what your mum's been prescribed. I'll need to tread carefully, as no doctor enjoys too much peer scrutiny. I know I don't!'

Rosie wasn't sure whether this was Simon trying to put a positive spin on events or whether he had genuine concerns. She was beginning to dread today's visit.

The drive through the grounds of Summerlands never failed to impress and the gardens had matured over the months since she had last seen them. Nevertheless, Rosie felt sick in her stomach as they parked the car outside Marjorie's villa. As she got out of the car, the door of the villa next door opened and Eva came out. Rosie knew the two women met regularly and had always been competitive about who could finish the *Telegraph* crossword first.

'Hello, Eva. How are you? Have you and Mum been doing the crossword again?'

Eva shook her head before putting her hand on Rosie's arm. 'Rosie, your mum isn't here. She's been taken to The Retreat.'

Oh, Mum. What on earth is happening to you?

Roberta appeared, blooming and filling the doorway with her bulk. She reached out and gave Rosie a hug.

'I'm so sorry, Rosie. Marjorie was fine last time I visited. Sure, she was a bit unsteady on her feet, but then she must have deteriorated very suddenly. I didn't expect this either; I don't really know what's happened. Can I come with you?'

*

Rosie, Simon and Roberta were standing under a palm tree in the Summerlands reception, waiting for Nicky.

'I feel like I'm still in Abu Dhabi,' Rosie said crossly, her face tense with anxiety.

'I'm so sorry, Mrs Jennings.' Nicky approached the little group and overheard. 'Next time I will meet you at The Retreat, once you know where it is.'

The Retreat was indeed a good walk away, right at the end of the Summerlands complex.

So far, it lives up to its name.

They approached an anonymous-looking building, surrounded by newly planted trees.

'It looks like they're screening it from the rest of the complex,' Roberta said.

A small courtyard with rattan chairs was deserted.

'Do you think the inhabitants will recover enough to sit in them?' remarked Rosie.

'Chin up.' Simon put his arm round her.

The reception had an unmanned desk, some hard chairs and a telephone. There were glass doors with security pads on either side, leading to two separate corridors. Nicky punched a code into the left-hand door and led them down a white empty corridor. It was completely silent and yet they could hear the sound of voices murmuring and a TV coming from somewhere in the building.

Marjorie was lying asleep in a room that was simply furnished with a hospital bed, two armchairs and a wall TV that was switched off. There was also an adjacent wet room. Rosie caught a sob that threatened to escape as the seriousness of her mother's condition hit her.

'Mum, it's me, Rosie.'

Marjorie's eyes fluttered. 'Madeira cake,' she whispered, and then lapsed into sleep again.

'I'll sit with Mum for a while,' Rosie gasped.

'I'll stay if you want me to,' said Roberta.

'And I have an appointment with Professor Hawley,' said Simon grimly.

*

As they drove home, Simon told Rosie what he had found out.

'I can't find anything untoward in the meds she was being prescribed before she fell ill. Statins for high cholesterol and medication for a hiatus hernia. Neither are associated with confusion or dizziness. Hawley says he has ordered a CT scan.'

The rest of the journey was spent in silence.

TWENTY-SIX

Rosie

The following day, Rosie had an appointment with Nicky.

'Such a shock for you,' Nicky said. 'Come into my office and we'll talk about it.'

Rosie followed her as she gestured towards the two sofas with the table and the tissues.

'Make yourself comfortable.'

'I didn't expect Mum to be this bad,' Rosie started to say, then bit her lip as tears threatened again.

'Let me assure you that our doctors are assessing her right now.'

'But I don't understand how she has deteriorated so quickly.'

'We're trying to find out what's going on. She's in good hands. Come to our talk this afternoon at two o'clock on palliative care. It'll give you a lot more information about what is happening to your mum, and it will help you come to terms with it.'

'I'll do that, thank you.'

Rosie felt she was sleep-walking through a bad dream, and she was irritated too.

I'm just being served platitudes.

The palliative care talk was being held in a small meeting room off reception. Rosie walked in to find three women about her age together with what looked like a family: mum, granddad, daughter and son. She caught snatches of their conversation, interspersed by someone sobbing.

'We love Mum, but we don't want her to linger and suffer…'

'I keep thinking, what more can I do, after all she's done for us…'

'I'm here to understand what's happening. I'll really miss her, but it's her time…'

Rosie sat down as discreetly as possible, trying to hide her shock. *My experiences are of duty, not love. What can I say to these people?* She felt at a loss. They were talking about the kind of relationships she had never known with her mum. Just then Richard Hawley entered the room.

'Good afternoon and welcome to Summerlands. Let me introduce myself. My name is Professor Richard Hawley and I'm the medical director. I have been involved in Summerlands from its very beginnings and I am very proud of what it has to offer its residents. Today I want to talk to you about some of the aspects of ageing that affect elderly people approaching the end of their lives.'

At this point, a woman started sobbing quietly again whilst the elderly man blew his nose and dabbed his eyes.

Richard Hawley smiled at the small audience and continued. 'One of the first things we notice is that residents no longer socialise. They become less concerned about their appearance and don't bother to cook proper meals. They also tend to sleep a lot more and doze during the day.' He paused. 'To add to this, many elderly people take a range of medications to manage the common diseases of old age. However, certain medications have the unfortunate side effect of impairing cognition and causing confusion.'

Rosie listened, aghast.

This is exactly what is happening to Mum.

'At some point, we have to acknowledge that a person needs what we call palliative care because they are dying.'

This statement generated further sobbing as the audience was left in no doubt that their loved ones were coming to the end of their life.

Hawley went on to describe palliative care as 'easing the symptoms rather than trying to cure' and described in detail the stages a person might go through as their body shuts down.

No! ... Why is this happening so quickly?

'The Retreat uses a range of drugs which ensure your loved one will be pain-free and peaceful to their last breath,' he concluded.

Which drugs?

He then sat there quietly, allowing the group to assimilate what they had been told. 'Please take your time, everybody. Help yourself to tea or coffee and biscuits. I am here to answer any questions you may have, and in my experience, you may find it a comfort to talk to each other.'

A mix of emotions was swirling in Rosie's head. No, she didn't want coffee. She was desperate for comfort, but not from strangers, and she could feel the beginnings of anger threatening. At their meek acceptance, at Yume's inadequate telephone call, at Nicky with her platitudes and at Richard Hawley, the patronising grim reaper. She wanted to scream at them all.

Not here, not in public.

The family were chattering together and helping themselves to coffee and biscuits. Richard Hawley was standing on the fringes of the group, his arm round a woman's shoulder as she sobbed.

Rosie walked out.

TWENTY-SEVEN

Marjorie

Richard Hawley entered Marjorie's room and gave his latest patient a cursory glance. He picked up her notes and read them again:

> Previous falls, dizziness and confusion afterwards.
> Fell at home. Put on care team watch.
> Found in bed with flushed face, rapid heartbeat, vomiting, dizzy, confused.
> Taking standard meds for a hiatus hernia, statins for high cholesterol.
> No history of a chronic condition.
> Admitted.
> CT scan clear.
> Continuous and excessive sleepiness interspersed with agitation and confusion since she was admitted.

Marjorie was restless, her face flushed. Richard checked her pulse, which was rapid. He yawned and was reminded that his girlfriend had kept him awake last night, and although it went against his principles, he needed a caffeine fix.

He pressed a call button, and Yume entered.

'Insert a cannula in her hand and give her a start dose of Elysium,' he ordered.

*

Marjorie was aware of a heavy and insistent ache that was radiating from the back of her right hand. She was having great difficulty moving any part of her body.

She heard Richard and Yume talking, and was seized with a sudden fear.

Dr Death.

Eva had mentioned the nickname that had been coined regarding the rumours about Richard Hawley. Marjorie had dismissed it at the time as mischief making.

I am in The Retreat, with Dr Death. No one ever comes out of here.

Her breathing changed as she began to panic. She eventually managed to move her head slowly from side to side, but when she tried to speak, she could make no recognisable sound. Her body started to tremble with the effort and the stress.

She sensed Richard leaning over her, watching. 'This is most unusual. I gave her a dose of Elysium to calm her. Why doesn't she respond like the others?'

Marjorie felt his presence inches from her head; she felt his breath on her face. Then she felt him lift her eyelid as he shone a light directly into her eyes.

'Check her pulse and blood pressure.'

There was a pause, then she felt Yume's light touch. She heard her murmur and felt Richard lean over her again. 'She's panicking. I'll give her another dose of Elysium.'

She heard a chair being dragged towards her bed. Richard took her hand in his and placed his head close to her ear. 'I know you are frightened, Marjorie, but there is no need. We are going to make all the pain and anxiety go away and you will feel wonderfully relaxed.'

She felt something tug at her hand as Elysium began to course through her veins with a renewed purpose. If she had not succumbed to the chemicals that now flooded her body, she would have witnessed the two doctors aghast at the suddenness of her death.

'I don't understand. How can she have gone so quickly?'

Richard turned to Yume, whose face was drained of what little colour she had.

'*Nidoto nai*,' she said, reverting to her native Japanese.

Not again.

TWENTY-EIGHT

Rosie

'I'm sorry, Rosie. There's no easy way to say this. Your mum has just passed away quite suddenly.'

Yume paused, trying to assess the silence at the other end of the phone. 'Are you alright?'

Rosie had dropped the phone, her face ashen, her lips white. She ran into the study and buried her face in Simon's shoulder, sobbing.

Simon made Rosie drink a cup of tea with a healthy slug of brandy in it, and some of the colour returned to her face. 'You did everything you could for your mum, you know,' he said for the umpteenth time.

'Yes, it's just the shock.'

He looked at her intently. 'When you're ready, I'll take you to Summerlands.'

'It's okay, I'm feeling much better. I'm just glad you're here with me.'

*

385

Richard Hawley's secretary told Simon that he was in a meeting with another doctor and could not be disturbed.

'Tell him it's Dr Simon Adams to see him about Marjorie Clark,' he said.

Simon was immediately shown into Richard's office. He was at his desk which was covered with paperwork. Yume was sitting on a chair at the side. Richard stood to shake Simon's hand, then motioned for him to take a chair on the opposite side. 'Take a seat. My condolences on Mrs Clark's death. We're just discussing it right now.' Richard flashed a brief smile, his manner business-like but perfectly at ease.

Simon got straight to the point. 'Could you tell me what the cause of death was?'

Richard immediately assumed his compassionate manner. 'Marjorie's death followed a pattern that we are familiar with once an elderly person starts to decline. Since she came into The Retreat, we have been giving her palliative care to ease her symptoms. I am satisfied that her death was from natural causes; in effect, old age caught up with her.' Richard spread his hands out, palms up in a conciliatory gesture, but Yume just looked down, avoiding eye contact.

Simon was silent for a moment, as if considering his answer. 'Do you mind telling me what drug you were using?'

Richard looked seriously offended. 'Only the best. A ground-breaking drug designed specifically to ease pain and anxiety for the Palliative Care Pathway.'

He then gave Simon a chilly and forbidding stare that in anyone else would have halted further questions.

You have not named the drug yet.

Simon had asked once, and he'd felt that Richard's answer was evasive. He certainly wasn't going to ask again. Instead, he paused and frowned, making his dissatisfaction clear. 'I am not happy with your diagnosis,' he finally replied. 'The last time Rosie and I saw Marjorie the only outward sign of decline was her balance. I can't accept that her deterioration in just over a week was due just to natural causes. As far as I am concerned, her death was sudden and needs more explanation. As a registered doctor, I shall be visiting the coroner to request a post-mortem.'

Richard looked rattled. 'I agree her death was sudden, certainly not the usual, but in my many years of specialising in gerontology...' He paused, unconsciously puffing his chest out. '...I have seen this happen before.'

'Well, I am not happy with that,' repeated Simon.

Richard was clearly struggling with his judgement being questioned. Simon also wondered if it was the potential for damage to his career and his aspirations that really mattered to him.

There was nothing else Richard could say, and he waved his hand in dismissal. 'Go ahead then. My records are at your disposal.'

*

Later, Simon drove Rosie back to The Retreat and she peered through the glass pane in the door of Marjorie's room.

I've never seen a dead person before, not even Dad.

Marjorie's eyes were closed. Someone had placed her arms across her chest and a single flower in one of her hands.

Like a saint.

She plucked up courage and entered the room, which was cool and smelt of plug-in air freshener. Silently she walked up to the bed until she was standing by her mum's head.

She looks like Mum; she looks asleep.

Rosie bent over her and gently kissed her forehead, something that would never have happened when she was alive.

Poor Mum, I hope she knows I did that.

Simon came into the room behind her. He moved towards her and placed his hand on her arm in a gesture of support. 'Are you okay?'

Rosie shook her head numbly.

Simon looked at her with tenderness and concern. He knew her well and guessed she was struggling to contain her emotions.

TWENTY-NINE

Rosie

Rosie and Simon broke the news of Marjorie's death to Theo over breakfast. He was distressed and broke down in tears. Simon could see that he had developed an affection for the crusty old lady.

And an insight into Rosie's upbringing, perhaps.

Hugo failed to materialise, and Rosie and Simon headed off alone to the coroner's office. Simon told the coroner that he was unhappy with Richard Hawley's diagnosis of 'natural causes' but rather that he felt the death was 'sudden and unexplained'. It was slightly unusual for someone to contest the attending doctor, but his clout as another MD, plus a phone call to Richard, was enough for the coroner to request a post-mortem.

Hugo had surfaced from his room when they returned. Rosie found him in the kitchen and brought him up to date, Simon hovering in the background to help if needed. Hugo, for the large part, remained impassive until Rosie mentioned the post-mortem. He was speechless for a moment, his eyes darting everywhere, then he focussed on Rosie with a haunted look. 'Why? I mean, I don't like the idea of the old girl being carved up. Do we have to?'

Rosie took him by the hand. 'Hugo, I'm really sorry to ask at a time like this, but can you tell me exactly what is going on with you? You look dreadful, and you're out all night into the small hours. If I get close to you, you ask for money. It's happened too many times, and when I want to know exactly what it's for, you back off. You're an adult and I'm disappointed that you don't seem responsible. You owe Theo money, who else?'

'It's none of your business,' Hugo retorted, his eyes flashing with anger. 'Go back to your luxury life in Abu Dhabi.' He avoided her as she reached out to him and, springing up from the sofa, he marched out of the room, bristling with self-justified anger.

Simon was way overdue to be back in Abu Dhabi, but he felt he couldn't leave until after the post-mortem results, and he was concerned about Hugo's behaviour. He spent his time observing life at the house. He and Rosie had decided that as they couldn't establish David's whereabouts to sell the house, it made sense for Rosie's boys to live there. Simon could see that while it had helped Theo become more independent, it had had the opposite effect on Hugo, giving him a false sense of security.

Gravy train springs to mind.

The post-mortem was scheduled for the next day. In the afternoon, Simon called in at the coroner's office to see if there was any news to report, returning to Rosie's house with a heavy heart. 'It's not what we want to hear. There's no conclusive cause of death yet, but the pathologist has noted scarring to the oesophagus and stomach lining and a marked lividity in these tissues and the liver. He is recommending a forensic examination.'

Rosie looked horrified. 'Oh no, I don't believe it. I've been through all this already last year with Linda's death.'

Simon moved towards her. 'I'm sorry. I've brought this on, but I know there's something not quite right here.'

'Of course, Simon. I trust your judgement, but we'll have to tell the boys, in case they hear about it in the papers.'

As it happened, the fact that Marjorie Clark's internal organs were under further investigation did not warrant a mention in the local press.

Still, Hugo was unhappy and rounded on Simon. 'You're causing Mum a lot of distress,' he blurted out. 'Is this really necessary?'

*

The days dragged by. Rosie and Simon were at breakfast when the post came. Simon went down the stairs to the hall to fetch it. Among the usual items was a brown envelope with the coroner's logo on the back. Rosie stared at it for a long moment.

'It's probably addressed to you, darling, as next-of-kin,' prompted Simon gently.

'No, it's addressed to you, Simon Adams MD. Please will you open it first?' said Rosie, dropping it next to his plate as if it was hot.

Simon read it through while Rosie distracted herself with the other post. At one point, he exclaimed under his breath.

'That bad?'

'You don't have to read it till you're ready.' He folded the letter up.

Rosie took a deep breath, reached over and unfolded the letter again. As she read, her breathing quickened and Simon caught her as she swayed on her chair.

Simon laid her on the floor. Rosie's breath was coming in ragged gasps. She was hyperventilating. He placed one hand just below her ribs and one on her chest, applying light pressure. 'Breathe in through your nose and out through your mouth.'

Just then, the doorbell rang.

Simon was distracted, then he remembered that Rosie had opened the electric gates and unlocked the door earlier for Roberta, who was due to visit.

'Can't… breathe.'

'Come in,' he shouted to Roberta, who was puzzled that there was no one to greet her. It was not like Rosie to be so casual.

'Upstairs!' Simon managed to gasp.

Roberta's face eventually appeared, looking startled at the sight of Simon and Rosie on the floor together. A jokey comment died on her lips when she saw their anxious faces and heard Rosie struggling for breath.

'I just happen to have a paper bag on me,' she said, reaching into a holdall slung over her shoulder. 'Here, breathe into this.'

She deftly scrunched the neck of the bag up, blew it open and handed it to Rosie.

Soon Rosie could sit up and was almost breathing normally.

'How did you know what to do?' she asked when she could speak.

'It used to happen to me a lot when I was going through my divorce from Will,' replied Roberta. 'It's a panic attack,' she added unnecessarily.

She looked at both Simon and Rosie, realisation dawning on her face. 'Oh, dear, is it bad news? Shall I go?'

Rosie got to her feet and gingerly made her way to the sofa. 'No. Stay, Roberta. I think you are just the person I need with me right now.'

Simon made coffee all round. 'Brandy or whisky in yours?' he asked Rosie. 'This daytime drinking will have to stop, though,' he joked.

'Shall we tell the boys tonight?' she asked Simon.

'Tell them what?'

Hugo was standing in the doorway, looking very hungover. 'Christ, is that brandy I can smell?'

'Come in, Hugo. Sit down, let me pour you some coffee and then I'll tell you,' said Simon. 'Is that okay with you, Rosie?'

'I'm better now, thanks. Gracious, that's the second time recently I've had a reaction to stress that I can't control. How on earth have I got this far in life without it happening before?' She took a gulp of her fortified coffee. 'I never really understood, you know. I thought it was a matter of willpower or self-control, but it isn't, is it? It's like your body takes over, whether you like it or not. It's scary.'

Simon began speaking to them all. 'Rosie and I have just received the coroner's report with the results of the post-mortem and forensic tests.' He glanced at Hugo, who was clenching his hands. 'The forensic tests established traces of cyanide in the tissues tested. Marjorie died as a result of ingesting cyanide.'

There was silence, absolute silence, from everyone.

'I'm not going to read out all the medical details, other than it would seem it happened before she went into The Retreat. There are traces of the usual sedatives from her stay there, but nothing else. The coroner will open an inquest and adjourn it, pending a criminal investigation.'

Roberta began to cry softly. Hugo stared straight ahead of him at nothing.

Rosie put her arm round Roberta to comfort her. She reached out to Hugo to beckon him over, but he grimaced and headed for the door. Simon looked aghast at the idea of being drawn into some sort of female bonding.

'I'm just going to look at flights back to Abu Dhabi,' he muttered as he too fled out of the room.

Rosie buried her face in Roberta's shoulder and allowed herself a few tears.

How can my life be turned upside down… again?

I feel like an actor in this weird play that is my life.

I just accept everything, don't I? The good, the bad – I don't fight back.

It's time I did.

Gently, she prised herself away from Roberta, and they looked at each other's tear-stained faces, both slightly embarrassed now at their mutual need for intimacy.

'Being pregnant makes me emotional,' said Roberta, brushing the tears away.

'I'll make another coffee, if you can stay. I just… need to talk about how I feel, and who better than one of my oldest friends?'

'Less of the old,' said Roberta, smiling again.

*

'How did Mum come to swallow cyanide?' said Rosie when they were seated again with mugs of hot coffee. 'She was in a good place physically and mentally, she was well looked after, or at least I thought so.'

'You couldn't have done more,' said Roberta.

'Yes, I could. I could have loved her,' Rosie cried.

'The guilt of those who are left,' murmured Roberta.

'And the anger. I have a lot of questions to ask of someone. Who gave it to her?'

'We could start with Yume,' Roberta suggested.

'I've never met her.'

'I'll introduce you.'

THIRTY

Richard

Richard Hawley had been sleeping badly since Simon's visit. Tonight he was wide awake and trying not to focus on the brightness of the streetlights and the neighbour's security light, trying not to play out the different scenarios that could be a consequence of the coroner's report. He heard the nearby church clock ring three, four and five o'clock, by which time he had given up on the idea of sleep and had driven to his local gym. He pushed himself to his limit to reduce his anxiety but to no avail.

He went straight to work in jeans and a polo shirt as opposed to the Italian suits that he normally wore. Worry lay heavily on his shoulders and sapped his usual energy, but he couldn't sit still. He walked around his office at The Retreat and looked at the evidence of his success displayed prominently on the walls for his visitors to admire. Gold-framed certificates demonstrated his achievements. Awards nominated by his peers were of particular satisfaction to him. His peers came to him for advice; the Government came to him for advice. He felt his anger rise.

And all I have achieved so far could be wiped out by an interfering cardiologist.

There was a knock at the door and the receptionist came in carrying a large brown envelope. Richard had arranged for the coroner's report to be couriered to him. He would normally have enjoyed some banal chatter with the young woman, but the contents of the envelope were the only thing on his mind. He looked around for his letter opener; he thought it crude to tear open envelopes. His anxiety levels clouded his memory and he couldn't remember where he had last used it. He dragged open drawers and cupboards before finally resorting to using his thumb.

He sat down at his desk and took out the bound document. He felt the beginnings of a tension headache and rubbed his temples. He began to read, and as he got further into the report, he was overcome by relief. His actions and the use of Elysium appeared to have been exonerated. The post-mortem had found lividity of the stomach and liver tissues and burning in the oesophagus which was indicative of ingesting small amounts of cyanide over a period. However, the amount of dispersal in the tissues indicated that she had not ingested any in the last three days of her life.

Which was when she was in The Retreat.

He closed the document, placed his hands on the desk, fingers splayed, and breathed deeply, enjoying the sense of calm that washed over him.

After a while, he began to realise that, while he was off the hook, there appeared to have been a murder committed and that would inevitably lead to further investigations. A police presence would cause concern amongst staff and residents. Questions were going to be asked and records inspected. He decided to phone Jason Brown and give him an update.

Jason's phone rang several times before it was picked up by his PA, Andrew Gordon.

'Hello, Andrew. Richard Hawley here. Can I have a quick word with Jason, please?'

Richard thought he heard a muffled conversation as if Andrew had put his hand over the mouthpiece.

'Sorry, Professor. Jason is in a meeting that will last all day. Can I give him a message?'

Richard knew that tactic. He had used it himself many times.

'No. No message. Just tell him I called.'

How had Jason Brown heard about it?

THIRTY-ONE

Sandra

Summerlands was awash with rumours. It did not have any post-mortem facilities and Marjorie's body had been collected by ambulance and taken to a local hospital. As most people discreetly exited in an unmarked funeral director's van, that was enough to alert the staff.

Sandra had been horrified when she heard about Marjorie's untimely death. She had not been involved in caring for her, Richard insisted on personally monitoring the palliative care programme. Yume was the only other person he allowed to work with him. She was relieved; it would have been awful if Rosie had found her to be under suspicion again.

As far as she was concerned, the odds were stacking up against Richard and Yume. He had established the Palliative Care Pathway system, he and Yume had been colleagues for a long time, and Yume was a member of A Dignified Death.

I need some answers from Yume, but will I like what I hear?

That evening they were at her house. Yume was relaxing and watching a TV programme. Sandra had lit a fire and was already halfway through a bottle of red wine.

Sandra realised Yume was staring at her.

'What?'

Yume muted the TV and patted the sofa next to her. 'Come, sit here and tell me, Sandra. Something's bothering you?'

'Bad thoughts,' replied Sandra, not looking at her. 'You wouldn't know about such things, Yume. You never seem to have any.'

'Now then, are you cross with me? Tell me what I've done to upset you.'

Sandra looked at Yume fully then. 'Okay, you are making me confront my own anger as usual. I'm unsettled about Marjorie's death.' She took another slug of wine. 'I'm already building up an aggressive defence in my head against an imaginary attack from Rosie. It's what I do best.'

She finished her wine off and refilled her glass. Yume knew better than to stop her. 'And I'm annoyed because there's maybe something that you haven't shared with me, something to do with you and Richard. The more I think about it, the angrier I get. Tell me, is there some secret between you about his Pathway project?'

There, it's out.

'It was nothing we did,' said Yume. 'It was cyanide poisoning.'

'Jesus Christ!'

'I was there with Richard at Marjorie's death, you know—'

'I guessed that.'

Sandra wrapped her arms around Yume in sympathy and gave her a hug.

Whatever Yume was going to say next was interrupted by a knock on the door.

It was raining, and DS Steve Mallory was sheltering under the porch.

Sandra had dated Steve nearly a year ago, but she'd not been in touch with him since she met Yume.

'Sorry, am I interrupting your evening?' he began.

'Steve, come in and let me shut the door. Have you met Dr Yume Yamamoto?'

Steve stepped inside. Yume was looking at him in amusement.

He's twigged already and doesn't seem to mind.

Steve's look of shock was gradually replaced by embarrassment.

A cosy evening by the fire is not on the cards. In fact, he is interrupting one.

'You work at Summerlands, don't you?' he said to Yume. 'You're on my list to talk to as well.' He paused and coughed nervously into his fist. 'Don't disturb yourselves, I'm not stopping. I just called to let you know that I will be at Summerlands tomorrow, interviewing all the staff.'

'Thanks for the heads-up, Steve,' said Sandra. 'But are you sure there isn't anything we can help you with right now?'

She and Yume both grinned.

'It doesn't look like there is,' he replied testily. 'I'll see you tomorrow then.'

As the door shut behind him, he thought he heard stifled laughter.

THIRTY-TWO

Yume

Yume was sitting cross-legged at home, still in her pyjamas. She had been truly horrified at the manner of Marjorie's death. It had taken her back to the events which had led to her being struck off.

There's me thinking that working with Richard will provide me with a mentor and show me the very best in geriatric care.

Yume didn't dislike Richard. She found him personable and knowledgeable, but his oversized ego and apparent lack of empathy were not what she believed to be the qualities required of a doctor.

Then, of late, patient care at The Retreat had become more like a production line.

Not one single patient has walked out alive. This isn't right.

She picked up the coroner's report from the table and began reading it again.

Cyanide poisoning.

The report's contents gripped her with a mixture of horror and professional fascination. The concept of investigating cyanide poisoning appealed to the scientist in her, but then there was that niggling doubt about that last dose of Elysium that Richard had given Marjorie.

What is going on in The Retreat?

She shuddered as the image of a line of people fading into the distance came into her head.

Euthanasia? No, that is too extreme a word, surely?

She checked her watch and jumped up from the sofa. She would just have time to dress before Rosie and Roberta arrived.

What am I going to say to them?

*

Half an hour later, Rosie and Roberta were sharing coffee and biscuits. Rosie had been introduced to Yume and immediately liked her. Apart from her exquisite appearance, it was something about her demeanour, her self-possession.

The atmosphere was surprisingly relaxed, and they were getting on well, opening up to each other.

'I have so many questions, and I don't know who else I can get some honest answers from,' Rosie began. 'Since I came back, I have been served so many platitudes, it leaves me angry.'

Roberta chipped in. 'I think it's this so-called accountability. Everyone is watching their own backs, while looking to put a knife in yours.'

'I've had years of that with my ex, and I'm not going to put up with it anymore,' said Rosie, jutting her chin out. 'Yume, I understand your position and I swear that anything you say will not be used against you.'

Yume looked from one to the other, checking their faces for a second. 'Okay, everything I say must remain *"Herkos Odonton"*.'

Roberta looked puzzled, but Rosie's face lit up. 'The classical Greek equivalent of "Top Secret", "The Hedge of the Teeth". Of course it will.'

Yume smiled her understanding and crossed her legs; she sat back on them, preparing to share her thoughts.

Rosie was elated. She would get some meaningful information.

She sat forward eagerly, and Yume began. 'The coroner's report states that poisoning must have occurred before Marjorie entered The Retreat. Her symptoms then mimicked old age but were obviously cyanide poisoning. We didn't know, and even if we *had*, it would have been too late to do anything.'

'What did you say… why?' stammered Rosie, looking shocked.

Yume continued. 'Sorry, I'll explain. There used to be a fascinating test for cyanide poisoning that created a pigment called Prussian Blue – now used by artists, by the way.' She gave a nod towards Roberta. 'It was unfortunately post-mortem, but from that, scientists developed a more sophisticated test that could be done on a live patient, which they swiftly followed up with an antidote. It only works within a three-day window, though, so there was nothing you could have done, even if you had known.'

Rosie pursed her lips. 'Small comfort in that.'

'What bothers me is that Richard just plugged her straight into the Pathway without any further investigation. I was there when she died; I found her death really distressing.'

She looked at Rosie, whose eyes filled with tears that she angrily brushed away.

Is this a good sign? I am responding to my emotions, not repressing them.

'If I wasn't a member of A Dignified Death, I might even call it euthanasia.'

'At least we have each other to talk to. Please don't feel guilty or upset, Yume, you're voicing your concerns. Something's not right, is it?'

'The police are looking into how she came to ingest cyanide, but I would also like to find out just what Richard Hawley is up to. He seems obsessed with monitoring and increasing the dosage of Elysium. I have a friend, Catherine, in the Department of Health who used to work with Richard. I'll phone her now.'

Yume dialled a number and eventually got through. After exchanging mutual greetings, she began to frame her request, but as soon as she mentioned Richard Hawley's name, there was a torrent of words from the other end. She ended the call and turned to face them. 'Catherine's reaction to Richard Hawley's name was surprising. She swiftly interrupted me and suggested that we meet up. Can you both come to London? I'm sure we can stay with my grandfather.'

They spent the next hour discussing logistics. They huddled together over Yume's diary to find convenient dates.

'And when were you going to tell me about your latest secret collaboration, Yume?' Sandra's voice came from behind the door, making them all jump.

The tension in the room was palpable. Roberta looked embarrassed; Rosie was on the edge of her seat, but Yume put a cautioning arm out. She then stood up and walked towards Sandra, stopping when they were face to face.

'Sandra, you are cross with me again? Please don't be. Rosie only phoned this morning, asking to come and see me, and you were working.'

Yume's reasonable words diffused the atmosphere and Sandra's shoulders relaxed. 'How come you're here now?'

'There was a phone call at The Retreat from a Catherine Day at the department. She used to work with Richard and she seemed to be checking us out. She said you phoned her, and I immediately smelled a rat.'

'Not a rat, you are exaggerating as usual. Come sit here with me, and I'll explain.'

Yume gently brought Sandra up to date, while Rosie and Roberta stared at them agog.

'Talk about *The Taming of the Shrew*,' Roberta whispered.

'Are they…?'

Yume eventually got up and positioned herself facing exactly midway between them, so she could turn easily to talk to them all.

She's good at body language.

She spoke softly. 'I would like to ask you all to put aside your differences for the meantime. We are strong women, and together we can be a force.'

She waited to let this idea sink in, then went on. 'Please understand my position. I will be sticking my neck out professionally. What I don't want to do is become a referee in your hatred game, Rosie and Sandra.'

She paused again, watching a variety of shocked expressions appear. 'We can't let negativity cloud our thinking and our actions. Do you agree?'

They all nodded, Rosie a beat after everyone else.

'I need your support on this one hundred per cent, Rosie,' she insisted quietly.

Rosie blushed. She felt like a five-year-old being told off in class.

I've come here for Yume's help, and these are her terms.

'You're right, and I agree,' she said as boldly as she could.

'Yume's good at this, isn't she?' said Sandra.

THIRTY-THREE

The Press

Sharon Lee, junior reporter, was kicking her heels. There was little of interest happening, so in common with other reporters working for local media, she had gone down to the coroner's court on the off chance there might be something newsworthy. The building was typical 1970s architecture, an unappealing blend of dreary grey concrete and glass. The corridors still retained the faint smell of stale tobacco despite it having been a few years since all the smokers had to get their fix outside.

The room in which the hearings took place was painted cream and was lit by strong fluorescent strip lighting. Rows of plastic seating at the back of the room were reserved for members of the public and other interested parties. The reporters sat here, the young ones grasping their take-out coffees whilst balancing their phones and laptops on the knees, the older reporters still favouring their dog-eared notebooks. A few bored people had come in from the rain, hoping for a whiff of scandal.

The inquest on Marjorie Clark's death was opened and adjourned by the coroner. Sharon noticed a plainclothes detective sitting nearby. She recognised him as DS Steve Mallory and pushed her craving for a cheeseburger and another latte to the back of her mind. Here was the promise of something newsworthy. As the coroner's voice droned on, she grasped the implications for a rolling storyline, and made copious notes.

Slipping out discreetly, she waited a short distance away and snapped Mallory as he came out. She then retreated to McDonald's to consider how best to find out more.

After a satisfying lunch, she went back to her office and researched the newspaper's library and database for background information and photographs. She found several stories about Summerlands and its wealthy clientele. The publicity that had surrounded the launch provided her with photos that would add wealth and glamour to the story. In a last-ditch effort to get a quote, she phoned and asked to speak to Professor Richard Hawley. The receptionist, who had already been coached on how to handle the press, explained that the professor was in a meeting and offered to send her a press release that had been prepared in anticipation of such a request. There was no time to delve into anything else. About four pm she presented the story to her editor, who seized it immediately for the front page and sold it to the national press.

The next day's headlines read, 'Suspicious death at Summerlands Luxury Retirement Complex'.

THIRTY-FOUR

The Police

The local Cheshire police station nearest to Summerlands was in a pretty rural village that had never dealt with a murder investigation before. DS Mallory arrived early and paused outside to enjoy the rich scent of flowers in window boxes and the drone of bees in the sunshine before entering. A small incident room had been hastily allocated. Mallory studied the room with amusement. There was a pinboard and whiteboard on the far wall, a specimen table in front, a couple of computer workstations either side and, finally, a row of chairs.

All vital equipment of a TV crime drama.

Because of the seriousness of the drug involved, DI Jack Holly had been drafted in to head the investigation. He now entered the room, followed by three younger officers.

'Please take a seat, everybody,' said Holly.

He began without preamble. 'The victim was Marjorie Clark, an eighty-four-year-old woman who moved into her own villa in the Summerlands complex two months ago. She deteriorated suddenly and was admitted to The Retreat, a care facility within Summerlands, where she died within four days. A post-mortem has found traces of cyanide in her tissues, diluted by the passage of time, which seems to rule out The Retreat.'

He paused to change tack. 'There's a forensic team at Summerlands right now. They're checking Marjorie's villa, and her room and medical stores at The Retreat. Mallory, I want you to interview all the staff at Summerlands.'

He handed Mallory a list of names.

'Dawson, I want you to examine all the medical records at The Retreat and get copies of Marjorie's medical records from her GP in Amersham.'

'Yes, sir.'

'King and Warner, I want you to make a list of all the relatives and friends who have visited Marjorie since she has been at Summerlands. Obtain their addresses and interview them.'

'Yes, sir.'

'And find out who the beneficiaries of her will are.' He pointed to a small pile of papers on the desk. 'There's a summary of your brief. We'll meet here again tomorrow morning. Just one other thing you need to know which might be relevant.'

He paused again to make sure he had everybody's attention. 'A year ago, Linda Hammond, a resident of Poynton in Cheshire, died aged forty-eight from a heart attack brought on by taking the slimming drug Svelta. Subsequently, it was found that within Sipher, the company that produced it, a high-ranking employee had falsified the clinical trial data to make it appear safer than it was. This employee is still at large and evading custody. There are several coincidences with that case and this one, which I have listed on the brief.'

Holly picked up the top copy from the desk and read from the last page.

Get on with it, Holly.

Mallory was poised to leave.

'The missing Sipher employee is David Jennings, the estranged husband of Rosemary Jennings, Marjorie Clark's daughter.

Furthermore, Rosemary Jennings was a close friend of Linda Hammond, as was Sandra Marsden, a nurse at Summerlands.'

He looked at them directly. 'I don't believe in coincidences, do you? Now go and find out what you can.'

*

By day three, the notice boards in the incident room were covered with information and DI Holly had called an early-morning meeting of the team.

'Thank you, everyone, for your efforts. We now have a list of the names of Marjorie's recent contacts and her medical records have been read, as have those of all the other people who have passed through The Retreat. The forensic team are still at her villa right now.'

Mallory turned away to pull a ghoulish face at Holly's choice of the word 'passed'.

'We're not in class, Mallory,' snapped Holly, who didn't miss much. 'Okay. Settle, everyone.' He continued, 'Who were her visitors at her villa in the weeks before she went into The Retreat?'

'Mainly Eva Phipps, her neighbour, Eva's daughter Roberta Kenyon, grandsons Theo and Hugo Jennings, then a collection of other neighbours and friends. There were also the Summerlands staff cleaner and handyman and Dr Yume Yamamoto,' replied Walters.

'Did you find out who was the beneficiary of her will?' Holly asked her.

'Yes, Rosie Jennings made me a copy. Apparently, the grandsons Theo and Hugo were the sole beneficiaries.'

'It comes back to family.' Mallory had his cynical face on.

'Where can you get cyanide?' King innocently threw in a vital question.

Mallory played his trump card. 'I think the cyanide was probably obtained on the internet, or through contacts. It's not exactly for sale on the high street. I suggest a warrant to seize the computers and mobile phones of everyone in the Jennings household.'

'Good idea, Mallory. Get it done. Anything else?'

'I checked the medical records and everyone at The Retreat was being given a drug called Elysium,' said Dawson.

'We should get it tested for cyanide,' said Holly. 'Just in case.'

THIRTY-FIVE

Rosie

Rosie was working at her roll-top desk in the corner of the family room. Years ago, she had dealt with her paperwork from here whilst keeping an eye on the boys, and the familiarity gave her some comfort now. Simon was out, finalising his flight back to Abu Dhabi.

She had been to the villa earlier to collect Marjorie's papers and was looking through them, not that there was much to deal with. Summerlands would take care of the household bills, and no doubt their own. She was also arranging Marjorie's funeral, now that the coroner had released the body.

She paused as she came across some recent bank statements, and her eye was drawn to regular cheques for three-figure sums. Her heart went cold as a search for the cheque book stubs confirmed the truth. Hugo Jennings.

Hugo has a complete lack of shame.

She felt shocked and angry. This was the last straw, taking money off an old lady. She resolved to confront him as soon as she could find him.

Rosie had endured two visits so far from Cheshire Police. The officers had looked so young and fresh-faced when they came to the door that it was hard not to think of them as children.

My own boys are no longer youngsters compared with these two.

She had felt strangely distanced at the interviews. She answered their questions and supplied them with a copy of Marjorie's will, along with the names and addresses of friends and family.

I'm not lying, but I'm deliberately not volunteering information either. I'm wary of something, and I don't know what.

The intercom on the gate sounded, redirecting her thoughts.

Blast, another policeman?

Minutes later, the figure of DS Mallory loomed large in the porch, and she opened the door to him and a policewoman carrying a large bag.

Mallory introduced himself and DC Dawson. He and Rosie uncomfortably recognised each other from Linda's inquest the previous year, although neither of them acknowledged the fact.

'May we come in, Mrs Jennings?'

Rosie was not so ungracious that she didn't offer them a seat, but she drew the line at refreshments; she was hoping they would be gone soon. Her hopes were dispelled when they sat on the sofa, making themselves comfortable. They produced a wad of paperwork and a collection of large plastic bags. There was a proprietorial feel about their actions that made Rosie hover nearby and observe Mallory more closely.

He definitely has his official hat on.

A feeling of dread came over her.

'I think you might want to sit down, Mrs Jennings. We have some new developments that relate to your mother's death.'

Rosie took the armchair opposite them.

'Mrs Jennings, you will have been aware that our forensics teams have been working in your mother's villa. They have discovered cake crumbs down the side of her chair that contain traces of cyanide.'

Rosie couldn't help herself. She gasped out loud, then steadied herself.

Be calm. I haven't done anything wrong.

'We've come to take any computers and mobile phones that you may have, as part of our investigations. I'm sorry that it's short notice, but it's our policy not to forewarn people for obvious reasons.'

'I guess we can do without them,' said Rosie with bravado.

I won't be intimidated.

'What about Simon's computer?' asked Rosie. 'He's out right now.'

'His too, I'm afraid. Are your sons at home?'

She called upstairs for Theo and Hugo, it being a Saturday.

Of course, they will pick a day when most families are at home.

Surprisingly, Hugo was in for once, and he and Theo came down to the family room.

They stood uneasily at the doorway as Mallory repeated his request. Hugo already looked pale, but his face blanched and he made to go out again.

'If you don't mind,' said Mallory in an even voice, 'we have a procedure for this. I would ask that you all stay here with me, and Dawson will accompany you, one at a time, to retrieve your computers and phones. Can you give me Simon's mobile number? I'll call him myself.'

Hugo looked as if he was going to throw up but rallied round, joking about a heavy night out last night. 'Who wants a cup of tea?' he offered.

They all declined.

*

Simon came home to a bizarre scene. He first saw Mallory and a policewoman bagging and tagging mobiles and computers on the table, and they nodded in his direction as if this was an everyday occurrence. He could then see Rosie and Theo huddled at the far end of the sofa with the TV on, he guessed as a distraction from the lack of conversation and the sound of Hugo throwing up in the downstairs loo. Lost for words, he stood with a perplexed expression until Mallory saw fit to brief him as to what was happening. He sat down next to Rosie and hugged her in a gesture of support. Mallory's head darted forward and back like a mother hen, desperately trying to keep an eye on them and Hugo.

After the longest time, all the equipment was bagged and labelled, and Mallory and his DC made a swift exit.

Rosie gave Theo a reassuring hug and called to Simon, who was in the hall seeing them out. 'Simon, I'm going to have a bath, I feel grubby somehow. I'll catch you later. I've got something to tell you.'

'Okay, darling.'

Simon went into the downstairs cloakroom. Five minutes later, he rushed out and grabbed Hugo by the collar as he tried to sneak out of the front door. 'Oh no you don't, my lad. I've got a few questions to ask you.'

THIRTY-SIX

Hugo

Simon's taxi pulled into Woodford aerodrome where a Lear Jet had been flown in. Despite private jets being a familiar form of travel to the wealthy citizens of the Middle East, Simon had still felt uncomfortable asking if he could take advantage of the company jet. Now it was essential.

This is the only way of getting Hugo out of the country before the net closes in.

Woodford manufactured military aircraft, many of which were sold in large numbers to governments in the Middle East, so the arrival of a private jet was not unusual, and the formalities were virtually non-existent. This was what Simon had hoped for.

As the plane taxied out, he looked at his fellow passenger, the son of the woman who meant so much to him.

How is this young man, who has so many advantages in life, so corrupt?

As he sat back in his leather seat, his mind recalled the events of the previous few days. He had been aware of Hugo's jumpy reaction to his phone calls and had been eavesdropping whenever possible to try and find out exactly what he had got himself involved in. Then there was his reaction to the news that his grandma had died from cyanide poisoning and not from old age as everyone had assumed. Hugo had appeared in a state of shock, then his mobile had rung and he had hurriedly left the room. His reactions that day had all the hallmarks of previous phone calls and Simon had followed him upstairs to his bedroom.

'Ten thousand… by the end of the week? I can't do that! Look, give me a few weeks. I'm due some funds coming in.'

Simon had confronted him. 'What's going on, Hugo?'

Hugo ended the call and brandished the handset above his head as if to hit Simon. 'None of your fucking business, mate.'

Hugo turned towards Simon, his face full of disdain, his jaw set. The two men found themselves squaring up to one another. Suddenly, Hugo attempted to push Simon to one side, but he was no match for Simon's strength and physical fitness. Simon grabbed him by the wrist making him drop the phone. He then held both his wrists in such a firm grip that Hugo howled with pain. Simon looked him straight in the eye.

'You are going to tell me exactly what's going on and don't even think about sanitising the facts. You are going to tell me everything.'

*

Simon shuddered as he recalled listening as Hugo capitulated and told him the extent of his gambling, the loans he had taken out, pawning his mother's jewellery, taking cheques from Marjorie. Simon had stressed that Hugo stealing Rosie's possessions was, in his eyes, unforgivable, but he knew that gambling was an addiction, an illness, and it could make people do terrible things. He had promised him he would help him to sort out his debts if he would quit gambling and get a reasonable job. He would help him have another chance; he was a wealthy man. He would, however, do it primarily for Rosie.

It was Hugo's reaction to the police taking his computer and mobile phone that had made the hairs stand up on the back of his neck.

He had grabbed Hugo at the door and yanked him outside. 'We're going for a drive.'

Simon parked at the front of the Egerton Arms. 'No, we're not having a drink. At least if you start any trouble here, you will be noticed. Now you are going to tell me everything, and I mean everything, this time.'

Now I wish I didn't know.

*

Simon had told Hugo nothing of his plans, apart from the fact that he was getting him out of the country as discreetly as possible. Hugo had brightened visibly at the sight of the Lear Jet and had embarked on a self-pitying rant about how he would have had one too but for his run of bad luck at the gaming tables. Simon told him to shut up, and after that, Hugo climbed into a seat away from him and fell asleep, or feigned sleep, for most of the flight, only waking up when the engines went into reverse thrust and the jet landed at a private airstrip just outside Abu Dhabi.

Simon was thankful he didn't have to make conversation. His mind was still reeling from this latest turn of events and he was feeling very uneasy about lying to Rosie. He wondered about their relationship and whether it was strong enough to bear the burden of the knowledge of his actions, and those of others. He would be the first to admit that he had neglected his first wife by working long hours, and he had been determined to look after Rosie, his new love.

Am I going too much the other way by shielding her from the truth? I don't think so.

He could not tell her about this latest atrocity after everything that David had put her through, and so soon after Marjorie's death. He knew she was a strong woman and he was making a massive assumption that she would not cope, but his desire to protect her had won.

He turned his mind to planning their next move. Taking his phone out of his briefcase, he familiarised himself with what David Jennings now looked like, where he worked and his phone number. Apparently, the man in the photo was known as Adam Verity, a highly successful property salesman and the young woman with him was his partner, Veronica.

A bit heavier, and with a beard, but it's him, smug bastard!

As they walked down the steps from the jet, Simon scoured the desert which lined the runway and breathed a sigh of relief as he saw the car waiting for them as arranged. Rashid got out and opened the rear door to the Lexus so Simon and Hugo could get out of the heat and into the air-conditioned coolness. Simon thought how wonderfully discreet he was. No questions, just his usual bright white smile.

'Dubai Marina, please, Rashid.'

THIRTY-SEVEN

David

Once the car turned onto the highway, Simon took out his phone and dialled the mobile number he'd been given for David. It was picked up after only a couple of rings and Simon, who was just wondering if he would recognise his voice, was forced to speak.

'Is that Adam Verity? I've been given your name as someone who can help me. I've just taken up a job here and I'm after an apartment on the Dubai Marina.'

Simon needn't have worried. David's antennae remained primarily attuned to money and he fired off some standard questions. 'My budget? Right. I'm thinking in the order of seven million dirhams, although I could probably go higher for the right property.'

The conversation continued with a discussion about rooms and marina views. Hugo remained totally disconnected and just stared out of the window at the desert landscape and the occasional camel. He didn't know who Adam Verity was – yet.

'I need to move quickly on this, Adam. You are actually my first call. I am hoping I could look at some properties this afternoon. Is that possible, do you think? You come highly recommended.'

Simon was betting on the man's ego having not been diminished, and he was right.

'The Grosvenor Two, at four o'clock, the bar by the upstairs pool, got it. See you there.'

Simon snapped his phone shut. Satisfied that the call had been as straightforward as he had hoped, he instructed Rashid to divert back to his villa. 'I think we could both do with a shower and change of clothes,' he said to Hugo.

Once back at the villa, home to him and Rosie, he felt a kind of unease at Hugo's presence, which somehow seemed to pollute something that was wonderful and unsullied.

'You can shower in here,' Simon said curtly as he led him towards the guest suite. 'And there should be some clean shirts in the wardrobe. Help yourself. We need to leave in fifteen minutes.'

He watched as Hugo stared at the floor, unwilling to look him in the face. Simon hated him, hated the charade, but he had to finish what he had started.

The journey from Abu Dhabi to Dubai was again made in silence with Hugo gazing out of the window. As they neared the city the desert was replaced by Western-style business parks as the four-lane highway headed towards the futuristic city of glass towers that was Dubai.

At the five-star Grosvenor Two hotel, they took the escalator to the opulent first-floor lobby to ask for directions, then they took the lift to the rooftop pool and bar. Simon looked around and realised that this was obviously a meeting place for both businesspeople and ladies who lunch. A bar ran the length of the pool where expensively dressed people perched on stools in front of colourful cocktails, which appeared to be accessories they didn't drink. Simon thought the place exuded an aura of what glossy magazines called glamour but he would call excess.

Perhaps I'm just getting old.

Surveying the seating options, he led Hugo towards a table and chairs that allowed him a full view of the lift whilst placing

Hugo opposite, so David would not see his son on his initial arrival. Simon felt confident he would recognise David despite the addition of a beard and a few extra pounds. He ordered beers and a selection of sliders, which arrived with great speed and were consumed at a similar rate.

They had just finished eating when the lift door opened. David stepped out, accompanied by a very attractive woman who looked a few years older than Hugo.

Veronica, Gail's friend. I recognise her from the picture. He's old enough to be her father!

David, dressed in designer jeans and a crisp, white open-necked shirt, surveyed the room looking for his client. Simon stood up, raised his hand and watched as David strode confidently towards them, leaving Veronica to trail behind him.

David stretched out his hand towards Simon and then paused. 'Adam Verity, erm, you look familiar. Don't I know you?' He then turned towards the young man who had remained seated but was now staring open-mouthed as if he had seen a ghost. Simon watched as the scene played out in slow motion, as if none of the actors was familiar with the script.

'Hugo?'

'Dad! What are you doing here?'

Simon took charge of the situation, aware of the need to stop things spiralling into a confrontation, something which would be viewed badly in this part of the world, where decorum in public was always expected.

'Please sit down and I'll explain.'

Father and son stared at each other whilst Simon shook the hand of an alarmed-looking Veronica and, ever the gentleman, pulled out a chair for her. She managed a weak smile.

David looked back at Simon and was first to speak. 'Who exactly are you and what is my son doing here?'

Simon was beginning to relish David's obvious discomfort. 'I'm Simon Adams, medical director at the Cardiac Centre in

Abu Dhabi. But we met many years ago at Manchester University when you went under the name of David Jennings. Your wife Rosie is a friend of mine and so I know your sons, Hugo and Theo.'

Veronica looked on, aghast, as a new reality dawned.

Simon continued. 'Hugo here is a chip off the old block, David. He has some serious gambling debts and is being pursued by people from the Manchester underworld who want repayment, and that may not be the worst of his problems yet.'

Simon watched as David tried to regain control. 'This has nothing to do with me, mate. I've been here for the last year. Come on, Veronica. Let's go.'

He stood up and pulled at Veronica's hand, but the young woman snatched it back. 'I'd like to hear what Simon has to say, so sit down, Adam, or David, or whoever you are.'

Simon spoke deliberately, making his scorn and anger obvious. 'Your son is also wanted by the police for questioning about Marjorie Clark's death, so he will sit very well with you, David. I believe you still have an international arrest warrant out in your name?'

He paused for effect here. 'I have it on good authority that by next year there will be an extradition arrangement with the UK. It just so happens that many of my patients are senior figures in the UAE. So I feel sure you will want to do what is right by Hugo.'

David looked cornered. 'And what exactly do you suggest I do?' he hit back.

'Take responsibility for him, and that'll probably mean settling his debts. Then, as both of you will be in the same boat evading the law, you'll have a common bond. Please don't forget what I said about my contacts. They're at the highest level in the police and judiciary. Any ideas you may have about not complying will not end well for you. Any threat to me or those close to me will result in your whereabouts being revealed.'

Veronica was speechless. He almost felt sorry for her.

I can't see her assuming the role of stepmother.

With nothing more to be said, Simon turned on his heel and left them. He was desperate to breathe air that wasn't polluted by avarice and lies. Father and son deserved one another.

THIRTY-EIGHT

Rosie

Rosie was at home and in shock. Hugo hadn't been back since the police had taken the computers. Then Simon had an emergency call the same evening; an important patient had been admitted to the hospital in Abu Dhabi, needing a heart bypass operation, and only Simon would do. A Lear jet had been dispatched to pick him up.

Hugo had been prone lately to disappearing for days, but this time Rosie was worried sick. She regretted that she had not had a chance to have that severe talk with him that she had steeled herself to undertake. She and Theo phoned round all his friends without success. She was waiting anxiously now for Simon to return from Abu Dhabi and trying to bury her thoughts by checking for any last-minute arrangements for Marjorie's funeral in two days' time. However, one sentence kept repeating itself, no matter how many distractions she created.

First David, now Hugo. This can't be a coincidence.

She could stand her isolation no longer, and phoned Roberta, who came round straight away. 'I'm only painting,' she said.

By mid-afternoon, Rosie had poured herself a large glass of wine. Now with Roberta beside her, drinking a tonic water, she felt calmer with her presence, and as the alcohol took effect, she unburdened herself.

'It can't be my fault... Hugo is just like his father... Let's face it, I don't really know either of them.'

'Agreed, not your fault.' Roberta was lying on the sofa. 'Isn't it *you* supposed to be lying on the psychiatrist's couch, though?'

Rosie smiled briefly. 'Surely Hugo will be back for his grandmother's funeral?'

'That would be normal behaviour, but this situation is not normal, is it?'

Roberta decided it was time to change the subject and turned the discussion to their approaching visit to London. 'A week is a long time and London is expensive,' said Roberta with a worried frown.

'You won't have to spend that much,' said Rosie. 'Yume has arranged for us to stay with her grandfather, remember?'

Roberta, who was a homebody, groaned. 'I won't keep up with everybody, I get so tired.'

'There'll be so much going on, you won't notice. As well as meeting Catherine, Yume's grandfather has contacts from the charity for the elderly he supports. Then there may well be some action required, depending on what Catherine comes up with. I do value your input, and you don't want to miss out on all this, do you?'

'Yes, actually, I do. It's not my world; I would be a spare part. I'd be happier staying here.'

'You know, I haven't told Simon about this yet. I'm following Yume's call to keep everything top secret. It feels strange, though.'

A key sounded in the door, and Simon came in, dragging a suitcase. She ran down the stairs to him and flung herself into his arms. They hugged each other for a very long time.

Eventually, Simon disengaged himself and held her at arm's length. 'Daytime drinking, Rosie? I can smell it on your breath.' He raised an eyebrow in mock surprise and then laughed. 'I think I'll join you.'

They were catching up, when the doorbell rang.

DS Mallory and DC Dawson were on the doorstep. Dawson was carrying a large holdall. 'We've come to return your computers,' Mallory began.

Simon made as if to take the bag from Dawson, but it wasn't proffered.

Instead, Mallory took a step forward. 'May we come in?'

It was a statement, not a question.

Simon stepped back and let them both in. 'This way,' he offered, taking them up to the family room.

'Shall I go?' Roberta sat up on the settee as the police entered.

'No,' said Rosie, 'you're family.'

The police duo stood, uneasily taking in the scene. Roberta was spread out on the sofa; the wine bottle was almost empty on the coffee table. Simon didn't offer them a drink. Instead, he moved to stand at the back of Rosie's chair in a clearly patriarchal manner and waited for them to state their business.

Dawson proceeded to lift items one by one from the bag, and, in the absence of anywhere else to put them, leant over and laid them on the coffee table. Rosie snatched her wine glass away.

'Laptop and phone, Rosemary Jennings; laptop and phone, Theo Jennings; laptop and phone, Simon Adams,' Dawson recited.

'Ahem.' Mallory cleared his throat and looked at the wall behind Rosie and Simon. 'We are retaining the laptop and phone belonging to Hugo Jennings.'

'No! Why?' Rosie cried, emboldened by the drink.

Simon reached over her shoulder and clasped her hand.

Rosie looked at Mallory, forcing him to look directly at her. He was clearly uncomfortable. 'I have to inform you that on Hugo's phone there are texts and calls between known underworld contacts. It appears that he owed a considerable amount of money to some unscrupulous people.'

Rosie gasped.

'I'm afraid that's not all. There were searches about poisons on Hugo's laptop, including cyanide,' he concluded dramatically, looking at the wall again.

There was complete silence.

'That must be a coincidence. I can't believe Hugo would try to get out of debt that way…' Rosie mumbled, then faltered, her face ashen.

'Obviously, we would like to question Hugo about this,' said Mallory. 'Is he at home?'

Rosie turned around to look at Simon and was puzzled. She expected a look of mutual support, even for him to take over and reply to the question. Instead, his face was full of conflicting emotions.

'He's not been home for a couple of days,' Rosie found herself saying.

'Do you think he has gone missing?' asked Mallory carefully.

'I haven't heard from him, but that's not unusual,' replied Rosie evasively.

'Tell him to either phone us or report to the police station as soon as he turns up. I have to inform you that Hugo is now a person of interest in your mother's death.'

Mallory saw himself and Dawson out, leaving Rosie and Simon rooted to the spot, and Roberta lying on the settee. Eventually, Simon came to sit on the arm of Rosie's chair and took hold of both her hands. She turned to look into his face again, and reluctantly his eyes met hers.

'What aren't you telling me?' she asked him.

*

Simon thought that it was uncanny, this sixth sense that women seemed to have. He was closer to Rosie than he had ever been to anyone in a relationship, yet now her eyes were a cold green that he had never noticed before. What to divulge?

Damage limitation, I think.

'I think I'll be going now,' said Roberta. 'I'll see myself out.'

Simon and Rosie hardly heard her.

'I heard snatches of phone calls.'

'You spied on him?'

Simon sighed. 'Come on, Rosie. You must know he has been taking money from Marjorie. We've both had our suspicions that Hugo was in debt.'

'That's not all, though, is it?'

Simon thought quickly.

I'll have to tell her more, but what?

'I had a talk with him. I even offered to help him settle his debts. But then I found he had pawned some of your jewellery.'

Rosie dashed upstairs to check. Minutes later, she was down again, in tears.

Simon made a move to comfort her, but she took a step back and faced him. 'You didn't tell me. Why? I thought we were a team?'

'Rosie, you were so upset about your mum I thought you had enough to handle. I have no experience with stepchildren. I just didn't know what to say to you. I tried to deal with him myself instead. I just didn't want to hurt you.'

Rosie's face softened slightly. 'I can understand that, but what else have you done that I don't know about?'

'I promise you that from now on I will consult with you first,' he fudged.

Rosie allowed herself to be hugged.

'We all need hugs right now,' Simon said, sensing that she was not completely reassured and that a wedge had driven itself between them that afternoon.

Neither of them spoke for some time, their arms around one another, Rosie resting her head on Simon's chest. As he stroked her hair, her mind was a maelstrom of unwelcome thoughts. Eventually she stepped back and looked at Simon with heavy eyes.

'Could Hugo really be so, so evil, that he's capable of killing my mum, his grandma?'

Simon went to pull her close again, but she resisted.

'It would seem that Hugo has not only inherited David's looks but also his amoral attitude to life. How did I not see it? Could I have done something?' She slowly shook her head at the futility of her thoughts.

'Where has he gone, Simon? Is he safe? Oh, darling, do you think he's a murderer?'

THIRTY-NINE

Yume and Avard

Yume's grandfather, Avard Harriman, was staring at a photograph on the mahogany desk that dominated his wood-panelled study. He was looking at a young girl standing between him and his wife, sporting a wide toothless grin, long gangly legs and poker-straight black hair. His granddaughter, his Yume.

Avard had been concerned to read in the papers of the suspicious death of one of the Summerlands residents. He wondered whether he should phone Yume, but she had phoned him instead.

'Hello, Jii-chan. Can I come down and see you next week?'

Avard immediately knew she was upset. Yume had never lost her Japanese good manners and would normally enquire first about his health and that of her grandmother.

'Yume-chan, how are you? I was just thinking about you. I have just read the news.'

'Oh, Jii-chan, I was there when the lady died, and it brought back everything that happened in Tokyo. But this time I am not responsible. The patient died because she was given cyanide before she came into The Retreat.'

Avard remembered how devastated Yume had been, years previously. She was talking at an unusually fast pace, something she always did when she was stressed.

Poor girl, it's bringing it all back to her.

'It's not just me that is concerned. There is the lady's daughter and a work colleague. We have allocated next week to come to London and try to find out exactly what is going on. I will explain the details later.'

'Of course, you must all come to stay, and I will help all I can.'

'Thank you, Jii-chan. How are you and Baa-chan?'

Avard was happy to hear Yume revert to her normal self. 'We're just great, Yume. Look after yourself. We look forward to seeing you all.'

*

Marjorie's funeral took place under a grey cloudy sky and a steady drizzle. It was a short service where a local vicar had done his best to reflect on the life of an elderly lady he had never met and who had died in unpleasant circumstances. Surprisingly, it was well attended by friends, reporters and various onlookers. Rosie had rented a small conference room at Summerlands for the wake. Despite her growing hatred of the place, it was convenient.

A week later, Simon had flown back to Abu Dhabi, and Rosie was on a train to London. Yume and Sandra had already arrived separately at Yume's grandfather's house. At Euston, she took a taxi to Westminster, and the Ichi-Riki sushi house.

Yume and Sandra were there with Catherine, who immediately introduced herself.

'I chose this place for Yume,' she said proudly. 'Also, it's one of the nearest restaurants to work. Do you all like sushi?'

Over lunch, she apologised for the manner of the phone call with Yume straight away. 'I make it a rule never to talk about work over the phone these days,' she explained. 'Especially now when there's a strange atmosphere in the department and unexplained things are happening.'

She went on to tell them that she had been a team member of the original Palliative Care Pathway project run by Richard Hawley for five years. Some months ago, shortly after the appointment of a civil servant, Jason Brown, she had been told she was no longer needed. More than a bit annoyed, she kept an eye on things, noticing that a small group comprising Jason Brown, Richard Hawley and two others continued to meet, though none of the meetings were minuted on the intranet. She had heard the words 'Avalon project' used.

'I will try to find out more about what's going on and get back to you tomorrow,' she promised.

*

Yume was sitting with her grandfather in the lounge of his London house. Her grandmother had made everybody welcome and had prepared an excellent supper. Now they had all discreetly retired, leaving Yume to talk with Avard alone.

'Jii-chan, I'm really worried about Richard's behaviour. He is using Elysium, a drug he helped develop. It's the way he's using it for every case that comes into The Retreat. I'm worried that he is hastening their deaths.' Yume's expressive face contorted with distress.

Avard was taken aback. He knew Richard of old and although the man was full of his own importance, with a reputation as a self-publicist, Avard had always felt he genuinely had the interests of older people at heart. 'Hold on a moment. These people are dying, right? Isn't he just making sure they have a pain-free death?'

'I think it goes beyond that. They're given Elysium, and then the dose is increased until they just gradually shut down. That's the only way I can describe it. The lady who just died didn't react like the others, though. We now know she had been poisoned with cyanide beforehand, but at the time, Richard just gave her an increased dose of Elysium and she died immediately.'

Is she reacting to her memories?

'It must have been devastating for you to watch,' he consoled her.

'There's more. You remember Catherine Day, who was a member of Richard's Pathway team? She tells me the whole team has suddenly been removed, and now the project has been renamed Avalon, with only four people. It seems to be driven by Jason Brown, a new director responsible for business transformation. She has seen Richard meeting regularly with him.'

Avard was beginning to understand Yume's concern. 'Business transformation? That invariably means saving costs. Why would someone in that role be interested in palliative care?'

'Catherine is trying to find out exactly what this new streamlined project team is trying to achieve.'

Avard looked uneasy. 'Yume-chan, the only way the Department of Health can cut costs is either by reducing the number of doctors and nurses or the number of patients. I don't like to contemplate what might be happening here. I will consult Tony Knight. He's a long-time campaigner and lobbyist for the interests of the elderly. But take care, Yume. There may be a lot at stake. I'll help you all I can.'

Avard clasped his hands over hers in a gesture of solidarity.

FORTY

Catherine

The women met Catherine the next day for lunch, at Pizza Express this time. It was further down the road but still within walking distance from the department.

Catherine arrived, crackling with energy. 'Sorry for the cloak-and-dagger stuff again. I just don't want to be seen to be doing anything out of the ordinary. I have found a way to get information, though. I've had a chat with Jim, a colleague who works with the Government's secure intranet, or GSI, as it's more commonly called. He's worked for the department for as long as I have, so I trust him.'

There was a pause while they put their food orders in, then Catherine continued. 'I didn't know Jim's views on the recent changes, so I approached the subject cautiously, asking him what his take on Jason Brown was. I shouldn't have worried – he was quite vocal with his suspicions. We met for a drink after work and he volunteered to access the GSI. Apparently, he was involved in setting it up and can still access its contents. He has never abused this privilege before, so he doesn't know what will happen. It would not be impossible for him to stumble upon emails between two parties which might shed some light on Avalon.'

With no further revelations, they chatted and concentrated on their lunch.

'Can you meet me at the Cinnamon Club tomorrow? It's in the old Westminster library, you will love the building,' said Catherine as she left.

'Do people lunch like this all the time in London?' said Sandra.

'Only if they have a salary to match,' replied Yume.

FORTY-ONE

Catherine

They met Catherine the next day at the Cinnamon Club as promised, but she was in a quite different mood. Gone was her bubbling energy. They had been admiring the building, but she hustled them quickly inside and selected a discreet table in a corner.

She looked nervous. 'I can't put any of this in writing, and please don't quote me either.'

'"Herkos Odonton",' said Rosie, parroting their earlier oath to Yume.

Catherine visibly relaxed. 'Thank you,' she replied.

They ordered their food, and then Catherine began speaking, except today, she didn't order anything. 'Sorry, I don't want to make a fuss, I can't eat at the moment – just water, please.'

She began talking haltingly in a low voice. 'It would appear that Jim has found spreadsheets that explore the savings to be made if death among patients in palliative care takes place three, six or nine months earlier than projected.'

'Woah, slow down, Catherine, can you say that again in ordinary speak?' said Sandra, putting her knife and fork down with a clatter, making them all jump.

437

'Yes, sorry, Jason's team have identified immense cost-savings that could be made if people in the final stages of life were to die sooner rather than later. From what I can see, Richard is complicit in all this and it's difficult to believe the minister himself is not aware of what's going on.'

Yume gulped a large mouthful of wine. She didn't know what she'd expected, but having her worst fears confirmed was a shock.

'So that's what Avalon is all about, terminating the terminally ill!' cried Rosie.

'I'm sorry, Rosie, I knew this would upset you especially. I don't know how far Richard's involvement has gone yet either,' Catherine began.

'My mum died from cyanide poisoning, so that's a separate issue which the police are investigating,' replied Rosie.

It's okay, Catherine, it's my son who's the murderer there.

Rosie abruptly changed the subject. 'How do we get evidence, though?'

Catherine reached into her pocket, pulled out a memory stick and handed it to her. 'That's got the emails and spreadsheets that'll leave no doubt as to what is being proposed. I have another copy which I'll stash somewhere safe in case yours gets into the wrong hands. Do you know what you plan to do with the information? You will be crossing some high-profile and very ruthless people, and I'm worried about your safety.'

'It's non-elective euthanasia, Catherine, there is no other way of looking at it,' said Yume earnestly. 'This goes against everything we stand for at A Dignified Death. My grandfather has contacted someone called Tony Knight. You may know him from his appearances in TV debates. He's an outspoken advocate for the rights of the elderly and would know the best way to use your information. We need to act quickly. Thanks again, Catherine, and please thank Jim.'

'I must go now.' Catherine was visibly nervous and anxious to get away. 'Jim and I both want this exposed.'

'Thanks for trusting us, we will use this information carefully.'

FORTY-TWO

Avard

Avard Harriman glanced out of his office window at the rain-soaked London street as he waited for a meeting of five people who had unwittingly become embroiled in what was likely to become the greatest scandal of the early twenty-first century. His central London home was an ideal location, on the basis that a retired American diplomat would be unlikely to attract the attention of the authorities.

He had been through the information on the stick the night before and familiarised himself with its contents. Now he had to disclose it to the two other people that his granddaughter trusted, plus his colleague Tony.

His thoughts were interrupted as Yume, Sandra and Rosie came to join him.

'We're just waiting for Tony now and then we can get started,' he said.

As if on cue, they heard Avard's wife answer the front door. They could hear a muffled conversation, then the door to the meeting room opened and a small, dishevelled-looking man in his fifties stumbled in, tripping over one of the cables and showering the room with papers that had been stuffed into the bag he was carrying. He pulled himself up by a nearby chair as the others gathered up his papers. After straightening his clothes, he introduced himself. 'Tony Knight. I do like to make an impact when I enter a room.'

Avard smiled. This was the Tony he had known for years. Behind the somewhat chaotic demeanour was a sharp mind and a commitment to the causes of the elderly.

'Right. Well, let's get this show on the road. I think I have the equipment you need already set up.'

The group watched in silence, the whirring of the projector in the background, as they looked at what Jim had uncovered. It started with spreadsheets showing the cost savings that could be achieved by bringing forward the deaths of elderly people undergoing palliative care.

'The most obvious savings could be made on drugs and other medical interventions,' said Avard. 'We are talking about millions of pounds, by the way. Further savings involve freeing up beds for elective surgery, the hidden benefit of which is that people there are more likely to return to work and pay taxes.'

There were murmurs of shock at such a callous approach.

He then moved on to a colour-coded graph. 'You can see here with absolute clarity how an earlier death than projected generates far greater cost savings. The blue line shows the savings if death occurs three months earlier, the green line six months earlier and the red line nine months earlier.'

Avard watched the audience shake their heads in utter disbelief at what they were seeing.

'And here is the evidence of the people involved.'

Avard moved on to show the email trail between the members of Avalon. This proved conclusively that although the project was being driven by Jason Brown, there was no doubt as to an awareness at ministerial level of what was being considered.

'I have taken the precaution of making a backup of this information and it is stored securely,' said Avard. 'Whilst Jim took great care to avoid any form of an audit trail of what he's done, a forensic investigation could uncover his activities. I think we need to act quickly.'

There was another silence. Everyone in the room was processing the information.

'We'll have a short break,' said Avard, 'and then we need to share our thoughts as to what we do next. I don't need to remind you that we are a closed group now. If any of this information is leaked to the wrong people, all our lives will be in danger.'

*

Yume spoke up first. 'I'm a member of A Dignified Death – in fact, many doctors are. We see suffering daily, and in most cases we can alleviate pain and make people well again. But none of us can live forever and where people are in unbearable pain or living in a situation of no hope, we believe there should be an option for people to choose to die. Many of us believe euthanasia should be available to elderly people too.'

Rosie was next. 'My mum died in Summerlands, where Richard Hawley works. Even though she was dying when she entered The Retreat, he just plugged her into what we now know as project Avalon.'

'I've looked after elderly people for years,' said Sandra. 'There is definitely a point where they start to fade, and drugs make them rally around temporarily. Watching this cycle repeated over and over again is tortuous for everybody involved.'

Avard realised that there might be differing views on the matter and it was best for everyone to have their say.

'Tony, what's your view?'

'If the Government were targeting an ethnic minority with their plans, it would be called genocide. I don't have any strong views on euthanasia; what gets to me is that they see the sick and elderly as a soft target.'

Avard stood up and walked towards the graph that had been left projected onto the wall. 'This,' he said, pointing to the graph, 'this is euthanasia on an industrial scale to save the Government billions. It has nothing to do with dignity, nothing to do with treating people as individuals; it has everything to do with saving money. I for one cannot ignore what I've seen.'

FORTY-THREE

Avard

Avard remained standing in front of the group. The role of chairman fell naturally to him.

'I have to warn you how catastrophic the publication of this data will be to the Government, and I know from my years as a diplomat how governments behave when they are backed into a corner.'

Everyone was listening.

'The minute they get any inkling of what we know, our lives will be in danger. We need to act now and make it public. We are just a small group of people and alone we have no clout. Exposure by the media is the obvious way to amass large-scale resistance, then everyone will jump on the bandwagon.'

There was a murmur of assent at the call to act quickly.

Avard continued. 'In my experience, any attempt by the media to publish will be shut down immediately by the judiciary in what will be called "the interests of public safety". Quite ironic, really, given what we now know about their ideas. No, we need to find another way.'

Tony had been quiet for some time, staring ahead, deep in thought. Suddenly, he stood up and raised his arms skywards. 'The Blogger of Baghdad!'

Avard looked up and grinned. 'Exactly, Tony, that's the way forward.'

The other three looked puzzled, and it was Rosie who asked for some clarity. 'You both obviously know what you're talking about, but can you explain it to the rest of us, as we don't have a clue.'

The group listened intently as, between them, Tony and Avard explained how a young man in Baghdad had used a personal website to tell the rest of the world what was happening in Iraq before and after the American invasion. What he wrote was shared with a worldwide audience and was picked up by various journalists.

'Right,' said Rosie. 'So, if I understand you correctly, you are saying we put what we have found out on the internet, so it gets into the public domain?'

Tony nodded before explaining the nature of what they were up against. 'We'll only have a very short time after our website goes live before the Government discovers it and calls in GCHQ – that's the Government's tech experts – to get it shut down. We'll need to contact the major media outlets beforehand and tell them that what is about to be made public is a news sensation and constitutes a threat to the lives of all us.'

'Which, of course, it is,' said Avard solemnly.

The group sat silently for a while, each contemplating the enormity of what they were considering before Avard continued. 'I understand quite a bit about how the Government monitors communications, but I don't have the skills to set up a website.'

Tony became animated again. 'My son, Michael, is a website designer. I'm sure he'll be glad to help. We'll need to write the content, but I'm certain he could set up a site for us.'

'Well, we've got the content, as you refer to it, on that memory stick,' said Yume.

Avard sensed a growing feeling of excitement and moved to urge caution. 'We have to approach it very carefully. If the information is produced verbatim, the path will lead very quickly to Jim and Catherine.'

'People don't want to read lots of detail,' Tony countered. 'We just need to get the main points across. Let's have a brainstorm and agree exactly what our message is going to be. We need to focus on producing bullet points. Yume, would you mind taking notes?'

Yume scribbled as the group began to come up with thoughts and ideas.

Government plans to introduce institutionalised euthanasia.
Secret meetings at the Department of Health.
Assisted dying for those in their final months of life.
Cost-saving initiative exposed as selective euthanasia.
Do we mention Elysium?
Do we name names?
Should we publish figures?
The graph will be very powerful.

Avard held up his hand. 'Okay, okay, we have lots to say, but we need to keep it succinct. Tony, I know you have lots of experience in getting a message across. Do you think you could come up with, say, a short paragraph that people could read quickly? And what do you all think about using the graph?'

'It illustrates exactly what they are contemplating,' said Yume.

'Yes, a picture paints a thousand words,' said Tony. 'I will come up with some strong copy to accompany it.'

Avard continued. 'Two things come to mind. We need to move within days, not weeks, and we need to be aware that we will all be in danger until this information gets into the public domain, and maybe after that. Now let's get an action plan together.'

For the rest of the rainy day, the group pooled their knowledge and agreed on a name for the website that was to go live that Saturday.

'Here's to the success of The Final Pathway.'

Avard raised his mug of coffee and the others followed suit.

Despite their outward bravado, they would all be looking over their shoulders from then on. They agreed to meet again in two days' time to review what Tony had written.

FORTY-FOUR

Avard

The rain had persisted all week. Clouds were gathered overhead, blocking the light. Their presence created an eerie atmosphere in step with Avard Harriman's thoughts, and he switched on the lights in his office to dispel them.

He'd been reliving his years as a diplomat, thinking about the dark forces that governments turned to when their actions needed to be shielded from the public eye. It wasn't just unelected despots or leaders in the Eastern bloc that clamped down on dissent in this way. He had witnessed the same approach from Western governments, who had 'assets' they deployed when their actions were not destined for public consumption.

And what we plan to expose will be seen in exactly that way.

The group were due to meet again that day, to see for themselves what The Final Pathway web page would look like before it went live. They had agreed that any phone or digital communication between them needed to be carefully handled in case of surveillance. In fact, the only contact Avard had received was a coded text from Tony who had 'confirmed his son was delighted to work on the pathway in Avard's garden and Tony himself had some ideas regarding the planting'. The memory momentarily lifted his gloomy mood.

By two o'clock they had all arrived. As he greeted each one, Avard scrutinised their faces with paternal concern. Apart from Tony, who was buzzing with adrenaline, the women looked as if they had not slept since the last meeting two days ago. He knew he had to get them thinking beyond their fear and back into supporting one another in making public the appalling truth they had uncovered. His wife had organised a buffet lunch which they picked at, their appetites obviously suppressed by the fear felt deep in their stomachs.

Avard disappeared and came back with a drinks trolley. 'This will oil the works,' he said, and wouldn't take no for an answer.

When they had all finished and relaxed a bit, Avard stood up. 'Okay, Tony, can you take over and show us what you've done?'

The normally garrulous Tony was now silent as he directed the projector towards the wall and turned it on. A single screen was displayed.

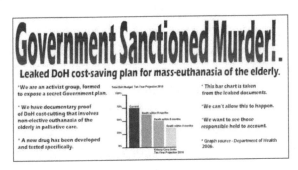

He looked around the room at their faces.

Avard was the first to speak. 'I'm impressed, Tony,' he exclaimed.

'Wow,' said Sandra, 'that cuts to the chase.'

'Brilliant headline,' said Rosie. 'It grabs your attention straight away!'

'Well written, Tony,' said Yume. 'I like your thoughtful handling of the word "euthanasia". You are emphasising how far it is from "pro-choice euthanasia" with the words "mass" and "non-elective".'

'I'm pleased you like that. You made us aware last Saturday that a lot of people believe in pro-choice euthanasia. It took me a while to select the right words, you know.'

Clearly gratified by the group's response, Tony began to explain in more detail what they were looking at. 'Okay, what you see here is a website with a single page. It has been set up on something called the dark web, and without boring you with the technical stuff, it's a communications network where you are ensured anonymity. Ironically, it was developed by the government in the US for intelligence sharing.'

This caused a few smiles.

'As Rosie noticed, I planned the headline to be stark and attention-grabbing. Under that, we have a single sentence that summarises the message. This leads on to the bar chart and the bullet points with succinct information of who we are, where we got our information and ending with a call for action.'

'Admirable. It certainly works,' Avard chipped in. 'Sorry, do go on.'

'It is important that you see "Graph source – Department of Health 2006", next to the bar chart. They would have to deny the existence of this file and we can rebut that by providing copies of the files Jim and Catherine obtained. Finally, the plan is for it to go live at 9.00am GMT this coming Saturday.'

Avard looked around at the group who were all now smiling, nodding and muttering their approval, and he was relieved to see they had been buoyed up by what they had seen.

We're back on track.

'Just one more feature,' said Tony with a cheeky smile. 'This screen is available as an image which can be emailed to people if and when The Final Pathway site gets shut down by the Government. I also had another idea. The image could be projected onto well-known landmarks around the country. It will take a bit of organising, but I know lots of organisations that would be willing to help. What do you think?'

'Brilliant idea,' exclaimed Rosie again. 'That will get media attention, and not only in this country.'

The rest of the afternoon was spent listing the media outlets that could be contacted and given log-in instructions.

As everyone began to leave, Avard made his parting shot. 'Jim and Catherine are in particular danger, as I'm sure you're aware. I have a holiday home in the West Country which I will offer to them. They can stay until we can ensure the safety of all of us. Once this is made public, the authorities will have their hands tied, but there are dark forces who will be seeking revenge.'

FORTY-FIVE

Richard–Saturday

Richard had already been to the gym and now he was back in his house. He always liked this time to himself. His normal ritual was to enjoy a mug of decaffeinated coffee and catch up on the news. Today, he took his drink into the lounge and sat for a while admiring the proportions of the Victorian room with its tall ceiling, fireplace alcoves, squared bay window and the view of his neighbourhood of leafy mature trees. He needed peaceful thoughts to replace the growing feeling that he, Professor Richard Hawley, was being taken for a ride with the Avalon project. His thoughts were interrupted by the shrill sound of his landline phone. His girlfriend had changed the ringtone and he hated it. He lifted the receiver to make it stop and intended to put it straight down again.

'Would you care to comment, Professor…?'

Intrigued, Richard held on.

'…as a specialist in elderly care, on a web page that has appeared online?'

'Who is this?'

'I'm Natalie Roberts, a research assistant at BBC News. We have been sent a link to a web page called The Final Pathway. It gives details of a leaked Government plan for mass euthanasia of the elderly. I was wondering if—' Natalie's young and sprightly voice was beginning to grate, and he stopped taking in what she was saying. He'd heard enough, though, to feel alarmed.

'I know nothing of this,' he interrupted testily.

'Let me email you the URL,' said Natalie. 'What's your email address?'

Richard was computer-savvy, but he hated this fad of reducing everything to initials. 'What's that?'

'A link to the web page,' replied Natalie patiently.

Richard reeled off his email address as he took the phone into his office to get his laptop. 'One moment,' he said, then, 'The link doesn't work.'

'It's been taken down already!' exclaimed Natalie. 'I made a copy, so I'll email that to you.'

Richard's computer screen filled with a single page. He suppressed a gasp of horror at the title. 'I repeat, I know nothing of this. That is my comment for now. I need time to read it properly. Thank you for bringing it to my attention.'

He put the phone down and stared at the web page. He was interrupted by the doorbell. He peered around the lounge door and glimpsed more people at the gate.

Reporters! ...at least they can't see me in the office.

Who is behind this, I wonder?

The landline rang again, and Richard pulled the plug from the socket. His mobile began ringing and he switched it off. He thought quickly and, switching his mobile on again, phoned the only person he could think of.

*

Yume answered on the first ring. 'Richard?'

'Have you seen a web page called The Final Pathway, Yume?' he demanded abruptly.

'Yes, I have.'

'I'm shocked, I know nothing about this.'

Yume realised she was holding her breath.

'Jason was hinting that Avalon would eventually consider pro-choice euthanasia when he recruited me. I was expecting to oversee a team of my choice; I anticipated months, maybe years, of meetings and discussions, but the only people that I've met so far are two monosyllabic accountants glued to computers. So far, Jason has just asked me to carry on incorporating Elysium into the Pathway programme and to monitor the results. This is the first I have heard of these three-, six- and nine-month projections.'

'Richard, I have been concerned at the use of Elysium at The Retreat and the increasing dosages.'

Richard sighed heavily. 'There is nothing sinister about Elysium. It is merely a superior mix of commonly used drugs. I admit my enthusiasm for it over others; after all, I helped develop it. Jason knew of this and he asked me to monitor its use in preparation for Avalon. He didn't have to try hard to persuade me. Perhaps I got carried away with experimenting with the exact dosage at critical stages. It wasn't intentional and I wasn't aware of it. I'm glad you brought it to my attention.'

Yume was surprised at Richard's candour.

'I would like to talk to you, but I'm surrounded by reporters and I need to get away from my house,' Richard added. 'Can you suggest anywhere?'

Not here.

'I'm not suggesting your place, Yume,' said Richard, echoing her thoughts. 'You might have reporters around as well. It's amazing how they make connections so quickly.'

'I think I know a place where they won't find you, and we can meet and talk about what we do next,' replied Yume.

Richard was strangely comforted by the 'we'.

*

Roberta was putting the finishing brushstrokes to a painting of the Caribbean island of Carriacou. She had captured perfectly the bright sun, the vibrant colours it created, the stall on the beach selling local fruit and vegetables. She sighed and tried to ease her aching back with her hands. The baby was due in a week, so they said at the hospital, and she tired easily.

She was in good spirits though, buoyed up by hormones and a forthcoming show of her work at a local gallery. It promised some sales and commissions that would tide her over the period after the baby was born.

There was a knock on the door, and Roberta got up painfully and walked slowly to open it. Yume was standing outside, and behind her stood a handsome man of a similar age to herself.

'Have you brought Prince Charming to rescue me?' Roberta asked flippantly.

Yume was used to Roberta's offbeat humour. 'No, I've brought you a lodger. Will that do?'

FORTY-SIX

Sharon–Saturday

Reporter Sharon Lee shouted an expletive as she shot upright in bed, spilling coffee and spraying toast crumbs over her unsuspecting boyfriend.

'Sorry, Mike,' she said, hastening to mop up the worst of the mess with her nightie, which she then threw into the corner of the room. 'At least I missed my laptop,' she added, making him growl and dive under the remaining dry sheets.

'It's my Saturday lie-in,' a muffled voice protested.

Sharon took the hint and, snatching her dressing gown from a hook on the door, took herself and her laptop into the kitchen, where she made fresh toast and coffee and sat at the table.

I don't believe what I've just read.

'Where is it?' she muttered impatiently as she tried to find the article again.

At last, she spotted the copy of a web message featured on the *News of the World* page under the headline 'Breaking News: Murdered in Their Beds!' She read through the text with a mixture of horror and excitement. There were already thousands of shares and comments expressing shock and calling for the Government to explain themselves. She noticed that a group called Ageing Matters were campaigning for a protest outside 10 Downing Street. A further post commented that the page had been taken down suspiciously quickly, speculating on a Government cover-up.

Sharon's reporter brain was kicking into overdrive. She thought of Marjorie Clark's murder at Summerlands. The latest statement from the police had said they were searching for her grandson Hugo, and the story seemed to have died, for want of a better word. Professor Hawley had issued a pompous statement of denial from his office.

Sharon dressed hurriedly and left a note for Mike on the counter. She wanted to follow this up, and the best place to get information on a Saturday was the computer in the library at work. She closed the front door quietly and unlocked her bike from the stand in front of her flat.

Half an hour later, armed with a latte, she inserted her card pass into the reader by the door at work. A skeleton staff was there at the weekend, but the paper went out every evening except Sunday and she wanted to gain an advantage. On what, she wasn't quite sure yet; she just had a hunch. The library was in a small back room crammed with racks of periodicals, local guides and gazettes competing for space with two computer terminals. She breathed a sigh of relief that one of them was free and nodded to her colleague at the other one. There were changes being mooted to get rid of the files and put in more screens, but the old guard still swore by paperwork.

The *East Cheshire Echo* had set up its systems to follow press, TV and radio, amongst other organisations. Sharon quickly scanned them. Most had copied the original web page with a variety of headings, promising an update shortly. Several had been successful in obtaining comments from key figures. Sharon gave a sigh of frustration; her local paper did not have the resources to find ex-directory or mobile telephone numbers. Then she found what she was looking for.

'Natalie Roberts, BBC researcher, contacted Professor Richard Hawley this morning and he has made the following comment:
"I know nothing of this. I repeat, I know nothing of this. I need time to read this."
Natalie has been unable to contact him for further comment.'

What does Professor Hawley really know about this?
It has all the hallmarks of a guilty reaction.

Sharon ploughed on instinctively. She opened the website for the Registrar of Births, Marriages and Deaths, and logged in to a special portal, available to interested organisations by subscription.

The website had improved its cross-referencing system, so although she didn't know any names, she was able to research recent deaths at Summerlands for which a medical certificate had been issued. She gasped. There had been four in the last month alone.

She tried Professor Hawley's landline, but it was engaged continuously.

Off the hook, or has he fled?

She phoned Dominic Maxwell's home number and he picked up.

'This is Sharon Lee of the *East Cheshire Echo*. I just wondered if you'd seen the web page that went live today, accusing the Government of planning mass euthanasia of the elderly?'

It was Dom's day off and his response was relaxed and curious. 'Is this a hoax?' he queried.

'The page has been taken down by someone now, but I can send you a link to the BBC website that has posted a copy.'

Dom repeated his email address to her and waited.

'I've got it now,' he said.

There was silence for a good while.

'Are you still there, Mr Maxwell?'

'I am shocked,' was Dom's brief reply.

'Do you have any comment, Mr Maxwell?'

'Why are you asking me?'

'I tried to phone Professor Hawley, but he is either not at home or he has left his phone off the hook. Do you think his hurried denial means that there is something else he knows about? Can you tell me why there have been four deaths at Summerlands in the last month while he's been in charge at The Retreat?'

There was silence, then Dom replied in a reasonable tone. 'I've no idea where Richard is. I will try and contact him. His denial will be genuine, as he is a professional man. Finally, I *do* know the latest monthly figures for deaths in The Retreat and I can assure you, it can happen, unfortunately.'

'Thank you very much, Mr Maxwell. I know it is the weekend, but may I phone you tomorrow to see if you have been able to contact the professor?'

Dom was impressed by her politeness.

She'll learn.

'Yes, of course,' he replied politely, and ended the call.

Sharon started preparing a headline for the newspaper's website: 'More Suspicious Deaths at Summerlands!'

Dom was searching for Richard's mobile number on his phone.

FORTY-SEVEN

Avard–Saturday

Avard was driving slowly down the winding Cornish lane. The high stone hedges made turning each corner a precarious activity, and he could see little of the magnificent coastal views that he knew they were hiding. It had taken him over five hours to reach the Lizard Peninsula from London, and the tiny fishing village of Porthallow took a further half an hour down a single-track road. It was the blissful isolation of the place that had first attracted him; it was such a contrast to London. Despite the effort it took to get there, he always felt able to unwind within hours of arriving.

And if it's this difficult to get to, it will remain unspoilt.

The village had fewer than fifty inhabitants and Avard thought it the ideal place of safety for Jim and Catherine. A single road led to a few terraces of whitewashed cottages that clung to the hillside and overlooked a wide shingle beach. The road ended at a local pub where the good beer and excellent food was a fraction of city prices.

As he descended the last hill, he turned his car sharply left towards his cottage. He was unsure of the nature of Jim and Catherine's relationship, but when he asked his wife her impressions, she just fell about laughing. 'Avard, you are such a typical man. It's on the cards they are more than just friends. You'd better warn them that you are coming and give them time to prepare the bedrooms.'

As he approached the door, he remembered her advice and decided to knock instead of using his key.

Just as Jim opened the door, a military jet screamed low over the village and out over the English Channel, banking steeply to the left. Catherine appeared just behind Jim and they both looked terrified. Avard realised they were reading too much into the plane's presence and he needed to put their minds at rest.

'Oh, I should have told you. RNAS Culdrose is a navy base on the Lizard. It's used for reconnaissance and search and rescue work. I should have warned you that they practise most days.'

Catherine and Jim relaxed visibly at this news and welcomed their guest to his own home.

'It's a lovely cottage, Avard,' exclaimed Catherine. 'I'm so grateful to you for letting us stay here to get away from the department. God knows what the atmosphere will be like. They like a good witch hunt! Do you want a cup of tea, or something stronger?'

Avard realised how naive Catherine was about the danger she and Jim would be in when the Government reacted.

They went into the cosy front room. Catherine and Jim took the sofa, and Avard stood with his back to the wood burner, enjoying the warmth and easing his aching muscles after the long drive.

'I thought I would get away for the weekend and come and see if you were safe and settled here,' he said. 'I fully expect that the media will be trying to contact me for a comment, but I am not the most prominent activist for elderly charities, so I will hopefully be left alone. The less I say the better, I think.'

'We've been watching the news coverage on TV, thanks to your supercharged antenna,' said Jim. 'The web page has galvanised people of all ages and walks of life to take action. Tony has been interviewed live, demanding answers from the Government, and there was a film report showing people gathering in neighbourhoods, parks and street corners. There's lots of reaction from everyone except the

Government. By the way, I love the way the screen image has been used on walls and buildings. There was coverage of crowds gathering at these sites too. I wonder how the others are holding up?'

'Good that you can keep in touch, but you know the Wi-Fi isn't secure for communication. The antenna is military equipment, but don't tell the locals. Well, Tony has a lot of experience handling the media and he's putting his skills to great use. I spoke to Yume before I left. She's planning to work at The Retreat as usual today. Rosie and Sandra have just been keeping their heads down. The really interesting news is that no one can find Richard Hawley. Yume says he phoned her, insisting that he knew nothing about the three-, six- and nine-month cost-savings that Avalon was planning. I want to believe him, if I'm honest.'

Jim and Catherine looked surprised at Avard's defence of the man.

'I can't see a way in which he wouldn't know about its objectives,' said Catherine.

'The online forums are very busy,' said Jim, changing the subject. 'People have used them to share a copy of the web page, and special interest groups are also sharing it. We've been following one called Ageing Matters. They are calling for a protest march on Parliament already.'

'The internet is a great force for dissemination,' said Avard. 'The Government, on the other hand, will be using all its assets, overt and covert, to get to the truth. They won't be able to stay silent much longer and they won't be able to cover this up either. One thing's for sure. Jason Brown will be feeling the heat.'

'Can't happen to a more deserving person,' said Catherine.

They wrapped up against the wind coming off the sea and wandered down to the pub for a hearty meal of homemade Cornish pasties washed down with local beer. Once back at the cottage they watched the evening news on TV. The Final Pathway was still the lead story and reporters had tracked down Jason Brown, who was seen pushing his way through an army of reporters and TV cameras to get to his front door. More importantly, the Minister for Health had stood down.

FORTY-EIGHT

MI5–Sunday

Elizabeth Furnival was only the second woman to occupy the role of Director General at MI5 in its hundred-year history. Gazing down from the top floor windows of Thames House on a quiet Sunday morning on Millbank, she drank her second strong coffee of the morning. She was a small, slim woman, with a grey haircut in a no-nonsense short crop. She looked competent and in control, with a hint of steely resolve in the set of her jaw. She was not unattractive, yet she had never married, and her sexuality was often the subject of office gossip. The reality was Elizabeth was wedded to her career, and any men in her life played second fiddle to her job. In her role as DG she was party to information that for most people would be the stuff of nightmares, but Elizabeth relished the challenge. Famed for her early-morning starts, she had arrived just after six am today and had timetabled today's meeting for eight am.

She had been made aware of The Final Pathway website within minutes of it going live the previous day and had immediately contacted her counterpart at the Government's communications headquarters, GCHQ. She found that they had already been instructed to find the site and shut it down, but this had taken

461

nearly an hour, by which time the inflammatory content had been widely distributed and people were becoming angry. Such was the public reaction that the PM had called a meeting of the COBRA committee late that afternoon. Elizabeth was mentally revisiting the circumstances of previous COBRA meetings. Some were the result of events beyond the Government's control, but others, such as the miners' strike and fuel protests, were a result of Government policy.

Is this something of the Government's own doing and they need damage limitation, I wonder?

One thing's for sure: this is an inside job, done with specialist knowledge of the intranet. The use of digital communications as an instrument of dissent moves our work into a completely new arena.

She had briefed the attendees for today's meeting late on Saturday. She had chosen them carefully: an IT trio she had used before with great success and two spooks. She needed the best the service had to offer.

She was in no doubt that there was a high risk of large-scale public disobedience which could potentially topple the Government. There were two main areas of investigation as far as she was concerned: the first was to find out who was behind The Final Pathway and the second was to determine if there was any truth in its message.

I'm not sure which takes precedence.

Elizabeth looked down at her coffee mug, which shook slightly, betraying the early stages of Parkinson's disease, something she had managed so far to keep between her and her doctor. The message in The Final Pathway now took on a more personal relevance.

Her thoughts returned to work again, with the arrival of the IT team she had chosen for this investigation. They were nicknamed the Three Ms, being Michael, Mark and Matthew. All were IT experts and Mark was an ex-hacker who had been convinced to work for 'the good guys'. Despite only having been briefed late on Saturday morning, their smiles indicated some progress. Following them were a couple of spooks who often worked together undercover, Erica and Craig.

'Okay, pour yourselves a coffee and let's get going. First, have you been able to identify who's behind all this?'

'I've conducted a forensic analysis of the department's intranet,' Michael began. 'The graph displayed on the website was created in September by a member of the Avalon team and—'

Elizabeth interrupted him, needing clarity. 'What is Avalon? Do we know?'

'From reviewing most of the documents, I would say it's a new programme for palliative care of the elderly.' Michael waited patiently to be asked to resume.

'Do you have copies of these files?'

Michael hooked his laptop to a projector, and they all watched as he displayed a slideshow of the documents that he had found. Afterwards, there was a discreet silence as they waited for Elizabeth's response.

'Do you have any names yet?'

'Yes,' said Michael. 'Firstly, the person responsible for the department's intranet is Jim Morris. Secondly, the Avalon spreadsheets have been created on two computers by two accountants, ID'd by codes and countersigned by Jason Brown, Director of Business Transformation. Most of the correspondence is between these three, but there is also another member of the team from outside the department, Professor Richard Hawley, who previously ran the Palliative Care Pathway project before it became Avalon. From the emails, it looks as if he has been trialling a new drug called Elysium and sending the results to Jason. It also looks as if he has very much been kept outside the loop, judging by the number of questions he has been asking and Jason's monosyllabic replies.' He spread three photographs on the table.

'Do you know of any disgruntled employees?' asked Elizabeth.

Mark spoke up. 'I have checked all the computers of the original Palliative Care Pathway team. Apparently, they were disbanded earlier on this year and reassigned to other duties. There was a lot of bad feeling expressed in departmental emails.'

'Does anyone stand out?' asked Elizabeth. 'Although I do think this is the work of more than a few employees. It's been very well-executed.'

'I have examined CCTV footage within the department,' replied Mark. 'There are two occasions when Jim was seen leaving the building with Catherine Day, who was a member of the disbanded Palliative Care Pathway team.' He added Catherine's photo to the table.

'So, who else has an interest in elderly care? Are there any other lobbyists?'

Craig spoke. 'There's Tony Knight, who has been interviewed by all the major media. He is playing a straight bat, taking the line that if it's true, it's industrialised euthanasia and heads must roll, etc. There is also retired diplomat Avard Harriman, who has a low-key role at various elderly charities.'

'We focussed on Avard because he is a member of the pro-choice euthanasia group A Dignified Death, as are Richard and Catherine,' said Erica. She added another photo of Avard.

'Richard is not at his home address in Manchester or at his place of work, Summerlands in Cheshire,' said Craig.

At this point, Matthew interjected, 'Summerlands? Well, that's a coincidence. I found an article online written by some local journo in Cheshire about suspicious deaths in the Summerlands Retirement Complex, as it's called. Richard is the medical director there. Avard Harriman's granddaughter, Yume Yamamoto, works there with him.'

'That's more than a coincidence,' remarked Elizabeth.

'Jim and Catherine are missing from their homes,' continued Craig. 'Apparently, they have been absent from work since Thursday as well.'

'Avard was followed from his London home to his holiday property in Cornwall yesterday afternoon,' said Erica. 'The door was opened by a young couple who looked like Jim and Catherine.'

'Well thought out by amateurs,' mused Elizabeth aloud. She turned to the team. 'The PM will be making a statement in the Commons tomorrow which will hopefully calm things down, but I'm not confident it will be enough. Fact or fiction, guilty or not, our task is damage limitation here. As you know, the minister has stood down so he can clear his name. We must stop the perpetrators in their tracks.'

FORTY-NINE

Richard–Sunday

Richard had spent the previous day checking the internet and the TV for the latest news. Now he was looking forward to discussing what he had heard with Yume. He had a few ideas.

Staying with Roberta was proving to be an interesting diversion. He had never had much to do with the art world apart from being a patron. In between news bulletins, he sat with her and they talked as she sketched and painted. It took his mind off his current predicament and gave him an insight into a world he didn't know anything about. He was used to working with a precision that demanded that everything be weighed, measured or quantified, with strict guidelines to be adhered to. He watched Roberta with fascination. She loaded her brush, made a few deft strokes on the canvas, frowned, added another colour, stood back, then mixed a completely different one. She seemed to respond emotionally, yet intuitively, to the materials and the subject, and he questioned her about it.

Roberta laughed. 'Well, there are rules like using perspective. Then you establish a light source and define where the shadows are. You can further create depth with tone and colour; after that it's down to experience, skill and, yes, personal interpretation of the subject, which could mean ignoring all the rules. It's not life or death, though, like your work.'

By late afternoon the light had gone, and they sat outside with a glass of wine each.

'I shouldn't drink, of course,' said Roberta, 'but I do treat myself to one glass occasionally. It goes straight to my head, though.'

Later, she retrieved a one-pot dinner from the oven, and they ate while Richard finished the bottle of wine and started another.

In this mellow atmosphere, they found out about each other's lives. Richard found Roberta easy to confide in and even told her the story of his mother. Roberta explained how she came to be pregnant and told him the story of her Caribbean adventure.

'I think your mother's death led you into promoting healthy ageing and then to your belief in pro-choice euthanasia. Do you think your helplessness at her death has now taken you too far, to the point of omnipotence, where you are toying with the dangerous power of life or death?'

No one had ever dared talk to Richard like this before. Yet he knew she had uncovered the truth. This strange hippy woman had turned a mirror on him. She made him want to go back and start on another path.

'Roberta, you are very perceptive, and I really appreciate your insight. I probably came very close to it without realising.'

They sat in companionable silence for a while. Then Richard spoke. 'What is your Danish skipper's name?'

'Jan Larsen, but why do you want to know?'

'Do you know if he's okay?'

'A policewoman told me he would soon be back on his boat. What happened was apparently a regular occurrence. The police make an arrest, then the big boys pay them off.'

'You haven't told him where you are. If I was him, I wouldn't want to let you go so easily. There is also a child that he doesn't know about. Is that fair?'

Roberta sighed. 'I've told you about my first marriage. I don't want that scenario again.'

*

Yume turned up at Roberta's the following morning with the latest news about Summerlands.

She looked at Richard nervously, but he seemed relaxed.

'I have invited Rosie to come,' she said, looking at them both in turn. 'She wants to hear what you have to say, Richard.'

'I'll make another coffee,' said Roberta, focussing on practicalities.

Richard was looking nervous now. 'Is she going to expose my whereabouts?' he asked.

Rosie arrived, and she and Richard were reintroduced.

'There are journalists hanging around everywhere,' Yume began. 'Apparently, a local reporter has insinuated that there are sinister connections between the Avalon project, Marjorie Clark's death, The Retreat, Elysium and you, Richard.'

'Yes, I know about her,' he replied with a dismissive tone. 'She contacted Dom Maxwell too. He then phoned me to discuss it.'

'And what did you say?' Yume asked.

'I said I knew nothing about any corporate manslaughter agenda behind Avalon. I was only asked to carry on trialling Elysium and monitoring its effects.'

Yume looked at him as if she were about to say something but changed her mind. He was her boss, yet her suspicions about his behaviour had helped trigger these events. 'What will you do, Richard? If you don't mind me saying, the fact that you can't be found is giving people a different message.'

'I wanted some space to consider my options. I realise I am guilty of getting carried away with the science of drug testing, to the point where I was ceasing to see my patients as people. Rather than let all my work be wasted, I would like to capitalise on the current situation and use it to showcase a cause that you and I have always believed in. A Dignified Death.'

Yume was transfixed. Of course, she should have known that Richard would find a way out of his predicament. She was disarmed, though, by his honest admission of guilt.

'How do you feel about my mum's death?' Rosie asked him, her bottom lip trembling slightly. 'Did you see her as a drug test or a person?'

Richard looked at her; she was an attractive woman, so he tried not to upset her. 'I would never have given your mother Elysium in the first place if I'd suspected she'd ingested cyanide. To me, she presented the classic symptoms of dying, I'm so sorry. Yes, I gave her a second dose; I was trying to help her. If I hadn't, she may well have suffered for longer.'

'Thank you, Professor Hawley,' murmured Rosie.

'What do you plan to do?' asked Yume.

'I will suggest an urgent meeting of A Dignified Death, where I will propose that we join Ageing Matters in their plans for a protest march on Parliament. We then need to work on a counter-proposal to the Government plan. It will be a campaign for pro-choice euthanasia to be legalised, and for the Power of Attorney to be extended to include physician-led euthanasia. We have talked about these things so many times; all we need to do is step up our campaign and use the platform that has been created by this crisis.'

FIFTY

Avard–Monday

Avard had spent all day on Sunday with Jim and Catherine, reassuring himself that they were safely hidden in his favourite Cornish village. It was a mixed blessing that there was no landline or mobile coverage at his cottage, only his secret but unsecured Wi-Fi. Avard had asked them to drive to the nearest town regularly and keep in touch by phone or email. His mind at rest, he decided he would leave the following day.

It was early Monday morning and still dark when he suddenly woke. He had been worrying about his wife in London; perhaps that was it. He wasn't superstitious, but suddenly he wanted to check in with her. Donning a coat over his pyjamas, he put on his walking boots. There was usually a phone signal at the top of the nearest headland, and he wouldn't ever use his Wi-Fi for fear of detection. He smiled to himself as he imagined her reaction at being woken at six am.

It was a fresh September day with a loamy smell of the autumn to come. Avard took a familiar footpath along the edge of a field that eventually led to a high wall and a gate, beyond which the ground rose steeply up. A half-moon gave him just enough light and he could hear the waves getting louder as he reached the top of the cliff. There wasn't a breath of wind and, looking back over the fields, he noticed white mist forming in the hollows. Was a fog coming in? If so, he needed to be quick and get down again. It had taken him nearly an hour as it was. Shaking off his unease, he dialled his home number.

The phone was picked up, and then there was silence.

'Are you there, my dear?' he ventured, trying to keep the alarm out of his voice.

'Avard, it's you! How could I guess you would call at this hour? This phone has been ringing for two days solidly, I swear it, all kinds of people asking questions. You didn't wake me, though, I was already awake worrying about you. I felt spooked for some reason.'

Avard let out his breath with a sigh of relief. 'I hope we haven't been,' he began.

He had paused, letting his wife's comforting chatter wash over him when suddenly there was a loud explosion and a ball of fire shot into the air from the direction of the village. It lit up the sky, clearly showing him its source.

His cottage – the whole building was an inferno!

There was no chance of saving it. He could just make out some figures running towards it and then hurriedly turning away.

'What was that, Avard?'

'Later, I have to go.'

Time ceased to exist as a series of realisations hit him.

What a fool I am, leading them to my cottage.

Will Jim and Catherine get out? Unlikely.

They are working faster than I gave them credit for.

Avard had seen many examples of brutality during his time as a diplomat, but he had never been involved in a direct target. He suddenly felt weary.

I am too old for this game.

He pulled himself together as his mind kicked into auto-drive.

Are they still around?

There is only one road into the village.

The blaze had turned the sky orange and Avard climbed down the seaward side of the cliff, using another path that led down to the beach.

Thank God I know this coastline well.

The tide was out. Another factor in his favour. He kept to the shadows as much as he could and, skirting the rocks, managed to make his way around the headland and into the far end of the bay. At the harbour, he could see a crowd of villagers and the arrival of two of the Cornwall Fire Service's specialised four-wheel drive pumping appliances.

It was beginning to get light and he considered his options. With a heavy heart, he realised he could not go back to the remains of the cottage just yet; he could still be a target. He struggled to keep to practical thoughts; his car was parked next to the cottage and would probably be a write-off.

Under the cliffs, away from the village, there was a disused lifeboat station. Since it had been de-commissioned, there had been a series of residents who had made attempts to turn it into a home. From the outside, the task seemed unrewarding and relentless, but Avard knew Bill, the latest resident, and had been inside to find a cosy, if eccentric, living space. Clad in his pyjamas with coat and walking boots, he realised that he must look a conspicuous figure. Ironically, Bill was probably one of the few people who could help him without batting an eyelid or asking difficult questions.

He saw that smoke was coming out of the chimney and Bill was at the door, watching the mayhem in the harbour. He made up his mind and headed over to him.

FIFTY-ONE

Richard–Monday

Richard and Roberta were catching the latest news on the TV when a bulletin came on, telling of a fire at the Cornish holiday home of Avard Harriman. Richard clutched his morning coffee cup tightly as scenes of the wreckage filled the screen and the newsreader gave details of the explosion and all-consuming blaze that had reduced the building to four blackened stone walls. So far two bodies had been found, burnt beyond recognition.

Avard?

The cameraman was filming from a discreet distance and panned across other onlookers who were being held back by barriers, then closed in on a reporter who was trying to interview someone.

Avard, thank God.

'And here is the owner, Avard Harriman. Sir, what can you tell us about what's happened here?'

Avard was wearing an old overcoat, walking boots, a shirt that looked like a pyjama top and, incongruously, a pair of faded jeans. Richard had never seen him dressed so shabbily. He looked dazed.

An equally eccentrically dressed man with long hair and a beard took his arm and led him away. 'Sorry, he's not in a fit state to answer questions.'

'Hiding in plain sight,' muttered Richard.

The reporter moved on to the group of onlookers.

'There are rumours of a Cornish Liberation group,' said one of them mysteriously.

'What do you mean, hiding in plain sight?' asked Roberta.

Richard turned to face Roberta. He liked this straightforward woman. 'Someone has blown the whistle on a secret Government plot and MI5 will be busy trying to find who they are, plug the leak, destroy the evidence and possibly the people concerned, then pass it off as something less, something more acceptable.'

Roberta's eyes were like saucers. 'Really?'

'This is where I want to come in, banging the drum for pro-choice euthanasia to be legalised. I have been hiding from the media, but also from MI5. I don't know, but I suspect that Avard may have been involved in trying to hide someone too. The point is, Avard is not running away. He is in the public eye, so this makes it more difficult for anyone to "get at him" without a reason. He is safer hiding "in plain sight", and I will too. I'll go to the Summerlands residents' meeting this morning and speak, as Dom has asked me to do.'

'Oh, good,' said Roberta. 'You can give me a lift.'

Does she understand what I just said?

*

Rosie was also going to the Summerlands residents' meeting. She was still desperate for any information that could help her make sense of Marjorie's death there. Simon had flown back to Abu Dhabi after Marjorie's funeral.

She felt a mess. She had been drinking too much and hardly eating or sleeping. The house felt strangely empty. Theo was quiet by nature and the closeness that she and Simon had enjoyed had been severed by something she couldn't define.

*

Yume was in her bathroom, getting ready for the meeting. She looked in the mirror, sighed and splashed her face with cold water to hide the evidence that she had been crying. She and Sandra had just had a long and tearful conversation, following the news bulletin. They had always known that Jim and Catherine would be in danger. Avard had repeated it many times.

And first in the firing line…

She knew she was experiencing the guilt of those left behind. To add to that, it was she who had started all this off, with her suspicions about Richard. Now she wanted some good to come out of all this. The Government would have to concede something.

*

Dom had had to put up with the media at the gates of Summerlands since Sharon's article had appeared online. Added to that, he had spent all day Sunday fielding phone calls and visits from irate residents and relatives. He decided to call an emergency meeting for them all to try and calm their fears. He knew he was a good speaker, but he was a little short of things to say.

The meeting room was already crowded to overflowing when he entered. The admin staff had set out as many chairs as they could into rows facing a raised platform on which stood chairs, a table and a microphone. When he took his position, the hubbub of voices petered out and the faces raised towards him looked decidedly unfriendly.

'Ladies and gentlemen, so many of you have contacted me in the last two days. I have called this extraordinary meeting to give you my reassurance in the light of recent events and to answer any questions you may have.'

Dom's direct approach and disarming concern for their feelings were hitting the right note.

'There have been two incidents recently that I know you have concerns about. Let me explain them from my perspective.'

Dom went on to summarise the events surrounding Mrs Clark's death, and the subsequent coroner's verdict; and then to describe the shock web page that had appeared online.

'The local press has been quick to sensationalise both these incidents and imply sinister connections with Summerlands. While I respect their freedom of speech and the need to sell news stories, I can tell you that there is no truth whatsoever in these allegations, and we will be looking to press charges against the paper concerned.'

He paused to let this sink in.

'Mrs Clark was already dying when she entered The Retreat, and a police investigation into her death is still ongoing. If you have any information that would be helpful, you can approach DS Mallory after the meeting.'

At the back of the room, Mallory raised his hand. 'Detective Sergeant Mallory will also be giving a short speech later and will answer questions. Now on to the web page which purports to reveal a Government plot for mass euthanasia. The same local paper has insinuated that Professor Richard Hawley, who is in charge of The Retreat, is not only involved but has been experimenting here at Summerlands, resulting in four deaths last month. Professor Richard Hawley is here himself to reassure you all and to answer any questions you may have.'

There was a murmur of surprise from the audience and Dom stepped down from the platform, feeling that the crowd was already less hostile than when he started.

Richard stepped up on the platform, smiling benevolently, supremely confident as usual. 'I know nothing of these Government plans for mass euthanasia,' he began. 'I have made caring for the elderly my life's work and I am an expert in the field. I have also been instrumental in developing the Palliative Care Pathway, which is now used in every institution from hospitals and hospices to care homes. This plan ensures that people who are dying are monitored stage by stage and given the appropriate medication.'

He paused to let people take this information in. 'I have met many people who did not want to prolong their misery, my mother included.' There was a collective gasp as he revealed this personal information. He looked at Roberta. She had encouraged him to say this. 'I am also a member of A Dignified Death; an organisation that believes pro-choice euthanasia should be legalised.'

The audience began muttering and he held up his hand for silence. 'Please hear me out. I was recently asked by the Department of Health to contribute my expertise to a new Palliative Care Project, Avalon. I was told we would be re-evaluating the existing scheme in response to projections of enormous figures for elderly care in ten years' time. I was asked to recruit new people, I anticipated many meetings, and yes, I expected that eventually, pro-choice euthanasia would be discussed. None of this has actually happened yet, so I am as shocked by the revelation of these plans as you are. A journalist has seen fit to jump on the bandwagon and create a link between this Government plan and four deaths at Summerlands, one of which was that of Marjorie Clark.'

He leant forward to emphasise his next point. 'This is nonsense. I stress I have nothing but the best care of you and your relatives in mind, and that has always been the case. My reputation goes before me.'

He looked around the room. 'I intend to take action, and tonight I will be meeting with members of A Dignified Death to plan a group protest to Parliament. We will be demanding clarification from the Government about the exact nature of The Final Pathway. If indeed it looks like there is a serious problem looming with a burgeoning elderly population, we as an organisation believe that there are better alternative solutions to be discussed. Be assured, we will be lobbying against what is no better than corporate slaughter in favour of pro-choice euthanasia. Now I welcome any comments and suggestions you may have. Thank you for listening.'

There was silence, and then scattered applause from some of the audience in response to the man's show of integrity.

Dom took the platform again, flanked either side by Mallory and Richard. The questions came thick and fast.

*

Roberta had been sitting with her mother Eva throughout the meeting. She was feeling uncomfortable and cramped on the hard seat and was ready to leave when Mallory approached them both.

'Hello, Mrs Phipps,' he said, looking at Eva. 'Some new evidence has come to light. Can you tell me if you ever ate cake with Mrs Clark?'

'Well, yes,' replied Eva. 'Hugo was always bringing her cake, and she always called me over to share a slice.'

FIFTY-TWO

Jason–Monday

Since The Final Pathway went live on Saturday, Jason had spent long hours in his home office, mentally role-playing the approach he would take when interviewed about Avalon.

Which bastard is playing God and publishing this stuff?

His ruthlessness had been subject to questioning before, but he realised this time the stakes were a lot higher.

There's only one thing for it. Richard will have to be thrown under the wheels.

This morning, despite his thorough preparation over the weekend, Jason had been caught off-guard by a visit at six-thirty am from two plainclothes police officers. He had been forced to answer the door in his dressing gown, having just stepped out of the shower, and he was annoyed with himself for agreeing so easily to their request to answer a few questions. Now he found himself sitting on a plastic chair, at a table with a chipped Formica top which looked like it hadn't been cleaned for weeks. He had been given a polystyrene cup of what was supposed to be coffee, which remained untouched. He looked down at his hands which were folded in his lap to avoid any contact with the furniture.

479

Why am I in this shithole? I'm above these things.

The room was windowless, and the stale air added to his feeling of grubbiness. A large mirror took up one wall. Jason presumed it was two-way, allowing scrutiny from people watching from the other side. He checked his watch. It had been over half an hour since he had been brought in here.

Just then, the door opened, and a man and woman walked in and sat down facing him on the other side of the table. The man was the first to speak, though he did not introduce himself or his colleague.

Keeping it deliberately impersonal.

'Mr Brown, thank you for agreeing to this interview. Hopefully, we'll not take up too much of your time.'

Jason noted he spoke without any trace of a regional accent.

Oxbridge, no doubt. These are not time-serving plods.

'Tell us about the Avalon project. We understand you are responsible for it?'

Jason saw where this was going and knew he needed to be as evasive as possible. 'Well, the project has actually been running for some years now, under the direction of Professor Richard Hawley. It promotes best practice in the care of the elderly. It was previously called the Palliative Care Pathway project, which is a bit of a mouthful, so I renamed it Avalon.'

His interrogators made notes, leaving an extended silence.

Trying to rile me – keep calm.

The woman took a paper from her briefcase and passed it across the desk to him. 'Do you recognise this document?'

Jason knew his answer had to be a rock-solid defence. 'Yes, of course. It's a spreadsheet that looks at the costs of caring for people in the final months of their lives. This accounts for a considerable proportion of health spending, and consequently the department needs to constantly monitor how much resources may be needed in order to plan accordingly.' Jason smiled at his interrogators, feeling that he had scored a winning point with his response.

'Thank you for clearing that up. Now, can you explain to us what Elysium is and how that fits into the Avalon project?'

'Elysium is a newly developed drug that is used in palliative care. That is all I know. Professor Hawley oversees trialling it, so I suggest you ask him.'

The man and woman continued to make notes, creating a further silence that lasted several minutes.

'Have you seen The Final Pathway website? We think whoever published this information must have been familiar with the Avalon project. Can you think why they would want to discredit the department and, by implication, you?'

Jason was beginning to feel the rise of his anger and resentment towards people like his interrogators. 'Look, I can't see what all the fuss is about. We model contingencies so we have the money and people in place to deliver services. End of. There will always be disgruntled employees who want to disrupt things.'

Jason tried to slow his breathing, but he suspected he was losing his cool. His face felt hot and his palms clammy. The questions continued to rain in.

'What is your view on euthanasia?'

How to draw things to a close?

'Why are you asking me all these questions? I am just an accountant.'

The man looked at his notes. 'It says here that you are the Director of Business Transformation. That seems like a role where you are expected to make big changes, to look at ways of saving money, for example. Am I right in that assessment?'

Jason looked at them both. The man's eyes seemed to bore into him. He leant across the desk towards them. 'Just what am I being accused of? Doing my job? When was that a crime? You will be horrified at how much of your taxes are wasted on keeping people alive beyond what nature intended.'

The man and woman smiled at each other and closed their notepads.

Jason sat back, arms folded, realising he had said too much.

'You are free to leave now,' said the woman. 'I fully expect we will need to speak to you again and we require you to surrender your passport. One of our colleagues will accompany you home to collect it.'

As they got up to leave, the man turned to Jason. 'Oh, and I think it would be prudent to retain the services of a lawyer. Good day, Mr Brown.'

FIFTY-THREE

Andrew–Tuesday

Andrew Gordon, Jason Brown's indispensable PA, had – to date – led a charmed life. His parents were wealthy and he had been privately educated before going up to Cambridge to study politics, philosophy and economics, where he was awarded a first. His father had then pulled strings to get him onto the civil service fast-track graduate programme. Andrew was outwardly a model employee; privately he thought his boss Jason was an uncouth oaf who, despite his best efforts, had failed to shrug off the evidence of his working-class origins. As far as Andrew was concerned, the job was a means to an end. However, it was now the reason he found himself that afternoon in an interview room at MI5's headquarters, facing two inscrutable agents of the state. He was beginning to feel uneasy.

'Can you tell me how long this is going to last? I have some arrangements made for this evening.'

The older of the two men answered, 'That depends. You appear to have been involved in activities which, now they have been exposed, are contributing to major unrest. We need to understand what has happened, and you will remain here until we get clarity from you about the Avalon project.'

Andrew was all too aware that The Final Pathway website had exposed the exact nature of the Avalon project. Should he ask for a lawyer or would that imply a level of guilt, he wondered? He decided against that idea.

'I'm on a graduate programme, and that means I get to spend some months in different sections of the department learning about what they do. I'm currently Jason Brown's PA, but it's all quite menial, really. I just do his bidding, so to speak.'

The faces of his two interrogators showed no reaction to his flippancy.

'Mr Gordon, what have you learnt about what they do in Jason Brown's department?'

This was the question he had expected, and he had already formulated his response. 'Jason and his team have been providing an analysis of costs incurred within the different areas of the health system. It's to ensure the department has the right resources to maintain a high level of service both now and in the future.'

Andrew looked at the men across the table, who stared back at him.

'That sounds very altruistic. Who are these good people in the Avalon team?'

'The team consists of four people: Jason, two accountants and Professor Richard Hawley, the Government's advisor on all aspects of ageing. I just make the coffee and manage the database.'

The men looked down at their laptops and exchanged glances before the younger man spoke. 'As I understand it, the Avalon project was previously known as the Palliative Care Pathway and its composition was different. There were more team members, some of whom had considerable experience in the care process. Why, I wonder, was it reduced to such a small team and Richard Hawley?'

Andrew knew exactly why the team had been reduced, but he wasn't about to offer any suggestions.

I need to deflect this away from me.

'I'm not involved in any of the decision-making. As I said before, my role is purely administrative.'

A few minutes of silence added to Andrew's discomfort. He watched as the men consulted their screens, pointing out things to one another.

'You said you were responsible for the database. Can you tell us exactly what the database contains?'

'Documents such as spreadsheets, correspondence, emails,' Andrew replied, trying to sound upbeat. 'I set up a filing system so that documents could be easily retrieved according to their content.'

The younger interrogator leant forward across the desk. 'To do that, surely you would need to be familiar with the contents of the documents?'

Shit.

'I didn't produce anything. I just filed it according to the subject. I can't recall what was in the documents.'

The men consulted their screen again before sitting back in their chairs, arms folded across their chests. The face of one of them softened slightly with what looked like a smirk. 'It says here you have a photographic memory and almost perfect recall. This is according to your Director of Studies at St John's College, Cambridge. He says your memory was one of the best he had ever encountered. Now, are you trying to tell us that you have no recall regarding the content of the database you administered? Because I find that hard to believe, and I think a jury would agree with me.'

Andrew knew he had been cornered and claiming ignorance of the project in detail was not going to work, yet he tried again, with the only defence he could think of. 'I am not involved in Avalon. The project is Jason Brown's.'

The older man looked at Andrew and shook his head. 'You had sight of what was being planned, which makes you an accessory to the crime.'

Andrew was angry and felt a burning injustice. 'I was just doing my job. I haven't done anything wrong. But I can see that

485

the Government would be seriously on the back foot if their plans were put out there...'

Andrew stopped short of saying more. The fact that his knowledge had great value was not lost on him. His interrogators, too, saw where his thought processes were going.

'Thank you, Mr Gordon. That will be all for now. Enjoy your evening.'

As Andrew left the room, the older man spoke urgently into his mobile.

FIFTY-FOUR

Andrew

It was nearly nine o'clock at night before Andrew got back to his third floor Pimlico apartment. His grandmother had owned the property since the early 1950s when it was built as part of the post-war reconstruction. Now she was living in a nursing home in Surrey near his parents, and she had insisted that Andrew use it.

He was alone, having been forced to cancel his date for the evening. He poured himself a large vodka tonic, opened the French windows onto the apartment's balcony and gazed over the roofs of the properties opposite towards the Thames. Across the river, the derelict Battersea Power Station still dominated the skyline. It had been de-commissioned a quarter of a century previously, yet it remained, serving as a reminder of the days before clean air was considered important. It had been the subject of a variety of ideas for its redevelopment, but so far nothing had come of any of the plans. Andrew's eyes followed the path of the river, east towards the City and St Paul's Cathedral, picking out the lights of Oxo Tower. It was a mild autumn night, and after his second drink he decided to put on a coat, stay outside and enjoy a spliff.

As he inhaled, the drug calmed his senses. He leant back in his chair, looking up at the clear night sky, and revisited the events of the day.

What I know is highly saleable. How much will the broadsheets pay to get the full story, I wonder? Will the red tops pay more?

He lit a second spliff, his mind whirring with potential opportunities.

I can write a book, an exposé. I won't be the first insider to spill the beans. I can sell the film rights. Who will play me, I wonder?

Cannabis always improved his mood, and he laughed at the idea.

Brown deserves everything that's coming his way. Smug twat. And the pompous Richard Hawley. Although, to be fair, he is always very courteous towards me, so maybe I'll portray him in a kinder light.

Andrew savoured the remainder of his spliff whilst considering just how much power his knowledge gave him. He was so absorbed in his thoughts that he didn't hear the footsteps approaching him from behind. The first and last thing he felt was an arm around his neck pulling his head backwards, snapping his spinal cord, before his body was thrown over the balcony, another victim of the deadly combination of drugs and alcohol.

FIFTY-FIVE

Rosie–Tuesday

Simon had returned from Abu Dhabi, unsure of his next move. He didn't want Rosie to stumble over a photo of Hugo out there as well. Yet it seemed pointless to him that she was staying in England. Was she waiting for Hugo? He couldn't tell her the whole truth.

He suffered a restless night and he thought Rosie had been feigning sleep too, but he didn't know for sure; they were hardly speaking. Eight am came and found them both sitting stony-faced on separate ends of the sofa, staring at the television. All the channels were providing commentary on the unfolding scandal exposed by The Final Pathway. Neither of them seemed to have any appetite for food and Simon had made them both a mug of coffee. Rosie seemed to be holding hers close, as if for warmth.

A poor replacement for a human touch.

The buzzer on the gate broke the silence and Simon jumped up and walked over to the intercom. DS Mallory stood there with his face pushed up to the screen. 'Mr Adams, it's DS Mallory.'

Simon opened the gate and walked down to the front door to let the man in.

'Dreadful weather,' said Mallory, making small talk. 'Is Mrs Jennings in?'

'Come in, DS Mallory.' Rosie appeared at the end of the hall, her voice flat and devoid of emotion as she led them into the kitchen. 'What can we do for you?' she asked wearily.

Simon put his arm around Rosie, who just sat still, staring straight ahead. He knew she must be processing the information and coming to an obvious conclusion.

'Mrs Jennings, have you been able to locate your son Hugo, or have you heard from him at all?'

Rosie shook her head.

'Mrs Jennings. If you know where he is, you would be obstructing us if you didn't tell us.'

Simon knew there was no use in Mallory pursuing this line of questioning with Rosie and adopted a moral stance. 'Look, Rosie doesn't know where he is. She's his mum and she is understandably upset that he has not been in touch and she's concerned for his safety. She buried her own mother recently. For God's sake, man, show some humanity.'

Simon's attempt to close down the questioning was futile, as Mallory continued. 'So, your son didn't attend his grandmother's funeral? Why do you think he has disappeared?'

Simon kept his arm around Rosie, who was now beginning to sob quietly.

Mallory pressed on. 'I have to ask you again, Mrs Jennings. Do you know your son's whereabouts?'

After a lengthy silence, Rosie lifted her head and spoke with a clear voice. 'I have no idea. No idea where my husband David is and no idea where my son Hugo is.'

The irony of her remark brought Simon up short.

And if you knew where he was and who he was with, where would that leave us…?

Mallory got up to leave. 'If you hear from him, please get in touch with me.'

Simon spent the next few hours avoiding starting a conversation that would be difficult. Eventually, Rosie sought him out and found him hunched over his computer in the office. She put a gentle hand on his shoulder, which he covered with his own.

'Simon. Let's go back to Abu Dhabi. What's here for us? Out there we have good friends, good jobs and the weather is so much better. Theo can fly out to visit.'

Simon felt guilty and confused. He knew that Hugo had poisoned Marjorie to get his hands on her money. He knew where Hugo was and who he was with. He felt they couldn't return to the UAE because of that, and he'd been looking for jobs in the UK.

'But, Rosie, don't you want to be here for Hugo, if and when he turns up?' Simon knew it sounded feeble and he saw the look of confusion on Rosie's face.

As he swivelled his chair around, he knocked the mouse, causing the computer screen to refresh. On display in front of them was a job advertisement for a cardiologist based in Liverpool.

Rosie's face took on a look of disbelief. 'Why are you looking at jobs in the UK, Simon? You're exceptionally well paid in Abu Dhabi. You have fantastic facilities there. I don't understand it.'

Later that afternoon, Rosie sat alone, a glass of chilled white wine in her hand, and considered her situation. She wondered if she had ever really known anyone properly. Was she such a poor judge of character or was she too ready to ignore what was staring her in the face? She drained the glass and poured another and began to review what had gone on that afternoon with Simon. After the revelation that he had been applying for jobs in the UK, he had left the house without saying anything more to her. Why had he not discussed that he wanted to come back to the UK? She wondered about going back to the UAE on her own, but then the reality of that situation hit home.

I'm dependent on Simon for my life out there. I don't earn enough at Al Wahah to even rent a small apartment.

She forced herself to confront what she now knew about Hugo. Her own son had pawned her jewellery, conned large sums of money from her mother and, she finally had to admit, was responsible for her death.

FIFTY-SIX

Avard

Avard was sitting at his kitchen table seeking comfort and waiting for the morning cup of coffee that his wife was preparing. He was disorientated after his Cornwall experience and unwilling to get to grips with the many issues that he knew were waiting for his attention. He thought of the meeting of A Dignified Death the previous night, which he had attended to show his support. Richard had been gratified to see him, and he had shaken his hand and held on to it for a moment.

'I saw the news this morning; how are you bearing up, my friend? Who would have thought that our work with the elderly would become so controversial and dangerous?'

Avard had acknowledged him with a wry smile. 'We will talk of this soon,' had been his non-committal reply.

He realised his wife was speaking to him and he hadn't heard a word. 'I'm sorry, my love. Can you start again?'

She looked at him with concern on her face. 'I was just saying that a young man came and serviced your computer yesterday.'

Avard looked startled. 'I didn't ask anyone to come in,' he began, and then his brain clicked into gear. 'I think I'll take my coffee into the study if that's alright.'

A minute later, his wife heard him shout and rushed in to find the normally tidy room was littered with papers and every drawer was open.

'My computer is missing too,' said Avard.

'Oh, no,' she wailed. 'He came to the door with his ID on a lanyard and acted like he had been here before. I was busy in the kitchen, so I showed him the study and left him to it. He just popped his head round the door when he had finished. I never checked – what do I know about computers?'

Avard turned to face her and put his arms around her. 'Please don't blame yourself. If the man hadn't got in this way, he would have broken in and the damage would have been far worse. Yume told me the same thing happened yesterday at Summerlands. They will be looking for any files that exist about The Final Pathway and they are looking for copies too. They won't stop until they have destroyed them all.'

In fact, Avard had spent a large part of the meeting the previous evening reassuring Yume and wiping her tears with his handkerchief. She had told him about the theft of both her computer and Richard's, but it had slipped his mind. He was more concerned about her anxiety.

'I am responsible for starting all this, and now poor Catherine and Jim,' Yume cried. 'Oh, Jii-chan, do you think we are safe?'

*

Avard wasn't sure whether his phone calls were being monitored; he was probably still being watched too. He took the tube to Green Park, then walked the short distance to a café in the park. The sun was shining, and it was warm for the end of September; in fact, it was an ideal day for being out and about in London. Avard bought himself a drink and watched the commuters and the tourists. He was joined at his table by Mark, a surgeon and fellow member of A Dignified Death whom he had asked to find out various things for him.

'I have checked with the relevant local police as you asked, and it looks like Jim's flat and Catherine's have been broken into and searched. I have also spoken to Richard this morning and he had already had a meeting with Jason, who was flapping because his computers have been taken away. More importantly, his two accountants have not turned up for work, and his PA Andrew has been questioned by MI5.'

Avard grimaced. 'I'm surprised Richard got in to see him, but I hear that Jason is busy trying to implicate him as a major player in The Final Pathway and will be looking for any information that can help him. Now, tell me what Richard has said about the arrangements for the march.'

FIFTY-SEVEN

Rosie–Wednesday

It was late afternoon when Rosie arrived back home, having spent the day keeping herself occupied buying baby clothes for Roberta's imminent arrival. Rosie knew her friend would never spend money on the sort of things she had chosen.

Our lives are so different. Roberta always has to consider the cost of things.

The thought made her uncomfortable and the memory of Sandra's description of 'Rosie's gilded cage' came back to her.

As she made a cup of coffee, she recalled the events of the last few days. The meeting she attended at Summerlands on Monday had not been the PR whitewash she was expecting. Dom Maxwell had seemed a genuine person and had faced the situation head on. Richard Hawley was adamant that he had not been party to the real nature of the Government's Avalon project and had been honest about his personal views and motivation.

But am I again being a lousy judge of character? Am I too quick to accept what I am told?

Then, recalling the conversation she overheard between DS Mallory and Roberta's mother, she shuddered involuntarily as she processed the implications.

Hugo takes cake to Mum when he visits. Cyanide is found in cake crumbs at Mum's villa. Hugo is missing.

She took her drink and sat in the corner of the sofa, curled her legs under her, and watched the sky colour as sunset approached. She felt at a loss. Simon had left the previous day without saying goodbye or explaining why he was applying for jobs back in the UK.

Is my situation too much for him?

Her thoughts were interrupted by the sound of a key in the front door. She got up, her heart pounding in her chest. Simon stood there. His eyes were red, and he looked like he hadn't slept. They walked towards each other hesitantly and then they were in one another's arms. Rosie buried her face in his chest, breathing in his scent as he stroked her hair gently.

Eventually, Simon held her shoulders at arm's length and looked directly at her. 'Rosie, I have things I need to tell you. I don't want us to have any secrets, so I must tell you everything and then it will be up to you as to whether we have a future together.'

Rosie felt sick as she heard the words, wondering exactly what she was about to be confronted with.

Simon took her hand as they walked back into the kitchen. 'I know where Hugo is. He is with David in Dubai. I took him there when I was pretty sure he was responsible for your mum's death. You remember the picture Gail showed you? Well, I followed it up and it was David. It struck me as a good solution at the time. I really thought that after everything that has happened the knowledge of what Hugo had done would be too much for you. I realise that I should have told you of my suspicions and let you make your own choices. I'm sorry.'

Rosie sat motionless, stunned. Over the last few days she had begun to come to terms with Hugo's actions, but this new information was hard to take in.

Simon knows where David and Hugo are.

'Say something, Rosie,' Simon pleaded. 'I was thinking of you, but I realise that I was very wrong to take matters into my own hands. That was why I was applying for jobs in the UK. If I'm honest, I didn't want you to see David and Hugo again.'

Rosie held her head in her hands, trying to come to terms with the enormity of Simon's actions.

Eventually she spoke, her voice trembling with anger. 'You were thinking of me? How long have you known of David's whereabouts? Don't spare me any details. I want the truth for once, Simon.'

'I confronted Hugo the night of the police visit, and he more or less gave himself away. It seemed a solution to get him out of the country before the police could arrest him.'

'And how was my errant husband?' Rosie asked with heavy sarcasm.

'Surprised. Angry at being exposed, and angry at being landed with his son and his debts. If he doesn't live up to the arrangement, he is in no doubt that I will make the authorities in the Emirates aware of his situation.'

They sat in silence for a while before Rosie spoke again. 'So, there was no urgent heart operation back in Abu Dhabi? You lied to me. What else haven't you told me? What other secrets do you have?'

Simon sat quietly for some minutes before looking straight at Rosie. 'I helped Linda with her abortion. I was still a medical student and she was desperate to get rid of it.'

'I can't take all this, Simon. I need some time to myself.'

She walked slowly upstairs and sat on the edge of her bed.

The bed I shared with a man I thought I knew.

A maelstrom of emotions gripped her. Anger at Simon's behaviour, frustration that matters that she knew nothing about had been dealt with without consulting her, sadness for her mum's death, and the raw pain of knowing that her son was a thief and a murderer. She was consumed by grief, beyond tears. Then she thought of her friend Linda. No doubt she was one of Simon's girlfriends at the time. Why didn't she see these things? Was she blinkered?

I am still naive at the age of forty-eight.

She heard the crunch of tyres on gravel and through the window she watched Simon drive out of the gates.

And out of my life?

FIFTY-EIGHT

Rosie

Rosie picked up the bedside phone and dialled Roberta. She needed to tell someone else what she had learnt. Roberta's friendship had stood the test of time and they had seen one another through crises before.

'Roberta, I don't know where to begin,' she managed to get out before succumbing to a loud sob.

'I'll put the kettle on. Come round, and we can talk properly.'

Roberta was already standing in the doorway when Rosie pulled up outside. 'Come on in. What on earth has happened? You look dreadful.'

Rosie smiled weakly at her heavily pregnant friend, who waddled into her kitchen and returned with two mugs of tea.

Roberta listened quietly, shifting her position from time to time to try and get comfortable as Rosie told her everything that had happened.

'I just can't understand how all this had been going on under my nose and I didn't suspect anything. Well, I suppose I knew Hugo was following in David's footsteps. He has the same moral compass, but Simon? He just took matters into his own hands and he said he was thinking of me!'

Roberta exhaled loudly and rubbed her large belly before speaking. 'I'm your friend. If I tell you what I think, will it spoil our friendship?'

'No, I need your help. If it needs saying, please tell me.'

'You give out signals that are attractive to men who want to – how can I put it – wear the trousers. You are a lovely, sweet person, but materially, you have always been given everything you wanted. You've never had to fight for it. First your parents, then David; and it's the same situation with Simon. He has a good job, earns lots of money and he is happy taking care of you. So, okay, he has taken this beyond caring to the point of lying; but I think Simon is genuine and really thought he was saving you from some awful facts. He got it wrong, but you have to accept some responsibility.'

The two women sat looking at one another.

'Am I really that pathetic?' Rosie asked.

Roberta continued, undaunted by Rosie's attempt to get some sympathy. 'You are an intelligent woman. You just need to think more independently. You don't need a man to look after you. You need to be your own person. Have you told Simon about your involvement in The Final Pathway's exposé?'

Rosie hung her head. 'No,' she said.

'Do you think you are both operating in patterns you have learnt from your last relationships?'

Back home again, Rosie considered what Roberta had said.

*

It's true, Simon and I have not developed a way of relating to each other.

Gradually, her thoughts crystallised into a series of actions.

There is a way forward for me. I'm sure Richard needs help organising the protest march, and I have a few ideas. I can't change what's happened to Mum, but I can help others have a dignified death.

Rosie dialled the Summerlands number. Sandra answered the phone.

501

'It's Rosie,' she said boldly. 'Is Richard Hawley still there?'

There was silence for a minute. 'He's in London, organising the protest rally,' Sandra replied.

'I would like to speak to him. Can you give me his number, please?'

'I wouldn't normally give out his private number.' Sandra hesitated, and then added in a curious tone, 'Why do you want to speak to him?'

'I want to help with the rally.'

'Good for you,' said Sandra.

FIFTY-NINE

Lee–Thursday

Lee Davis, Jim's flatmate, was eating breakfast cereal and watching TV when his ears pricked up at the sound of a familiar name. Jim Morris? He was a bit fed up with Jim, to be honest. He had hardly seen anything of his flatmate since he'd met up with Catherine. Normally reliable to the point of being boring, Jim had been notably absent of late, skipping his share of the chores. Then there was a break-in where Jim's stuff had been taken. Lee had begun to wonder what he'd got himself embroiled in. What was Jim doing on national TV, though?

He listened, and shock registered as he heard that a holiday home in Cornwall had been burnt to the ground as a result of a gas explosion, and that two bodies had been identified from dental records as Jim Morris and Catherine Day. Jim had not really been a close friend and Lee wondered when he should advertise for a new flatmate. No doubt Jim's relatives would come and take his stuff away.

Stuff... he remembered the envelope that Jim had given to him and asked him to stow somewhere safe. He rooted under his bed and pulled out a pair of trainers. He extracted the envelope from inside one of them.

'If I don't come back, hand it in at *The Independent* newspaper offices.'

A voice from the grave...

Lee shuddered and crossed himself like any good Catholic. He would take it there straight away and be rid of his obligation.

*

The newspaper's offices were only a short walk away. Lee was wheeling his bike, as he had to get to work afterwards. At some point, he felt he was being followed. It was pure instinct, a mere ruffling of the hairs on the back of his neck. He turned around and saw nothing. He then quickened his pace and reached the crossroads just in front of the office.

Suddenly a man darted out from the side street and grabbed the handlebars of Lee's bike. It was a high-spec model, worth over a thousand. Lee dreaded it being stolen.

He propelled the bike into action, mounting the saddle he headed straight for the glass doors of the newspaper office. At the last moment, he leant forward and kicked one of the doors open, leaving the would-be thief to crash into the other. Lee was an experienced trials biker. When the police and ambulance were called, it seemed a clear case of attempted theft, but Lee wondered about what was in the envelope.

*

Jeff Holt, journalist at *The Independent*, was seated at his desk when an email arrived from reception, asking him to pick up an envelope that had been handed in in a rather dramatic way. Intrigued, Jeff made his way there personally. It had been screened by security and had been seen to contain a memory stick. Other than that, there was no indication as to its value. He heard the details of its dramatic arrival and decided it needed priority.

There was still another procedure to go through. Jeff plugged it into a stand-alone PC, dedicated to checking out data from an unknown source; it was a regular occurrence for USBs to arrive with malware. Jeff opened the contents and was astounded. He knew all about The Final Pathway web page that had appeared on Saturday. He was looking at the documentary proof.

He reached for his phone and spoke to his editor urgently.

*

Later that afternoon, Elizabeth Furnival and two grey-suited men met in the small wood-panelled meeting room that adjoined her office. The first of these men was the Home Secretary, William Bullivant, a staunch right-winger, who had demonstrated his willingness to clamp down on free speech when it didn't serve the interests of his party. The second was the Cabinet Secretary, David Miller, a career civil servant who had risen to the top of the tree and who now had fingers in every aspect of Government policy. The men's armed protection officers waited outside, ready to intervene to safeguard their charges.

'Please take a seat, gentlemen.'

Elizabeth was glad this meeting was taking place in her territory. She had decided to dispense with the niceties of refreshments. Time was short after what had now unfolded.

'I think it was Harold Wilson who said, "A week is a long time in politics," and this last one certainly bears testimony to that. Shall I summarise the situation with The Final Pathway as we now find it?'

David answered first. 'Yes, please, Elizabeth. I am assuming you have an update to have called this meeting.'

'Indeed, I have. As you know, my team's efforts have focussed on containing any further dissemination and to identify and remove those responsible. Whilst we've been successful in silencing some of the perpetrators, the data that underpinned the allegations is now in the public domain.'

505

Elizabeth paused before providing the information that demonstrated that their efforts had been thwarted. 'Unfortunately, it is now in the hands of *The Independent* newspaper, and earlier this afternoon they asked the department for comment.'

Both men looked grim.

David spoke up. 'The PM is worried. He has just appointed a new Minister of Health who has vowed to restore faith in our health service, etc., etc., but our soundings are that things are getting febrile out there. Home Secretary, I take it you have the resources you need to police next week's march effectively?'

William straightened his tie and produced a smile that did not quite reach his eyes. 'Police leave has been cancelled and I have the army on standby. We will be cordoning off streets in London this evening to allow us to manage the large numbers expected.'

Elizabeth found the man tiresome but didn't let it show. She continued. 'Gentlemen, I think we have an opportunity to deflect some of the flak. We interrogated Jason Brown earlier this week and I think he might be the person behind the initial cost-saving idea. You could certainly issue a statement that infers it was the work of a lone wolf and not Government-led. Whether this is totally true remains to be seen but it might de-fuse things before the march.'

David looked relieved. 'That is very helpful, Elizabeth. I'll get our PR team on it immediately.'

'But it doesn't say much about how we vet our senior Government officers, does it?' replied Elizabeth.

SIXTY

The March–Friday–
a week later

The day of the march on Parliament dawned. A blanket of grey cloud lay over Westminster, darkening the river and casting a dull light on the normally sand-coloured stone buildings. Rosie looked on the scene with equanimity, and the knowledge that at least there was no rain forecast.

The internet had been buzzing with arrangements all week. Ageing Matters and A Dignified Death were spearheading a campaign which had been officially called 'Our Death Our Choice'. Local splinter groups had developed to organise transport to London or stage their own protests, but the main event was being orchestrated from an office hastily set up in a rather dilapidated empty shop in Camden. A steering committee had been formed, led by Richard Hawley and assisted by Tony Knight and Avard Harriman. Working tirelessly in the background, coordinating the activities, was Rosie Jennings.

Following her initial phone call to Richard, she had turned up to a meeting at a hotel in London the previous Friday, where everyone had agreed that the march should take place as soon as possible to capitalise on the mood of outrage and anger being expressed by the population and in the media. By the end of the day, Rosie had secured premises for them to work from. By Monday they had planned the route, Tony's son had put up internet pages with information, and Rosie had set about obtaining the necessary permissions.

Despite the short timescale, there was a tremendous amount of sympathy from officials in the local borough council and the police. Rosie made a point of visiting them all in person and found that everyone had experienced the untimely death of a relative and wanted to talk about it. Many had read the story of Marjorie Clark, and Rosie sometimes had a hard time getting away. They all promised to fast-track her application.

Richard Hawley had been uneasy when Rosie first phoned and offered to help. But he couldn't fault her determination, or her motives.

'I want to make sense of Mum's death.'

Now he realised she had been instrumental in getting the march organised, and she'd contributed some novel ideas to get the attention of the media. He didn't know much about women her age and thought her frenzy was perhaps due to hormonal imbalance. Then he mentioned Simon once and she froze him out. Maybe it was something to do with him then?

A media headcount was putting the number of people attending in the region of half a million and the police were concerned about the flow of people, but Rosie assured them it would not be a problem. People coming by coach would start their march in the early morning at Gower Street. Londoners would start at Victoria Embankment, both aiming to meet at Westminster at midday. There they would stage a protest, then walk together to Hyde Park, where there would be speeches.

Like many others, the marches began with people carrying placards. Some were in uniform – nurses, carers, doctors, nuns.

Everyone else wore hospital gowns, their faces and hair whitened. Everybody was completely silent. Rosie's idea.

The silence was powerful, emphasising the messages on the placards.

Elderly Genocide – We Demand Transparency
Pro-Choice Euthanasia – Our Death Our Choice

The uniforms contrasted sharply with the hospital gowns, depicting the able and the sick. Richard Hawley found tears in his eyes. Splinter groups of drama and dance students, actors and artists took their chosen themes and developed them into performance art, all in silence. Rosie spotted Sandra and Yume in a group of Gay Pride marchers, identifiable with their pink and rainbow colours. The media muscled in with their cameras, recording the spectacle.

As the first people approached Westminster Bridge, the uniforms and others depicting the able filtered down the South Bank and crossed over Lambeth Bridge, milling into Victoria Park. They also crossed Westminster Bridge and started to fill Parliament Square and the surrounding green spaces. By contrast, the people in hospital gowns either boarded a series of boats moored on Westminster Pier or crossed over to the South Bank, disappearing amongst the trees in front of St Thomas' Hospital. It was like watching a choreographed dance. Rosie had positioned volunteers at strategic crossroads, making sure the right groups kept together.

This activity continued for some time – until midday, in fact – then it seemed to pause and stop. There must have been a signal, because the boats on the pier started their engines and began to make their way under Westminster Bridge. Richard, who had not been party to the details on this, realised it had been timed to catch the attention of the MPs planning to lunch on the terrace and in the dining room.

What followed was pure theatre. The boats lined up just off the Parliament embankment, keeping their position in the water. In one fluid movement, all the people stood up on deck and turned to face the gawping diners. With their pale faces, they looked like the poor souls they were meant to depict, and crowds began to appear on the terrace as word got around. Just as the MPs were getting uncomfortable with the silence, and with being eyeballed, there was a shout from the opposite bank and 'porters' shot from under the trees, each pushing a hospital trolley containing a gowned 'patient' whom they proceeded to manhandle into the river. The patients swam over to the boats and were hauled on board. The porters returned with more loaded trolleys.

Richard was panicking. 'Oh, shit,' he exclaimed. 'We'll be in trouble for this.' He turned to find Rosie at his elbow. 'What about health and safety, trespass, and theft for a start?' he spluttered.

'Don't worry,' she said calmly. 'It's all above board. The people in the water are lifeguards; the trolleys and porters' uniforms were lent by the hospital to actors and stuntmen. The boats have been lent by their owners, and unless we land at the Parliament building, we are not trespassing. Oh, and the river police have closed this stretch of the river for the stunt.'

Richard looked at her with new respect.

They turned their attention to the spectacle in front of them. The people in the boats were holding up placards demanding answers; the boats were getting uncomfortably full when suddenly everyone lay down. The pile of bodies needed no further interpretation.

There was a buzz of conversation on the dining terrace and the spell was broken. The boats headed back to Westminster Pier.

*

The Prime Minister turned to his new Minister of Health.

'Feelings are running high – always the same when it's family. We need a scapegoat for this debacle. Then we need to address the looming problems in elderly care. Any ideas?'

SIXTY-ONE

The March–the aftermath

There was a palpable sense of elation amongst the marchers at its overwhelming success. Hours after the protest had finished, they were still congregating in coffee shops and pubs near the various London stations. The white-faced groups who had walked the London streets, placards held high, had been a traffic-stopping spectacle, and the media were wasting no time in talking to them in pursuit of public-interest stories for that evening's TV and the next day's papers.

Richard, Rosie, Tony and Avard retired to a pub on the riverside which had recently been revamped to create a traditional ambience with wood-panelled walls and plush seating. A blackboard described the real ales on tap and the rib-sticking specials of the day.

The group were sitting around a table looking through the menus. Richard looked at the three people who had been instrumental in making the day such a success. He felt a sense of gratitude and admiration that they had put themselves in danger for something they believed in.

'This is my shout,' Richard insisted, 'my treat for all your help and support.'

They looked through the menu which was unquestionably calorie-dense. Health guru Richard looked at Rosie with concern. She seemed to keep rereading the options.

With her figure, probably not the sort of food she would normally eat.

'Fish and chips for me, please, Richard,' said Rosie, 'and a glass of Sauvignon to wash it down.'

Richard was taken by surprise. 'Right then, Rosie. Tony? Avard?'

The others placed their orders and Richard headed to the bar to order.

As he waited to be served, he took in the sight of a group of supposed in-patients drinking pints and considered how his attitude had changed over the past few weeks.

I really like these people. They stand up for what is right. And here they are, dressed in hospital gowns, with their faces and hair white.

He came back to the table with the drinks and looked at a smiling Rosie. 'Rosie, you must be really happy with the way the march has gone. You are an organisational genius.' He raised his glass and made a toast. 'To Rosie. A great job done.'

After devouring their food, and into their second round of drinks, Richard spoke to them about his plans. 'You all know how strongly I believe in pro-choice euthanasia, and I want to capitalise on the momentum we've achieved today. There may not be another opportunity like this for many years.'

He looked directly at Rosie. 'Rosie, your skills are just what is needed if we are to press ahead while we have the initiative. Would you be willing to work on the campaign going forward?'

'I'd love to,' Rosie said without hesitation.

Avard and Tony grinned, and Avard turned to Richard. 'Richard, please feel free to use my house for the campaign. I think you need a London base and we can set up the conservatory as a workspace.'

'That would be great,' said Tony. 'Most of my media contacts are in London and we need to keep the pressure on. Rosie, can we meet up to agree a communication plan ASAP?'

'What about tomorrow?' replied Rosie.

*

They walked out of the pub and said goodbye. Rosie was staying with Avard, so they turned towards the tube station.

'Congratulations, Rosie.' Simon stepped out to greet them. 'Congratulations, Mr Harriman. A brilliant protest with a powerful message. Let's hope it has results.'

His eyes were on Rosie, pleading. 'Can we go and talk somewhere?'

Avard looked at Rosie. It was her choice. He waited.

'I'd like that,' she said, turning to look at Simon.

'I'll see you later then.' Avard set off walking again, hiding a smile.

Simon took both her hands. 'It was wrong of me not to tell you about Hugo. I stupidly thought you needed to be shielded from the truth. You're a strong woman.'

'I didn't tell you about The Final Pathway either, but that was for security reasons beyond us.'

'We both probably saw the things we wanted in each other, not the whole person. Are you willing to try again?'

'We *do* think alike, Simon, that's what I would like.'

'I've booked into a hotel,' said Simon.

'Let's go.'

Rosie took his arm.

SIXTY-TWO

Rosie

Rosie and Simon talked over dinner at the hotel for hours. The dining room décor was dated, but the ambience was perfect, with subdued lighting, candles on the tables and soft music. They chose a discreet corner.

'Ideal,' murmured Rosie, feeling like she was on their first date all over again, discovering a new Simon.

They spent the first hour apologising to each other, gazing into each other's eyes.

'I can't believe how I patronised you, taking you to the UAE, finding the "little woman" a job, dealing with Hugo. You are a force to be reckoned with, Rosie.'

'Hindsight is easy, Simon. We both started off with the roles we knew from our first marriages. This tragedy has changed us.'

Their talk turned to David and Hugo.

'Our hands are tied,' said Rosie, unconsciously clasping hers together. 'If we shop David to the authorities, we also shop Hugo. We will have to wait to sell the house, till something happens or he is declared dead.'

'How do you feel about Hugo now?'

'He's an adult, I have to hold my hands up.' She spread her hands apart and then laughed as she realised.

Simon caught one of them and held it. 'I haven't heard you laugh for ages, you know.'

'I feel happier that he is with David than loose in the house in Chelford getting up to God knows what,' Rosie went on. 'I've never been able to control him; it was David who did that.'

'What about Theo? Do you think he knows where David and Hugo are?'

'We can't tell Theo,' said Rosie. 'He and his girlfriend can look after the house, but if I tell him, he will have to tell her. Theo is more perceptive than we give him credit for, you know. He has never asked me, but I'm sure he has his ideas. The truth? No. It's best left buried.'

'I've given up the job in UAE, you know.'

'Oh, Simon, it's because of my family.'

'Rosie, I'm not going anywhere unless you choose to be there too.'

'I miss the sunshine.'

'You pick a country, and we'll go there.'

SIXTY-THREE

Kate

Kate Turner was seated in her office at the Department of Health, mulling over her impending meeting with the Prime Minister. She had been a surprise appointment to the role of Minister for Health three weeks previously after the sudden resignation of Ken Hunt. Kate sighed, stood up and began to pace the floor, rehearsing what she planned to say. She was a tall woman, often described as 'statuesque', known for her penchant for tailored trouser suits and eye-catching jewellery. These assets helped her make an impact wherever she went, a fact that always surprised her. During the two weeks of her tenure, public fury at the disclosures of The Final Pathway had increased dramatically. This, together with the protest march, had gathered unwanted media attention from all around the world. The whole situation had the potential to get out of control. She had to be seen to act.

'This job is a poisoned chalice,' her husband had told her, and she was beginning to agree with him. This morning she had been summoned to meet the PM, Adam Redgrave, a man she found to be superficial and who had demonstrated on numerous occasions an underhand willingness to sacrifice colleagues in order to protect his own career. In anticipation of the meeting, she told her staff to prepare statistics. Not wanting to replicate Jason Brown's figures, Kate had asked them to focus on the projected numbers of elderly people over the coming years and the percentages of those who would have serious, life-compromising illnesses. Now she wondered how to approach the subject and stop the PM going into denial mode.

The department is aware that this looming problem has been around for years. The figures are staggering. It's got to be addressed now. No more heads in the sand.

She closed her attaché case, just as her assistant buzzed through to say her car was waiting at the back of the building. Since she took up the role, her security had been stepped up. Decoy cars and plainclothes protection officers were now an everyday part of her life. She had received a number of death threats which she had dismissed as the work of 'nutcases', but the police were taking no chances.

Outside, there was a convoy of three identical Range Rovers. She was ushered into the last in the line. After setting off, each car took a different route towards Downing Street, accompanied by unmarked police cars front and back. As Kate's car approached the Downing Street gates, it passed a tented community of journalists from all over the world who were waiting for the next instalment in The Final Pathway saga. Kate kept her head down as instructed, but she was all too aware of flashes from the cameras of photographers hoping to get a shot of the woman who was now at the centre of the story.

Once inside Number Ten, she was greeted by the PM's private secretary, who led her up a wide staircase past pictures of former prime ministers and into a room where the current incumbent was seated at a desk.

'Kate. Good to see you.' Adam shook her hand and indicated that she should sit opposite him. 'How can we defuse what is becoming a rather difficult situation?'

That is the understatement of the year.

'What do you think our options are? Personally, I think we need to place the blame fairly and squarely at the door of those within your department whose activities have precipitated this crisis and bring them publicly to book.'

Kate considered what she had just heard, and it tried her patience. 'Prime Minister, I think that is part of the way forward. However, it has brought the debate over end-of-life care into prominence. Faced with the exposure of so-called Government-led plans, the feeling amongst the people is that they would rather have the choice of when and how they die. Also, now that the numbers have been made public, people's minds have become focussed on the issues involved. They are not stupid; they know it will cost money.'

Kate wondered if she had gone too far but pressed on. She took the documents from her case and laid them out. 'As you can see, the figures speak for themselves.'

Adam studied them for some minutes before replying. 'So, what do you suggest?'

'Going back to your first point, I agree that those within my department who have abused their role should be dealt with via the criminal justice system. It's been suggested to me that there is a good likelihood of a conviction for misconduct in public office. But the more difficult problems to deal with are the End of Life issue, as it is now being called, and then the proper long-term funding of elderly care.'

Adam looked surprised at Kate's directness. 'I'm pretty sure that the furore will not die down. People are wound up and want answers.'

There was a pause, where he appeared to mull over her words. *Nice piece of theatre, Adam.*

'Okay,' he finally said. 'I think we could set up an inquiry into the options. Get some academics and civil servants on board and it could report back initially as early as next summer.'

Kate realised the man had not grasped the mood of the country at all. The public was not going to be satisfied by an inquiry which she felt was Government-speak for 'kicking the can down the road'. She was appalled at how ready he was to dismiss the views of millions of people.

She felt that this was the time for total honesty, even if it meant she would be reshuffled shortly. 'With respect, Prime Minister,' she said, 'everyone knows inquiries are a mechanism to delay making decisions with the hope that the problem will go away. The people want action now! The Government needs to consider putting forward legislation that allows a patient in palliative care to choose to die, especially if they are suffering unbearably.'

Adam was clearly taken aback. 'Kate, you are talking about euthanasia. The Church will not accept it.'

Kate was amazed that he was so out of touch. 'The great majority of the population don't go to church anymore,' she replied.

Adam had clearly run out of instant responses on the first issue. He moved on to the second. 'How do you propose elderly care will be funded?'

'How about increasing taxation?' said Kate. 'Like in Denmark and Sweden. Or a new type of national insurance paid by the over-forties, like in Japan? I think the population will listen to these options, having seen the alternative.'

Kate had said what needed to be said. Adam looked flummoxed. Here was a man who had a reputation for swerving the question whilst appearing to 'engage with the issue'. Now he had been confronted with a straightforward analysis of the problem and presented with solutions, and he didn't seem well equipped to respond.

After a period of uncomfortable silence, he spoke. 'Well, you obviously have a good grasp of what needs addressing. Do you think you could put forward a paper which suggests solutions that we can bring to the Cabinet for discussion next week?'

'Yes. I can do that,' said Kate, managing to disguise her shock.

The pair rose together and shook hands. Their proximity revealed Kate to be half a head taller than him and Adam momentarily looked diminished. He solved the problem by immediately sitting down again and buzzing for his secretary to summon Kate's car.

As she was driven through the streets of London, Kate considered how to best approach what she had been asked to do. She knew what the problems were and she had a grasp of possible solutions, but it would not be an easy sell in some quarters. She needed to get advice from those with more knowledge of the detail. That was going to be the challenge, and she only had a week.

SIXTY-FOUR

Jason

Jason had instructed a lawyer to accompany him to police interviews. The man had been described to him as 'top-notch' by one of his former friends from the East End whose career choices had needed frequent use of such skills. There had been several interviews now, and his lawyer had given him the bad news that today would be 'make or break', meaning he would either be free to go or be charged. This information had unnerved Jason, who had assumed he was paying the lawyer all this money to get him off.

The two were now seated at the familiar chipped Formica table as two police officers entered the room and introduced themselves. Jason sat with his arms folded, jaw set, staring at a point on the wall behind the men. He did not intend to give any ground. However, his cool demeanour was soon to be shattered.

'Mr Brown, this interview is being conducted under caution. You do not have to say anything. But it may harm your defence if you do not mention, when questioned, something that you later rely on in court. Anything you do say may be given in evidence.'

Jason felt slightly sick and a shiver ran down his body. He looked at his lawyer, who looked remarkably relaxed. Jason lowered his gaze and fought to compose himself as the police officer continued. 'Mr Brown, I would like you to clarify for me certain assertions you have previously made regarding the Avalon project. You informed me that the project had been running under the direction of Professor Richard Hawley. Is that correct?'

Jason wondered where this line of questioning was going. He was beginning to feel horribly out of control. 'Yes, that's correct.'

The man looked down at his laptop screen before speaking. 'We have trawled through all the electronic communication between the four members of the Avalon project and there are only two emails from Professor Hawley, both of which are responses to requests from you for information. It appears to me that you were directing matters, not Professor Hawley.'

Jason sat there silently. A cold sweat began to travel slowly down his back.

The questions continued. 'The two new members of Avalon were accountants. Is that correct?'

'The project needed competent analysts,' Jason replied, but he knew he was beginning to sound defensive and his voice sounded weaker.

The man continued. His voice, by contrast, was strong and confident. Jason recognised the change in dynamic. He hated it but could do nothing. 'Were those two team members recruited by Professor Hawley? And did he instruct them regarding their respective roles in calculating cost-savings should people die three, six or nine months sooner?'

Jason said nothing.

'Can you tell me whether it was you or Professor Hawley who dismissed the previous members of the Palliative Care Pathway project and renamed it Avalon?'

Jason's lawyer whispered in his ear. Jason looked at his interrogators. 'I have nothing more to say.'

The officers looked directly at the once-arrogant Jason Brown, now a diminished version of his former bombastic self.

'Jason Brown, I am charging you with misconduct in public office.'

Jason was half aware of the caution being repeated before he slumped forward, head in his hands, his body shaking and his lawyer's hand on his shoulder.

SIXTY-FIVE

Eva

Eva got up painfully from her chair and peered out of her lounge window for the umpteenth time that day. If she was honest with herself, she would have admitted to feeling a deep sense of loss at Marjorie's death, as well as a good dose of anxiety, but she had been schooled from an early age to curb such introspective and self-indulgent thoughts.

She was born between the two world wars, into a household damaged by the first one. Her father had inhaled mustard gas in the trenches, her mother's brother was killed in France and her grandfather had died of a broken heart, so they said. Granny came to live with them and set up court in the spare bedroom, banging on the floor with her stick. Most families had been touched like this in some way and there was only a brief respite before the Second World War. Hers became the generation that soldiered on.

Roberta was due to visit, and there was another source of anxiety. From an early age, Roberta had exhibited a total lack of understanding of her parents' values. She operated on an emotional level that they could never comprehend. Part of Eva condemned her actions; the repressed rebel inside her applauded.

There was a knock at the front door. Roberta had a key and Eva wondered whom it was. She opened it to an attractive, smartly dressed woman about Roberta's age.

'Hello, Mrs Phipps, I'm Linda Morris. I work for Dom Maxwell, and I'm just calling round to see how things are with you after the death of your neighbour and friend, Mrs Clark. Can I come in?'

'Well, I suppose so,' said Eva, who was secretly glad of any company right now. 'I'm expecting my daughter soon,' she added, just to put Linda in her place.

'No problem, Mrs Phipps,' Linda replied.

Linda was, in fact, from the marketing department and adept at getting people to open up. Soon, Eva was confiding in her the gossip and the fears of the elderly Summerlands residents.

'There are rumours that no one ever comes out from The Retreat once they go in,' said Eva dramatically. 'Mrs Clark was keeping quiet about her symptoms because she was scared. Who knows? If she'd said something sooner, she might still be with us today.' She glared at Linda for effect.

'Professor Hawley will be saddened to hear that,' Linda replied automatically, trying to play things down.

'Oh, him,' said Eva, and, leaning forward towards Linda, she added in a whisper, 'We call him Dr Death.'

SIXTY-SIX

Dom

Dom Maxwell was pacing the floor of his office, deep in thought, waiting for the arrival of Richard Hawley. He noticed absentmindedly that the newly planted trees and shrubs in the border outside his window were growing well, framing a glimpse of the lake, just as he had planned.

It must be done. A new broom sweeps clean.

At last, his secretary announced Richard's arrival.

'Show him in,' replied Dom automatically.

The person that opened the door and bounded in took him aback. He was expecting Richard to look at least a bit chastened. Instead, he was crackling with energy.

They shook hands and exchanged pleasantries.

'Take a seat,' said Dom, gesturing towards two easy chairs that were positioned round a low table by the French windows. 'Can I offer you tea or coffee?'

He rang for his receptionist.

When they were seated with drinks, there was a pause.

How do I sack a senior director?

'Did you hear about the protest march on Parliament last Friday?' Richard burst out.

'Yes, I saw it on the news. It was quite spectacular. Of course, we had our own protest to deal with outside the gates here,' Dom replied mildly.

Richard immediately looked contrite. 'Forgive me, Dom,' he replied. 'I completely forgot that you would be at the receiving end here too.'

Dom nodded his head in acknowledgement. 'It wasn't too bad; a bit of shouting went on. The protesters here were divided, though. Some were reacting to the Government plan, but others were demanding answers for the deaths here.'

There was another pause. 'Yes, that local newspaper has stirred things up,' mused Richard.

'Yes, they have,' said Dom. 'I have to be seen to be taking action to uphold our reputation, so I'm suing them for a start.' He paused for effect. 'Can you suggest anything else?'

'I think I should step down as medical director,' Richard volunteered, to Dom's surprise. 'This murder is not good for my reputation or yours and will cling to me if I don't. Besides which, I want to commit more of my time to the End of Life debate.'

Dom was secretly relieved that it had been easy so far. 'I'll be sorry to see you go, Richard,' he replied sincerely. 'Your reputation has helped us launch Summerlands. Of course, there will still be questions to be answered.'

There was another pause as they both considered what to say next.

Richard spoke first. 'I am aware that, because I dealt with the palliative care and I believe in pro-choice euthanasia, I am seen as a suspect, despite the post-mortem evidence,' he began.

Do you know they call you Dr Death here?

Richard went on, choosing his words carefully. 'I was using a new drug that I helped develop. Then there were three other patients in palliative care at the same time as Marjorie Clark was murdered. It's no wonder that I have been considered a prime suspect.'

'There is also the fact that you were recruited to the Avalon project at just about the same time,' Dom reminded him.

'Well, that was a farce. I wasn't consulted about anything. I've thought long and hard about this. If Jason Brown had asked me how to kill off the elderly population, I would have recommended a virus, not an overdose of medication.'

He seemed to collect himself. 'I have been asked to appear on TV in various current affairs programmes, including *BBC Breakfast*. I have nothing to hide.'

Dom was impressed with the man's self-belief. He seemed changed somehow, more transparent, less arrogant, yet it still felt as though there was something he hadn't said. Whatever it was, he hoped it would stay buried, for both their sakes.

'Who will you appoint in my place?' asked Richard, changing the subject. 'I would recommend Yume Yamamoto. She has worked with me for five years now and is up to speed with the procedures that are in place at The Retreat.'

'Yes, indeed, I was expecting you to recommend her. She would be a good choice.'

There seemed little else to add to the meeting.

'Let's hope your TV appearances can settle the unrest here,' said Dom, as Richard rose to leave. 'I wish you every success. Let me know how you get on.'

'I am fairly confident. I have asked Rosie Jennings to carry on working with me as my PA. That woman has incredible ideas, you know.'

SIXTY-SEVEN

Roberta

Sandra was visiting Roberta at home and found her in bed.

'Tut, you need to take some exercise,' she said. 'I'm on my way to my Pilates class, come with me.'

'Your ankles are looking puffy,' said Kate Sellars, the Pilates teacher. 'I'm not sure you should be doing any exercises at all.'

'My ankles are a bit swollen, that's all,' Roberta protested.

'When is your next hospital appointment?' asked Sandra.

'Oh, dear, there's been so much going on recently that I think I've missed a couple. They make so much fuss these days.'

Sandra had a blood pressure monitor in her car and the resultant test was sky high. 'I'm taking you straight to hospital, Roberta. You're overdue and you need to be under the observation of a doctor.'

Sandra didn't want to alarm Roberta, but she was seriously concerned. High blood pressure and swollen ankles were both symptoms of pre-eclampsia, and although Roberta had had two pregnancies with no such complications it didn't bode well.

At the hospital Roberta was examined, exclaimed over and assigned a bed on a maternity ward.

'You've been stupidly neglecting yourself,' scolded Sandra.

'I'm so sorry.' Roberta's eyes were bright with tears.

'And I still think you should have told Jan about the pregnancy and given him a chance to at least offer to help you.'

'I'm so confused I find it hard to explain why anymore. It started with a point of principle that I wouldn't let another man feel trapped.'

'Oh, I give up trying to discuss it with you. I'll come back and see you tonight with Yume. Is there anything you want me to fetch from your house? Make me a list.'

*

That evening, Sandra went with Yume to Roberta's house, collecting toiletries, clothes and some knitting.

'Roberta won't tell anyone the sex of her baby, but this wool is blue,' observed Sandra.

They were in the living room and had left the front door on the latch.

'Shh, I think I just heard somebody come in,' whispered Yume.

Sandra looked around for a handy weapon but could only find the TV remote.

Just as she crept behind the living-room door, a large hand reached round and grabbed her by the wrist. It belonged to a giant of a man with white-blond hair and flashing blue eyes.

'You won't hurt me with that. I'm Jan – now, tell me about Roberta's baby,' he said firmly.

Wow, Roberta, what a catch.

Sandra couldn't take her eyes off him.

*

Jan, Sandra and Yume were sitting together on Roberta's sofa, drinking tea and discussing her.

'Who is this Richard Hawley? He wrote to tell me that Roberta is having my baby. His letter was waiting with the port authorities at the same island where she left me. Is he a new lover?' He glared

530

fiercely. 'I realise I am just thinking of myself and *my* life, so I came to see what's going on with Roberta,' he added.

'Richard is certainly not her lover!' cried Sandra angrily. 'Jesus, is that all you men can think about? And yes, you are just thinking of yourself, unlike Roberta, who was thinking of you.' Sandra glared at Jan for emphasis. 'She didn't want your lifestyle to be compromised.'

'But how can she think I would not want our son?'

'Did Roberta tell you about her first marriage?'

'Ahh, yes, now I understand.' Jan put his head in his hands. 'That's Roberta, she is good and honest. I feel I hardly deserve her.'

Suddenly he jumped up, knocking his tea over. '*Av for fanden!* Why are we here? I must go and see her.'

*

Roberta wasn't in her bed in the ward and Sandra went to the nurses' desk to find out what was happening.

'Mrs Kenyon is in a delivery room,' a nurse informed her. 'Are you a relative?'

'I'm her friend and I brought her in here,' said Sandra impatiently. 'I'm a nurse and I was worried about her blood pressure.'

Yume and Jan were right behind her.

'I'm her friend too,' said Yume, 'and I'm a doctor.'

'I'm the father,' Jan chipped in.

The nurse stared at them all for a long moment. 'Well, I guess you're all suitably qualified then. The doctor decided to induce labour. From what I hear, everything is happening very quickly. I'm sorry, but I didn't have any of your phone numbers to let you know.'

*

Roberta was lying on her back on the bed, panting and wailing alternately whilst breathing in gas and air for pain relief. Sandra and Yume poked their heads round the door.

531

'You took your time,' she said crossly.

'It's my fault they're late,' said Jan, following them into the room.

Roberta burst into tears.

'Don't let me put you off,' said Jan, kissing her forehead. 'I'm so glad I'm in time to see my son be born.'

Sandra and Yume left them together and sought out the midwife, who assured them that everything was progressing normally, but fast. On their way back, Sandra bumped into Rosie coming out of the ladies' room.

'Oh my God, Rosie,' Sandra blurted out. 'Congratulations on the march. I could tell your touch, it must have been you, old Hawley hasn't got that kind of imagination.'

'Thank you,' said Rosie.

*

Back in the delivery room, they all watched as a blond-haired baby made his entrance into the world. Jan placed him on Roberta's chest, hugging them both. Everybody had tears of emotion in their eyes.

SIXTY-EIGHT

Afterwards

Rosie, Sandra and Yume could hardly tear themselves away from the hospital delivery room and the tableau of Roberta, Jan and their new baby. For a moment the world was standing still, filled with happiness and love.

Rosie was the first to collect herself. 'I think we're superfluous here now,' she remarked.

'We need to leave them in peace to catch up with each other,' said Yume.

'Jesus! Let's go and wet the baby's head,' exclaimed Sandra.

Buoyed up with euphoria, they said their goodbyes and piled into a waiting taxi outside the hospital, giving directions to their favourite wine bar in Alderley Edge. Yume sat between Rosie and Sandra, easing any constraints, and they kept their talk to safe subjects, like the baby's name: Christian.

'Wasn't it funny how Roberta and Jan both seemed to decide on the same name?'

'Kindred spirits?'

'Do you spell Christian with a "K" or a "C" in Danish?'

Outside the wine bar they paused, each remembering their

different get-togethers there not so long ago, now eclipsed by recent events.

'Onward and upward,' muttered Sandra as she pushed open the door for the others to enter. It sounded like an incantation.

They ordered glasses of wine and fussed with their coats and their seats in lieu of conversation, which seemed to have stalled now that they were facing each other. The wine came, and they raised their glasses.

'To Roberta, Jan and Christian.'

'To their future. May it be happy.'

Small talk followed, with exclamations on the timing of Jan's appearance.

'It was Richard's doing. Apparently, he and Roberta had candid chats when he stayed with her,' remarked Yume. 'I think they did each other good.'

'Cheers to Roberta – Mother Earth.'

They drained their glasses and ordered a bottle of wine.

Rosie spoke next. 'Richard is to be an advocate for the End of Life Act, as it is now being called. I will be working as his PA until Simon gets another job.'

There was silence, and Sandra and Yume looked at each other.

Rosie didn't miss their glance. 'Is something wrong?' she asked them.

Yume looked away, but Sandra answered. 'You know we've both worked closely with Richard at Summerlands? You know there have been concerns about the way he was using his new drug, Elysium.'

Rosie recoiled. She felt her judgement was being questioned, but then she jutted her chin forward, determined to stand her ground. 'Whatever Richard did, he was not responsible for my mum's death, so I have no personal issues against him in that respect. As for trialling the new drug he had developed, I think he was just doing what he was trained to do. He's told me he was uneasy about Avalon from the start, so I think he would have raised questions very soon.'

Rosie looked directly at Yume and Sandra. She could see understanding in Yume's face, but Sandra's showed scepticism and… scorn?

How dare she mock me? David's long-term mistress!

Rosie felt a wave of overwhelming anger at this injustice. Then she remembered Yume's pep talk. Fuelled by two large glasses of wine on an empty stomach, she turned to face Sandra. 'I can see you question my judgement, Sandra. Yet you are just as guilty as I am of taking the easy options with David. Taking the lavish lifestyle that we now know was based on fraud and a complete lack of respect for life. There is no comparison between him and Richard. David is a psychopath with no feeling towards mankind. If Richard is guilty of anything, it is only inflated self-importance.'

Sandra looked shocked. This was a new Rosie that she hadn't known was there.

'Rosie, you are probably right,' she ventured.

*

Sandra was feeling a sense of unreality. Her head was spinning from the wine, more so than it had ever done at the booze- and drug-fuelled parties during her nursing training.

I'm out of practice.

'We should get something to eat,' said Rosie.

There was a TV on the far wall, a new addition to the wine bar that they had all noticed and none of them approved of. Yume was the first to spot the headline running along the bottom of the picture: 'Former Department of Health Minister Kenneth Hunt and Director of Business Transformation Jason Brown have been charged with misconduct in public office.'

SIXTY-NINE

Roberta

Roberta was back at home, worrying about her mother and how she was taking the news of Christian's birth. Since then, she had only talked to her on the phone, and Eva had quickly changed the subject. After much discussion, Roberta and Jan decided to take the bull by the horns and pay her a visit. Walking up the path together, they saw that Eva was peering anxiously through the window as usual. She looked startled to see them and took her time coming to the door. She opened it just wide enough for them to enter, with a severe look on her face, but she unbent slightly to proffer her cheek to Roberta.

Jan took it all in his stride, having been well briefed by Roberta, who had talked to him earlier.

'Mother will be sulky and childish and show her disapproval, then she will start asking questions about things she can further disapprove of. It's a stance, carried forward through generations of women in her family. I do feel sorry for her, but it's hard when I am a target.'

'Don't worry, I have a few ideas, Roberta.' Jan had squeezed her hand in support.

Jan attentively helped Eva to her chair. Once she was seated, he introduced himself and proffered his hand. Eva was visibly impressed. Jan was easy on the eye and a definite improvement on Roberta's ex-husband Will. He then drew up another chair and sat down to be more at her level. Roberta stifled a giggle and carefully propped Christian up on the sofa between two cushions so that Eva could take her time and look at him. She offered to make a cup of coffee whilst Jan engaged Eva in conversation, expressing his concern about how she was dealing with Marjorie's death.

Soon Eva was in full flow. 'Of course, Marjorie and I were well-suited, and I shall miss her company, but we didn't live in each other's pockets, you know.'

Eva then had to explain the English idiom 'in each other's pockets' to Jan, which caused her to smile. She was also very matter of fact about the cyanide poisoning. 'Cyanide is in more things than you think, you know. It's frightening, really.'

'I think you are a very brave lady,' Jan observed.

'I used to belong to an amateur writers club, and I wrote several short stories, so I pride myself in having an enquiring mind.'

'Would you like to meet Christian? I am happy to bring him to meet you, his *mormor*. It's Danish for grandma.'

*

Later, Roberta and Jan called in at the main Summerlands building and proudly showed Christian to manager Nicky. They were made to sit down on the sofa in her office and treated to more coffee and biscuits. Dom, who was passing by, heard laughter and poked his head round the door out of curiosity.

'It's good to have happiness here at Summerlands,' he remarked after he had been introduced.

Jan turned to him. 'The end of life should be celebration like beginning, yes? I wonder how this can work in this Summerlands, though; divided by wealth as it is.'

'Why do you say that?' replied Dom, intrigued.

'In Denmark, we look after elderly people in a different way. We pay big taxes to care for everyone, young and old. We are not a hierarchal society and there is no very rich or poor.'

'I'd be interested to hear about it,' replied Dom sincerely. 'When you can spare a moment from your family, of course.'

SEVENTY

Rosie

Rosie and Richard were in the conservatory at Avard's house, practising the likely questions he would be asked at his forthcoming TV interview. She had insisted that they set the scene correctly, with chairs placed at a suitable angle to each other and glasses of water on a coffee table between them. Richard had been amused and slightly irritated.

'I have done a lot of interviews, you know,' he said pompously.

Rosie gave him a long look and he noticed her eyes were a chilly green today.

*

Rosie started with a resume of Richard's background, then the questions began.

'Professor Hawley, your reputation goes before you, but more recently it has been tainted by accusations of murder, and involvement in Government genocide plans.'

Richard recoiled and tried to speak, but Rosie held up her hand. 'Marjorie Clark died on your watch at Summerlands, of cyanide poisoning. You were also a member of the Avalon team, yet you claim to know nothing about The Final Pathway. You have half an hour to rescue your reputation.'

Richard attempted to grin, but it faded under the withering look that Rosie gave him.

Of course, she has a vested interest in knowing the answers.

He felt as though his head was in a noose. This woman was not playing. He pulled himself together. This was indeed a test. If he could convince her, he could convince anyone.

'Is it true that you saw your appointment at Summerlands as an opportunity to experiment further with your new palliative care drug, Elysium?'

Richard was ready for her. 'I have specialised in creating palliative care plans for the elderly for the whole of my career. I have striven to prescribe the right dosage of medication for each person during this time. It is a near-impossible task when everyone is already taking a combination of drugs. If you accuse me of experimenting, you can include the rest of the medical profession. Elysium is a superior mix of familiar drugs, based on my experience over the years. Of course, I will advocate and use it in preference to other drugs.'

He glared at Rosie, but she was ready with the next question. 'Why did you agree to join the Avalon project? How was it going to differ from the original Palliative Care Pathway?'

'I was given to understand that the department would be looking into forecasts of almost impossible numbers of elderly people in care in ten years' time. It is a sensitive subject and I was to keep it under wraps for the time being. I expected there to be many meetings and then petitions to Parliament and yes, I anticipated that pro-choice euthanasia would be considered. Instead, my team from the Palliative Care Pathway was disbanded and replaced by a couple of accountants. Now I see it was merely a number-crunching exercise for the underhand plans that have been exposed.'

'What did the Director of Business Transformation want from you?'

'He wanted the kudos of my name, of course, to add respectability to his project. He lured me in with the mention of using my new drug.' Richard paused. 'I was vain enough to take the bait,' he muttered.

Rosie looked surprised but carried on. 'What motivates you to work in palliative care with elderly people? Is it the power to control life and death?'

Richard looked startled. 'I watched a relative die from drug abuse and that led me to study toxicology. I then moved on to specialise in the drugs needed in palliative care. I am an advocate of a good life with good health, diet and exercise. When the health fails, and it will happen to all of us...' Here he leant towards Rosie to emphasise the point. 'I would like everyone to have a good death, the death of their choice – not mine, and not to a Government timetable.'

'Professor Hawley, who do you think blew the whistle on The Final Pathway plan?'

'I assume it was someone at the department, concerned about the secrecy surrounding Avalon. I don't know who else could have gained access to the statistics that were being produced.'

'It was common knowledge that you were working on Avalon. Is it possible that there were concerns about what *you* were up to?'

Richard looked suddenly shocked.

Yume?

He pulled himself together.

'Yes, it's possible,' he muttered. 'But as I have explained, it was not the case.'

Rosie waited, but nothing else was forthcoming.

'And finally, you have now resigned from Summerlands and turned your attention to lobbying for the End of Life Act, a new title that wallpapers over the word "euthanasia". It looks like this could also be a wallpapering exercise to redeem your reputation. What exactly will you be doing?'

Richard cringed. Rosie was giving him a hard time, and she meant it.

541

'A monstrous Government plan has been exposed. I want to harness the mood of the people and offer them a better option in a cause that is dear to my heart.'

He thought of his birth mother and an unwanted tear threatened.

Rosie looked at him, alarmed. 'Thank you, Professor Hawley,' she said quietly.

SEVENTY-ONE

Kate

The media was continuing to stir the mood of the population with TV programmes, phone-ins and interviews featuring all walks of life, from campaigners and specialists to the man in the street. Heart-wrenching stories of negligence in care and untimely deaths were featured on daytime TV, in magazines and online. Samaritans and mental health organisations were inundated with calls from desperate people, reliving the guilt and anxiety they felt over the death of a loved one and turning it into anger against the establishment.

Richard, Rosie, Tony and Avard had no problem keeping the end-of-life debate in the public domain. Richard had given his TV interview and had appeared on other current affairs programmes, promoting the campaign for legislation. Rosie, however, was getting increasingly concerned about the hysteria and drama that was taking over reasoned argument.

'Look at this, Richard,' she exclaimed.

They were in Avard's conservatory, reading the newspaper headlines and checking morning TV. It was a daily ritual over a cup of coffee and usually convivial, but not today.

Rosie turned the sound up on the TV to catch a harassed-looking reporter being jostled in a crowd outside a hospital. 'Police have been called to this hospital in Birmingham, to disperse a picket who are stopping doctors and nurses from entering the building to do their work,' he gasped.

The camera panned out to a sizeable crowd, some carrying placards saying: 'We Demand Legislation, Not Extermination'. It held the shot for a few moments, establishing the hostile mood of the demonstrators. Then it zoomed back to the reporter, who had managed to get himself into a quieter spot and had cornered a frightened-looking youth wearing blue scrubs under a parka jacket. 'Julian, you are a junior doctor here, unable to get into work. Can you tell me what is happening?'

'These protests have been escalating since the publication of The Final Pathway. It started with relatives coming onto the wards, demanding to know every detail of a patient's care plan. We hardly have time to do our job, never mind discuss it. The sheer number of people turning up is becoming a problem, especially in A&E. We have called the police several times to restrain anxious relatives who think we're either not doing enough or doing something sinister.'

Rosie looked shocked. 'What is the Government doing about this, Richard?'

'You know that Avard, Tony and I are meeting with Kate Turner, the Minister of Health, today? Well, she's putting together a proposal for legislation of the End of Life Act for the Cabinet to consider next week. She's already convinced the PM that it's an emergency, God knows how.'

*

'You are the first people I have chosen to consult, being specialists in the care of the elderly. I shall also be talking to other organisations and charities in the next few days. I am aiming to put forward a draft plan of the procedures to be implemented, should the Cabinet vote yea. If they do, I shall be looking to draw on your experience again. If they don't, well…'

Kate Turner was addressing Richard, Tony and Avard in a meeting room next to her office. They all knew each other, and the tone of the meeting was informal, apart from the seriousness of the situation.

'How did you persuade the PM to rush this legislation through?' asked Richard.

'I impressed on him the dangerous mood of the public. I then expressed the opinion that the Government that responds to this crisis, instead of avoiding it like previous governments, will gain the most support in the future. I expect it put him in mind of the elections coming up.'

There was a ripple of suppressed laughter around the table.

*

Kate had been up since five am putting the final touches to the presentation she was giving to Cabinet colleagues that morning. Now she was eating a dinner of fish pie with her husband Ted. Home was a three-storey townhouse in a sweeping crescent in Notting Hill. They had lived there for the past twenty years, ever since she had been elected as an MP. Its situation had meant that she could walk to the local Underground station and catch the Circle line to Westminster. Now she was a member of the Cabinet, it was a ministerial car at the door and protection officers, day and night.

She finished the wine in her glass and turned to her husband. 'That was just what I needed after today. Comfort food and a large glass of wine.'

Ted smiled and kissed the top of her head before collecting the plates and topping up their glasses. 'Do you want to talk about the presentation?' he asked.

Kate grabbed her glass and sat down on the settee. She kicked off her shoes, tucked her legs underneath her and watched her husband arranging the items in the dishwasher with a precision that made her smile.

'I think it went well. They all had copies of my paper to read over the weekend so, looking at the figures, they could be in no doubt that it's a problem that successive governments have chosen to ignore. The Final Pathway has ensured that continuing with that approach is not an option.' Kate took a mouthful of wine, savouring it in her mouth before slowly swallowing it and enjoying the buzz of relaxation it induced. 'We'll see. The Cabinet will reconvene tomorrow and vote on it yea or nay.'

She picked up the TV controller and mindlessly turned it on. The top story was yet again the continued fallout from the revelations of The Final Pathway website. Hospitals were recruiting extra security personnel to deal with angry relatives. MPs had been inundated with letters and emails from constituents demanding action, and a twenty-four-hour protest camp had started up outside Westminster, which doggedly voiced its demands hour after hour.

Kate looked at the coverage, becoming more concerned at how things were spiralling out of control. 'I hope my colleagues have seen all this and realise the strength of feeling in the country.'

Ted drained his glass before speaking. 'And, of course, there is an election next year.'

'Good timing, I hope,' said Kate.

'Perfect storm,' said Ted.

*

Adam Redgrave, PM, turned off his TV. He knew that by now the news would have been syndicated across TV channels around the world. The same would apply to repeats of coverage of the protest marches, which kept The Final Pathway and its message constantly in the headlines.

Not exactly good PR for the country.

It was the increasing public disorder by groups who normally would not be visible that was giving him real cause for concern. His party represented middle England, who were not prone to this sort of dissent.

Civil unrest...

He poured himself a large Scotch on the rocks, swilling the ice around the glass.

And then there's the general election next year...

He had realised some days ago that it was looking likely that he would probably need to get new legislation in place. He had taken advice as to the available mechanisms for fast-tracking new laws and had been assured that it was possible to do so.

Time to get things in place and for the dust to settle before the election campaigning begins.

SEVENTY-TWO

New Year's Eve 2006

Rosie was at a black-tie ball at the Lowry Hotel with Simon. They made an attractive couple as they danced. Rosie was wearing a fitted velvet dress in a deep shade of purple that showed off her trim figure, and Simon looked handsome in his dinner suit.

It was nearly midnight and Rosie thought over the events of the last few months. The Cabinet had voted yea to the End of Life Act and Kate Turner had appeared on TV, outlining the procedures the Government would have to go through. At the same time, and in her no-nonsense manner, she reassured the country that everything would be available for public scrutiny, and nothing like The Final Pathway was ever going to happen. The demonstrations had ceased, and reaction had dwindled on the internet to the regular posts on charity websites and the usual handful of conspiracy theories and witch hunts. Richard was in demand as a consultant, his TV appearances having re-established his credentials as a caring gerontologist with a human touch. He was keeping Rosie busy.

The band finished playing, and Simon looked at his watch.

'Shall we stay on the floor for the New Year?' he said.

'I think so, that would be nice,' replied Rosie.

The band struck up a slow number and the master of ceremonies started a countdown. At midnight, everyone was cheering; balloons and confetti were cascading from nets under the ceiling.

Simon took her hands. 'Happy New Year, Rosie,' he said, and kissed her full on the mouth.

*

Sandra and Yume were at an après ski party in Chamonix, France. Yume had persuaded Sandra to take up skiing, a sport she had never even contemplated. But she was now enjoying the thrill of speed and learning to control her body and respond to the demands of the piste.

Most of the après ski parties were rowdy and New Year was no exception. At midnight they were dancing to Leona Lewis's 'A Moment Like This', and indeed, at that moment, she felt that her life was perfect.

Then a niggling thought of things not resolved came into her mind. She had been composing a text to Steve Mallory for a while – nothing romantic, it was to do with David's whereabouts. She looked at Yume guiltily. 'Time to lay the ghost,' she said aloud and pressed send.

'What was that?' asked Yume.

'Happy New Year, Yume,' responded Sandra, kissing her.

*

Jan, Roberta, Christian and Eva were in Denmark, for Christmas and New Year, staying with Jan's parents, Karen and Erik, in their retirement home. Roberta had been surprised at the invitation, and that it included herself and Eva. But there were guest rooms, and they were all made to feel at home.

Jan's parents turned out to be delighted with the grandson they never thought they'd have.

549

Karen hugged Roberta. 'Jan will never have a traditional life, but then perhaps he has met another free spirit, eh?'

It was a shock for Roberta to find out that Jan's father was suffering from dementia. Jan had never mentioned it and she didn't know what to expect at the home. She was pleasantly surprised. They were shown into a communal room by Hanne the manager. It had floor-to-ceiling glass windows that looked onto a courtyard garden in the centre. There was a living area with an open kitchen, and they found Jan's parents helping to prepare lunch. Other people were sitting around, enjoying the bustle and aromas of food being prepared. The mood was light and bright.

'If you can peel potatoes, you are still useful,' joked Erik.

Hanne explained, 'The Danish government's philosophy is to integrate elderly people, to keep them active in the community for as long as possible. When they have to come to a home, we carry that on. We all do all the cooking, laundry and cleaning together. We deliberately engage them to participate in household chores. If you can hold a broom, you can sweep the floor. And residents can have a glass of wine at dinner.' She gave Eva a wink.

The time flew by. All the residents made a fuss of baby Christian, and Eva spent time playing cards or chatting to some of them, who all spoke good English.

'No one is going to learn Danish.' Karen laughed.

Roberta and Jan toasted the new year with a glass of schnapps, and Jan sent a text to Dom Maxwell: 'Living it up in Denmark with my parents. You should come here and see Danish elderly care for yourself!'

SEVENTY-THREE

2007–Six months later

It was a bright June day with clear blue skies, and Rosie was in the family room, looking through the French windows at the vapour trails that criss-crossed the sky. She thought about her husband and son, both of whom were now thousands of miles away in the UAE. The symbolism was not lost on her.

The doorbell rang, announcing the arrival of her two oldest friends. Roberta struggled in with baby Christian in his car seat and Sandra followed, bringing in a bag of baby essentials, out of which she pulled a bottle of pink champagne and two birthday cards.

'Happy Birthday, Rosie! Stick this in your fridge.'

Rosie led the way to the kitchen and put it in the freezer. 'That'll be quicker. Mustn't forget it…'

Christian was asleep and they all admired him before Roberta put his chair a little away from them in a quiet corner.

Rosie opened the cards. Both contained messages of love and friendship. She kissed each woman in turn. To Rosie's surprise, Sandra's eyes welled up and she bit her lip, then shrugged her shoulders defensively.

'Well, you know, we go back over thirty years,' she muttered.

Rosie was taken aback by such a display of emotion from Sandra, but her natural reserve stopped her from doing or saying anything in response.

We're closer friends now than we ever were then. Time and events mellow you.

'I've done some lunch, let's go through.'

Rosie rescued the champagne, put it in an ice bucket, and they sat at the table sipping and chatting as Sandra reverted to her normal outspoken self.

'We should all drink to "liking life".'

The three chinked glasses.

'Is the job with Richard permanent then?' asked Roberta.

'I don't know. Ever since the End of Life Act was passed, Richard's been in great demand as a consultant. He advises healthcare providers about what they need to have in place to ensure that patients' wishes are respected. Because it was fast-tracked through Parliament, they are all playing catch-up. Then there are relatives and medical staff to consider, and a lot of work to be done advising on power of attorney and living wills, but I love it.'

Roberta walked over to check Christian, who was still sleeping soundly.

'How's Jan?' Rosie asked.

'He flew back to the Caribbean yesterday. He's going to pick up his yacht and sail it back across the Atlantic.'

Rosie looked surprised. 'Back here?'

'No, the plan is for him to bring it to the Mediterranean and Christian and I will fly out to join him. We're going to try family life on board. My painting has always been inspired by bright skies and colours.'

'What, live on a boat with a baby?'

Roberta laughed. 'A lot of families do it. It's worth a try.'

'Not for me,' said Rosie, pulling a face. 'I like my comforts too much.'

She distributed the final drops of champagne across the three glasses, settled a second bottle in the ice bucket and turned to face Sandra. 'Tell me what's been happening at Summerlands. I always thought Dom Maxwell seems a decent sort. He didn't do anything to deserve all that bad publicity.'

'A lot has happened. Jesus, where to start? The Retreat doesn't do in-patients anymore, it's just a walk-in centre. Yume runs it now. She's a great doctor, but it's taken some time for people to start using it after what happened.'

She held her glass out and Rosie obliged, opening the second bottle.

'And Dom?'

'Poor Dom. A lot of the homeowners were spooked and used a buyback clause in their contracts. Dom's had to buy their properties at market value and – surprise, surprise – hasn't had any success reselling them.' She leant forward and dropped her voice conspiratorially. 'It's a bit hush-hush, but he's been dealing with the local council and they are using the villas to house vulnerable elderly people who can't buy a property. With a contribution from the council and a deal from Dom on the rent, they're gradually being reoccupied.'

Rosie raised her eyebrows in surprise. 'Mum would have been horrified at that. How have the remaining owners reacted?'

'Most of them left are the wealthy ones who bought the duplexes around the lake. For a lot of them, it's just a UK base and they have properties in other parts of the world. Dom is making them into a separate gated community.'

Roberta chipped in. 'Mother has sold up to Dom and moved into sheltered housing. She has her own apartment but can socialise when she chooses, which suits her down to the ground. She was very impressed with the home in Denmark where Jan's parents lived.'

'Yes, that reminds me,' said Sandra. 'Dom has changed his plans for the two Summerlands down south. They are being renamed Fellowship for a start; then Dom was really interested in the things Jan has told him about the facilities built for the elderly in Denmark. Apparently, they are geared towards keeping people highly independent, cooking and cleaning for themselves and others, and having people able to come and stay. So more like home, I suppose.'

'I think less dependency when you are old can only be a good thing,' said Rosie. 'This new tax the over-forties will pay to finance their future care means that the country can build more accommodation like this. It should be good news for Dom.'

The women were now getting towards the end of the second bottle of champagne and tongues were becoming looser. Rosie noticed Roberta, who had recently finished breastfeeding and had not been drinking for months, was looking happily heavy-eyed.

Sandra, on the other hand, was becoming more voluble. 'Rosie. I want to see David suffer. What about you?'

The champagne had freed up Rosie's inhibitions too. 'Yes, I do, most of the time. When I think of Linda and the thousands of others who took Svelta, I could murder him.' She gave an ironic laugh as she realised her choice of words.

She paused and frowned, then eventually she spoke. 'I have thought a lot about this, and there is another connection, between the deaths from Svelta and Elysium. More distant yet more powerful.'

'What's that?' said Roberta, struggling to concentrate, slurring her words.

'Feeding the Gods.'

'What do you mean?'

'It's a term for the human sacrifice to the gods that was part of the Aztec religion in the fourteenth century. The only thing that's changed since then is that the gods are now the pharmaceutical companies.'

'Profound.' Roberta was clearly struggling to understand. 'Very profound.'

'Jesus, tell us again when we're sober,' cried Sandra. 'And let me continue. I have been in contact with Steve Mallory recently.'

'You're not rekindling your fling with him, are you?' asked Rosie.

Seeing their surprised faces, Sandra burst into laughter. 'No, no, not like that. We keep in touch, but only as friends.'

'That'll be a first for you, then,' muttered Roberta.

'I texted him that there was a rumour that David Jennings was living in Dubai. Apparently, talks are underway between the UK and UAE to put an agreement in place for the extradition of criminals. He says to wait, as it will probably be in place this time next year.'

'Oh, let's drink to that,' slurred Roberta.

'Yes. Just one phone call will be all that's needed,' added Sandra.

'We can wait. After all, they say that revenge is a dish best served cold, eh, Rosie?'

ACKNOWLEDGEMENTS

We would like to thank the many people who have contributed to the production of *Feeding the Gods*, from John Wagstaff, who told us about growing up in a mining family in Yorkshire, to our beta readers, Alison Timms, Dee Blow, Angela Zajac, Kate White, Bianca Stott. Thanks also go to Tony Fyler of Jefferson Franklin Editing, for his early critique of our manuscript; Bob Buxton, who copy-edited our initial drafts, and Andy Monks, who came up with the idea for the cover.

We would like to thank Miles Hawksley of Daniel Goldsmith Literary Consultants for his valuable and constructive assessment of the book.

Finally, thanks go to the team at The Book Guild, who have been instrumental in the publication of *Feeding the Gods*: Jeremy Thompson MD, Philippa Iliffe, Jack Wedgbury, Rosie Lowe, Hayley Russell, Jane Rowland, Jonathan White and Megan Lockwood-Jones.